Copyright © 2025 by Viola Estrella

ISBN 979-8-218-76140-0 (trade paperback)

Library of Congress Control Number: 2025918107

Little Amish Girl

For my mother, who was once a little Amish girl. You lived a fierce life, and I'm so proud of you.

Preface

Some stories come from imagination. Others grow from truths too deep to ignore. *Little Amish Girl* was born from both.

My mother was once a little Amish girl. She grew up in a strict Old Order Amish community in Indiana, where tradition ruled with quiet, unforgiving authority. Behind the kerosene lamps, home-baked goods, and reverent prayers lived pain that few outside the community ever saw. My mother endured that pain. She carried it, buried it, and later in life, began to speak it aloud.

She left the Amish in the early 1970s, alongside my father, because they could no longer reconcile the teachings of the church with what they believed was right. For that choice, she was shunned. She was no longer welcome at her family's table. Literally. Years ago, I accompanied her to visit Amish family in Indiana. We met at a diner, but when we arrived, they quietly pulled our two tables apart. They could not be seen eating with someone who had left the faith. We didn't stay, and my mother cried all the way back to the car. I tried to make her laugh, tried to brush it off. But the wound had been reopened. That day was only one of many when this religion, her own roots, cut her deeply.

Little Amish Girl is fiction, but it asks a quiet, aching question: What if someone like my mother had been taken out of that life earlier?

What if she had found help? What might her healing have looked like, sooner?

Before my mom passed, she offered Amish phrasing suggestions for this book. She was happy I was writing it and was excited to have a copy in her hands one day. Sadly, I wasn't able to give her that in time, but I know she's smiling down at me now.

She also left behind essays she wrote while earning her GED—reflections of her Amish upbringing. Those stories were a gift, and I'll always cherish them along with her memory.

This novel is dedicated to her, and to all the girls and boys who were never given a voice.

May they find one here.

-Viola

Prologue

The stench hit her first—rank, rotten, and *wrong*. Ivy recoiled and clamped her hand over her mouth. Wind from the storm tore at her coat and whipped her hair across her face, but she barely felt it. Her eyes locked on the barn. The structure loomed in the moonlight, its jagged silhouette crooked and sinister.

Something waited inside. The presence seeped from the seams in the wood and slithered around her body.

She wasn't supposed to be in this place.

So why had she come?

Dragged here as if she had no control over her own body and mind.

"Stay out of the barn, Ivy. You don't want to know what's inside."

Ruth's voice echoed in her head, thick as molasses, coating her mind as she stepped forward. Ivy hadn't seen her sister in years, didn't even know where she was, but she thought of her constantly.

And in sleep, Ruth found her.

Ivy reached for the door with trembling hands and yanked it open. The wood groaned. Hinges screamed.

Darkness swallowed her. Airless. Pressed close.

A crooked beam hung low above, a lone kerosene lantern dangling from it. Its dim glow fluttered against the otherwise dark walls.

Using all her strength, she slammed the door shut. The wood shuddered in its frame as she fumbled with the iron latch, fingers stiff from the cold.

The storm still howled outside. But underneath the wind came another sound, riding the air like a warning:

"Get out. Get out. Get out."

She turned slowly, her eyes adjusting. Dust floated through the lantern's glow. The old hayloft. The rusted trough. The ladder she once climbed with bare feet and skinned knees. It was all here—older, quieter, but unmistakable.

Then she saw her.

Ruth lay crumpled on the dirt floor, her limbs twisted, her body caught in something shifting, writhing. Ivy's breath hitched. Rope. It had to be rope.

But it moved.

She looked closer.

A snake, black and slick as oil, coiled tight around Ruth's ribs, its body flexing with each shallow breath she managed to take. The tail wound around her like a noose, squeezing, squeezing—waiting.

Ivy clutched her stomach, nausea twisting inside her.

"Ivy, help me!"

Ruth's voice was raw, desperate. She lay tangled in the dirt, wide-eyed with terror as the snake's massive coils tightened around her.

Ivy's breath caught. She lurched forward—

The snake's head shot up.

Its jaw unhinged, fangs flashing in the lantern light. It struck so fast that Ivy barely yanked herself back in time, her pulse hammering against her skin. She glanced down at her wrists, at the veins bulging beneath the surface, the thrum of her heartbeat roaring in her ears.

A hiss forced her to look up. The serpent's body constricted, Ruth gasping under its crushing hold.

"Let her go!" The scream caught in her throat and stayed there.

Let her go, let her go, let her go.

The snake's tongue slithered out, tasting the air. And then—

It spoke.

"Stay out of the barn, Ivy."

The words slithered through the air, sinking into her skin like tar.

Ivy froze.

The voice, deep, twisted, seething with something dark, wrapped around her. It slunk into her bones, filling her with something heavy and wrong.

The barn tilted. The ground shuddered beneath her feet. Ivy stumbled, catching herself against a wooden beam, her breath ragged.

"Stay out of the barn, Ivy."

The serpent bared its fangs, its grin a jagged stretch of gleaming white.

"Or you'll end up just like her."

"I said let her go!" Ivy tried again, but the words strangled inside her.

The snake lunged.

Ivy reeled back again as its fangs snapped inches from her face. Her fury boiled over into something helpless and raw. She wanted to fight. She needed to rip the thing away from Ruth. To *do something*.

But fear held her in place.

Ruth choked on a breath, her eyes pleading. "Ivy!"

Ivy lunged—

And fell.

Her back hit the mattress hard, her body jerking upright with a strangled gasp. The room was dark. Too dark. Too silent.

But it didn't feel empty.

The nightmare clung to her, suffocating, settling in the dark corners.

Ivy pressed a trembling hand to her face, forcing air into her lungs.

The dream never changed. She always woke up before she could save Ruth.

And worse—she didn't know if she ever would.

Chapter One

Her father chose violence and religion over her, her church chose silence, and cancer chose the only person who ever truly loved her. So, at twenty-one, Ivy Schrock chose herself, a whisk, and a worn-down bakery on the edge of downtown.

At 4 a.m., Indianapolis belonged to the restless. The occasional car rumbled past, streetlights flickered, and the city sat in limbo, caught between night and morning.

Ivy knew that feeling well.

Being caught between what was, what is, and what might be.

She'd been awake for hours, jolted from sleep by another nightmare —the same one that always ended with her sister Ruth screaming and no one coming. Not then. Not ever.

Now, she stood in the kitchen of *Butter and Bliss*.

Here, she was in control.

Here, she wasn't a victim.

Here, she was someone.

Today was the grand opening of her bakery—the beginning of

5

everything she'd dreamed about. The thought sent a rush through her, quick and bright, like the first sip of strong coffee after too little sleep.

"Speaking of coffee..." Ivy washed her hands and made herself another cup. Today would be huge, and she needed to be awake enough to be able to revel in the glory of it all.

Her own bakery. *Her* name on the lease.

And no one standing over her shoulder telling her who to be.

Someone dear had told her to follow her passion. Someone Ivy had loved and now grieved.

Ivy inhaled, and the smell of fresh dough took her back to her childhood unexpectedly. She'd stood at another counter once, her small hands pressing into flour-dusted mounds, trying to mimic the sure, practiced movements of her *mamm,* her biological mother. The kitchen in their Amish home had been their safe space—their morning ritual before the rest of the house woke up.

A memory and moment that felt untouchable.

Until the pounding footsteps from upstairs broke the stillness.

Dat, getting ready to work the farm. *Dat,* always in a terrible mood. *Dat,* reeking of liquor at all times of the day.

Ivy had pressed her fingers deeper into the dough, as if working harder could make her invisible. Her *mamm's* hand had covered hers in a brief but firm squeeze.

Keep working.

So, she had. It was what she knew how to do. To be of help. To be as perfect as could be so she didn't cause any trouble.

Ivy shook the memory away, but a shiver skittered down her arms as another flashback took her to the last day with her biological family. The day her life altered forever.

"Stop it, Ivy," she said.

That day was a long time ago.

That *life* felt like it belonged to someone else.

Here, in her present, there were no hushed silences, no more hiding, no more bruises and broken bones.

Only the warmth from the ovens, the first of sunlight filtering through the windows, and the quiet beat of her heart, reminding her she'd built a *new* life for herself.

Something to keep her mind busy and at ease. Something to help with the loneliness.

Ivy turned and checked the muffins baking in the oven. Almost done.

Soon, customers would walk through those doors, drawn in by the promise of warm pastries and hot coffee. They would sit, talk, and fill the space with laughter and conversation.

And she would be here, in the middle of it all, making sure everything ran the way she'd imagined.

She wanted this place to feel safe—a deep breath, the kind of warmth people carried in their memories of home, even if they'd never really known one. It had taken two years of sleepless nights and more setbacks than she cared to count, but she'd done it.

The bakery downstairs, her apartment upstairs—her dream, fully realized.

She moved to the front of the shop, adjusting the seating and straightening the bookcase near the window. It was filled with books she'd handpicked, everything from well-worn classics to contemporary favorites. This building was more than a bakery—it was a space where people could linger, where they could lose themselves in a story while sipping coffee and nibbling on something warm from the oven.

The bell above the door jingled, and Ivy turned to see Fiona stepping inside, cheeks flushed from the early-morning air. A high school junior with curly red hair and an easy, infectious warmth, Fiona had been eager to help ever since Ivy hired her to run the register part-time before school started.

"Morning," Fiona said, shrugging off her backpack. "It smells amazing in here."

"Morning." Ivy smiled. "Thanks for coming in early. First day—no room for error."

Fiona grinned. "Don't worry. I told all my friends they *have* to stop by today on the way to school and try the blueberry muffins."

"You're an angel, Fi," Ivy said. "Let's make sure they leave with no regrets."

"You got it, Ivy. Let me know where to start."

As they moved around, finalizing last-minute details, the door chimed again. Ivy looked up as Camron stepped inside, his broad frame filling the doorway. He carried a bouquet of white roses in a clear vase, looking slightly uncertain but pleased with himself.

Ivy raised an eyebrow. "Flowers? Didn't expect that. Thank you, Cam."

Camron smiled. "Figured you deserved something nice today."

She accepted the bouquet, grateful for the sentiment, and set the vase on a nearby table. Camron was kind and undeniably handsome, stable in a way she should probably appreciate more. As her contractor, he'd helped her bring this building to life, and somewhere along the way, they'd started spending time together outside of work.

Camron Woodward was comfortable. Easy.

But he was *not* electric. Not the way she'd once felt before—when a single glance could set a fire inside of her, when every touch carried a charge. With Camron, there was no spark, no quiet thrill buzzing beneath the surface.

Camron was a nice man. A good man.

But nice and good weren't guaranteed to last.

Yep, Ivy had her walls up because walls were meant for protection.

His gaze moved around the bakery, taking it all in. "It looks incredible, Ivy. You did it."

She took a moment to look around as well, seeing the space with fresh eyes—the golden loaves of bread waiting behind the glass, the bookshelves by the window, the cozy chairs tucked into the reading corner.

"I did," she murmured, almost to herself. Then she said, "*We* did," a little louder. "I couldn't have done it without you."

She poured him a fresh cup of coffee. Black with a packet of sugar, just the way he liked it.

"For you." She handed him the cup.

"Thanks." Camron took the coffee and then glanced at his watch. "I wish I could stay, but I've got a new job to get to. Wanted to stop by and say congratulations."

Ivy gave him a friendly smile. "Thanks for coming by."

He lifted his coffee cup in a small toast. "To *Butter and Bliss*. It's going to be something special." He kissed her forehead and headed out.

Ivy closed her eyes, exhaling.

The grand opening is today!

She'd spent years imagining this day. And now, here it was.

No turning back.

She straightened, adjusting the flowers in their vase before moving toward the kitchen.

There was work to be done.

Chapter Two

Then

Ten-year-old Ivy stood as straight as she could beside her *mamm*. Her hands clenched in the fabric of her dress, willing herself to be perfect. Her hair was braided so tight her scalp tingled beneath her pinned cap and black bonnet. Today, Ivy would not give her *dat* a single reason to be angry.

The general store was a world of bright packages and unfamiliar noises, tempting in ways she couldn't explain. But she kept her hands to herself, resisting the urge to touch, to explore. She and her *mamm* were only here for flour and essentials—everything else came from home, from the farm. She'd been allowed along only because she'd stayed home from school that day, a rare treat that turned into an outing.

Her *mamm* stopped and gestured toward the public restrooms. "*Be gute*," she said, using a mix of English and Pennsylvania Dutch as they often did.

Be good. Ivy knew how to do that. She was the youngest of seven children, and she'd learned what to do and what not to do from watching her older siblings. Her brothers and sisters had their ways of getting into trouble, but Ivy had always been the quiet one, the one who followed the rules, mostly to avoid the sharp eye of their father. He was strict, and his punishments were swift and harsh, leaving little room for mistakes. Ivy clutched the cart handle as she watched her *mamm* walk to the indoor bathroom.

And then Ivy was alone. She shrank under the weight of curious *Englisch* gazes. The buzzing of the fridges, the beeping at checkout, the chatter of people who didn't follow her church's rules—it was overwhelming. This wasn't her world. She wished she were back at home, tending to the horses. Especially Twinkles. Twinkles was her favorite.

Movement in the cookie aisle caught her attention. A boy, not much older than her brother Jonas, reached for a bag of cookies and, without hesitation, tore it open, popping one into his mouth.

Ach du lieber. Oh, my goodness.

What was he doing?

Before she could look away, his sharp green eyes found hers. He grinned, bold and unbothered, and to her shock, walked straight toward her and pressed a cookie into her palm.

"Don't tell anyone," he said with a wink.

The color of his eyes reminded her of the rhubarb leaves in her *mamm's* garden. Along with a mischievous sparkle of gold in the middle.

Ivy's fingers curled around the cookie, her breath catching. It felt dangerous in her palm—an act of defiance wrapped in sugar. A stolen cookie. Given by an *Englisch* boy.

Before she could react, a stout man in a store uniform barked, "Hey! I told you not to come in here anymore!"

The boy bolted. The man lunged, catching his arm, and the open bag of cookies spilled across the floor. A commotion erupted as the boy twisted, then tore free, disappearing through the doors in a blur.

And then her *mamm* was beside her, seizing her arm with a force that stole Ivy's breath. "*Was hoscht du?*" What do you have?

Ivy opened her trembling hand, revealing the cookie.

Her *mamm's* expression darkened. She plucked the cookie from

Ivy's palm and dropped it onto a shelf with swift disgust. "*Scham dich.*" Shame on you.

Mamm's gaze darted around, and Ivy noticed a deacon from their church had seen the entire event. He shook his head in disapproval, and Ivy's stomach dropped. Her *mamm*'s grip tightened as she ushered Ivy out of the store without another word.

She'd failed.

Dinner that night was suffocating. Seven siblings sat in silence, forks scraping against plates. Their *dat* had returned from the fields in a foul mood, the sharp scent of liquor hanging in the air.

Ivy barely touched her food—her stomach knotted with dread. She'd learned to gauge his mood and to mimic her older siblings, who avoided his gaze, keeping their heads down.

Then, her *mamm* spoke. "Reuben, I need to tell you something," she said quietly. But the words echoed in Ivy's ears.

Ivy stiffened.

Her *dat* looked up, bloodshot eyes narrowing. "*Was isses?*" (What is it?)

"Well," *Mamm* began, "Ivy had an encounter with an *Englisch* boy at the market. He stole cookies and gave her one. She was holding it when I found her. Deacon Joseph Schwartz witnessed everything."

Silence. Heavy. Inevitable.

Her *dat's* glare burned through her. "Is this true?"

"Yes, *Dat*. I'm sorry."

Her older sister Ruth, beside her, squeezed her hand. "It was nothing. A mistake."

Her *dat* slammed his hand on the table. "A mistake?" He shot up from his chair, looming over them. "How many times must this family be shamed?"

The chair scraped against the floor as Ruth stood, stepping between them. "She didn't know, *Dat*."

His nostrils flared. "Do not talk back to me, Ruth."

The slap came fast. Ruth crumpled to the ground.

Ivy barely had time to gasp before his fingers latched onto her arm, yanking her from her chair.

The blows came hard and fast, pain bursting across her body. She tried to hold in her cries, but they tore free, swallowed by his rage. She begged him to stop, but her words dissolved in the air, meaningless.

The last thing she remembered was the floor rushing up to meet her —before everything went dark.

Ivy's eyelids fluttered open, but the world around her was a blur. Dim, unfamiliar lights cast soft shadows across the room, and the rhythmic beeping of machines filled the silence. Her mind was foggy, a haze that made it hard to remember anything clearly. Where was she? The sterile smell and the strange, uncomfortable bed were nothing like the familiar warmth of her bedroom.

She could barely hear hushed voices beyond the door, the murmurs penetrating the haze of her thoughts.

"How did she get here?" a woman's voice drifted in. "The Amish around here don't usually bring their children to hospitals."

"It's really sad," said a second woman. "Her older sister ran away from their home to the nearest neighbor with a phone and begged them to call for an ambulance. When the ambulance arrived, this little girl was unconscious. Apparently, the father had beaten her. And from the looks of her x-rays, this wasn't the first time."

"Wow, I hope the sister is okay. That was very brave of her."

The second woman replied with a sigh, "Yeah, me, too. You never know what's going on in these secretive Amish communities."

Her sister. *Ruth?*

Ivy tried to move, to make sense of their words, but her body felt like an old oak tree branch with deep roots, unable to move. Her arms and legs were sore, a dull ache that made it impossible to shift even a little. She wanted to open her eyes wider, to see more, but they were too heavy as if weighed down by invisible fingers.

"The father was arrested," the murmuring continued, "but he'll probably get off. The police never seem to get too involved when it comes to the Amish."

Her father... Ivy tried to piece it together. The memory slipped through her grasp, broken fragments buried under a thick blanket of confusion. Her older sister... something about Ruth. Was it Ruth? But before she could grasp onto a coherent thought, a wave of exhaustion swept over her, pulling her back into a deep sleep.

When she finally opened her eyes again hours later, everything looked blurry. Her head throbbed, and her body ached. When she tried to shift even a little, pain shot through her ribs and arm, piercing and mean—a reminder of what had happened. Tears stung her eyes as the memories rushed back.

Dat had been so angry with her.

And Ruth...Was Ruth okay?

Ivy glanced around the bright white room and found she was alone, the silence broken only by the soft beeping of the strange machines. Her breaths came in ragged gasps as she tried to understand where she was and how she'd gotten here.

Where was her family? Was this another punishment?

She couldn't remember a time when she'd been alone outside of her home. This wasn't how the punishments worked. Usually, after *Dat* was done, they'd go to bed and wait for *Mamm* to come and tend to any cuts, bruises, or pains.

Maybe what Ivy had done was different... somehow worse.

A woman walked into the room wearing strange blue clothes that matched top to bottom. She reached up and pulled back a curtain, and her face softened into a smile as she looked at Ivy.

"I'm Nancy, your nurse," she said. "Good to see you're awake."

Ivy pinched her lips shut and winced at the pain it caused. Her whole face felt swollen, her upper lip held together by stitches.

"It's going to be okay, Ivy." Nancy patted Ivy's hand. "We're here to help you get better."

Ivy knew she shouldn't speak to this woman, but she had to know. "Is Ruth okay? My sister?" She made sure to speak English, so she'd be understood.

Nancy looked over the paperwork on her clipboard. "Um, I can sure try to find out. We don't have a patient called Ruth that I know of."

Ivy carefully nodded her head, but the pain brought new tears to her eyes.

"Oh, dear. Try not to move too much." Nancy strode to the machines and poked a few buttons. "Let's get you some relief." She picked up a syringe with a long, pointy needle and brought it to Ivy's arm.

"No." Ivy squirmed, causing shooting pains.

"It's okay, sweetie. I'm going to insert it into your IV." Nancy pointed at Ivy's arm, and Ivy realized there was something taped to the inside of her elbow. "It won't hurt a bit, I promise."

Chapter Three

Now – Seven months later

Butter and Bliss wasn't just a bakery anymore—it was part of the neighborhood's rhythm. The front door chimed constantly, welcoming a steady stream of customers who were after their morning caffeine fix, favorite pastries, or a fresh loaf of Ivy's homemade bread. The scent of butter and espresso clung to the air, mixing with the low hum of conversation.

Ivy had built this. And every long, exhausting hour had been worth it.

She'd hired two part-time employees—Fiona, finally on a steadier schedule, and Mila, a single mom with a knack for balancing a dozen coffee orders and a toddler on her hip. Mila would be in by seven, in time for the morning rush.

Outside, March winds rattled the windows, but inside, Ivy was where she felt like she belonged. In the kitchen, she pressed her palms into soft dough, shaping loaves of rosemary olive bread with the kind of instinct that came from years of practice. This was her favorite time of day—the quiet before the storm.

Then, a loud thump against the front window shattered the early-morning stillness.

Ivy flinched, a jolt of adrenaline spiking through her. Her hand hovered near the bread knife on the counter, her pulse kicking up as she moved toward the storefront. Through the glass, she spotted a man sitting on the sidewalk, hunched into his tattered coat. A cigarette dangled from his fingers, a thin curl of smoke rising into the cold air. His breath turned to steam, mingling with the faint glow of the streetlights.

His jacket was worn, frayed at the edges, and dirty, as if he had been wandering the streets for a while. At first glance, she thought he might be homeless. A few passed through the area—she often left out day-old bread for them.

But something about him tugged at a distant memory.

She flipped on the front lights, hoping he'd take it as a sign to move along. Instead, he stubbed out his cigarette, pushed to his feet, and turned to face her with a slow, crooked grin.

Ivy's breath caught.

It wasn't just anyone.

It was Gram. The boy who used to be her foster brother.

The boy who'd once given her a stolen cookie in a grocery store.

Her grip on the bread knife loosened, though her heart still hammered. He'd changed so much, and yet, there was no mistaking those familiar leaf-green eyes, still filled with that same flicker of mischief and rebellion. His hair was longer, his face more weathered, but it was him.

She unlocked the door and held it open. "Gram?" she whispered, disbelieving.

His grin widened, hands buried in the frayed pockets of his jacket. "Long time, no see, Little Amish Girl."

The nickname made her chest tighten. She hadn't heard it in years.

Ivy swallowed hard. "What... what are you doing here?"

He shrugged, glancing past her into the bakery. "Passing through." His lips were cracked, like he hadn't spoken—or been heard—in a long time. "Heard your name the other day. Figured I'd check out the bakery. See how you're doing."

She didn't know what to say; her words stuck in her throat. The last time she'd seen him had been years ago. He was older than she was, almost like a big brother—always protective. Now, he stood in front of her bakery, worn down by whatever road had led him here.

A shaky breath left her lips, relief and concern tangling together. "Do you want to come in?"

Gram hesitated, his gaze shifting toward the bakery's door, then back to her. "Yeah," he said, "I could use a cup of coffee, if you don't mind."

She stepped aside, letting him pass into the warmth of the bakery. The scent of sugar and yeast wrapped around them as she locked the door behind him.

Ivy prepared a cup of coffee for him, wondering what had happened to him since they last parted ways. Since she'd lived in the mobile home park with one of her foster moms... what was it? Over eight, nine, or so years ago. And why, after all these years, had he come back into her life?

She grabbed a freshly baked muffin from the counter. Without a word, she walked over to the table where Gram sat, setting both the muffin and the coffee cup down before pulling out a chair to join him.

Gram didn't immediately reach for the muffin. Instead, he wrapped his hands around the warm cup of coffee, staring down into it as though he could lose himself in the dark liquid. His once confident demeanor faltered, and as Ivy studied him, she could see the embarrassment etched into his expression—the slight slump in his shoulders, the way he avoided her gaze.

"How are you, Gram? What's been going on?"

For a long moment, Gram didn't say anything. His jaw clenched as if he were trying to figure out what to tell her, or maybe how much to admit. Finally, he let out a slow breath and looked up, his leaf-green eyes clouded with something between shame and resignation.

"It's not going well, Ivy," he said. "I lost my job months ago. Some... bad choices on my part. I've been trying to find something else, but no one's hiring me." He paused, his hands tightening around the coffee mug. "Eventually, I couldn't keep up with the rent on my apartment. Got evicted in December."

18

A dull ache settled in Ivy's chest, making it hard to breathe as she listened.

"I've been staying at the shelter across town for most of the winter," he continued, his gaze dropping to the table. "But it's crowded. Too many people needing a place, not enough beds." He gave a short, humorless laugh. "Last night, there wasn't any space left for me, so I wandered around. Then I saw your bakery." He glanced up at her, a ghost of that old grin playing across his face. "Figured, why not stop by? See if you were here. See if I could get warm for a bit."

Ivy drew in a slow breath, trying to keep her emotions in check. She couldn't believe how hard things had become for him, and the thought of him spending the night in the freezing cold made her stomach turn. This was the boy she'd once looked up to, the one who had protected her when they were both lost in the foster system. And now he was the one who needed help.

"Why didn't you come sooner?" Ivy asked. "I would've helped you."

Gram shifted uncomfortably, his fingers still gripping the mug as if it were the only thing grounding him. "I didn't want to drag you into my mess," he muttered. "You're doing great now. I didn't want to show up and ask for a handout."

Ivy shook her head. "You're not dragging me into anything, Gram. You were there for me when I needed it, and now it's my turn to be there for you." She paused. "You're not alone in this." She said the words that had resonated with her long ago from her foster siblings.

Gram's face flushed slightly, and she could see the conflict in his eyes —wanting to accept the help but also battling his pride.

"Thanks," he said after a long silence. "I... didn't think things would get this bad, you know?"

Ivy offered a small tilt of her chin—the kind of gesture that said she got it without needing to say much. Life had a way of blindsiding people when they least expected it. She reached across the table and nudged the muffin toward him.

"Here," she said. "Eat. You look like you could use it."

He chuckled. "Gee, thanks, Little Amish Girl." His gaze shifted over her. "Not so Amish or little anymore."

Ivy gave him a grin and a wink, watching as he reached for the muffin and popped a piece into his mouth. She knew him well enough to see he wasn't comfortable accepting help. No way was she going to let him walk away without offering something more. Her mind was already racing with possibilities, and as much as she didn't want to overwhelm him, she also knew what needed to be done.

"Gram," she said, leaning forward. "I have an extra bedroom upstairs in my apartment. You can stay there for a while, at least until you get back on your feet."

He stopped mid-chew. "Ivy, I don't think—"

"Don't argue with me," she interrupted, her tone firm but warm. "It's not much, I know, but it's a warm bed, and it's better than the shelter or the streets. Plus, I could really use extra help here in the bakery. It's not much pay, but it's something. You could work here until you find something else. I mean, if you want to."

The shifting expressions on his face revealed his fight against the offer, but Ivy could see in his eyes that he was tempted—he was tired of the way things had been. He rubbed the back of his neck, his gaze dropping to the table as he wrestled with his thoughts.

"I don't want to be a burden," he said.

"You're not a burden, silly man," Ivy said. "You're family. And you've helped me when I needed it most. Let me do this for you."

There was a long, loaded pause. Ivy could sense the tension in his silence, the inner battle waging behind his eyes as he wrestled with accepting her kindness. Then, at last, he gave the faintest tilt of his head —a silent surrender.

"Okay," he said. "I'll stay. Just until I get back on my feet. And I'll do my fair share."

"You'd better." Ivy smiled, happy he'd agreed.

Gram let out a breath. "Thanks, Ivy. I don't know what I'd do without you."

"You won't have to find out," she said, standing up and grabbing another muffin from the counter. "Now eat this, and then we'll talk about getting you settled in upstairs."

That morning, as Gram slept upstairs, safe in a warm bed, Ivy moved around the bakery, preparing for the morning rush, feeling a sense of peace settle over her. She'd always looked up to Gram, even when life had knocked him down, and now she could be there for him in a way that truly mattered. He would get through this, and so would she.

Chapter Four

Then

Ivy sat up in the hospital bed, her bruises fading, though her left arm remained in a stiff white cast and her ribs ached with every breath. The bright white walls trapped her, a constant reminder that she was far from home.

Had her family shunned her? She'd heard stories in church about those who strayed too far into the *Englisch* world, only to be cast out, forgotten. Was that what was happening to her now?

The door creaked open, revealing a woman in elegant modern clothes—silky blouse, tailored coat, and a gentle smile that didn't quite erase the tiredness in her eyes.

"Hello, Ivy," the woman greeted, stepping into the room. "I'm Emily, your caseworker. How are you feeling?"

Ivy shifted slightly in her hospital bed, keeping her stiff guard up. "Fine," she mumbled, not wanting to talk too much to these English people and further her separation from her family. She'd remained mostly silent during her stay here, and she didn't plan on changing that.

Emily pulled a chair closer to the bed and sat down, giving Ivy a reassuring nod. "I'm here to understand what happened, Ivy. You don't have to talk if you don't want to, but I want you to know I'm here to help."

Ivy glanced at Emily but remained tight-lipped, her arms wrapped protectively around herself.

"I spoke to your mother," Emily said.

"My *mamm*. What did she say? Is she here for me?" Ivy glanced over the woman's shoulder, but no one else was in the room.

"Unfortunately, she's not able to be here. And well, she isn't able to bring you home either."

Ivy's heart pounded. "Why?"

Emily cleared her throat and continued in a gentle voice, "I also spoke to your neighbors who'd called the police and ambulance the night you were hurt. They said Ruth had told them it was your father who hurt you. Is that true?"

Ivy's mind raced, torn between her loyalty to Ruth and the fear of exposing her family's dark secret. She remembered the times Ruth had stood up for her and defended her against their father's anger. If Ruth had spoken the truth, it would be okay for her to do the same.

Tears welled as she whispered, "Yes. My *dat* gets upset with me sometimes. And he does punish me." She wouldn't speak for her brothers and sisters.

Emily tilted her head. "And he's the one who punished you and hurt you this time?"

"Yes." Ivy's nose burned as she tried to hold back tears. She stared at the floor, silent.

Emily's hand reached out, resting softly on Ivy's. "I'm sorry you had to go through that, Ivy. But I'm here to help you. We're going to find you a safe place to stay until we can figure out a permanent plan. In cases like this, we'd hope to find an Amish family for you to stay with—perhaps even a relative, so you'd be familiar with the surroundings. However... we can't seem to find one that has room at this time."

At those words, Ivy's whole insides crumbled. The weight of everything came crashing down, and before she could stop herself, tears streamed down her face.

"No, please," she managed to get out. "I don't want to go somewhere else. I... I want to go home."

"I understand, sweetie. Unfortunately, that's not an option right now. But we'll do everything we can to take care of your needs until we get this sorted out."

She thought of her uncles and aunts who lived in a nearby Ohio community. They didn't come around much, and they didn't seem to care for her *dat* too much. He'd always said he was the black sheep of the family. They probably wouldn't want his daughter staying with them.

She thought of her *mamm*'s brothers and sisters who also lived in Ohio. She'd met a few of them a couple of years ago. They'd seemed cold toward her parents... disapproving in some way. Her *mamm*, usually a hardhearted woman, had cried when they'd treated her that way. So, Ivy definitely didn't want to stay with any of them.

"I want to go home," Ivy said again, feeling helpless.

Emily squeezed Ivy's hand gently, her voice soothing. "I know it's scary, Ivy. But I'm going to do everything possible to make sure you're safe and protected."

"I'm fine at my home. I'll behave, I promise. And the church will forgive me and my *dat*. You'll see." Ivy's chest heaved as she sobbed. She clung to Emily's hand.

"I'm afraid it's not that simple, Ivy. But you're not alone," Emily said. "I'm here to guide you through this journey, to help provide the support you need."

But what she needed was to cocoon herself in her bed, pull the covers over her head, and forget this ever happened. She needed what was familiar.

Emily's car pulled up to a bright yellow house, nothing like the simple farm Ivy had left behind. She clutched her bag strap, her stomach twisting at the sight of the too-big windows and colorful curtains. Emily had explained this would be her foster home, and Ivy would have foster parents—or simply adults who would take care of her.

So that morning, Ivy had braided her hair tightly, secured her cap with pins, and put on the plainest dress she owned, clinging to the last bit of normalcy she had left.

And now, as she stepped out of Emily's car, her gaze darted around at the neighborhood. The homes were close together, so unlike the wide, expansive acreage Ivy had lived on with her family. She cast a nervous glance at Emily, who gave a warm, reassuring pat on Ivy's back.

An elderly woman with warm eyes and a kind smile approached the front door. The silver-haired woman stepped closer, her gaze widening ever so slightly, a fleeting glimpse of something that hinted at deeper understanding.

"You must be Ivy," the woman said, a little too chipper. "I'm Mrs. Anderson. Welcome to our home."

The woman gave her a smile, but her gaze shifted carefully over Ivy's cast and lingered for a second on the scar above her lip where she'd needed stitches. At least she couldn't see the ache Ivy still felt deep in her ribs.

Ivy blinked hard, willing her eyes not to water. Crying never did a bit of good. She kept her chin up, looking Mrs. Anderson right in the eye. If she were going to be here, she'd be brave. Mrs. Anderson kept smiling, all warm and kind. Maybe Mrs. Anderson wouldn't judge her for what had happened.

Ivy's fingers stilled as she clutched the hem of her plain black dress, resisting the urge to fidget. She said a quiet, quick goodbye to Emily and followed Mrs. Anderson inside, her eyes sweeping over everything in sight. The house smelled different, and there were so many things that seemed strange. A little knot of worry tightened in her stomach, but Ivy held her ground. She'd face it head-on, whatever "it" turned out to be.

The living room was a world away from her simple Amish surroundings of wooden furniture, oil lamps, and plain curtains. Intricate furniture adorned the space, and Ivy's gaze lingered on the vibrant colors and fancy patterns. Flowers and swirly designs that piqued Ivy's imagination.

In the corner of the room, a man sat in an armchair. Ivy's gaze met his briefly, and a shiver ran down her spine as she saw a glint of something troubling in his eyes.

This man didn't want her there, she could tell. She'd have to stay clear of him.

"That's Mr. Anderson over there," Mrs. Anderson said quickly, adding, "would you like to see your room, Ivy?"

"Yes, ma'am." Ivy followed Mrs. Anderson up the stairs, her footsteps echoing in the quiet house. They reached a room at the end of the hallway, and Ivy's gaze settled on the bed. It looked comfortable and welcoming, covered with colorful blankets and big soft pillows.

A stuffed animal was propped against one of the pillows. The teddy bear looked older, like it had belonged to another child at one time. One eye was missing, and its fur was wearing away. It was broken and alone, like she was. Ivy picked it up and cuddled it against her chest. Sitting, she ran her hand over the pink lace sewn onto one of the many assorted pillows.

It was... pretty.

"This will be your room while you're here, Ivy," Mrs. Anderson said, glancing at the old teddy bear in Ivy's arms. "I hope you find it cozy."

Ivy offered a small nod, grateful for the warmth in Mrs. Anderson's words.

"You can unpack your bag. There are some empty drawers over there." She gestured to a dresser.

"Okay, ma'am."

"Well, I'm sure you must be starving for some hearty food. Hospital food isn't the best." Mrs. Anderson gave a small laugh, but Ivy noticed it didn't reach her eyes. "Feel free to look around the room. I'll be right back."

As the woman left, Ivy let her fingers drift over the lace fabric on a pillow. The afternoon sun seeped through the yellow curtains, painting the room in a warm, cozy light, all bright and colorful—so unlike anything back home.

Alone again, Ivy swallowed hard, trying to keep the knot in her throat from getting any bigger. The past few weeks rushed back to her, clear as day. She remembered the bruises that had finally started to fade, the sting of the scar on her lip, and worst of all, the memory of Ruth crumpling to the floor.

Her chest tightened as she wondered if Ruth was okay. Were her brothers and sisters still back home, maybe talking about her as if she were a story from another life? Did they miss her at all, the way she missed them? Or had she become a stain on their memory, something to whisper about when no one else was listening?

She gazed out the bedroom window, stealing away tears as she watched a few cars drive by on the street below. Not a horse and buggy in sight.

Mrs. Anderson entered the room again, holding a tray with a sandwich, a bowl of soup, and a cup of water. "I thought you might be more comfortable eating up here. Are you hungry?"

Ivy's stomach rumbled in response. "Yes, ma'am."

She watched as Mrs. Anderson set the tray on a desk by the window. The aroma of the chicken soup filled the room, giving off a familiar comfort.

Ivy ate slowly at the desk, being extra careful not to spill or leave any crumbs behind. Every now and then, her eyes met Mrs. Anderson's, who was sitting on the bed watching her. There was something in Mrs. Anderson's eyes—a softness, a kind of worry—that Ivy wasn't used to.

After the meal, Mrs. Anderson led Ivy through the house, showing her the various rooms and explaining the routines of their household.

"Do you know how to use the toilet, Ivy?" she asked, a curious expression on her face. "Emily explained your home didn't have indoor plumbing. You had to use an outhouse."

"Yes, ma'am, I use this kind at school. And I used one at the hospital."

"Right." Mrs. Anderson sighed with what sounded like relief. "You go to elementary school. To public school?"

Ivy lifted her chin. "Yes, my community doesn't have an Amish school close by, so we have to go to the *Englisch* school. But my *mamm* says we don't have to go past the eighth grade," she said, remembering how her parents complained about them having to go at all. The church warned the members not to give in to the *Englisch* people's worldly ways while they were attending school.

"Interesting. We'll get your school arrangements figured out in the coming days. I'm sure Emily will help us get you enrolled in the neighborhood school."

Ivy would have to go to a new school, too? She swallowed back the overwhelming fear and tried to concentrate on Mrs. Anderson's voice.

She was pointing at the bathtub area in the bathroom. "Have you used a shower, sweetheart? Or a bath?"

Ivy glanced at the bathtub with a strange showerhead. She preferred to wash from a basin with water heated on the wood-burning stove like at home, but surely, she could figure out this contraption. She'd used the sink at school and in the hospital, and the nurses helped her with bathing. And she'd read many books where the characters had to use indoor plumbing like this. "I..."

"Not to worry. Here's a quick tutorial." The silver-haired woman stepped aside from the bathtub and pulled and twisted the knobs. Water streamed from the pipe. "We won't worry about this tonight, but tomorrow you'll try it out."

"Yes, ma'am."

Knowing her *dat* and the church allowed her to use the school's utilities, she let herself relax. Like in the hospital, she had no choice in the matter. And if her *dat* disapproved, he'd simply need to come and take her home. But it didn't seem that was going to happen.

Eventually, they returned to the room where Ivy would sleep, and Mrs. Anderson gestured toward the bed. "It's getting late. If you need anything, don't hesitate to ask. There's a bathroom down the hallway if you need to use it or brush your teeth."

Ivy's voice caught as she watched Mrs. Anderson leave. After a moment of hesitation, she lay down, her body sinking into the soft mattress. It was more comfortable than anything she'd ever known, but everything about it felt strange, as though she were a guest in someone else's life.

The weight of exhaustion tugged at her eyelids, and she fell into a deep sleep.

Sometime after, she awakened with a start. She needed to pee. Bad. But... she glanced around, foggy-brained. Where was she?

Ivy froze with fear. Then she remembered—she was at Mrs. Anderson's house.

And it was dark. So dark she could hardly see anything around her.

She needed to pee bad, but thinking about the strange hallways made her heart beat faster. She didn't know what might be out there, and the longer she waited, the more scared she got.

What if she couldn't find the toilet Mrs. Anderson had shown her? And what if she ran into Mr. Anderson with his grumpy face?

Her chest tightened, and her stomach ached as the minutes ticked by, her worry growing bigger and bigger.

At home, she had Ruth to wake up and take her out to the outhouse. In the hospital, a nurse was always nearby. Now, she was alone in a dark home—no lit candles, no lanterns to light the halls.

Eventually, she gave up, her bladder engorged too painfully, and she reluctantly wet the bed. The shame was overwhelming, and tears stung her eyes as she tried to clean up as best she could. Tears turned into quiet sobs, and as exhaustion took over her body again, she fell asleep.

Hours later, morning light filtered through the window, revealing the damp mess still beneath her. Ivy panicked as she remembered what had happened. She scrambled to her feet, her hands trembling, and her cheeks burned with humiliation. As she attempted to tear the sheets and blankets from the bed, Mr. Anderson entered the room.

His eyes narrowed with disgust as he took in the sight before him. "What's this mess? What did you do?"

Ivy's gaze dropped to the floor, her hands shaking as she clutched the damp sheets.

Mrs. Anderson hurried into the room, her face etched with concern. "What's going on?"

Mr. Anderson gestured angrily at the wet spot on the bedding. "I can't handle this, Maggy. I can't have another damaged child in this house. I just want it to be us. I'm too damn old and tired for this crap."

Mrs. Anderson's eyes flickered between Ivy and her husband, a conflicted expression crossing her features. "But Harold, it was an accident, I'm sure."

"I don't care. I don't want this. I warned you I was on my last straw after the last one."

"Emily assured me she's a nice young—"

"I said I don't care, Maggy. For the last time, you're not going to

29

replace our boy with someone else's child. This fostering business has got to stop."

Mrs. Anderson gulped, her eyes reddening. "I understand," she murmured and stepped forward, placing a gentle hand on Ivy's shoulder. "Ivy, I'm so sorry," she said softly. "Let's get you cleaned up, and we'll need to call Emily to find you a new place to stay."

Ivy's throat tensed as she realized what was happening. She sniffed back tears as Mrs. Anderson helped her to the bathroom with a fresh dress and underwear and then left to make the call.

As Ivy shimmied out of her dress awkwardly with her casted arm, she allowed more tears to fall. She'd messed up again, and she feared she'd never find her way home.

Chapter Five

Then

Emily drove Ivy to her new home—a worn-out two-story house at the bottom of a hill. Faded white paint, a yard half-wild with tangled grass and scattered toys. It wasn't perfect, but at least it looked like kids actually lived there. Relief settled in Ivy's chest.

The wooden steps creaked as she followed Emily up the porch, her fingers tightening around her bag. She thought about how her *dat* and brothers could fix the loose railing in no time, how Ruth was better with tools than most of them. But Ruth wasn't here. Ivy swallowed the lump in her throat and focused on the door, wondering who would open it.

Emily knocked. "You're going to meet Sophie Harris now. She's kind and generous. You might even make some friends."

Ivy straightened, tucking a loose strand of hair into her cap as the door swung open.

A woman with wild curls and a skirt bursting with color stood there, bracelets jingling as she moved. Her dark eyes twinkled under caked, dramatic makeup. "Welcome, sweetheart," she said with a raspy warmth. "I'm Sophie. Come on in."

Inside, chaos ruled. Kids darted through the living room, shrieking with laughter. A teenage girl sat in the corner, headphones on, lost in her own world. Toys, art projects, and an old TV blaring cartoons filled the space. The mess was overwhelming. Ivy had grown up in a house full of kids, but back home, there were rules. Chores. Order. Here, she was stepping into a tornado.

"Thank you for taking her in on such short notice, Sophie. I'm afraid I'm overbooked today, or I'd stay longer."

"No worries," Sophie said. "We'll be fine. I'll show Ivy around and get her settled in."

Emily's phone beeped in her hand, and she answered it as she made her way out.

Sophie's smile remained wide and toothy as Emily disappeared out the front door, though Ivy sensed a hint of curiosity in her twinkling eyes as she turned to beam at her.

"Ivy," Sophie said, glancing over Ivy's dress, "I'm so happy to meet you. I'm sure you're going to be a great help around here. I hear Amish girls are *excellent* cleaners."

Ivy's fingers worked the folds of her plain dress, searching for a scrap of comfort. She took in the chaos around her, careful not to let her eyes get too wide. The shift from her neat little home to this disaster zone felt jarring—disorienting in the worst way. A tiny smirk tugged at her mouth. If *Dat* saw this, he'd throw a fit big enough to echo through next week.

"Yes, ma'am." She cast her gaze downward, trying to be humble but truthful. "My *mamm* says I'm a good cleaner. A good baker, too."

Ivy could make herself useful here, at least.

"Wonderful. I think you'll fit in very well. That's Maya and Ashley over there." She pointed toward the young girls. "And that's Hannah over there. They'll be your foster sisters while you're here."

Ivy licked her dry lips and dared to let her gaze roam around the room at the strangers who were nothing like her real sisters. A flicker of movement at the entrance drew her attention. Her heart thumped as she recollected the boy's face.

It was him—the boy from the grocery store. The one who'd stolen those cookies and thought it'd be oh-so-clever to hand her one.

His green eyes locked on hers, recognition sparking. Then he grinned—shared history written in the curve of his mouth. Oh, they had a secret between them—only she was the one who'd paid for it.

His gaze landed on the scar on her lip and the cast on her arm, and his grin faded. He *knew* now. Knew what had happened to her.

"Hey there, Gram." Sophie's colorful bracelets jingled as she approached the boy. "Where've you been?"

"Out." He shrugged. "Exploring the thrilling world beyond these disgusting walls."

Sophie chuckled. "Well, tell us how you really feel." She turned to Ivy. "This is Gram—like a gram of sugar."

"Or a gram of something else." Gram rolled his eyes. "Dad liked his weed a little too much, I guess. Could've been worse. He could've named me Doobie, like my brother."

Ivy didn't understand what that meant, and she didn't ask.

"Anyway," Sophie said, "Gram is one of our resident explorers. Gram, how about you show Ivy around the house? She's new here, and I think you can be a great guide."

A half-smile curved on the boy's face, his snarky edge softening a bit. "Yeah, sure. Why not? Come on, newbie."

Ivy kept her expression carefully neutral as she followed him. The house was worn, with peeling paint, creaky stairs, and cracks snaking along the walls. Dust clung to the air, settling into the corners where cobwebs stretched undisturbed.

"This place is always a mess," Gram said. "You'll get used to it."

They stopped at a bedroom with a twin bed across from two toddler beds. "This is probably yours," Gram said. "You'll be sharing with Maya and Ashley."

Ivy clutched her bag tighter.

Gram's gaze swept over her dress. "You got other clothes? You don't *have* to wear that Amish stuff anymore."

"I... I don't want to change," Ivy said. "I still have a chance to go back home to my family, and I don't want to give them another reason to shun me any longer."

Gram knitted his brow, his confusion evident, but he didn't press the issue. "All right, suit yourself," he said. "If you got that broken arm and scar on your lip from that family, you might reconsider wanting to go back."

Ivy lifted a single shoulder to shrug, wanting to let the boy know she was brave, and her wounds weren't that bad.

"So, how old are you?" he asked, moving on with the conversation.

"I'm almost eleven."

Gram whistled. "So, ten. You're just a little girl. A *little Amish girl.*" He shook his head, amused. "Never thought I'd have one for a foster sister."

Ivy swallowed. She felt even younger, even more out of place.

Gram leaned against the doorway. "I'm fifteen," he said. "I'm working on getting emancipated so I can get out of this fucked-up foster care system and be on my own. I can totally take care of myself more than any of the asshat adults I've ever met."

Ivy winced at the bold language. If she'd spoken like that at home, she would've met a harsher punishment than the one that had landed her here.

Gram tilted his head, his rhubarb-leaf-green eyes narrowing a bit. "You don't say much. That your style, or...?"

Ivy held his gaze and gave a simple, "No."

Gram chuckled. "All right, no need to be so serious. It's gonna be okay," he said. "I got your back, Little Amish Girl. You'll see."

Gram's words made her feel a little better, even if she didn't plan on saying so. She gave a small nod, keeping her relief hidden. He went on ahead downstairs, and she followed, sticking close to him as the noise from the rest of the house washed over her again.

As they returned downstairs, her gaze drifted to the teenage girl with headphones. Ivy studied the strange tattoo on her stomach—a bleeding rose. Something about it unsettled her.

Gram introduced them. "Hey, Hannah, this is Ivy. She's new."

Hannah lifted one side of her headphones to reveal an ear. She cast a glance over Ivy and then out the window again. "Whatever. Like I need another reason to think I'm living in a freak fest."

Ivy's cheeks burned. She'd always been different from the *Englisch* kids at public school, but here, she was *alien*.

Gram shrugged. "Don't mind her. She's moving out soon anyway."

Moving out? Ivy didn't understand. How could a teenager just leave?

Sophie's colorful presence returned to the room, and Ivy stiffened, unsure about how to act around this particular adult. She seemed so different from any *Englisch* woman she'd ever seen with her clanging jewelry and heavy makeup.

"Gram." Sophie smiled warmly, "I need to run to the grocery store. Do you think you can stick around for a bit and watch the kids for me?"

"Sure," he muttered. "I don't have anything else to do."

As soon as Sophie left, Gram leaned in. "She's not coming back with groceries, *FYI*. She's going to the bar. She'll be back later, drunk off her ass."

Ivy's stomach clenched. Her *dat* drank too much, too. And it never ended well.

"But it's fine," Gram said. "You'll be okay. I babysit all the time."

Ivy swallowed hard, scanning the room. She'd learned to read danger, to see it coming before it struck. She wasn't sure if Sophie was dangerous yet—she'd have to keep a close eye out.

"I'm watching TV," Gram said, slouching into the worn couch as *The Walking Dead* theme played. The living room, like the rest of the house, was a mess—mismatched furniture, scattered clothes, dirty dishes.

Ivy hesitated, glancing at the gruesome scene on-screen—a zombie tearing into a man's neck. She wasn't supposed to watch TV, especially not something this awful.

"Sit wherever," Gram said, gesturing to a recliner buried under laundry. "Push it on the floor if you want. I'm sick of cleaning up after everyone."

She perched stiffly on the edge, eyes widening at the horror unfolding. *Were all Englisch shows this gross?*

"If you're hungry, grab something from the kitchen," Gram said over the screams. "We eat whenever we feel like it."

Relieved to not have to watch this show any longer, Ivy rose from the recliner and escaped into the kitchen, where the young girls were still coloring. One of them—Maya?—yawned. The other one, Ashley, she thought, looked pale and tired as well. They were probably hungry, too. They didn't look like they were very well taken care of. At least in her home, she never went hungry.

"Hi, my name's Ivy." She gave a small wave with her casted arm. "I don't think Sophie mentioned that. I'm going to be staying here for a bit. Do you girls want something to eat? It's about supper time."

"Yes, please." They both cheered.

Ivy helped herself to what she could find in the refrigerator. Some slices of cheese and bread were a good start. Curious little faces followed her every move. Ivy handled the bread and cheese, the fingers on her casted arm clumsy but determined. She was out of her element here in this modern kitchen, but she used her common sense.

"You making them a sandwich, too?" Gram said from the doorway.

"Mm-hmm. It's a cheese sandwich. That's all you got here right now. Do you want one?"

"Nah. I stole a hot dog and chips at the park. Some birthday party celebration with lots of kids. No one ever pays attention to me."

Ivy wrinkled her nose. "You should stop stealing."

Gram raised an eyebrow, a smirk tugging at the corner of his mouth. "So you do remember me from the store."

Ivy's cheeks warmed. "Only because you were making such a scene."

"Sure, whatever." Gram shook his head and shrugged. "Let me know if you need anything. And thanks for offering them a sandwich."

Ivy murmured a few Amish curse words she'd learned from Jonas and continued making the sandwiches.

"What?" Gram halted and spun around. "Those words might be in your secret language, but they sound familiar. I know what you said to me."

"Sorry," Ivy said quickly. She hadn't meant for him to hear her.

Gram stepped toward her, and she flinched. She shouldn't have used such language. What if he told Sophie, and she got kicked out of this home, too?

His eyebrows bunched. "Do you think I'm gonna hit you?"

Ivy froze, staring up at him, not able to answer.

36

"You have to chill. I'm not going to hurt you, no matter what you call me. I'm not like that." His gaze shifted over her as he took several more steps away from her. "Relax. I'll leave you alone. You're safe, okay?"

Ivy pulled in a few deep breaths as he left the kitchen, thankful he wasn't about to throw her out or hold her slip-up against her. She relaxed and let her shoulders drop, the tension easing out slowly.

She glanced at Maya and Ashley. They were both staring up at her with wide eyes.

Ivy cleared her throat. "How about cheese sandwiches?"

"Yes!" they both shouted. "I *looove* cheese," Maya said in a cute monster voice.

"Okay." She smiled and set the plates down in front of them. Thinking they needed something to wash down the sandwiches, she grabbed two plastic cups, poured water out of the faucet, and set them on the table as well."

"Thank you, Ivy," Ashley said.

"You're welcome. Now, eat."

She ate at the table with the girls, careful to chew with her mouth closed. She'd learned her lesson to do this early in life. Her brothers hated it when anyone chewed loudly around them, and sometimes they shouted at her.

The sound coming from the living room still rattled her. Screams, shouts, whispers, then the gory sound of ripping flesh, followed by more screams. Maya and Ashley didn't seem bothered as they gulped down their food. They were probably used to it.

"Are you two sisters?" Ivy asked, curious.

"We're twins. But we don't look alike," Maya said.

"I see. How old are you?"

They both held up four fingers. "Almost five. We go to preschool," Ashley added, her Rs sounding like a *w*.

"Oh, how nice. Do you like it?"

Maya shrugged a thin shoulder. "We get to play on the playground."

"Unless Miss Dove is grumpy. Then we have to take a nap," Ashley said.

Their tiny, scrunched-up faces told Ivy they didn't care for naps.

"What happened to you?" Maya pointed at Ivy's cast. "Did you fall?"

Ivy wasn't sure how much to tell the young ones, if anything at all. "I... I got punished for doing something bad, is all."

"What'd you do?" Ashley looked concerned.

Ivy sighed, not sure how to explain without scaring the girls. "I got caught holding a stolen cookie," she said finally. "My church frowns on stealing."

"What?" Gram's voice boomed from the living room, and Ivy froze, suddenly noticing the TV had gone quiet.

Gram barged into the kitchen, looking somewhere between shocked and guilty. His gaze landed on her, and he softened, rubbing the back of his neck.

"Wait... am *I* the reason you got beat up?"

Ivy looked down.

"It was just a cookie," he muttered. "You looked so *sad* standing there. I didn't think..."

His guilt lifted something in her.

"You didn't force it on me," she said with a small shrug. "I knew the rules."

Gram ran a hand through his hair, looking wrecked. "If I'd known... I'm sorry, Ivy."

His sincerity surprised her.

Ivy placed a hand on his arm, surprised by the comfort his apology brought. "You didn't know. It's okay. Really."

"Well," he said, "you're not getting punished here. Not if I have anything to do with it."

Her cheeks heated under his serious leaf-green gaze, a storm brewing.

"Thank you," she whispered, a little awkwardly.

"Anytime. Really." He exhaled, running a hand through his hair again before heading back to the living room, muttering curses under his breath.

Ivy sat there stunned. A boy... being nice to her? *That* was new.

After eating, Ivy washed the dishes, wrapping her cast in a plastic bag for protection. She liked the convenience of running water, she thought, feeling a tinge of guilt. But she remembered she didn't have a choice. There were no water pumps or outhouses to be found. She *had* to use the indoor plumbing.

Gram peeped his head in at one time. "Are you doing the dishes on your first day, Little Amish Girl?"

Ivy nodded.

"Impressive," he said with a wink. "I see you, Newbie."

He was being silly. She bit back a smile and wiped down the counters. She guessed this house wasn't so bad for now.

That evening, Ivy found herself watching over Ashley and Maya, making sure they cleaned up their crafts and paints, stashing them away in a basket on the kitchen shelf. She wasn't sure that's where all the items belonged, but they had to go somewhere.

The girls giggled and joked as Ivy followed them up the staircase. It was getting late, Ivy was tired, and there was no sign of Ms. Sophie... shoot, she'd forgotten her last name.

And these girls could sure use a cleaning with their grimy faces and oily hair.

"You should take a bath and get into your pajamas," she told them, trying to sound like Ruth—responsible and in charge.

"Nooo! We're not dirty." Ashley stomped her foot.

"Yeah," Maya chimed in. "Sophie doesn't care."

"You'll sleep better if you're clean," Ivy said, using her *mamm*'s old reasoning. "Go grab some pajamas and I'll meet you in the bathroom."

To her surprise, they didn't fight her. They skipped off to grab pajamas, and Ivy went to scrub the murky bathtub and fill it with clean water, careful not to wet her cast.

The girls bounded in minutes later. "What about bubbles?"

"Bubbles and toys?" Ivy shook her head. "You only need water and soap to clean yourselves. Now get in."

They pouted but climbed in, splashing wildly. She poured water over their heads, scrubbing their hair the way *Mamm* and Ruth had taught her with the bar of soap.

"What are you doing?" a female voice called out from the hallway.

Ivy turned to face the rude teenage girl, Hannah, whom she'd encountered earlier. Exhausted and grumpy from being wet, with a sore arm, she dismissed the girl and kept pouring water over the girls' heads to rinse out the soap. It'd been a long day.

"I said, what are you doing?" She said with an edge.

"I heard ya," Ivy said, turning to look at the girl again. "I'm giving these two a bath."

Honestly, what did it look like she was doing?

"Sophie gives them a bath." Hannah's nose was crinkled.

"Well, Sophie's not here." Ivy pointed out the obvious. "So, I'm giving them one. They needed it bad."

"Oh." Her perplexed gaze zipped from one girl to the next, and then she pointed at two bottles sitting on the edge of the tub. "Next time, use the shampoo and conditioner on their hair. It's not the 1800s anymore. And if you run the conditioner through their hair, it'll be easier to brush afterward."

Before Ivy could question anything, Hannah disappeared into the depths of the hallway.

A drop of sweat skittered down Ivy's cheek. It sure was hot in this house, especially since she'd been moving around so much. She swept a stray hair back behind her ear and decided to unpin her cap and place it to the side.

"I like your braids," Maya said. "Can you do that to my hair?"

Ivy smiled. "Sure. But first, pajamas."

Ashley leaped from the tub before Ivy could wrap her in a towel, water pooling on the floor.

Silly little girls.

Ivy dried them, helped them dress, brushed their damp hair, and wove it into braids.

As she tucked them into bed, the clock read 9:18 p.m. Late. And Sophie still wasn't home.

"Does Sophie read to you?" she asked, grabbing a book from the floor.

Maya yawned. "No, she tells us to go to bed."

"Well," Ivy said, flipping open the book, "I'll read while you get comfy."

The girls cuddled under their blankets as Ivy read *Green Eggs and Ham*. Within minutes, both were fast asleep.

She slipped out quietly, washed her face, brushed her teeth, and changed for bed.

From downstairs, the TV blared again—more screams, more gore. *How could anyone watch that?*

She slid under the covers, staring at the ceiling.

So much had changed in one day.

She was different. Braver.

Or maybe simply more comfortable in a house with other kids.

At least here, there was no *dat* to fear. No punishments looming.

Just a messy home, a loud TV, and a *snicklefritz* of a teenage boy who—against all odds—had her back.

With that thought, she let her eyes drift shut.

Chapter Six

Now

Ivy tugged on her coat, stealing a glance at the small mirror by the door as the familiar shuffle of footsteps sounded behind her. She didn't have to turn around to know who it was—or what was coming next.

Two months had passed since Gram moved in, and he still felt more shadow than presence—hovering, observing, always one breath away from offering an opinion she hadn't asked for.

She caught his reflection in the mirror, his arms crossed, his expression set in that *older-brother-knows-best* way she knew all too well.

"Where are you going?" Gram asked, voice casual. But his eyes? Too sharp for casual.

He'd cleaned up since moving in—gotten a haircut, kept his face shaved. His wardrobe was limited, but always neat. And when he wasn't acting like an overbearing weirdo, he actually looked pretty good. Handsome, even.

Ivy sighed, turning to face him as she tied her scarf around her neck. "I'm going out with Camron," she said, trying to keep her tone light. "We're grabbing dinner."

Gram cleared his throat as he leaned against the doorframe. "He treating you okay?" His words were simple, but there was an edge to them, a warning lingering beneath the surface.

Ivy chuckled, shaking her head. "Yes, he's treating me fine, Gram. You don't need to worry."

But Gram didn't look convinced. His eyes narrowed slightly, the frown on his face deepening. "I'm not a fan of the guy," he muttered, almost to himself.

Ivy raised an eyebrow, half-amused, half-exasperated. "Really? And why's that?"

"There's something off about him," Gram said, shifting his weight, his arms still crossed as if to make himself seem even bigger than he already was. "I can't put my finger on it, but I... don't like him."

Ivy rolled her eyes, giving him a playful shove on the shoulder. "It's your imagination, Gram. Camron's a good guy. You're being paranoid."

Gram didn't budge, his expression still serious. "Maybe. But if he does you wrong, you let me know. I'll take care of him." His tone carried a lightness, but something darker ran beneath it. The edge in his voice hinted at the old version of himself—the part of him that had always been fiercely protective, maybe even too much so.

She paused, the memory of the past surfacing in her mind. The time when Sophie's boyfriend stumbled into Ivy's bedroom, sitting on her bed too close, causing her to scream in fear. Gram hadn't hesitated, not for a second, to run into her room and beat the guy to a pulp.

The thought made her stomach twist, and she looked up at him, a little more seriously now. "Gram," she said quietly, stepping closer. "I'm an adult now. I can take care of myself, and I need you to recognize that."

He met her gaze, the tension stretching between them, unspoken and unmoving.

After a long pause, Gram finally shrugged.

"Fine," he said. "But be careful, okay?"

Ivy smiled, reaching out to squeeze his arm. "I will. And you need to back off a little, okay? I appreciate the concern, but I've got this."

Gram sighed, running a hand through his hair. "Fine. I'll zip my lips."

With one last grin, Ivy slipped on her shoes and grabbed her purse. "Good. Now, don't wait up for me. I'll probably be back late."

As she opened the door and stepped out into the cool spring evening air, she couldn't help but feel a mix of emotions. Gram's protectiveness had once been a source of comfort, but now it felt like a burden she wasn't sure she could carry. She was an adult, and while she understood his concern, she knew she had to stand on her own.

Still, as she walked down the metal staircase and down the street to meet Camron, a small part of her couldn't shake the memory of Gram's past. He'd always meant well, but there was a fierceness in him that sometimes made her nervous. She hoped he really would back off this time.

Dinner with Camron didn't go well either, unfortunately.

The restaurant was quiet, the soft clinking of silverware and the low murmur of conversation creating an intimate atmosphere. Camron sat across from her, his brow furrowed as he cut into his steak. His usual easygoing nature seemed strained tonight, and Ivy sensed something was on his mind. She knew what it was, but she waited, giving him the space to bring it up.

As they finished their meal, Camron set his fork down, glancing at her over the candlelight. His voice was steady, but Ivy could sense the tension in the air.

"Ivy, can we talk about something?"

She met his gaze, lifting her chin. "Of course. What's on your mind?"

Camron shifted in his seat, fingers tapping on the edge of the table. "It's... about Gram."

And there it was. Ivy placed her fork down and gave him her attention. "What about him?" she asked, trying to keep her tone calm when she felt defensive. Protective.

Camron sighed, rubbing the back of his neck, clearly uncomfortable. "Look, I know he was your foster brother, and I respect what you're doing by helping him out. But it's been two months now, and I'm concerned."

Ivy leaned back, crossing her arms, guarded. "Concerned about what, exactly?"

Camron hesitated, watching her carefully. "I don't mean to overstep, but don't you think Gram's getting a little too comfortable? He's living in your apartment, working in your bakery... he's always around. It worries me how much space he takes up in your life and how much of an influence he has on you."

Space? Influence? He spoke as if she were easily swayed, as if she lacked the ability to make her own choices. The implication didn't settle well, to say the least.

"Gram isn't a problem, Camron." Ivy leveled him a look. "He's been through hell, and I'm giving him a chance to get back on his feet. That's it. If you're expecting some big conspiracy where he's pulling my strings, you're wasting your time."

Camron sighed, his jaw tightening. "That's not what I mean. I'm not saying you shouldn't help him. But I've seen the way he watches you —still acting as though you need his protection. As though I'm some obstacle he has to work around." His fingers curled around his napkin, knuckles pale. "It doesn't feel right, Ivy. It isn't."

Ivy raised an eyebrow. "We've been through a lot together, Camron. You know that. He's had my back when no one else did, and now I'm returning the favor. That's what loyalty looks like."

"Yeah, but you don't need him to protect you anymore," Camron countered. "You're running a business, handling your own life. Meanwhile, Gram's still—" He stopped short, shaking his head. "I don't want him holding you back."

Ivy squared her shoulders. "Let's get something straight," she said, her voice stern, "I am an adult. I might be twenty-one, and people still look at me like I'm some clueless kid, but they, and you, have no idea what I've lived through—what I've carried to get here. No one's holding me back. I'm exactly where I want to be, doing what I want to do. Gram's not some lost cause I'm babysitting; he's family. And I don't need you treating me like I don't know what I'm doing."

Camron exhaled slowly, searching her face. "I get that, Ivy. I do. But don't you think at some point, he has to stand on his own? You've done more than enough for him." He hesitated. "I don't want to see you being taken advantage of."

Ivy leaned forward, locking eyes with him. "I'll decide when enough is enough. Not you. If we're going to be together, you need to trust me to handle my own life. Can you do that?"

For a long moment, neither of them spoke. Camron's expression wavered, a mix of reluctance and something softer. Finally, he sighed, dropping his gaze to the table. "I don't want him to come between us."

"He's not," Ivy said simply. "I'm here, aren't I? But if this relationship is going to work, you need to understand that Gram is a part of my life. That's not going to change."

Camron's mouth tightened, his shoulders still rigid. "All right. I'll back off. But I really hope you're right about him."

Ivy forced a small smile, but she knew this wouldn't be the last time they had this conversation. As the waiter dropped the check between them, a wave of unease settled in. She'd always been able to keep the people in her life balanced—knowing where to place each one so nothing toppled over.

But this time, the weight felt uneven, and she wasn't sure how much longer she could keep everything from slipping.

Chapter Seven

Now

Ivy had every intention of getting a full night's sleep—really, she did. But the book in her hands had other plans. Each chapter sank its hooks in deeper, unraveling enough to demand she keep going. She told herself one more page, then one more chapter, but the truth was, she wasn't avoiding sleep. She was avoiding the nightmare.

The one where Ruth was trapped. Where Ivy tried to reach her but never could.

The dream clung to her, slithering at the edges of her consciousness even when she was awake. It was trying to tell her something, some message buried beneath the horror of it. But Ivy didn't want to dig too deep into the logistics. She was too afraid of what she might remember —of what might claw its way back from the past if she let herself think too hard. Maybe it was just a dream, a cruel reminder of how she and her siblings had spent their childhood cowering under their father's wrath. Or maybe... maybe it wasn't a dream at all.

Her pulse quickened at the thought, fingers tightening around the worn edges of the pages. If she stayed awake, she wouldn't have to see

Ruth tangled in those monstrous coils again—wouldn't have to hear that sickening, hissing voice.

She barely registered the exhaustion waiting to ambush her in the morning—until a soft knock shattered the quiet, yanking her out of the story and back into the real world.

Ivy sighed, reluctantly slipping a bookmark between the pages before setting the novel aside.

She slid out of bed, padding toward the door with quiet, measured steps. Peering through the peephole, her stomach clenched. Camron. He stood outside, at the top of the metal staircase, shifting unsteadily under the dim glow of the overhead light. Even through the distorted glass, she could tell—he was drunk.

This was so unlike Camron. He rarely drank more than two drinks at a time. But now, seeing him sway like that brought back memories of her father. She remembered nights filled with the same unstable movement and the same unsettling feeling of helplessness.

Bracing herself, she unlatched the door and pulled it open enough to meet his gaze. The confirmation hit her instantly. His eyes were unfocused, his grin lazy and lopsided—missing the warmth she had come to expect from him.

"Hey," he drawled, dragging a hand through his already messy hair. "Thought I'd drop by. Maybe... stay the night?"

Ivy's brows pulled together as unease coiled in her gut. She partially shut the door and blocked his entrance with her body.

"Camron, you've been drinking. It's late. That's not happening."

He let out a chuckle, hollow and edged with something brittle. "Not happening, huh? What, because Gram's here?"

Ivy exhaled, folding her arms, refusing to take the bait. "No. Because you're drunk, and I'm not interested in having this conversation when you're like this. Let me call you a ride. We can talk tomorrow."

Camron's expression darkened, the hurt in his eyes quickly masked by something colder. "Oh, I see how it is," he muttered. "My friends warned me. Said this would happen. Told me you were probably sleeping with the guy."

The words landed like a slap, but Ivy barely flinched. Instead, a slow, simmering anger took its place. She met his gaze, unwavering. "I'm not going *to* entertain that kind of accusation. And I'm sure as hell not going to stand here and argue with a drunk man at my door. Go home, Camron. We'll talk when you're sober."

Before he could get another word out, the door behind her creaked open wider. A familiar presence filled the space beside her, solid and unmoving.

Gram.

She glanced up and became wary of his expression.

His face was carved from stone, his green eyes locked onto Camron with an unmistakable warning. "You heard her," he said. "Time to go."

Camron let out a sharp, humorless laugh, his mouth curling into something ugly. "Oh, here we go. The homeless knight in shining armor to the rescue." He dragged a hand through his hair, his eyes glassy with frustration and booze. Then he turned his attention back to Ivy, his expression twisting into something pitiful. "You know what? I'm done. I can't do this. I can't be with someone who's clearly hung up on another guy—especially one who's sleeping under her roof."

Behind her, Ivy could feel Gram bristle, but before he could react, she lifted a hand, motioning for him to stand down. "Gram, go back to your room. It's fine."

There was a hesitation, a hint of reluctance in Gram's stance, but eventually, he gave her one last look before turning away, his heavy footsteps disappearing down the hall to his bedroom.

Ivy stepped fully onto the outside staircase, pulling the door shut behind her. The cool night air brushed against her skin, grounding her as she met Camron's gaze head-on. "If that's how you feel, then I won't stop you. I'm not going to fight for something that shouldn't need fighting for."

Camron's gaze narrowed. "You're... okay with it? Just like that?"

"Just like that," she repeated. "If you don't trust me—if you don't trust *this*—then we shouldn't be together. Simple as that."

Camron stared at her, as if searching for some sign she was bluffing. But Ivy wasn't. She refused to buckle under the pressure of his insecurity.

His voice dropped, quieter now. "You never really let me in, did you?"

Ivy exhaled, her fingers tightening slightly around the railing. "Maybe not," she admitted, though she wasn't sure if she was saying it for him or for herself.

He let out a slow, bitter sigh, shaking his head. "I could never understand you. Not like he does."

A sharp pang went through her, but not for the reasons he thought. It wasn't guilt or regret—it was recognition. Because deep down, she knew he was right.

But that was a door she wasn't ready to open.

"Goodbye, Ivy," Camron said.

She didn't stop him. She didn't try to fix it or soften the blow. She watched as he turned and walked away, his footsteps clanking against the metal stairs before fading into the night.

When he disappeared around the corner, she let out a slow breath, rolling her shoulders to shake off the lingering tension. There was no regret. No ache. Only the quiet certainty that this had been inevitable from the start. Camron had always been reaching for something she couldn't give. And she wasn't about to apologize for that.

She stepped back inside, locking the door behind her before making her way to her bedroom. The lamp by her bed still cast a warm, golden glow over the pages of her book, waiting for her as if nothing had happened. She slipped under the covers, picking it up again, her fingers skimming over the words.

She knew she should sleep—she had to be up early for the bakery—but the story pulled her back in. A welcome escape.

Her thoughts shifted to Gram for the briefest of moments before she pushed them aside. That was a complication for another day. Right now, she had a business to run, a life to build, and pages to turn.

Everything else could wait.

Chapter Eight

Then

Laughter and the pattering of small feet woke Ivy. Sunlight streamed through the curtains as she blinked, momentarily disoriented. Then she remembered—her first morning in the new foster home.

She checked the bed. *No accident.* Thank goodness.

In the daylight, the room looked like a toy tornado had hit. Stuffed animals were everywhere, some perched on her bed as if waiting for a chat. Dolls lay tangled in a pile of brightly colored clothes, and a bookshelf overflowed with well-loved storybooks. Crayon drawings were pinned to the walls—some drawn directly on them. A toy chest gaped open, its contents spilling out. A lullaby tune hummed softly from a forgotten toy.

Ivy sat up, rubbing her eyes. Maya and Ashley's giggles filled the space, their laughter making Ivy smile.

"Good morning," Ivy croaked.

"Hi!" Ashley bounced on her feet. "Come downstairs. We're hungry."

"Okay." Ivy patted her braids, still intact, and pinned on her prayer cap as the girls dashed downstairs. She dressed quickly, maneuvering her cast through the sleeve, grateful her church had switched to eyelets instead of sharp pins.

Downstairs, the TV blared, and Gram was sprawled on the couch, unmoving.

"Still wearing the Amish shit?" he said when he saw her.

"Don't be rude," Ivy shot back before she could think better of it.

Gram gave a dry half-smile. "Whatever. I have school, and Sophie'll take the girls to preschool. You'll be here alone."

Ivy shrugged one shoulder, trying to seem brave.

"Your caseworker will probably register you for school. *If* she's any good." He scoffed. "Mine doesn't give a shit about me."

Emily seemed nice enough, but Ivy wasn't ready for a new school yet. Her *dat* allowed her and her siblings to go to public school since there wasn't an Amish school within miles of their house. The bus picked them up every morning and took them to school. Ivy was used to sitting beside one of her siblings. The thought of them had her wondering if they were all in the same school now, and if they were doing okay.

Her heart hurt thinking about missing them.

To distract herself, she helped the girls pour cereal and milk, watching them eat as memories of home surfaced—gathering eggs, baking bread, Ruth cooking breakfast, *Mamm's* morning coffee soup. The scents, the sounds. Tears stung her eyes. *Be strong, behave, and one day, you'll go home.*

Sophie entered in a colorful robe, makeup smudged under her tired eyes.

"Good morning, loves," she said, heading straight for the coffee.

Maya beamed. "Guess what, Sophie? Ivy gave us a bath and braided our hair!"

"And now our hair is curly!" Ashley clapped her hands.

Sophie turned to them, and Ivy held her breath, worried she'd overstepped.

"So pretty," Sophie said, then winked at Ivy. "Less work for me this morning. Thanks, sweetie."

Relief spread through Ivy. She'd been useful. Ruth would be proud.

"I like to help," she said.

Sophie smiled. "I adore you already." She took a sip of coffee. "I was out late. Sometimes I need to blow off steam—maybe don't tell Emily. Caseworkers can be dramatic about kids being home alone, even though I know you're all so self-sufficient."

Ivy hesitated. "No, ma'am, I won't tell. Everything was fine."

Sophie patted her shoulder. "Good girl. And call me Sophie. Ma'am makes me feel ancient." She sipped her coffee. "Hey, do you mind getting these monsters dressed?"

"Yes, ma—Sophie."

Sophie's eyes warmed. "I have a feeling we'll get along well."

Ivy swallowed hard, not sure if that was a good thing.

Hours passed, and Sophie hadn't returned. Ivy didn't mind. Alone time gave her the chance to get her bearings.

She scrubbed the kitchen, mopped the floors, and soaked laundry in the tub, uncertain how to use the electric washing machine in the dark basement. The machine at home had a simple tub, a washboard, and a crank that allowed her to wring out the wet clothing. She'd once gotten her finger caught in between the two rollers when she was smaller and dumber. Luckily, her sister Esther had been with her to release the crank and set her free, but dang, how that had hurt. She'd cried and cried until Esther couldn't take it anymore and told her to hush before *Dat* heard her and spanked her.

That had shut her up real quick.

Ivy shook the memory from her mind and hung the damp clothes over the porch railing to dry.

Everything took longer with her cast, but she managed.

Worn out and hungry, she made her way to the kitchen and fixed herself a sandwich. They were running low on bread and a few other things, so Ivy wrote out a shopping list, hoping Sophie wouldn't mind.

The front door creaked open then, and Sophie called out a "Hello," sounding tired but cheerful.

Ivy peeked at her from the kitchen, quickly cleaning up the crumbs from her sandwich.

"Welcome home, Sophie," Ivy said softly, hoping her efforts to clean would be appreciated. She walked to the living room to see Sophie's eyes sweeping the room, taking in the spotless floors and the absence of toys and clutter that had taken over the space.

Ivy wouldn't ask where Sophie had been all morning—she didn't want to be rude.

"Ivy, this is incredible," Sophie said warmly. "The place looks wonderful."

Her cheeks flushed with delight. "I wanted to surprise you and show you how much I appreciate you letting me stay here."

"I have one question, though." Sophie gestured outside. "Why is there laundry hanging on the porch?"

Shoot. Ivy had forgotten to bring those in. "At home, we had a clothing line to hang and dry our clothes," she tried to explain. "I thought it would be the best way."

Sophie barked out a laugh. "Ah, I see. Well, I'll show you how to use the dryer. That'll be easier and quicker. Let's bring them in. They look dry."

Together, they gathered the clothes, and Ivy watched as Sophie dumped her pile on the couch in a heap. She made a face and carefully laid out her pile of clothes over the top of the furniture, hoping not to wrinkle them.

"We'll fold these later," Sophie said. "Let me show you how to use the machines."

Hesitantly, Ivy followed Sophie down into the basement. It smelled like detergent and damp concrete. Sophie explained the machines, demonstrating the settings. Ivy focused, determined to remember.

"You did a great job today," Sophie said, squeezing Ivy's shoulder. "Thank you."

"I don't mind. It's what I'm good at."

Sophie smiled. "Well, one more thing—we need to get you registered for school."

"Right now? I... uh." Ivy's stomach clenched. She knew her school was closer to her rural Amish community, miles from here, but she wished she could still go to it. Starting at a new school without her siblings would be scary.

"You'll be fine," Sophie said. "I'll be with you."

The school was big—too big. Ivy swallowed hard, gripping the straps of her bag as she stepped inside. The halls buzzed with voices, laughter, and the sharp clang of lockers slamming shut. A bell shrieked somewhere above her, making her jump.

So many eyes. Watching. Staring. Whispering.

Not one of them dressed like her. No plain dresses. No caps. No other Amish kids. She stood alone.

Her black shoes tapped too loudly against the shiny floor, each step echoing like a reminder that she didn't belong here. Back home, her school had only a handful of children, all in simple clothes like hers. Here, everything was bright, fast, and strange.

She lowered her head, wishing she could disappear. But there was nowhere to hide.

Sophie crouched down, looking Ivy right in the eyes. "You all right, sweetheart? We can find you some different clothes if you'd like."

Ivy shook her head firmly. "I'm fine."

Sophie gave her hand a quick squeeze. "Then let's get you registered."

The office smelled strange—too clean. The kind of place that never saw dirt or fresh air. Ivy stood still as a woman with glasses flipped through her file. Her gaze darted to Ivy's dress, her mouth pressing into a thin line.

"You attended public school before?" the woman asked.

"Yes, ma'am," Ivy answered, sitting up straighter. "I learned English, reading, writing, and math."

The woman hesitated, her fingers hovering over the keyboard.

"Ivy is bright," Sophie said firmly. "The only difference is what she wears."

A long pause. Then the woman cleared her throat. "We'll do our best to make her feel welcome."

Sophie kept hold of Ivy's hand as they followed the woman down the hall. Ivy tried not to look too much at the other children who passed by, but she could feel their eyes on her—curious, amused, uncertain.

They stopped at a door labeled "3B." The woman pushed it open, and the sound of chatting students spilled out.

"This will be your homeroom," she said. "Mrs. Thompson is your teacher."

At the front of the class stood a young woman with bright blonde hair and an even brighter smile. "Class, we have a new friend joining us today. Everyone, say hello to Ivy."

She was met with a mix of greetings—some friendly, some quiet—and a few muffled giggles.

Ivy stood tall, swallowing down the nervousness creeping up. Sophie had said it plain and simple. *The only thing different was her clothes.*

"Thank you," she said, lifting her chin.

Sophie squeezed Ivy's hand. "You'll do fine," she whispered.

The administrator ushered Ivy and Sophie back to the school's entrance. "I'll finish up the paperwork, and if I find any issues, I'll give you a call, Ms. Harris."

"No problem," Sophie said. "You can reach out to Ivy's caseworker as well if you need to. I gave you her information."

Sophie led Ivy out to the parking lot and into the car. She drove back into their neighborhood and pointed to a stop sign on the corner. "You'll need to wait here for the bus. It'll take you straight to school." She pointed in another direction. "Do you see right down this street is our home? It'll be a quick walk."

Ivy nodded, understanding. "I had to do that at home too, but I waited for the bus with my sisters and brothers." Jonas, Esther, Joseph, Leah, and Eli.

Ruth had finished up her required education and didn't have to go to school anymore. She'd mostly worked in the barn, helping *Dat.*

Sophie's expression softened. "I know it's different here, but you'll make friends. And remember, I'm always here for you."

"Thank you, Sophie. I'll try my best."

Sophie wrapped her arm around Ivy's shoulders, pulling her into a comforting hug. "That's all I can ask for, Ivy. You're going to be fine."

Ivy hoped so. Her world was changing dramatically, but she'd have to remain brave and strong.

The evening routine was different this time. Sophie stayed home and made Hamburger Helper from a box. Ivy didn't complain. Sometimes her *mamm* had to make meals this way because it was faster and easier, though her *dat* had always turned his nose up at it. He liked homemade noodles and sauce. Homemade casseroles. Homemade bread. All from scratch.

Ivy's stomach rumbled as she remembered the smells that had filled the house.

Sophie gave everyone a serving of the beef stroganoff with a side of corn, and Ivy followed the others as they marched their plates into the living room and sat in front of the television.

A comedy show was playing, it seemed, since every so often the audience in the background would laugh. Hannah and Gram laughed along with some of the jokes. Jokes that Ivy didn't quite understand. Maya and Ashley didn't seem to get it either, but they were concentrating on scarfing down their dinner.

"My goodness," Sophie said, "didn't you girls eat lunch?"

"Yeah," Ashley said, "but it was gross. Green veggies and gross nuggets."

Maya added a gagging sound.

"Well, you need to eat your lunch, girls. I don't want to be accused of not giving you enough nutrition."

"Right," Gram said. "Eat your shitty lunch so Sophie doesn't get in trouble, get us taken away, and then lose her foster parent checks. She wouldn't be able to get lit every other night then."

"Excuse you, Gram." Sophie shoved gently at Gram's shoulder. He was sitting on the floor, his plate on the coffee table. "Don't be rude. And I'm not like that. I actually *care* about my foster kids, if you haven't noticed."

"Sure, sure." Gram rolled his eyes, and Hannah swatted him across the head. "Ouch, what was that for?"

"For being annoying." Hannah gestured to the television. "Shut up for once. I can't hear what's going on."

Ivy watched the interactions with interest. The way the children were allowed to curse and disrespect Sophie and each other was fascinating. They had no severe repercussions. No punishments. And they weren't afraid to say what was on their minds.

"By the way, Sophie," Gram continued, "I noticed that Ivy made a grocery list. Any chance you're going to the store anytime soon? I'm hungry for cookies." He winked at Ivy.

Ivy flushed.

"Sure, I'll make a grocery run in the morning while you guys are at school." Sophie glanced at Ivy. "I noticed you have flour, sugar, and yeast on the list. What's that for?"

"Oh, well," Ivy started quietly, fearful that Hannah might swat at her, too. "I can make some bread. And maybe some biscuits and noodles."

"Wow," Gram said. "You can do all that, newbie?"

"Yes, my *mamm* taught me how."

"Got it. Is that the person who beat the crap out of you?"

"Gram!" Sophie's fork clanked on her plate. "Don't speak to her that way."

Ivy swallowed hard. She didn't answer him—she wanted to forget that night. Instead, she turned toward the television and bravely said, "Gram, you should listen to Hannah and shut up."

"Nice," Hannah said. "Get him, Ivy."

Gram chuckled, shaking his head. "Little Amish Girl's fitting in just fine."

Chapter Nine

Now

Ivy and Gram worked side-by-side in the bakery kitchen, their movements falling into an easy rhythm as they frosted cupcakes and added the final touches of sprinkles. She wouldn't say it out loud, but there was something about working with him that... clicked. Like they'd been doing this forever. Like he belonged here.

Sunlight streamed through the kitchen windows, warming the countertops, catching the fine dusting of flour on their aprons. Ivy focused on piping buttercream, trying to ignore how close Gram was standing. How the heat of him was there, steady and distracting.

Which was ridiculous.

Especially since she'd broken things off with Camron last night. Shouldn't she be mourning the loss of her relationship?

Except... she wasn't.

Because deep down, she knew the truth—she'd never felt this kind of pull toward Cam. Not like this. And now that she'd admitted that to herself, she couldn't unfeel it.

It wasn't fair, the way Gram's presence settled next to her, solid and familiar, like a fire she wanted to sink into. Or how her pulse jumped whenever his arm brushed hers.

She was not the kind of girl who got flustered over a guy.

Not since Beck, at least.

Oh, geez. Now her mind was veering toward him.

She still thought about Beck more than she should—where he was now, if he was in Colorado, if he'd found someone new.

Ivy shook off the spiral of thoughts, forcing herself to focus. There was dough to knead, cakes to decorate, and no time for whatever nonsense her heart was trying to pull right now.

Outside the bakery, the city was waking up, the last traces of winter giving way to fresh spring air. The trees along the sidewalk had finally started budding.

But something about Gram felt different this morning.

He was quiet, his usual easy chatter absent.

As he started rolling out dough for the pies, he finally spoke. "I heard what happened last night with Camron." He didn't look up, but kept his focus on the rolling pin. "The breakup."

Ivy's hands stilled, her fingers pressing into the soft dough beneath her palms. Of course, he'd heard. His bedroom was off the front entrance, and the walls weren't exactly thick.

She exhaled, forcing a small smile. "Yeah, I've survived worse." The words came out light, but they sat heavy in her chest.

Gram finally glanced over, meeting her gaze with those sharp green eyes, softened by something unspoken. He nudged her shoulder, enough to be felt but not enough to push.

"You know I'm here, right?" he said. "If you ever need to talk."

It was such a simple thing, but somehow, it settled something in her.

She pressed the dough beneath her hands with more purpose. "I know."

And somehow, she really did.

The moment stretched, unspoken, dangling between them, until the front door chimed, pulling Ivy back to reality. A gust of wind followed Fiona inside, catching strands of her red hair as she pushed them away from her face.

"Morning," Fiona called, shrugging off her jacket as she made her way to the counter. "Guess what I read on my way here."

Ivy pulled off her apron and tossed it onto the nearest hook. "What's up?"

"There's an article going around about abuse in the Amish community," Fiona said, scrolling through her phone. "It made me think of you."

Ivy stiffened, her pulse skipping. "Let me see."

Fiona handed over the phone, and Ivy's eyes scanned the screen. The words hit her harder than she expected—stories of hidden pain, of women and children suffering in silence, trapped within the rigid control of their communities.

She forced herself to finish reading, but by the time she handed the phone back, her fingers were trembling.

"Ivy?" Gram tilted his head.

She swallowed hard, trying to ground herself. "I'm fine," she said, but the slight tremor in her voice betrayed her. "It... brought up some things."

Fiona touched her arm. "I'm sorry, I didn't mean—"

"No, it's okay." Ivy forced a tight smile. "I haven't thought about my family in a long time." She hesitated, her next words slipping out before she could stop them. "Maybe I should try to find them."

Gram set down the rolling pin, turning toward her, and crossing his arms. "You think that's a good idea?"

"I don't know." She exhaled, running a hand over her apron. "But maybe it's time."

Later, after the morning rush had passed and the bakery had settled into a lull, Ivy sat alone in the office, staring at her phone. The article still lingered in her mind, stirring up ghosts she'd spent years avoiding.

Taking a breath, she typed her last name—Schrock—into the search bar, not expecting much. Her family had always kept to themselves. The Amish world didn't spill onto the internet easily.

But then, something caught her eye.

Reuben H. Schrock.

Her breath hitched.

She clicked the link, her eyes scanning over the obituary. It was brief—his age, his dedication to the Amish faith, the family he'd left behind.

Her mother's name was listed. So were her siblings.

Except Ruth.

Ivy had expected it. But seeing it still sent a cold, hard knot twisting through her stomach.

Ruth, her first protector. The one who had whispered reassurances when their home was chaotic. The one who had taken the brunt of their father's anger to shield Ivy from it.

She'd heard Ruth had been placed in foster care, too. But she had never looked for her. Maybe she'd wanted to believe Ruth had found a good home. Maybe she'd been afraid of what she'd find.

But now, staring at the absence of Ruth's name, she realized what she hadn't let herself see before.

Had their family continued to shun Ruth?

Was she safe?

Was she alive?

Ivy's fingers clenched around the phone. Ruth had always been the strong one, the one who stood between Ivy and the worst of their father's wrath.

So why did it feel like she had disappeared outside of Ivy's nightmares?

A wave of emotions surged through her—curiosity, fear, frustration. And beneath all of it, something heavier.

Regret.

Guilt.

She had meant to look for Ruth. She really had.

Fueled by a sudden urgency, Ivy typed in her siblings' names, one after another. Most led to dead ends. Until she found Jonas.

Jonas Schrock, listed under a business directory.

Amish furniture maker.

Her heart pounded as she typed his name and his city into the search bar. A recent auction listing appeared. Jonas had purchased a house.

She stared at the address. Something about it tugged at her memory.

It was close.

Too close.

Her breath shallowed. Was it—could it be—near their family home?

Either way, she had a lead. She knew where to find Jonas. And if anyone had answers about Ruth, it would be him.

But what would Ruth think if Ivy suddenly reappeared in her life? Would Jonas even want to see her?

Doubt crept in, but something inside her refused to let go. She had spent years avoiding her past, pretending it didn't matter. But the part of her that still ached for closure knew the truth—she *needed* to do this.

Ivy texted herself Jonas's address as Gram peeked his head into her office. She met his curious gaze and let him in on her plan.

"You sure you don't want me to come?" Gram tossed a rag over his shoulder and leaned against the doorway, watching her closely. "I can hold things down here, but... you don't have to do this alone."

Ivy smiled, touched by the offer. "I'll be fine, Gram. This is something I have to do on my own."

He frowned but didn't argue. "All right," he said reluctantly. "But if you need anything, you call me. I mean it. I'll come running."

"Got it." Ivy stood and walked to him, squeezing his arm before grabbing her coat and heading out the door.

As she merged onto the busy street, the bakery shrinking in her rearview mirror, a knot tightened in her stomach. She had no idea what she was walking into, no clue how it would feel to stand face-to-face with the ghosts of her old life.

But she wasn't turning back now.

Chapter Ten

Then

Ivy walked to the bus stop, her black bonnet secured over her prayer cap. She'd put on her least-worn dress—it was her first day at the new school, and she wanted to look her best. She knew she stood out, but this was how she was supposed to dress. And she wouldn't do anything more to separate herself from her family.

The crisp May air carried the scent of dew as she clutched her tote bag, her nerves thrumming. A group of kids stood by the curb, all jeans and brightly colored shirts.

As Ivy stepped closer, the whispering started. A few sideways glances. A couple of snickers. She stared at the ground, pretending not to hear.

Then a boy with messy blond hair stepped forward, smirking. "What's with the old-lady clothes? You Amish or something?"

Ivy barely had time to answer before he reached out and yanked the string of her bonnet. The sudden pull sent pins scraping against her scalp, making her wince.

"Stop," she said, gripping the fabric to keep it from slipping.

The boy laughed, reaching to tug again—until another voice cut in.

"Leave her alone, Derek."

Ivy looked up to see a girl about her age with dark hair and fierce eyes stepping between them. She crossed her arms and glared at him. "Why don't you pick on someone your own size?"

Derek scoffed, stuffing his hands in his pockets. "Whatever." He backed off, but not before shooting Ivy one last sneer.

The girl turned to Ivy. "I'm Molly. Sorry about him—he's my brother, and he's a big ol' jerk."

Ivy retied her bonnet. "Thanks. I'm Ivy."

Molly grinned. "You have really pretty eyes. I've never met an Amish girl before. I see them around, but none live here. I have, like, a hundred questions." The girl spoke so fast that Ivy had to take a moment to absorb her words.

Before she could answer, the bus pulled up.

Molly waved her along. "Sit with me?"

Relieved, Ivy followed her new friend. Maybe today wouldn't be so bad.

School went by fast. Unlike her old school, they switched rooms for different subjects, which was confusing at first. At least Molly was in her library class, making things easier.

They strolled through the library aisles, Molly pointing out books Ivy had never seen before—certainly not at home. Ivy's church didn't allow these sorts of books, but she couldn't help but pick one up and scan over the cover. A girl stood on a rooftop, looking daring and brave, like she might laugh in the face of trouble.

Ivy wanted a little of that courage. And the book looked exciting. She gulped down her nerves and decided to check out a couple of books in the series. No one from the church would know, and she could hide them in her backpack. It wasn't like she was changing her outer appearance. This could be her secret, and she didn't have older brothers and sisters looking over her shoulder. Or a *dat* who might find out and whip her.

After school, Ivy was surprised to see Gram waiting for her at the bus stop. His arms were crossed over his chest, and he glared at each child as they stomped off the bus. Once he saw Ivy, he winked at her and gave her a warm smile.

"You okay?" he asked.

"Yes."

"Are you sure? Because I saw that fucking kid over there"—he pointed to Derek as he stepped off the bus—"pulling on your hatstrings this morning."

Ivy didn't correct him that it was a bonnet, not a hat, because she suddenly felt nervous for Derek. "It's fine," Ivy mumbled.

"Yeah, he did," Molly added in. "My brother's an idiot—barely passed sixth grade."

"Molly, shut up!" Derek's cheeks turned a bright shade of red.

The bus drove away, leaving the kids to find their way home. Derek turned and strode quickly down the sidewalk.

"Hey." Gram moved after him, grabbing his shoulder. He towered above the boy, who must've been about twelve years old.

"I didn't mean anything by it," Derek said. "I was playing around."

A knife appeared in Gram's hands, and Ivy gasped as he held it to Derek's neck. He said something under his breath to Derek, who stared up at him with wide eyes.

Molly stiffened beside Ivy. "Is he going to hurt my brother?"

"I don't know," Ivy said honestly.

Then just as quickly, the knife disappeared, and Gram sauntered back toward Ivy.

"He's not going to bother you anymore," he said to Ivy and turned to Molly. "And he's not going to bother you either, okay? Don't tell your parents, and we all call it even, got it?"

Molly swallowed. "Okay, I won't." She turned to Ivy and waved. "See you tomorrow!"

"See you tomorrow." Ivy waved back, her hands shaking.

She stayed quiet as she walked back to the house with Gram beside her all the way. She was glad he stood up for her, even if it had been extreme, but she was also worried he'd get her in trouble again.

"Hey," Gram said. "Don't tell Sophie about the knife. She'd have to report it, and I'd get sent away. This place sucks, but it's better than the others I've been in."

Ivy stopped to look at him, making sure he understood how serious she was. "I won't tell, but don't do that again. And don't steal anything anymore. I don't want to get in trouble again. I want to go home, and I won't be able to if I get caught being bad again."

Gram frowned. "I can't tell you how sorry I am for that, Ivy. I didn't mean for that to happen. You looked so sad and scared standing there in the store. You looked like you needed a cookie. I... geez, again, I'm so sorry."

"Just don't do anything like that again," Ivy remained firm, staring up at this teenage boy, who looked a bit handsome this close to her. His dark tan contrasted with his green eyes.

"I won't. I promise."

"Okay, good. Let's go inside. I want to get started on the bread."

"Hell yeah." He pumped his fist. "Let's hope Sophie got everything you need. Homemade bread sounds tasty."

That evening, Sophie left to go to the bar again—she hadn't lied this time but asked that Ivy not tell Emily.

Ivy was keeping a lot of secrets from Emily, and that worried her.

But she agreed. After hearing Gram say that this was one of the better foster homes, she didn't want to find out about the others. She wanted this one to last for as long as she was being punished.

She spent the evening kneading dough, letting it rise like her *mamm* had taught her. Gram helped set the oven—way easier than hauling wood for the stove at home.

For dinner, Ivy made homemade noodles from the flour and eggs, rolling them out as thin as possible before cutting them into slices and tossing them into the boiling pot of water. She drained them, placed them in a casserole dish along with some cut-up fried smoked sausage, and then melted cheese on top.

Everyone, even Hannah, showed their gratitude for the meal as they sat in front of the television and continued watching *Friends*, a comedy show about *Englisch* friends living in the same building and hanging out together. Ivy found herself giggling at certain parts. The characters were all so silly.

For dessert, Ivy toasted slices of her homemade bread and smothered them with strawberry jam. Maya and Ashley loved the tasty treat. Gram seemed impressed by the "newbie's" baking skills. And Hannah turned it down, saying she didn't want to get fat from all the carbs.

The grumpy teen headed up to bed, and Gram rolled his eyes at her departure and then gave Ivy a wink.

The next several weeks followed a loose routine—if Sophie's unpredictable presence could even be called that.

Emily checked in twice—once to take Ivy to the doctor to remove her cast, and once for a routine visit.

When Ivy asked if she could go home, Emily shook her head. "I'm sorry, Ivy. But *please* know this is *not* your fault."

Ivy doubted that. If her *mamm* and *dat* could ask for forgiveness at church, why couldn't she? If she could simply apologize for the stolen cookie, everything could go back to normal.

But she stayed quiet. Sophie's house wasn't *so* bad. She had a purpose—cleaning, cooking, watching over the girls.

Everything had settled into a rhythm.

Until Sophie started bringing a man home at night.

Chapter Eleven

Now

Amish Country hadn't changed much. Ivy drove past an endless stretch of cornfields, the landscape both familiar and foreign. The soil was the same rich brown she'd once walked barefoot. Red covered bridges still arched over slow-moving creeks.

Horse-drawn buggies trundled along the dirt road, their wheels kicking up dust. A few drivers glanced her way as she passed, their expressions unreadable beneath broad brims and the steady rhythm of reins.

The gravel road leading to her brother's house jarred the car with every bump, as if trying to shake loose memories she hadn't asked for.

Near the barn, a cluster of barefoot children shrieked with laughter, chasing each other in a game she instantly recognized.

Ivy's hands tightened around the steering wheel as she slowed.

Her nieces and nephews.

They turned toward her, small faces creased in confusion, their eyes tracking the strange car. The sight of them sent a sharp pang through her chest. She'd never met them, yet she recognized them in the tilt of their chins, the hesitant way they stood, the way their brows knit together as they studied her like an outsider.

Because that's what she was now.

She cut the engine, inhaling deeply before stepping out. The wind carried the scent of hay and tilled earth, crisp and clean. The porch steps groaned under her weight, same as they had when she was a child. The door looked the same too—solid, weathered, the knots in the wood unchanged.

Her heartbeat thrummed in her ears as she knocked.

The door swung open, and there he was.

Jonas.

Older. Harder. His face, once full of boyish mischief, had sharpened with time. Broad-shouldered, rigid, his blue eyes swept over her, lingering on the jeans and sweater she wore. His expression remained unreadable, but the set of his jaw told her enough.

For a long moment, neither of them spoke.

Then, finally, he exhaled. "Ivy."

No welcome. No warmth.

She hadn't expected anything else.

"Jonas," Ivy said, trying to keep the emotion out of her voice. She could already feel the distance between them. He hadn't seen her in years, but it felt as though he'd already judged her.

He stepped aside, silently inviting her in. The house smelled of burning kerosene lamps, so different from the flour and sugar of her bakery—the scent that wafted up to her apartment daily. Ivy took a seat at the table, but Jonas remained standing, his arms crossed.

"You can't sit at my table," Jonas said, eyes downcast. "You're no longer one of us."

The words hit Ivy like a punch to the gut, but she kept her expression neutral, refusing to show him how much it stung. She should've expected this, but it still hurt.

"I didn't come here to fight, Jonas. I want to know where Ruth is."

Jonas scoffed, his lips curling into a sneer. "Why? What do you want with any of us?" He shook his head, bitterness dripping from his words.

"She's my sister, and I care about her."

"Pfft. She tried to come back home at one point a couple of years ago after our *dat* passed, but *Mamm* wouldn't allow it. Ruth had changed too much. Like you, she fell into the sin of worldliness. And like her, you have to deal with the consequences of God's wrath."

A chill tightened around Ivy's chest, sinking deeper as he spoke about Ruth. The guilt surged, raw and sharp—she hadn't seen her sister in years—hadn't tried to find her. She'd been shunned by her family. Turned away as if she weren't human.

"Do you know where she is?" Ivy persisted.

He sneered. "I heard she's living in Fort Wayne, doing ungodly things. Maybe you'd fit right in with her. Both of you, so eager to leave our family behind."

"How do you know?"

"Our cousin, Thomas. He saw Ruth a while back. Working at a strip club, of all places. She was... buck naked," he spat the words out as though they tasted bitter. "Thomas said he spoke to her after the club closed. She told him she wasn't using her real last name so no one would know what she was doing. So no one could find her."

Ivy's stomach clenched, hearing where Ruth had ended up. More than that, the hypocrisy stung. Thomas had been at that club too, sitting there with no shame, yet somehow Ruth had been the one being dragged through the mud. But there was no point in arguing this with a brainwashed mind. Amish were taught that a woman's body needed to be hidden. And a man could ask for forgiveness for his sins—and he'd get it, no doubt.

She stared at Jonas, waiting for more, but he only shook his head, anger still radiating off him.

Her mind spun with the information. Ruth...dancing in a club, hiding her name? It didn't sound like the sister she knew, the protector she'd had growing up. But how well did she really know Ruth anymore? How much had she changed?

Ivy felt the tears threaten but held them back.

"Thank you for your time." She stood up, hands trembling at her sides.

She turned to leave, her heart aching, but she couldn't stay there any longer.

"Like Ruth, you made your bed," Jonas said as she reached the door.

71

"Now lie in it. I'll tell *Mamm* that ya stopped by, though I don't think she cares too much."

Ivy's hand gripped the doorknob. "Jonas, I didn't leave because I wanted to. I wanted to come home—"

"It doesn't matter," he cut in, his voice firm, final. "You're tainted by the *Englisch* ways now. There's no coming back from that."

Her breath caught, but she forced out, "Where is Mom?"

"What do you care?"

"God damn it, Jonas. Tell me."

He sneered. "She never left home. Now, why don't you get out of here with that filthy mouth of yours?"

Ivy tightened her grip on the doorknob, fed up with this callous, angry man. "You know, Jonas," she said, "you'll always have a small mind as long as you live in this small community and never try to understand anything outside of it."

Jonas's face turned a deep shade of red, his jaw clenched as he stood there, fists balled at his sides.

"Get out, Ivy," Jonas said through gritted teeth. "You don't know anything about me."

"Glad for that, at least." Ivy turned on her heel and opened the door, her breath hitching when the small boy collided with her. His wide eyes looked up at her in confusion, and when Ivy saw the dark bruises on his face, her stomach twisted.

Her knees pressed into the ground as she knelt, her pulse thudding like a warning drum.

"Hey there," she said, keeping her voice gentle despite the swirl of nerves inside her. The boy's gaze darted to her, wide and wary, before he quickly looked away, stepping back, his small body tense and guarded, as if he might disappear.

Ivy stood back up, her gaze locking on Jonas. "If you're hurting him or any of your kids the way our father hurt us, you'd better believe I'll find out, and I won't hesitate to call the police." Her voice was cold, and the warning in her tone left no room for doubt. "You think your community—your church—can protect you? Let's see what happens when the authorities get involved."

Jonas glared at her, his lips parting as though he wanted to lash out, but no words came. Shame flashed in his eyes, and for a second, Ivy saw the boy she used to know—scared, broken, and trapped. But the moment was fleeting, and the anger rushed back just as quickly.

"Leave," he spat. "Don't come back."

Ivy didn't need to be told twice. She turned and walked out, the screen door slamming shut behind her. The cool air hit her face as she stepped outside, but it wasn't enough to cool the heat of her rage.

Chapter Twelve

Then

Ivy sat on her bed, undoing her braids, preparing to brush out her hair. On the bed next to her, there was a tidy stack of books she'd checked out from the library. She eyed the pile, mentally picking which one to dive into next. With summer vacation in full swing, she finally had the time. Molly had shown her how to get a library card at the town library— lucky for her, it was close enough to walk to.

The door creaked open, and in walked Hannah, leaning against the doorframe with that bloody rose tattoo of hers peeking out from under her cropped T-shirt. Ivy swallowed, her hands pausing in her hair. Hannah hardly ever looked at her, let alone came into her room.

"Wow, Ivy," Hannah said, a smirk playing on her lips. "Didn't realize you had all that hair. You always keep it hidden under that funny cap of yours."

Ivy glanced up, still wary but a little defiant. "We're not allowed to cut it," she said.

"Really? So bizarre." Hannah stepped closer, a smile on her face. "Mind if I brush it for you?"

After a moment of hesitation, Ivy handed Hannah the brush. "Okay." Her sisters used to brush her hair, and she enjoyed the soothing touch.

As Hannah gently worked through Ivy's hair, she asked, "So, why do you still dress Amish? You're not living with them anymore."

A pang of defensiveness tightened Ivy's chest. "It's my religion. The church forbids colorful clothes. If I disobey, I'll go to hell."

Hannah let out a laugh, but there was something sharp in it. "Then I guess I'm going to hell along with everyone I know. All my friends, Sophie, Gram, the girls..."

Ivy had to consider this. She remained silent, feeling the brush move smoothly through her hair.

Hannah continued, "Want me to braid it? Like a French braid, maybe?"

"Um. Sure." Ivy didn't see the harm in it. As Hannah skillfully divided Ivy's hair, Ivy said, "Maybe God would forgive you for being worldly if you asked for forgiveness."

Hannah's hands paused for a moment. "I don't believe in God. After everything I've been through, if there was a God, he wouldn't have let me suffer so much... let me see so much."

Ivy turned slightly to look at her, wondering what awful things the girl had to go through to end up in this home. "Sorry. I..."

"Don't worry about it." Hannah resumed braiding. "I'm curious. Have you ever had to ask your church for forgiveness?"

"No, but my father has had to ask a lot."

"Why?" Hannah asked.

Ivy paused, trying to choose her words carefully. "He... lost his temper a lot. And he drank too much. The church doesn't allow this."

Hannah's eyes narrowed. "Is that who beat you?"

Ivy nodded, a sudden sadness massing in her chest. "Yes, but the church will probably forgive him. Again."

"That sounds like a fucked-up church." Hannah scoffed, shaking her head.

Ivy bit her lip, thinking hard. "It's the only way of life I've ever known. I'm not supposed to question it."

Hannah finished the braid, tying it off with a gentle touch. "Maybe you should question it, Ivy. It doesn't look like that church is helping you at all now."

Ivy looked down at her hands, Hannah's words sinking deep, heavy, and unshakable.

"Maybe you're right," she whispered, a seed of doubt beginning to sprout within her. She fiddled with the edge of her dress. "I think I've been shunned."

Hannah looked at her, confusion written all over her face. "Shunned? What does that mean?"

Ivy took a breath, trying to find the right words. "The Amish can cast away people for not obeying the rules or for leaving the community. It means they're not supposed to talk to you or help you. You're cut off from family and friends."

Hannah's eyes widened. "How did you break the rules? You're a little girl."

Ivy's cheeks flushed with a mix of shame and anger. "The deacon of our church saw me holding a stolen cookie at the grocery store. I didn't steal it, but I was holding it when he walked by. My father lost his temper when he found out."

Hannah's expression turned fierce. "I've done way worse than steal a cookie. If anyone ever tried to beat me like that, I'd kick their ass."

Ivy giggled, a small, hesitant, and foreign sound.

Hannah smiled back at her. "Look, most of the time, it's the grown-ups who mess things up. You didn't deserve to be beaten, no matter what you did. What your father did was wrong. He should be asking you for forgiveness, not the stupid church."

Ivy's eyes burned with the threat of tears, but she did feel a little better. "I've never thought of it that way."

Hannah wrapped an arm around her, making Ivy tense. She wasn't used to affection. "You're a good kid," Hannah said. "Not a total freak."

Ivy leaned into the embrace, tears prickling her eyes as warmth spread through her chest. "Thank you, Hannah," she whispered, wondering what she'd done to get in this girl's good graces. The rudeness had disappeared, and now Ivy thought she was a different person. A nice person who cared about her.

Hannah pulled back and shrugged. "Anytime. But don't go telling Gram that I got soft. I'll never hear the end of it."

"Your secret is safe with me." Ivy swiped her sleeve over her damp eyes and grinned.

"You know," Hannah said, a hint of excitement in her voice, "I'm going to be released from the foster care system next month. I'm planning on moving in with a friend, but I'll keep in touch, maybe."

"I'd like that," Ivy said. "Next month is my birthday, too, on the fifth."

Hannah's eyes widened in surprise. "No way. My birthday's on the sixth."

A grin spread across Ivy's face. "Really? That's so neat."

Hannah leaned back, something clearly running through her mind. "What if we have a combo party to celebrate before I move? Then I can go out with a bang."

"That sounds like so much fun. I've never had a real birthday party before."

"No shit? Well, that's about to change. We're going to have the best birthday party ever. I promise."

Ivy's hands flew to her mouth in delighted surprise. "What should we do for the party?"

Hannah tapped her chin, her eyes sparkling with ideas. "We could have a movie night, maybe order some pizza. And definitely cake. Lots of cake."

Ivy laughed, her earlier worries momentarily forgotten. "I would like that. I can't wait. And I can make the cake."

"Of course you will." Hannah gave her a gentle shove on the shoulder. "You're like some sort of weird genius when it comes to baking and cooking." She stood up and made her way to the door. "I gotta go. My friend and I are going to try to find a job at the new mall, and I need to change into something that covers this tat." She gestured to the tattoo on her stomach.

"What does that design mean, anyway?" Ivy couldn't help but ask.

"I got it to scare away boys and creepy men. They get too handsy sometimes, and I don't like that."

"Oh." Ivy didn't quite understand, but she went along with it.

"Hannah?" Ivy said before the teen could retreat. "Thank you for being nice to me."

Hannah scoffed. "Girl, don't ever thank someone for being nice to you. You should demand that shit, got it?"

"Got it," she forced herself to say.

Hannah walked out of the room, leaving behind a hint of her fruity perfume. Ivy sniffed in the pleasant scent and picked up her cap, twisting the strings around her fingers. Maybe tonight she wouldn't wear it. Nobody here cared. And the church wouldn't find out, she didn't think.

And well, if they did, she could ask for forgiveness, she supposed.

If she ever got the chance to go back.

...Maybe she didn't even want to.

She shook that thought out of her head, remembering how much she missed Ruth. Her fingers played gently over the French braid Hannah had given her. What would Ruth think of this, how her braid flowed over her shoulder rather than tied up close to her scalp?

She'd probably understand. Her older sister was always open-minded, and at times she did question the church... out of their parents' earshot, of course. She'd most likely think that Ivy needed to find her own path right now. She'd say something like, "It's hard, Ivy, but everyone's journey with faith is different. Do what you think is right."

Ivy let the prayer cap fall to the bed. She stood boldly and left the room, heading downstairs. There was dinner to make.

Weeks later, during the night, Ivy was jolted awake by the sound of Sophie's laughter, loud and unrestrained, mixing with a man's deeper voice. It was Sophie's new boyfriend—the one who always made Ivy's skin crawl a little whenever he was around. The two of them sounded like they'd stumbled in from the bar, slurred words and laughter echoing down the hallway.

Maya shifted in her bed but stayed asleep, while Ashley snored softly nearby.

In two days, both girls would be leaving the house. A nice young couple was adopting them, and they couldn't stop talking about their excitement—separate bedrooms, new toys, a fresh start.

Ivy was happy for them, truly, but the thought of saying goodbye weighed on her. She hoped she'd be able to keep in touch by writing letters, though she'd have to ask Sophie if that would be allowed.

The laughter from downstairs grew louder as Sophie and her boyfriend stumbled up the stairs and into Sophie's bedroom. Ivy swallowed, trying to push down the unease that always came with this man's presence. Sophie knew better than to bring someone like him into the house, but when she drank, she changed—like her father had.

She rolled over onto her side and kept an eye on the door, which was open a slit because the girls were scared when it was closed all the way.

The laughing and talking finally stopped. Ivy's eyes grew heavy, and she fell into sleep once more.

What seemed like seconds later, Ivy woke with a start, cold sweat prickling her skin, fear jolting through her. She glanced up.

Sophie's boyfriend sat at the edge of her bed, staring at Maya and Ashley's sleeping forms. His breath reeked of alcohol.

Ivy's blood turned cold.

"What do you want?" she whispered.

He turned to her, grinning, his hand creeping under her blanket.

Ivy yanked back. "Get away from me!"

"Shhh. I'm not gonna hurt ya." He reached for her again.

"No!" she kicked at him, and he grabbed her ankle.

Suddenly, Gram burst in, a baseball bat gripped tight.

With terrifying force, he swung.

The man crumpled to the floor. Gram didn't stop. Another swing. Another. Blood splattered.

Sophie rushed in, screaming, "Stop it! Gram, stop!" She grabbed his arm, trying to pull him back, but he shrugged her off, his anger still burning, his gaze fixed on the man sprawled on the floor. "I'm calling the police!" Sophie yelled, running out of the room.

Maya and Ashley woke up, their cries piercing the night. Ivy jumped onto their bed, holding them close, shielding them from the sight of the violence.

"It's okay, it's okay," she whispered, trying to calm them. But the sounds of the bat hitting the man, the man's groans, and Gram's grunts of effort were impossible to ignore.

Finally, Gram stopped. The man lay still, his blood pooling on the floor. Gram stood over him, breathing heavily, feral. He turned to Ivy, his eyes wild.

"Get them out of here," he said roughly.

Ivy didn't hesitate. She gathered Maya and Ashley and rushed them downstairs, bypassing a sleepy-looking Hannah who stood in the hallway.

She glanced around and then followed Ivy downstairs. They all huddled together on the couch, the girls clinging to her and Hannah, their small bodies shaking with sobs.

Then—the wail of sirens.

Police stormed the house. They took Gram away in handcuffs, his face blank, his clothes soaked in blood.

An ambulance wheeled the man out on a stretcher.

Sophie stood in the doorway, mascara streaked down her cheeks. "I'm so sorry," she whispered.

Ivy was too stunned to speak.

As the flashing lights vanished into the dark, one thought clung to her—

She would never see Gram again.

Ivy was relieved when Emily confirmed she could stay with Sophie, as long as Sophie promised not to bring any more men home. Sophie agreed without hesitation. Though most of the blame had fallen on Gram, Ivy knew the truth—he'd only been protecting them.

She overheard that the man Gram attacked would survive, though he suffered a concussion, broken ribs, and needed stitches. Gram, however, was sent to juvenile detention—*a prison for kids*—Sophie explained when Ivy asked.

"Will he be okay?" Ivy needed to know.

Sophie sighed. "Gram's tough. He'll be fine. But hey, you get his room now."

The next day, a day earlier than planned, Maya and Ashley's new adoptive parents arrived along with their caseworker.

The feeling around the house was bittersweet. The girls would get a forever home, but Ivy wouldn't get to see them anymore. She'd lost Gram and now the girls.

"They'll take care of you, and you can probably visit," Ivy whispered, kneeling down beside them.

"We don't want to leave you," Maya sobbed, clinging to Ivy.

"You'll be okay," Ivy whispered. "You'll have a real family now."

The couple was young and friendly looking. The man was tall and broad-shouldered with sandy blond hair and kind blue eyes. The woman had curly auburn hair that cascaded around her shoulders and a warm, welcoming smile. They both wore casual clothes that suggested comfort and care.

"Please be good to them," Ivy said to the couple. "They're good girls."

The couple gave Ivy's plain dress a quick, curious once-over. "We will, sweetheart," the man assured her. "Don't worry. We already love them to pieces."

In the kitchen, their caseworker was speaking softly to Sophie.

Ivy turned to the couple again. "They like to sleep with the bedroom door cracked. Maya hates ketchup, and Ashley won't eat her vegetables without ranch dressing. The generic kind is fine and less expensive. They like to be read to at bedtime. It helps them go to sleep."

The woman smiled at Ivy, seeming impressed. "Thank you so much for all the advice and suggestions. We'll make sure to take good care of them. You've been wonderful."

A jumble of sadness and relief whirled inside her as the couple, the caseworker, and the girls finally left. She hoped deep down that Maya and Ashley would be happy in their new home.

In the weeks that followed, Sophie moped around the house, her eyes always red and puffy. She wasn't going out to the bar anymore, which was a good thing, but she looked sad all the time.

Ivy cooked dinner for Sophie and Hannah. Just the three of them were left. After dinner, she escaped into her books—she and Molly had started a reading competition to see who could finish the most books before summer ended.

And Molly's brother, Derek? Without Gram around, Derek went back to tormenting Ivy, yanking her braids and calling her a freak. She avoided him by inviting Molly over instead of going to her house, but she couldn't escape him completely. She hated him—and, deep down, feared him, too.

───────

On the evening of Hannah and Ivy's dual birthday celebration, the house smelled of freshly baked cake, warm vanilla, and melted butter. Ivy had spent the afternoon carefully measuring, mixing, and frosting—every swirl of icing smoothed with the same level of care her mother had once used to bake for her family.

Now, the living room was bright with decorations—balloons swaying from the ceiling, banners stretched across the walls, and colorful confetti scattered over the coffee table. It looked like a real birthday party, something Ivy had never experienced before.

Sophie set the last of the paper plates on the table as the door swung open. Hannah strolled in, fresh from work, shaking out her hair as she kicked off her shoes. "I'm starving. Tell me we're ordering pizza."

"Already on the way," Sophie said.

Hannah grinned, plopping onto the couch. "Good. I need some greasy goodness in my life."

Ivy hovered nearby, nervous but excited. She still wasn't used to all this attention on *her*.

Sophie clapped her hands. "Before we eat, let's do gifts. I think you girls are going to love them."

Ivy's heart gave a nervous flutter as she sat down on the couch beside Hannah. Two gift bags sat on the coffee table, a floating helium balloon tied to each one.

"Here." Sophie handed Ivy one bag and Hannah the other. "Go on, open them at the same time."

Ivy hesitated, then peeked inside. A pair of brand-new black leather shoes stared up at her—sturdy, well-made, *hers*. She traced the smooth leather with her fingertips, feeling a lump rise in her throat. Her old shoes were too tight, the soles thinning. These were perfect.

She clutched them to her chest, voice small. "Thank you, Sophie."

"There's more," Sophie encouraged.

Ivy reached in again, pulling out a bag of red licorice, a paperback book she'd been wanting, and soft new socks. Then, at the bottom of the bag, she found a gift card. She glanced at Sophie in confusion.

"I figured we could go shopping," Sophie said gently. "Your dresses are getting snug. We can find fabric for new ones, or maybe... look at other clothes. Whatever makes you feel comfortable."

Ivy hesitated. The thought of wearing *Englisch* clothes made her stomach twist, but she also knew she couldn't keep growing out of her dresses forever. Slowly, she nodded. "Okay."

Hannah, meanwhile, had pulled a pair of new jeans from her bag. "*Yes!* These are the ones I wanted." She held them up triumphantly before slinging an arm around Sophie in an uncharacteristic hug. "Thanks, Soph."

Sophie laughed. "You're welcome. Now let's eat."

The pizza arrived, and they settled into the living room, plates piled high. Laughter filled the space as they ate, the warmth of the evening wrapping around them like a soft blanket.

Sophie lifted a glass of apple cider. "Happy birthday to the two best girls I've ever known."

Ivy felt her heart swell at the words. She'd never been called that before—*one of the best.* But even as happiness bloomed inside her, she couldn't shake the hollow ache of missing Gram, Maya, and Ashley. The house felt quieter without them. Too still.

After dinner, they cleared the plates, and Hannah grabbed the remote, flipping through the channels.

Then the lightness in the room shifted.

"So, Sophie," Hannah said, her tone sharper now, "are you planning to take in more kids after I'm gone? That's kind of your meal ticket, isn't it?"

Sophie sighed. "Well, yes, I have relied somewhat on the foster care income, but I need a rest after everything that's happened. Ivy and I will have to cut back a little bit, that's all."

"Yeah, probably a good idea," Hannah said, a hint of bitterness in her tone. "And I hope you're not going to go back on your word and bring any men home."

The sudden tension in the air had Ivy stiffening in her seat, her hands clasped tightly on her lap.

"You don't have to worry about that, Hannah," Sophie said, looking at her fingernails. "Concentrate on your own life, and everything will be fine."

Hannah whipped around to face Sophie. "Yeah, I get it. But I need to make sure Ivy's safe. She's still innocent, which is how it should be, and you need to make sure it stays that way."

"Hannah, don't ruin the evening by getting upset." Sophie raised her hands in a defensive motion. "I won't let anything happen to her, okay? I've never let anything happen to you, remember?"

Hannah's tongue worked the side of her cheek as she seemed to contemplate this. "Not that you know of."

Sophie's face darkened. "What the hell does that mean?"

"I mean, I'm not exactly a virgin, Sophie. You being gone every other night to the bar gave me plenty of time to make sure of that."

"Listen." Sophie stood and jammed her hands on her hips. "I'm not going to sit here and allow you to speak to me this way. I don't care whose birthday it is, understand?"

"Boo-hoo." Hannah rolled her eyes. "Why don't you go drink off your emotions like you usually do?"

"Is that what you want?" Sophie's voice wavered, eyes shining with the threat of tears. "You don't want me here?"

"I don't give a shit," Hannah said, giving the TV her attention again. "Do what you want. You always have."

Sophie's face went red. She grabbed her purse and yanked the strap over her shoulder. "Thanks for ruining Ivy's birthday." Then she stormed out, slamming the door behind her.

The house fell silent.

Ivy swallowed hard, the warmth from earlier gone.

Hannah exhaled through her nose. "I'm going to give you some advice, okay?"

Ivy bit her lip.

"No matter what happens, *you* have to protect yourself. If a guy ever touches you in a way that makes you uncomfortable, you *fight*. Scream, kick, bite—whatever it takes."

Ivy's stomach twisted. "Okay."

"If Sophie ever leaves you alone and you don't feel safe, *call Emily*. And tell Sophie you *will*. She'll listen if she thinks she might lose you."

Ivy hesitated. "But Gram said this home was better than others."

Hannah scoffed. "Gram's an idiot, but yeah, this place isn't the worst. Just make sure Sophie *fears* losing you. And if you get moved again, stand your ground. Don't let anyone push you around."

Ivy exhaled slowly. "I got it."

"Good." Hannah leaned back into the couch. "But I really hope you never have to use my advice."

Unease still churned in Ivy's stomach, but she managed a small hum of agreement.

Then Hannah grabbed the remote again. "Now, how about *The Princess Diaries*?"

Ivy hesitated. "No zombies?"

Hannah snorted. "No zombies. No blood. Promise."

Ivy relaxed slightly, curling into the couch with the throw pillow.

She was eleven now. A year older. And still not home.

No word from her family. No letters. No messages.

Maybe it was time to stop waiting.

Maybe this *was* home now.

Chapter Thirteen

Now

Ivy stepped inside, and the club swallowed her whole. Smoke curled in the air, mixing with the foul scent of sweat, cheap cologne, and something stale that clung to the walls. Colored lights pulsed through the haze, casting sharp flashes over glistening skin and the slow, practiced movements of dancers twisting around polished poles.

Men hunched at tables, eyes locked on the stage, faces slack, lost in the lull of the music, the dim glow of neon, the press of bodies. The bass pounded beneath Ivy's feet, rattling up her spine, merging with the clatter of drinks and the occasional burst of raucous laughter. Everything felt loud, overwhelming, too much.

She had been to one club already tonight, bracing herself for the possibility, hoping—praying—she wouldn't find what she was looking for.

But then she saw Ruth.

Ivy's breath hitched.

Her sister stood on a platform a few feet away, her body thin, nearly swallowed by the dark shadows and flashing lights. A strip of fabric barely covered her hips, and her arms wrapped around herself as if she could disappear into her own skin. But it wasn't the outfit that gutted Ivy. It was Ruth's eyes.

Those blue eyes, the ones that used to blaze with mischief and defiance, were dull now, vacant. The fire was gone.

Ivy's chest tightened. Ruth looked older—too old for her years. Her face was sharper, the hollows beneath her eyes deep, her skin drawn too tight over her bones. This wasn't exhaustion; this was life grinding her down, piece by piece, until nothing was left.

And yet, Ruth kept moving. Slowly. Detached.

Ivy's stomach twisted.

Then, as if she'd felt the weight of Ivy's stare, Ruth's gaze drifted toward her.

Something flickered—recognition, shock, maybe even shame. Her hands flew to her chest, a rush of color rising to her cheeks.

Ivy's heart pounded.

This was her sister. The one who had once shielded her from their father's fury. The one who had whispered promises of escape when the nights had been too long, too terrifying.

And now, Ruth was the one who needed saving.

Ivy didn't think. She moved.

Weaving through tables, past leering men and half-drunken conversations, she made her way toward Ruth, her pulse hammering with every step.

This wasn't the Ruth she remembered. But she was still Ruth.

Ivy's eyes locked with Ruth's. Time seemed to freeze. Ruth's face, gaunt and weary, twisted in shock, her wide blue eyes darting around the room as if searching for an escape. Ivy saw it all—the spark of recognition, the panic tightening Ruth's features, the sheer horror of being exposed in front of her little sister. But beneath the shame, there was something else. A kind of fear Ivy couldn't quite name.

"Ivy," she said, her voice barely audible over the pounding music. "What are you doing here?"

Ivy's throat squeezed, a storm of emotions churning inside her. She could feel the stares from the other people in the room, but none of that mattered right now. All that mattered was her sister.

Ivy took a calming breath as she faced Ruth. "I've been looking for you," she said. "We need to talk."

Ruth sighed, her expression worn, exhaustion settling into the lines of her face. She glanced around the room, her shoulders curling inward as if trying to make herself smaller. Her gaze dropped to her bare skin, and a trace of something unreadable crossed her features—regret, maybe, or resignation. She let out a slow, unsteady breath and shook her head. "Not here. Not like this," she murmured.

"Let's go somewhere else then," Ivy persisted. "I'm not leaving without you."

Ruth hesitated, her thin shoulders slumping. "Okay," she said. "Let me grab my things."

She hurried off the platform and disappeared behind the curtains. Ivy waited awkwardly by the stage, her pulse still racing from the encounter. The room around her seemed to buzz louder now, her emotions amplifying every sound—the thumping bass, the distant conversations, the laughter of men watching the other dancers. Watching her with curious gazes.

The smoke stung Ivy's eyes. The club's noise continued to thump against her eardrums, and the longer she stood there, the heavier the minutes dragged, stretching unbearably. She checked the back entrance again, half-expecting Ruth to emerge, but the curtains barely shifted.

Doubt crept in. Maybe Ruth had changed her mind. Maybe she wasn't coming at all. Ivy's pulse quickened—what if she stood here, waiting for someone who'd already decided not to show? She could turn back, slip into the car, and drive away. Pretend this night had never happened.

Her feet twitched toward the door.

No.

She clenched her jaw, forcing herself to stay put. She'd come this far —she wasn't leaving without Ruth. Even if it meant standing in this suffocating club for hours, she'd wait.

The curtain finally opened, and Ruth stepped out, drowning in an oversized hoodie and faded jeans. Her hair was damp from whatever quick clean up she'd managed, and her face was milk-white without makeup.

As Ruth reached her, a tall, broad-shouldered man emerged from behind the curtains. His muscled arms, straining against the fabric of his shirt, flexed as he crossed them over his chest. His dark eyes locked onto Ruth with unsettling displeasure.

"Where do you think you're going?" His voice sliced through the air, low and forceful.

Ivy tensed, watching as Ruth's entire posture shifted. She went from hurried to cautious, her shoulders hunching.

"I'm just—just going to talk to my sister," Ruth stammered, her gaze dropping to the floor.

The man looked at Ivy, his eyes narrowing suspiciously before flicking back to Ruth. "You can't leave. We've got rules, and you know it."

"I'll be back tomorrow," Ruth said, her voice small. "I promise."

Ivy didn't like how he hovered over Ruth, his presence too imposing, too threatening.

"I don't care where you go," he said, shaking a finger at her sister, "but you'd better show up tomorrow. Don't make me come looking for you again." He glared before turning on his heel and walking away.

"What did he mean by that?" Ivy asked.

Ruth let out a breath. "It's not important. Let's go."

The tension between them simmered, heavy in the silence. Ruth carried it in her shoulders, in the way her eyes avoided Ivy's. They stepped outside, the cool night air hitting Ivy.

She spotted a small, fluorescent-lit diner across the street. "Let's go there to talk."

Ruth nodded, and they walked side-by-side to the diner. Ivy's mind raced with questions, but she stayed silent for now, waiting for Ruth to feel comfortable enough to talk.

Inside the diner, the smell of grease and burnt coffee filled the air. Ivy slid into a booth, watching as Ruth sat across from her, fidgeting with her slim hands. The once confident, strong sister she remembered seemed so far away now, replaced by someone haunted by years of hardship.

The waiter, a lanky man with graying hair and a stained apron, stood beside their booth, pen poised over his notepad.

"Coffee, please," Ivy said.

"Same," Ruth murmured, not meeting his gaze.

The man's hand paused above his notepad. "You want anything to eat? Pie's fresh."

"No, thank you," Ivy said, while Ruth surprised her, saying, "Apple, I guess."

"Got it. Be right back." The waiter shuffled away, leaving them alone again.

Ivy studied Ruth as she traced the rim of her water glass with one finger. She wanted to ask a hundred questions, but she forced herself to start small. "Apple was always your favorite," she said.

"Guess some things don't change." Ruth let out a short, humorless laugh.

"Talk to me, Ruth," Ivy said, keeping her voice as gentle as possible while still wanting to get to the truth. "What happened to you?"

Her sister scoffed. "What happened to me? Do you think there's something wrong with me? 'Cause I'm a dancer doesn't mean there's anything wrong with me."

"Of course not. It's..." Ivy's eyes drifted over Ruth, who fidgeted with her oversized sweatshirt sleeve.

"It's hot in here," Ruth said, sounding dazed as she glanced around the diner. She yanked the sweatshirt over her head, revealing a fitted T-shirt and...

Faint bruises dotted the crease of her elbow, stark against her pale skin. Ivy hadn't noticed the marks in the dark club, and she couldn't help but release a sharp sigh.

Ruth crossed her thin arms around her body, hiding the evidence.

Ivy didn't know much about drug use, but she wasn't so naive as to not notice the signs.

A tight, dry lump formed in her throat, but she forced herself to swallow it down. This wasn't the time to ask, not when Ruth barely held herself together. Ivy had come to help—to offer something, anything, better than this. That was what mattered now.

Ruth leaned back against the cracked vinyl of the booth, a bitter smirk on her gaunt face. "So, what do you want, Ivy? You show up out of nowhere and want to insult me. There's nothing wrong with stripping. It's legal, and I get paid."

"I didn't mean to offend you. I want to understand—what your life was like, and what it's like now."

"It's fucking perfect," she spat, making Ivy flinch. "Can't you see?" Ruth laughed, but tears glistened in her blue eyes.

Ivy persisted. "Would you consider coming home with me? I don't live far from here. Only a couple of hours away. I own a bakery now with an apartment above. I have room for you."

Ruth's smirk faded into something more guarded. "I'm fine where I am. I don't need your pity, Ivy. I don't need you or anyone."

"But I care about you, Ruth," Ivy said, determined.

"Right." She rolled her eyes. "I've looked you up over the years. I know about your bakery. Good for you—you got lucky in the foster care system. Doesn't make you any better than me, so don't try to look down on me."

Ivy pressed her lips together, the words stinging more than she wanted to admit. "I'm not better than you. I want to help... like you helped me."

The waiter passed by, leaving their coffees and a piece of apple pie.

Ruth dug into the slice as if she'd been starving. Ivy cupped her coffee and warmed her hands. She glanced out the window, watching the cars pass on the darkened street. For a moment, Ivy thought Ruth wouldn't reply. Then, with a sigh, Ruth rubbed a hand over her face, exhaustion etched in every movement.

"That night, I tried to protect you from him. I did," she said. "I wasn't strong enough or big enough."

"I know. And I'm so grateful for all the times you guarded me from him."

Ruth sniffed and pushed her plate away. "That seems like a different life now."

Ivy's fingers traced the rim of her glass. "Yeah. It does to me, too."

"Foster care sucked for me," her sister continued, glancing at the ceiling. "I was angry and lost. So, they put me in a group home, and I got angrier, and I fought everyone who tested me. Everyone who tried to touch me or be near me." She banged her hand on the table as if demonstrating. "They gladly released me when I turned eighteen, and I did the only thing I could think of—I went home. *Dat—*" She shook her head. "Dad was dead, and I thought Mom would let me back home. I begged her to give me a chance, but she stuck up her fucking nose at me and told me to leave."

The waiter loudly cleared his throat as he strode by again.

Ruth shot him a glare and began again. "She said I looked dirty and worldly, and the church would frown on me coming back. She said I never should've called the police on our father. She said the reason you were taken away was my fault. That..." She went still, lashes sweeping down. "*Killed* me. I was only trying to protect you. I never wanted to hurt you."

Ivy's chest tightened as she listened. She'd always known their upbringing had left wounds, but hearing it from Ruth hit her harder than she'd expected.

"Oh, Ruth, I understand that. Believe me, you saved me in ways you don't realize. I'm so sorry our mother said that to you. It's not true. Not any of it. You didn't do anything wrong. In fact, you did the only thing that was right at that moment. Something our mother should have done long before."

At that, tears trailed down Ruth's face. "She really should have."

"Yes. But it was you. And I want to thank you and pay you back for everything you sacrificed for me."

Ruth swiped the tears away. "What do you mean exactly?"

"You don't have to live this way if you don't want to. There's still time to change things." Ivy held her hands up. "Only if that's what you choose."

"And do what, Ivy? Bake bread with you? Pretend I'm someone I'm not?"

"You can be whoever you want to be," Ivy said firmly, leaning forward. "You're not stuck here, Ruth. I know things are complicated, and I know I can't fix everything. But I'm here now. I won't disappear on you. And I won't turn you away. *Ever.*"

Ruth's blue eyes held the familiar spark buried deep beneath layers of pain. For the first time, Ivy saw a glimmer of the sister she remembered. Brave. Kind. Caring.

Fierce.

After a long moment, Ruth let out a slow breath and whispered, "I don't even know who I am anymore, Ivy."

Ivy reached her hand across the table, resting it on top of Ruth's. "Then let's figure it out together. You can stay with me. I have a roommate, but he won't mind. We'll make room."

The words hung between them, fragile yet full of possibility. Ruth stared at their hands, and it appeared that the walls she'd built around herself were starting to crack.

Chapter Fourteen

Then

Summer vacation ended too quickly, and Ivy's first day of school arrived with a mix of anticipation and dread. She was starting fifth grade, and it was the first time she wouldn't be wearing her Amish clothes to school. She'd outgrown them. In their place, she chose simple summer dresses—no prints, only solid, darker tones that reminded her of the ones she used to wear. She hoped the change would help her blend in more, but anxiety gnawed at her.

She walked to the bus stop, her steps slow and hesitant. Her long braid swayed gently with each step, reaching almost to her waist. When she arrived, she spotted her friend Molly immediately. Molly waved excitedly, her ponytail bobbing as she bounced on her feet. Ivy smiled back, feeling a bit of her nerves ease.

But then, she saw Derek, Molly's older brother, leaning against a tree. He'd been teasing her all summer, but she'd mostly managed to avoid him. Now, she was stuck near him, waiting for the school bus.

"Hey, Ivy," Molly greeted her with a hug. "Guess what? We're going to have the same homeroom teacher this year. Isn't that awesome?"

Ivy nodded, trying to focus on Molly's excitement. "Yeah, that's great."

Derek sauntered over, his lips pulled into a taunting grin. "Well, look who decided to join the modern world," he sneered, peering at her chest. "You're going to need a bra soon, though, Ivy. Something to hide those little things peeking out."

Heat flooded Ivy's cheeks, and she glanced down, wishing she could disappear.

"Leave her alone, Derek." Molly glared at her brother.

But Derek wasn't done. He grabbed hold of Ivy's long braid and tugged.

"When are you going to chop this off? It hangs down to your butt. You can dress however you want, but you're still the creepy Amish girl who everyone talks about behind your back."

Ivy bit back the tears, her throat tight, the words pressing upward like broken glass she couldn't swallow.

You're going to have to stand up for yourself, Ivy. No matter what happens, you're the only person who's going to look out for you.

Hannah's words sprang to her mind, and she gulped down her fear. Hannah, who'd moved out a week ago.

"What's wrong with you, Amish girl?" Derek grabbed her braid and yanked. "Don't have your criminal foster bro to protect you anymore?"

Ivy clenched her fists and shoved at Derek. "Leave me alone!"

Derek laughed, and Ivy couldn't take it anymore. She turned and ran, her feet pounding the pavement as she fled back home. She burst through the front door, her breath ragged gasps. Sophie was still asleep, so Ivy grabbed the phone and called Emily, her caseworker.

"Emily, it's Ivy. I can't go to school. I can't."

"Ivy? What happened?"

"A boy makes fun of me. He says everyone talks about me. He grabs my hair, and he won't leave me alone. I don't know what to do."

"Okay, honey. Where's Sophie?"

Ivy bit her lip, lying quickly. "She's in the shower."

"I'll come over as soon as I can, and we can come up with a solution. Sound okay?"

"Yes."

"Will you be okay until then?"

"Yes, ma'am."

"Good. Hold tight. I'll make some phone calls to rearrange my schedule, and I'll be over as soon as I can."

Sophie woke up soon after, her movements slow and groggy as she wrapped her robe around herself. Again, dark makeup smudged around her eyes. She shuffled into the kitchen, narrowing her gaze at Ivy.

"Why aren't you in school, Ivy?" Sophie yawned and sat beside Ivy. She smelled of stale alcohol from the night before.

Ivy took a deep, shaky breath, gathering her thoughts before explaining everything. She recounted Derek's relentless bullying, the cruel comments, and how he had embarrassed her in front of everyone at the bus stop. She described how she'd used Hannah's advice to stand up for herself, only to end up running home in tears.

"I can't stand him, Sophie," Ivy said. "He makes fun of me, and all the other kids still think I'm weird. They talk behind my back. I don't want to go to that school anymore." She paused, afraid to tell her the next part. "I... I called Emily. She's going to come over."

"I'm so sorry, Ivy." Sophie pulled her into a tight hug. "I should've been more aware."

Ivy thought she apologized an awful lot, but it was nice to hear she wasn't in trouble for missing school and calling Emily, at least.

"I'm going to get dressed before Emily gets here. Do you want to come with me or are you okay down here by yourself?"

"I'm okay."

She straightened up the kitchen and swept the floor before Sophie joined her again—her face washed clean of smeared makeup and her clothes clean.

As Sophie made herself a cup of coffee, there was a knock at the door. Ivy went to open the door for Emily, who walked in, her expression a mix of concern and surprise as she took in Ivy's new attire.

"Ivy, are you okay with wearing these new clothes?" she asked gently. "I know we haven't really talked about this."

"Yes, I'm fine." There's nothing more she could do about it anyway.

"Good." She glanced at Sophie as she walked into the living room. "Let's sit down and talk about what happened."

Ivy rehashed the morning, aware of their eyes on her, uneasy and unsure of how they'd respond.

Emily turned to Sophie after Ivy finished explaining, her expression serious. "I'm concerned Ivy is taking on too much, too soon. Maybe we should consider homeschooling for a while."

Sophie pursed her lips. "Homeschool? How would that work?"

"Quite a few of my kids homeschool, and they like it. Ivy will need access to a computer, which I can find easily." Emily's attention centered on Ivy. "You'll need to spend a few hours a day doing coursework. It'll be guided and fairly simple for you, I think, considering how well you adjusted to school in the latter part of last year.

"That sounds like a good idea," Sophie said. "Ivy, would you be okay with that?"

Ivy hesitated, her mind torn. She'd be learning from home, so she'd miss out on having homeroom with Molly and talking to her. But she wouldn't have to worry about what Derek and any of the other kids thought of her.

"I think so," she said tentatively. "We have computers at school, but I don't have that class yet. I'm not sure how to use one."

Emily smiled reassuringly, her eyes kind. "We'll figure it out, Ivy. I'll help you set up a computer for homeschooling, and Sophie can help you use it."

"I know how to use a computer," Sophie said. "I can teach you, Ivy."

Ivy exhaled slowly, the pressure in her chest easing. The prospect of not having to face Derek and the other kids was comforting. "Thank you. I think this will be good."

Emily left, promising to talk to the school and bring over an old computer to help Ivy get started. As Ivy sat at the kitchen table, a sense of peace settled over her. She knew she would miss Molly, but for now, this was the best decision for her well-being. She had the support of Sophie and Emily, and that was enough to help her feel safe and cared for.

Six weeks later, Ivy tapped at the laptop keyboard while working on her homeschooling assignments at the kitchen table. She'd grown to love using the computer in the short amount of time, exploring the vast resources the internet had to offer. A world of information lay at her fingertips, empowering her with newfound skills.

Outside, a storm raged, the rain pounding against the windows and the wind howling through the trees. The lights flickered intermittently, and Ivy glanced nervously at the computer screen, hoping it wouldn't shut down before she finished her coursework for the day.

Sophie strode into the room, chewing her nails—a nervous habit Ivy had never seen before from her foster mother.

"It's coming down too fast," Sophie muttered, peering outside. "I've never seen it storm this much. The street's starting to flood."

Then, the power cut out. The house fell silent. And Ivy lost her homework. Shoot.

But it seemed she had bigger things to worry about. She walked to the window and stood next to Sophie. The water on the street swallowed the sidewalk and crept up Sophie's car tires. Their house, sitting at the bottom of a hill, was quickly becoming an island.

"What should we do?" Ivy asked, her voice barely audible over the roar of the storm.

"We'll be okay," Sophie said, trying to smile, but it didn't quite reach her eyes. "It's the house I'm worried about. Let's be smart and start moving some things upstairs, off the floor."

Ivy got to work. She helped Sophie carry framed photos and important papers to the upstairs closet. Then they moved small appliances, Sophie's favorite rugs, and any other furniture they could manage. They needed to save what they could.

Outside, the storm raged—rain battered the windows, wind slammed against the house, and thunder rattled the walls with each distant strike. Lightning split the sky, each flash striking uncomfortably close, illuminating the chaos for a fleeting, blinding second before plunging everything back into darkness.

"I'm starting to get scared," Ivy admitted, her body trembling.

Sophie's eyes darted around, thinking fast. "We'll be okay, I promise." Her voice was calm, but Ivy could see the worry on her face. "But if the water keeps rising, we'll need to get to higher ground."

Then came a loud knock at the door, and Sophie opened it.

Molly's dad stood there, soaked and breathless. "Water's rising fast. You need to come up to our house. It's safer."

Fear tightened Ivy's chest—Derek lived there. But alarm sirens wailed in the distance, making the choice for her.

Sophie grabbed essentials—clothes, important papers, a few sentimental things. She threw a raincoat over Ivy and took her hand. "Stay close."

They waded through the thigh-deep water, each step a struggle. When they reached Molly's house, Ivy's heartbeat slowed.

Inside, Molly's mom ushered them in, worry etched on her face. "You're safe now."

They huddled in the living room, a battery-powered radio crackling with flood updates. Derek, for once, was quiet. Fear had wiped away his usual smugness. Molly clung to her parents, her eyes wide.

Ivy curled up beside Sophie, her head resting on her foster mother's lap. Sophie stroked her hair, a comforting rhythm against the chaos outside. Despite everything, Ivy felt safe. Slowly, she drifted to sleep.

By morning, the floodwaters had swallowed Sophie's house. People paddled through the streets in canoes, rescuing stranded neighbors.

Ivy stood at the window, staring at the water-logged remains of her home. "Where will we go?" she asked softly.

Sophie exhaled. "I need to call Emily. We'll figure it out."

Dread curled in Ivy's stomach. "I don't want to leave you."

Sophie pulled her close. "I don't want you to either, sweetheart. But I have to go stay with my sister in Michigan, and there's no room for you there."

Ivy's chest ached. First Gram, then Maya and Ashley, then Hannah —and now Sophie.

Emily arrived later that afternoon, her face gentle but firm. "Ivy, we'll find you a good place."

Sophie knelt, cupping Ivy's face. "You're strong, sweetie. You'll be okay."

Ivy swallowed the lump in her throat. And as Emily drove her away, the sun shining as if nothing had ever happened, she knew—her world had changed forever.

Chapter Fifteen

Now

Ivy couldn't believe Ruth had actually said yes. The storm inside Ivy finally calmed. After years of wondering, of fearing the worst, Ruth was finally back in her world—walking away from a life that had diminished her, a life that wasn't worthy of her. And she was choosing to. Choosing Ivy.

She'd tackled the snake in her nightmares, had wrestled it away from Ruth's body, and thrown it into the darkness where it belonged. But even as she breathed through the rush of relief, there was still something gnawing at the edges of her gut, something uneasy, coiled tight beneath the surface.

Because in the dream, the snake always came back.

They drove in silence toward Ruth's apartment to grab her things. Ivy glanced at her sister, still half-waiting for her to change her mind. Ruth sat slouched in the passenger seat, arms crossed, her fingers tapping a restless rhythm against her sleeve. She looked exhausted, but at least she was here.

Ivy smiled. "I'm happy you're coming with me."

Ruth let out a soft scoff, not quite a laugh. "Yeah, well... we'll see if you still feel that way when I start taking up all your space."

"You forget I grew up in a house with nine people and one *outdoor* bathroom," Ivy teased. "I can handle a roommate." Or two. Ivy hoped Gram wouldn't mind making room for Ruth.

Ruth didn't answer right away. Instead, she picked at a loose thread on her hoodie, her expression unreadable. "I should tell you something," she finally said.

"Okay," Ivy said carefully. "Go ahead."

Ruth exhaled sharply, staring out the window. "The owner of the club..." She hesitated, shaking her head slightly. "He doesn't let girls walk away."

"What do you mean?"

Ruth sighed, rubbing at her temple. "I mean, he's possessive. He treats us like we belong to him. And honestly, he was upfront about it. He told me that if I wanted to work for him, he'd take care of me, but that came with a price. I promised him loyalty and to work for him for however long he needed me."

Ivy was confused. "So, you can't quit? Is that what you're saying?"

"He depends on us to run his business. And at first, it felt nice being needed. But... no, we can't quit. And if he finds out I'm leaving, it could be a problem."

A chill ran through Ivy. "Are you saying he's dangerous?"

Ruth turned to her then, her blue eyes dark with something Ivy couldn't quite name. "I'm saying... we should hurry, Ivy."

"Jesus, Ruth. He doesn't own you. You *can't* be owned. You have rights."

Ruth swallowed, her gaze locked on the windshield as if watching ghosts in the glass. "He's found girls before. Brought them back. He... he did it to me once. I tried to leave, and he made sure I understood that I couldn't."

A wave of fury surged through Ivy. The thought of someone controlling her sister and treating her like property infuriated her.

"If he comes after you," she said, "we'll call the police. He can't get away with holding you prisoner."

Ruth let out a bitter laugh. "It's not that easy. Or it hasn't been. He's all I have. He's made that clear."

"You have me now," Ivy insisted. "You're not going back there."

Ruth didn't answer. Her chin dipped, hands curling in her lap as if bracing for a truth she wasn't ready to face.

When they reached Ruth's apartment, Ivy parked on the cracked pavement outside a run-down building. The hallway inside smelled of stale air and dampness, the lights overhead casting a yellowish glow that made everything feel washed out.

As they climbed the creaking stairs, Ruth spoke over her shoulder. "I don't have much. I've been staying with a friend... kind of."

Ivy didn't press. There'd be time to talk later.

Inside the apartment, a sagging couch sat against one wall, covered in a thin, threadbare blanket. A coffee table was littered with empty beer cans and an overflowing ashtray. Ivy's eyes landed on a used needle and a glass pipe.

Ruth caught her staring. "That's not mine," she said quickly.

Ivy kept her expression still, fighting the twist in her gut. She wanted to believe her sister—but this version of Ruth felt unfamiliar. A stranger in pieces she used to know.

Moving with urgency, Ruth gathered her belongings—a handful of clothes, a toothbrush, and a battered notebook she tucked away carefully. Everything fit into a single worn duffle bag.

"I don't have much," she said again, zipping up the bag.

"You have what you need," Ivy assured her. "Let's go."

As they stepped back into the hallway, Ivy glanced at the apartment one last time. Something about it felt final. Ruth wasn't leaving behind a place—she was leaving behind a whole version of herself.

Ruth fell asleep not long into the drive, her head resting against the window, her breath slow and steady. Ivy didn't mind. It gave her time to absorb everything—Ruth agreeing to come with her, the weight of what she'd survived, and the lingering unease over what Ruth had said about the club owner.

By the time Ivy pulled into the parking lot behind the bakery, she hesitated before waking Ruth. She looked so much younger in sleep, the sharp edges of exhaustion smoothed away. But they needed to get inside.

"Ruth," Ivy said softly, giving her sister's arm a gentle shake.

Ruth stirred and sat up, her eyes darting around as if piecing together her surroundings. Without a word, she unlatched the car door and stepped out, stretching.

As Ivy and Ruth reached the top of the metal staircase, the apartment door swung open before Ivy could reach for her keys.

Gram stood in the doorway, one hand on the frame, his sharp green eyes darting between Ivy and Ruth. He stepped aside, wordlessly letting them in.

The scent of coffee hung in the air, and Ivy spotted the half-empty mug on the kitchen table, steam still curling from the rim.

Gram closed the door and crossed his arms, leaning against the counter, his expression unreadable. "Ivy," he said before his gaze shifted to Ruth. "And you must be the sister." His features eased as he extended a hand. "Nice to meet you."

Ruth hesitated for half a second before shaking it. Her grip barely held, and her wary glance suggested she hadn't decided whether Gram was friend or threat.

"She's staying with us," Ivy said. "For as long as she needs."

"You can have my room," Gram said easily. "I'll crash on the couch."

Ruth blinked, surprised. "I... I don't want to take your room."

"You're not taking it." Gram shrugged. "I'll be moving out soon anyway. And I'm pretty much a professional couch sleeper, given my past."

Ruth glanced at Ivy for reassurance.

"You're welcome here," Ivy said gently. "We'll make it work."

Something in Ruth's posture softened. She adjusted the strap of her bag and followed Gram down the hall to his room.

Ivy stayed behind, lingering in the kitchen, exhaling a slow breath. She pressed her hands to the counter, letting the moment settle over her. There was still so much to unpack—so much Ruth hadn't said yet.

But she was here.

Safe.

And for now, that was enough.

Chapter Sixteen

Then

Emily drove Ivy through the rain-soaked streets, the sky now clear and blue as if the storm had never happened. The landscape shifted from city streets to open fields, white farmhouses, and horse-drawn buggies. Ivy pressed her forehead against the car window, scanning for familiar sights.

"Is this where I used to live?" she asked, trying to remember.

Emily glanced over. "No, but it's another Amish community."

Ivy sat back in her seat, her heart tugging in two directions. It wasn't her home, but it was close enough to remind her of everything she'd left behind.

"Am I going to be staying with an Amish family?" Ivy fidgeted with her cotton dress, an *Englisch* dress her family and church would not approve of. Not to mention her new laptop that Emily had gifted her, which required electricity to use. She'd surely be scorned for having that in her possession.

"I'm afraid I still couldn't find any open Amish foster parents for you. But the family I'm taking you to is very conservative and religious. My hope is that you'll be a good fit in this home."

"That's okay. I'll wait until my family can take me back."

Emily gave her a small, sad smile.

They left the farmland behind, arriving at a quiet suburban neighborhood. The two-story house was tidy, with a manicured lawn and flower beds lining the walkway. Ivy clutched her laptop bag, her stomach knotting as Emily parked.

"This is it," Emily said, shutting off the engine. "The Thompsons are good people. Sharon, the mother, will be looking after you. She has two little boys and another foster girl about your age."

Ivy swallowed, trying to calm her nerves. Emily led her to the front door, and a moment later, it swung open to reveal a tall, stern-looking woman with dark hair pulled back into a tight bun. She was wearing a long plain skirt and a buttoned-up top in the same color.

"Hello, Emily," the woman said with a thin smile as she scoped out Ivy from head to toe. "This must be Ivy."

"Hi, Sharon," Emily said. "Thanks so much for taking Ivy in on such short notice. You are a gem."

"It's no problem." She waved them inside, her long arm pointed into the foyer.

Ivy stepped inside, her gaze darting around. The interior was spotless, with everything in its place. It smelled faintly of lemon polish and something baking in the oven. From somewhere in the house, she heard children laughing.

A teenage girl with long, dark hair and a no-nonsense expression appeared in the hallway. She reminded Ivy a bit of Hannah, though without the tattoo and cropped T-shirts. She wore baggy jeans and an oversized soft pink T-shirt.

"This is Ivy," Sharon said to the girl. "She'll be staying with us for a while."

"Hi, I'm Tara," the teen gave her a small wave. "I'll show you around."

Emily squeezed Ivy's shoulder. "I'll check in on you soon. You're going to be okay."

Ivy met her gaze, then turned to follow Tara through the house, taking in the pristine living room, the well-organized kitchen, and the playroom where two toddlers played contentedly with their toys.

"That's Lucas and Liam," Tara said. "They're twins. I still can't tell them apart."

Upstairs, Tara led Ivy to their shared room, a simple space with a pair of twin beds, a dresser, and a closet. "That one's yours," Tara said, pointing to the bed by the window.

Ivy set her bags down and sat on the edge of the bed, feeling overwhelmed.

Tara leaned in, lowering her voice. "Listen, I need to warn you about a few things. Sharon's super religious, like, crazy religious. She'll expect you to go to church and follow all her rules. And Alex, the foster dad, is gone most of the time because he's in the military. So, it's just us and Sharon, which isn't so bad."

Ivy nodded, trying to absorb everything Tara was saying.

"Keep your head down, help out around the house, and never, ever leave a mess," Tara continued. "Sharon will go ballistic if things aren't perfect. Trust me on this."

A hard knot gripped her stomach. "Thanks for the warning."

"Also, no cussing or backtalk. Dinner's at five sharp—be on time. And she prefers modest clothes, but looks like you already have that covered."

"Okay," Ivy said, grateful for the insight.

"The bathroom's down the hall," Tara said, offering a small smile. "If you need anything, ask, okay? It gets pretty lonely here, so I'm really glad to finally have another foster sister."

"Thank you." Ivy bit her lip nervously.

Tara sighed, giving her a sympathetic look. "It's not so bad once you get used to it. And if you need anything, let me know. We're in this together."

Ivy managed a small smile. "Okay."

Weeks passed, and Ivy quickly learned the routine of her new home and the patterns of her foster mother, Sharon. Every Sunday morning was the same: Sharon, with a determined air, would gather Ivy, Tara, and the twin boys, and usher them out the door to church. It was a nonnegotiable event, no matter how much Ivy might have wished to stay behind in the quiet solitude of her room.

The church itself was a stark contrast to anything Ivy had known before. The large, imposing building seemed to loom over them as they entered, and the atmosphere inside was dense with an energy she couldn't quite place. The pastor, a towering man, led the service with an intensity that made Ivy squirm in her seat. His face turned a deep shade of red as he delivered his sermon, his words sharp and filled with a kind of righteous fury that Ivy found unsettling.

She stood out in this environment, out of sync with everything around her. The sermons in her Amish church had been calm, peaceful, and introspective. The simple wooden benches, the quiet, reflective words of the minister—they were a world away from the loud, fervent declarations she now found herself surrounded by.

As the pastor's voice rose to a crescendo, Ivy stole a glance at Sharon. Her foster mother was nodding vigorously, tears streaming down her face, seemingly moved by the pastor's words. It was a sight that left Ivy feeling even more alienated. She didn't understand what could be so moving in this anger-fueled diatribe, but Sharon seemed to be deeply affected.

The twins were in Sunday school, and Tara, seated on the other side of Sharon, looked bored, her gaze wandering around the room, her mind clearly elsewhere. She had likely been through this routine too many times to care, her face a mask of indifference. But Ivy felt the weight of every minute, each one dragging on as the pastor continued his tirade.

When the service finally ended, Sharon wiped her eyes and turned to the girls with a soft smile, as if the tears were a balm for her soul.

"Wasn't that powerful?" she asked.

Ivy gave a tight smile, unsure how to respond. The experience had left her drained and tangled inside.

As they filed out of the church, she caught sight of the sign out front: *First Assembly of God*. Her Amish church had always warned its people to steer clear of places like this, claiming other religions were dangerous or false. Ivy wasn't sure anymore. With everything she'd seen and been through, she wondered if any of them were truly good.

Unease stayed with her, crawling beneath her skin and refusing to let go.

More weeks passed, and Ivy noticed a shift in the atmosphere of the house. Sharon, who had always been serious, seemed to become more withdrawn and emotional. Ivy would often find her foster mother in the living room, a well-worn Bible in her lap, tears streaming down her face as she read. It was unnerving to Ivy, who was used to Sharon's stern, composed demeanor. The tears came more frequently, especially after church, and Ivy didn't know what to make of it.

One day, Sharon approached Ivy with a proposition that made her stomach churn. "Ivy, dear, I think it's time you considered getting baptized in our church. It's important, you know, for your salvation."

A tremor ran through Ivy. The thought of being baptized in Sharon's church, with its fiery sermons and unfamiliar customs, filled her with dread.

"I'll think about it," she mumbled, trying to deflect the conversation.

But Sharon didn't let it go, and over the next few days, she brought it up repeatedly, her tone growing firmer each time. Ivy tried to avoid the topic, but it became harder and harder to do so. Tara, sensing Ivy's discomfort, pulled her aside one evening.

"Do it, Ivy," Tara said. "It's just water. They dip you in, and it's over. Then she'll stop bugging you about it."

"I don't want to, Tara," Ivy said, frustrated. "I don't even know what I believe anymore."

Tara sighed, her expression softening. "I get it. I don't believe in all this either, but sometimes it's easier to go along with it, you know? Keep the peace."

Christmas approached, and the house took on a festive air, though it didn't quite reach Ivy and Tara. Sharon's husband, Alex, returned home for the holiday, but his attention was solely on his twin toddlers. Ivy and Tara were largely ignored, which suited Ivy fine—Alex's presence was intimidating, and she preferred the quiet of their shared room.

On Christmas morning, Ivy listened as Sharon and Alex celebrated with Liam and Lucas downstairs. The sound of laughter and torn wrapping paper filled the house, but upstairs, it was eerily silent. Ivy and

Tara stayed in their room, the absence of Christmas cheer palpable. A pang of loneliness gripped Ivy, a stark reminder that she didn't truly belong here.

But then, to Ivy's surprise, Tara handed her a small envelope. "Merry Christmas," Tara said with a shy smile.

Ivy opened it and inside found a gift card to the local bookstore. Her eyes welled up with tears as she looked at Tara.

"Thank you," she whispered, pulling Tara into a tight hug.

Sharon seemed to forget about the baptism while her husband was home. December slipped into January, then February, and March.

Spring arrived, bringing with it blooming flowers that added a touch of brightness to the house. On Easter, the family gathered in bursts of energy—egg hunts, laughter, and too many sweets. Ivy and Tara stayed nearby, watching from the doorway. No one told them to keep their distance, but no one pulled them in, either. They were part of the scene, but not the celebration. Present, but still on the outside.

By May, the school year wrapped up. Ivy finished fifth grade without much trouble. She'd grown increasingly comfortable with her computer skills and was now devouring a book a week—tales of girls braver and louder than she felt.

Summer blurred by in slow motion. Heat clung to the neighborhood, and the days stretched out—lazy, aimless, all running into each other.

Ivy turned twelve quietly, without cake, without candles.

Then, the morning after her birthday, she woke to blood on her sheets.

She hadn't been feeling any different, but when she noticed the blood, her breath hitched, shallow and quick. She didn't know what was happening to her, and a deep panic set in. Maybe something was seriously wrong. She needed help, but the thought of going to Sharon with this—whatever it was—made her stomach churn.

Instead, Ivy sought out Tara, who was in their shared room, staring at her flip phone.

"Tara, I think something's wrong with me," Ivy whispered.

Tara immediately put down her phone, her brow furrowing with concern. "What's wrong?"

Ivy hesitated, feeling a wave of embarrassment wash over her. But she had to say it. "I'm... I'm bleeding... down there." She pointed downward, her face burning with shame and fear.

Tara looked surprised, and then a small giggle escaped her, but it was quickly followed by a kind smile. She reached out and squeezed Ivy's hand. "Oh, Ivy, don't worry. It's okay, I promise."

Ivy looked at her, confused and still scared. "It is? But why am I bleeding?"

Tara stood up, still holding Ivy's hand, and led her to the bathroom. "It's your period. It's something all girls get when they reach a certain age. It means your body is growing up."

Ivy stared at her, wide-eyed. "My period?" She'd never heard of such a thing, not even in any of the books she'd read... not that she could remember anyway.

"Yeah, it happens to every girl. It's totally normal," Tara assured her as she opened a cabinet and pulled out a box of pads. "Here, let me show you how to use these."

Tara patiently explained how to use a pad, walking Ivy through it step by step. She pointed out where everything was stored in the bathroom, so Ivy would know where to find them next time.

As she talked, Ivy began to feel a little better, the tight knot of fear loosening. "It'll happen every month now, so it's something you'll get used to. And if you have any questions or worries, you can always look things up on the internet. Or you can ask me, okay?"

Ivy glanced at her, the relief starting to settle in. "Thank you, Tara. I didn't know... I was really scared."

Tara smiled and hugged her. "I know it's scary when it first happens, but you're going to be fine. It's part of growing up."

Calm settled over Ivy. With Tara's help, she managed to push aside the panic and embrace the idea that this was a normal part of life—a part she could handle, especially with a foster sister like Tara by her side.

Later that month, Alex was deployed again for his military duties, and Sharon fell back into her depression. Her insistence on Bible readings returned, this time with an added urgency. After each reading, she would sternly warn Ivy that without baptism, she was doomed to hell.

Ivy, trying to keep the peace, would promise to think more about it. But the pressure continued to build until one day, Ivy found herself cornered in the kitchen, Sharon's intense gaze locked on her.

"Ivy, it's time," Sharon declared, her tone brooking no disagreement. "You need to be baptized. You can't stay in my home if you're not."

Ivy summoned all her courage. "Sharon, I don't want to. It makes me uncomfortable, and I'm not ready."

Sharon's face hardened. "I see," she said, then turned and walked off, leaving Ivy cold and rooted to the spot.

Later that day, Ivy overheard Sharon on the phone. "Emily, it's not working out with Ivy. She's resistant to our ways, and I think she needs to be placed in a home that's a better fit for her. Can you make arrangements?"

Ivy's heart plummeted as the reality of the situation hit her. She was being moved again, discarded like a problem no one wanted to handle. The loneliness she had felt during that past Christmas deepened, and she wondered if she would ever find a place where she truly belonged.

Chapter Seventeen

Now

Ivy stood in the bakery kitchen, prepping bread dough. She'd slipped into the kitchen hours before the sun rose, hoping the rhythm of her work would ground her. Her thoughts raced, too keyed up to sleep after bringing Ruth home.

She hadn't expected to hear the soft creak of footsteps behind her.

"Couldn't sleep either?" Gram stepped into the kitchen, sleeves rolled up, ready to work.

"Too much on my mind, I guess." She offered him a tired smile. "Thought I'd get an early start."

Gram didn't say anything else. He washed and dried his hands, then stepped beside her and picked up the dough she'd left on the counter. Together, they kneaded in silence. The rhythm of their hands softened the tension in the room.

But it wasn't long before Ivy's thoughts bubbled up to the surface, and she spoke the worry that had been bothering her since they'd left Ruth's apartment.

"I'm worried about my sister," Ivy admitted quietly. "I saw some...

things at her place. Drug paraphernalia. A needle. She said it wasn't hers, but..." she trailed off, not needing to finish the thought.

Gram's hands paused. "You're worried she's using." He glanced over at Ivy, his eyebrows knitted.

She shifted her weight and gave a small, almost imperceptible movement in response. She thought about telling Gram how and where she'd found her sister, but kept that to herself. That was Ruth's truth to share, not hers.

"I'll help keep an eye on her," Gram said. "If she's doing drugs, we'll make sure she gets help."

Ivy's heart ached with both gratitude and concern. She didn't want to lose Ruth—not after finally finding her again.

"Thank you, Gram. I... I don't know what I'd do if something happened to her. Seems as though she's been through a lot in her life."

There was a long pause before Gram spoke again. "I went looking for my brother a couple of years ago," he said. "I wanted to reconnect, to see if he was okay. But by the time I found him, it was too late. He'd died of a drug overdose."

Ivy stopped what she was doing and looked up at him, her heart squeezing painfully. "I'm so sorry, Gram."

He shook his head. "It was hard. But I made peace with it. Or at least, I tried to. But seeing someone go down that path... it doesn't leave you. If Ruth's struggling, we'll be here for her, okay? We'll make sure she doesn't end up like that."

Ivy swallowed hard, the lump in her throat refusing to budge. She hadn't known that about Gram's past. The depth of his own loss made his presence now even more comforting.

He understood what was at stake.

"Thank you," she said. "And... for giving up your room. I appreciate you accommodating her."

Gram gave her a small, lopsided smile. "I should be the one thanking you, Ivy. You took me in when I had nowhere else to go. You're kind and... well, you're a lifesaver. I was in a bad spot, and you helped me through it."

Before Ivy could respond, Gram reached out and pulled her into a hug. It was warm, comforting—like all the other times he'd hugged her.

But this time, something felt different. More charged, more intimate. Ivy melted into his embrace, her worries momentarily quieted by the solid warmth of him.

When Gram pulled back, his hands still resting on her arms, he paused, looking down at her with a strange expression. Then his lips twitched into a mischievous smile. "You know," he said, brushing his thumb over her chin, "you've got flour everywhere. Pretty sure you could open a bakery on your head."

Ivy reached for her hair, and then laughed—a real, genuine laugh that bubbled up from deep inside her, cutting through the tension that had weighed her down. She glanced in the small mirror on the counter, realizing he was right—her hair was dusted with flour from the morning's work.

She swatted his arm playfully. "I guess I'm a walking advertisement for Butter and Bliss, then."

Gram chuckled, and Ivy felt the tension in her shoulders ease as she brushed flour from her hair.

"Thanks, Gram," she said. "I needed a laugh."

"Anytime," Gram replied, his grin softening into something more genuine. "I've got your back, Ivy. Always."

As the moment faded, Ivy allowed herself to linger in the feeling of comfort. She cared about Gram, and it was becoming clearer that her feelings for him were deeper than she'd realized. But now wasn't the time to dive into those emotions. Not with Ruth needing her focus, her help.

She needed to concentrate on her sister. The rest—the feelings that stirred whenever Gram was near—would have to wait. For now, they both had work to do, and Ivy was determined to see Ruth through this. Whatever it took.

Chapter Eighteen

Then

One year and almost four months since entering foster care...

The year had stretched and reshaped her. Ivy couldn't quite explain it, but everything she'd been through had aged her. The little girl she once was had slipped away back in that first foster home.

Now she was in another house, another strange place that didn't feel like hers, trying to make sense of it all over again.

This home reminded her of Sophie's when she first arrived—messy, cluttered, and loud, with a kind of unsettled energy hanging in the air.

Gina, the foster mom, was small and soft-spoken, her blonde hair streaked with dark roots, a sign she'd either been too busy or too worn down to bother with upkeep. She moved carefully, with a hush in her presence that suggested she didn't want to disturb the air around her, always edging toward the background.

Her husband, Harry, couldn't have been more different. He wasn't especially big or tall, but his voice boomed through the house, cutting through every conversation. Just standing still, he seemed to take up more space than anyone else, his overconfidence radiating in a way that made Ivy's skin crawl. Old acne scars roughened his face, and his blue eyes, though bright, never sat still long enough to feel safe. Ivy lowered her gaze when he was near—so did Gina—and it didn't take long to realize this was the kind of house where shrinking might be the only way to survive. Again.

They had two other foster children. Mikey was three, and Sugar was four—both full of energy, always tumbling underfoot, their giggles and occasional cries echoing through the house. They needed so much attention that it made Ivy's head spin watching Gina keep up with them. But Ivy had her own room, and for that, she was thankful. It was small, with no windows and only a dim table lamp casting a weak circle of light. Still, it was hers, and in a house like this, that was a gift.

She did what she always did when thrust into a new home—settled in quickly, quietly. She cleaned, took care of Mikey and Sugar when Gina needed help, and stayed out of the way. If she made herself useful, maybe this place wouldn't feel as awkward. Maybe Harry wouldn't notice her at all.

Harry worked construction and came home at odd hours, his boots thudding heavily across the floor. His clothes carried streaks of dirt and cement dust, and the scent of sweat and earth clung to him, ingrained deep. He rarely bothered to shower after work, and Gina never said a word about it. She didn't speak up about much. Instead, she greeted him with a faint, worn-out smile and reheated his dinner while he cracked open a beer. Sometimes she leaned in and kissed his cheek, her movements hollow, mechanical—more routine than affection.

Ivy couldn't decide if Gina's quiet endurance made her strong or worn down. Maybe both. Either way, it left Ivy wondering if that was what life was supposed to look like—everyone too tired to say anything real.

Harry wasn't a kind man. He grumbled constantly, finding fault with everything. The meals Gina prepared were never good enough. Her appearance was always wrong in some way. The house was too messy, too cluttered—an accusation that grated on Ivy, who had taken on much of the cleaning herself.

At least, Ivy thought, he wasn't cruel to her, Sugar, or Mikey. His contempt was reserved solely for Gina, a woman who seemed to wither under his constant barrage of criticism. Ivy watched the dynamic between them and wasn't sure if she felt pity or frustration.

Gina was so eager to please, so determined to maintain some semblance of peace in the household, yet nothing she did ever seemed to be enough for Harry.

The nights were the hardest for Ivy. Lying in her small, dark room, she would hear the muffled sounds of Harry's shouts through the thin walls, his words sharp and cutting, though she couldn't make out exactly what was being said. Gina's responses were usually soft, almost inaudible, a striking difference from Harry's loud and abrasive tone.

Ivy would clutch her pillow and squeeze her eyes shut, trying to block it all out, but the tension seeped into her dreams, turning them into restless, uneasy nights.

Despite the turmoil, Ivy tried to focus on the small positives. She had her own space, even if it was small and dark. She had books to read, and Mikey and Sugar, though tiring at times, brought some joy into the otherwise bleak atmosphere. She reminded herself daily that she needed to get through it—to survive until something shifted.

But deep down, a part of Ivy knew that surviving wasn't enough. She craved something more, something out of reach—a place that offered safety, worth, and a true sense of home.

Weeks turned into months, and Ivy threw herself into her schoolwork like never before. She was excelling, her grades reflecting her dedication and focus. It filled her with a sense of pride she hadn't known she was capable of.

The idea of finishing grade school, high school, and maybe even going to college began to feel like more than a distant dream—it felt possible, tangible, something she could reach out and grasp if she tried hard enough.

When she'd lived in her Amish community, the idea of education beyond what was legally required had never even crossed her mind. The world had been small and restrictive, and her future had seemed equally so. But now, things were different. The hunger for knowledge had taken root within her, growing each day. The computer and internet access she now had revealed a world she hadn't known existed—a world full of possibilities.

With it, she became boundless, as if the limits that once confined her vanished. The more she learned, the more she wondered if she could ever go back to the life she once knew, where the boundaries of her world were so narrow.

As the days passed, Ivy found herself grappling with an emotion she hadn't expected.

Anger.

At first, it was a quiet murmur, something she could ignore. But the more time she spent away from her family, the louder it grew, pressing against her ribs until she might explode. It wasn't just anger at being left behind—it was rage at all the things they had done to her.

Her father. His heavy hand. His thunderous voice had turned every room into a battlefield. The bruises lingered for weeks, and the fear stayed rooted deep in her bones. He hadn't treated her as a daughter, not even as a person—only as something to strike when his temper snapped.

Ivy could still feel the sting of his belt across her back, the sharp slap of his hand against her face. She clenched her fists, her nails digging into her palms. How could a father, her *dat*, do that to his own child? Wasn't he supposed to protect her, to love her?

And her *mamm*. Ivy's throat tightened at the thought of her. Quiet, distant, always looking the other way. Her mother hadn't laid a hand on her, but she might as well have. Every time her father's anger erupted, her mother would sit in the next room, silent, pretending not to hear Ivy's cries. Not once had she stepped in to stop him, to shield Ivy from the blows. Ivy could see her mother's face so clearly—her lips pressed tight, her eyes cast down. She'd let it happen. Over and over again, she'd let it happen.

The thought burned in Ivy's chest. What kind of mother did that? What kind of mother allowed her child to suffer, to live in fear? Ivy wanted to scream at her, to shake her, and demand an answer.

And then there was the way they had let her go. Her father, who had struck her so hard that she'd been taken away. Her mother, who hadn't fought to keep her. Neither of them had lifted a finger to stop it. The people who were supposed to love her the most had been the ones to hurt her the deepest.

Her hands trembled as she thought of it all, her mind racing with questions she'd never get answers to. Did they even miss her? Or were they relieved she was gone, one less child to deal with?

The anger filled her now, bigger than the sadness, bigger than the fear. It wrapped around her like armor. She didn't want to feel this way —so bitter, so betrayed—but it was better than feeling small and broken. Better than being the scared little girl they'd tried to make her believe she was.

No, she wasn't going to be that girl anymore. If they didn't care about her, then she would have to care about herself. Someone had to.

The anger burned within her, feeding her determination to succeed, to prove to herself that she was worth something, even if her parents couldn't see it. She would show them—show everyone—that she could make something of herself, that she could build a life far beyond what they had ever imagined for her.

Because in the end, Ivy realized, she was the only one who could shape her future. She was the only one who could decide who she would become. And she was determined to make something of herself, no matter what it took.

As Ivy's thirteenth birthday approached, she noticed something unusual about Gina—an effort, a warmth that no one had shown her in a long time. Amid the chaos of a household filled with toddler-sized tantrums and Harry's intimidating presence, Gina still managed to find these quiet moments for Ivy. She asked about school, about the books Ivy was reading, even about the little drawings Ivy would make in the margins of her notebooks.

It was enough to make Ivy wonder if Gina really saw her—not as another mouth to feed or chore to manage, but as a person. And when Gina suggested a plan for her birthday, Ivy nearly choked on her disbelief.

"Ivy, you're turning thirteen," Gina began one evening, her face bright despite the exhaustion that usually weighed it down, "and that's a big deal. I thought we could do something special. Just you and me. My neighbor promised to watch Mikey and Sugar for a few hours. So how about a girls' day? We could go shopping, maybe even get your nails done."

Ivy wasn't sure she'd heard right. A day for her? No screaming kids, no dirty dishes waiting in the sink? The idea was so foreign, almost impossible.

"Really?" she asked. "You want to do that... for me?"

"Of course I do. You deserve a day where you feel special, Ivy. So, what do you say?"

The thrill hit Ivy before she could stop it, warming her chest and making her heart thud in excitement. "I'd love that," she said quickly, and then, more quietly, "Thank you."

The day seemed like it belonged to someone else—a dream from a world Ivy never imagined calling her own. Gina led her into a store and let her choose her own clothes. Ivy ran her hands over the soft lavender sweater and smiled as Gina grinned in approval.

The sweater was the first piece of clothing Ivy had ever owned that didn't carry the weight of her past or tie her to the Amish. It was soft and light in her hands. Then Gina handed her a pair of jeans to try on. Jeans. Ivy hesitated before slipping them on, her fingers fumbling with the unfamiliar material.

When she finally stood in front of the fitting room mirror, she hardly recognized herself. Her cheeks turned pink as she stared at her reflection. The jeans hugged her legs, a bold shift from the plain dresses she used to wear. She wasn't a girl trying to fit in anymore—she looked pretty. Strong. Brave. Independent.

She was thirteen, a teenager now, after all.

At the nail salon, Ivy sat stiffly in the chair until the lady painting her nails started humming a tune that made Ivy relax. She watched the careful strokes of lavender polish transform her nails, matching the shade of her new sweater. The indulgence seemed almost silly, but she loved seeing her hands—soft, clean, cared for.

By the time they reached the café for lunch, Ivy drifted like a balloon, buoyed by unexpected happiness. The scent of fresh bread and coffee filled the air as Gina ordered sandwiches and slices of chocolate cake for dessert.

"Thank you for today, Gina," Ivy said, trying to find the right words. "It's been so fun."

Gina reached across the table and gave Ivy's hand a gentle squeeze. "You're welcome, sweetie. You're a special girl. Don't ever forget that."

The words touched her deeply. Ivy flushed, caught off guard. No one had ever told her that before.

That feeling lingered as they climbed into the car, but it didn't last. Somewhere between the turns of the road and the quiet hum of the engine, the warmth began to fade. A slow unease crept in, tightening around her.

By the time they pulled into the driveway, dread had settled in fully. Harry's car was already there—he was home early.

Gina's smile faded as she noticed it, too.

When they walked inside, the tension was palpable. Harry was waiting in the living room, his face twisted in anger.

"Where the hell have you been?" he shouted, making Ivy flinch. "I get home, and there's no dinner, nothing in the fridge. What the hell, Gina?"

"I'm sorry, Harry," Gina's voice shook. "It was Ivy's birthday, and I wanted to do something special for her. I'll get dinner ready right now."

But Harry wasn't in the mood to listen. His anger escalated quickly, the frustration of the day seeming to bubble over.

"You think that excuses neglecting your duties? You think a stupid shopping trip is more important than having dinner ready when I get home? How much money did you spend anyway?"

"It was from my allowance," Gina spoke quietly, her head down.

"Your allowance is for necessities. You know how upset I get when you waste money on crap."

"I know, I know." Gina held up her hands in surrender, her petite body shrinking even more. "I won't do it again. I felt like her thirteenth birthday was an important one."

"Fuck these foster kids," he spat out. "I should be number one in your life."

"You are, I promise. Settle down, Harry. I'll go get Sugar and Mikey, and then I can make you dinner."

"Settle down? Are you kidding me? Where the hell are the other two?"

"Next door. Tammy said she'd watch them."

"Oh, now you're getting friendly with the neighbors and asking for favors. I can't believe this. I work so hard for you and these kids, and you go and embarrass me."

"Harry, it's really not a big deal. Tammy is—"

"Don't talk back to me, Gina!"

Before Ivy knew what was happening, Harry moved toward Gina, his hand raised in anger. Everything seemed to slow down. Ivy's pulse drummed in her neck as she instinctively stepped between them, her small frame blocking Gina from Harry's path.

"Don't!" Ivy shouted, her voice trembling but resolute.

But Harry's momentum carried him forward, and he struck Ivy instead. The blow sent her staggering back, pain exploding across her face. Gina screamed, rushing to Ivy's side, while Harry stood there, momentarily stunned by what he had done.

Without thinking, Ivy pushed herself away from Gina and bolted toward the door, fear and determination mixing and guiding her. She wouldn't allow violence, wouldn't stand for it anymore.

She ran out of the house, her vision blurred by tears, and sprinted to the neighbor's house, the only place she could think to go.

She pounded on Tammy's door, desperation in every knock. Tammy opened the door, her eyes widening in shock when she saw Ivy's tear-streaked face and the swelling bruise on her cheek.

"Tammy, please." Ivy gasped, her breath coming in ragged bursts. "Can you call the police?"

Tammy didn't hesitate. She pulled Ivy inside, locking the door behind them, and grabbed her phone. Within minutes, the police arrived, their lights flashing ominously outside the house.

Harry was calm when the officers questioned him, his demeanor cool and collected. He denied everything, claiming that Ivy had tripped and hit her face. But Ivy, determined, told them what had really happened.

The officers took note of her story and, after a brief discussion, called social services.

An hour later, Emily arrived, her face a mask of concern and quiet anger.

"Ivy," she said, carefully bracing Ivy's cheek. "I'm taking you somewhere safe."

Ivy nodded, feeling a strange mix of relief and sadness. As they left the house with her clothing in a plastic bag and her laptop safely in a backpack, she couldn't bring herself to look back. She clung to Emily's hand, but this time as a thirteen-year-old girl. A teenager.

As Emily drove her away, Ivy stared out the window, emotions swirling—anger, betrayal, loneliness.

But she'd stood up for herself. Like Hannah would have. Like Ruth had for her.

She felt something new now.

Strength.

And no one would ever take that from her again.

Chapter Nineteen

Now

The cash register chimed as Ivy and Ruth sorted through the bills, the bakery quiet now after the afternoon rush.

Ivy glanced at Ruth, taking in the subtle but steady changes in her sister. A little more color in her cheeks. A little more weight on her frame. The dark circles under her eyes weren't as deep. She looked better. Healthier.

And she talked more now—about customers, about ridiculous reality shows she'd gotten hooked on, about nothing in particular. Sometimes, she even laughed. It didn't happen often, but when it did, warmth reached into the quiet space between them—sudden and bright, unexpected as sunlight slipping through a cracked windowpane.

Ivy didn't say anything about it—she knew Ruth brushed it off— but deep down, she held onto the hope they were both finding their way back to something that felt like home.

"I swear that guy today was flirting with you," Ruth teased, tucking a loose strand of hair behind her ear as she stacked the last few bills.

"The one with the dorky tie and glasses? He asked way too many questions about the bread."

Ivy rolled her eyes but grinned. "He just likes sourdough."

"Sure, sure." Ruth smirked, shaking her head.

Ivy was about to argue when the front door suddenly swung open with a forceful thud, rattling the windows.

Both girls froze. The easy warmth of the moment evaporated.

Ivy's stomach clenched as she turned toward the door. A man filled the entryway, his massive frame blocking out the light from the street. He was broad-shouldered, thick-necked, and had a scar on his cheek.

Ivy recognized him from the strip club. The man who hadn't wanted Ruth to leave.

Crap.

"Gary," Ruth said, stepping back. She sucked in a sharp breath. The color that had returned to her face drained instantly.

The man moved toward them, his boots thudding against the tile, each step a ticking of a bomb.

"Ruth," he shouted. "Get your shit. You're coming with me."

Ruth's fingers gripped the counter edge, knuckles white. She looked at Ivy, her wide eyes silently begging, but she didn't move.

Ivy's pulse pounded in her ears. Her body reacted before her mind could catch up. She planted herself between her sister and the man, her back straightening, her chin lifting.

"She's not going anywhere," she said.

The man's lip curled, amusement flashing across his face before turning to something darker.

"You don't know what you're messing with, kid. Get the fuck out of the way."

Then, with no warning, he grabbed the nearest table and flipped it. Cups, plates, silverware—everything crashed to the floor, shattering on impact.

Ivy jumped at the sudden violence, but she held her ground.

"You're gonna regret this," he spat. "Ruth, you remember what happens to girls who leave me."

"I'll go," Ruth choked out, panic clawing at every word. "If it gets him to stop—I'll go. I'll go, Ivy, please—"

"No." Ivy's hands shook as she reached for her phone, her fingers fumbling over the numbers. "I'm calling the police."

Gary's eyes flashed with fury. He lunged forward and slammed his fist into the wall. The impact shook the shelves, sending a framed picture crashing to the ground. A deep, jagged hole remained in the plaster.

"Ruth!" he roared. "Now!"

Before Ivy could react, another crash sounded—this time from the back door. It banged open, slamming against the wall.

Gram.

He strode in, dark eyes flashing, fists already clenched. He took one look at the scene—the overturned table, the hole in the wall, Ivy standing protectively in front of Ruth—and his expression turned lethal.

"Who the hell is this?" Gram's voice was low, dangerous.

The man turned, sizing him up, then sneered. "None of your damn business, asshole. I'm here for Ruth."

Gram tilted his head slightly, a smirk playing at his lips—something wild, almost amused. "See, that's where you fucked up."

Then he lunged.

The two men crashed to the floor, fists flying, chairs skidding as their bodies slammed into tables. Ivy gasped, her heart hammering as she watched Gram's fist connect with the man's jaw, a sickening crack echoing through the bakery.

Ivy's hands scrambled for something—anything—to help. Her eyes landed on a rolling pin.

She snatched it up, barely thinking, barely breathing.

The fight was a blur of movement—punches, grunts, the scrape of boots on tile. The man grabbed Gram by the shirt, slamming him against the counter. Gram gritted his teeth, but the momentary struggle gave Ivy the opening she needed.

With every ounce of strength, she swung the rolling pin.

It connected with the back of the man's head with a crack.

A strangled sound escaped his lips, his body going slack. He crumpled to the floor, unmoving.

Silence.

Ivy stood frozen, the rolling pin still clutched in her hands, her breath coming in gasps. She could feel her pulse in her fingertips, her body trembling with adrenaline.

The phone in her pocket crackled.

"911, what's your emergency?"

Ivy dropped the pin on the floor as she raised the phone to her ear. "I—I hit him. He's unconscious. We need help. Send the police and an ambulance. Now."

The woman on the other end of the line asked questions that Ivy didn't have answers for, so Ivy continued to repeat the request. Police. Ambulance.

God, she hoped she hadn't killed the man.

Gram pushed himself up, wiping blood from his nose with the back of his hand. His knuckles were raw, his chest rising and falling in sharp breaths. But he barely acknowledged the pain, his focus locked on Ruth.

"Who is he?" Gram clenched his battered fists.

Ruth swallowed hard, her eyes still wide with shock.

"The owner of the club I danced for," she whispered. "Gary. He thinks he owns me."

Gram's jaw ticked. The blood dripping from his nose didn't seem to register.

Ivy had only seen him this furious one other time. The time he'd beaten Sophie's boyfriend to a pulp, which had changed his life forever. But they were adults now, and they were defending themselves.

"He controls everything," Ruth said, her voice ragged. "Breaks girls down until they believe they've got nowhere else to go. I was one of them." She swiped at her eyes. "I didn't see a way out... not until Ivy."

Ivy's stomach knotted. She hadn't expected him to follow Ruth, not here. Not this far. The man was unhinged.

"I knew he'd come," Ruth whispered. "I just didn't think it would happen this way. He never went after anyone outside his circle before. Only the girls." Her voice cracked. "I'm so sorry."

"It's not your fault," Ivy said, pulling her sister into a hug.

The distant wail of sirens cut through the silence.

Moments later, a squad car pulled up outside, red and blue lights flashing against the bakery's glass windows. Two officers stepped inside, guns holstered but hands at the ready.

One knelt beside the unconscious man while the other approached them.

"What happened here?"

Ivy swallowed hard. "He attacked us. He came for my sister. He was trying to kidnap her. But we stopped him. He gave us no choice."

The officer scribbled notes while his partner checked the man's pulse and called for backup.

"We'll need statements," he said. "But first, we're taking him into custody." He motioned toward the blood on Gram's face. "Do you need medical attention?"

Gram swiped at his nose and sniffed. "I'm fine."

The officer's gaze flicked to Ivy. Her hands were still trembling, the rolling pin now abandoned at her feet. Blood speckled her white apron.

"You?"

"No." Ivy shook her head. "Get him out of here. We need a restraining order. Please."

The officer gave a quick signal, and his partner moved in to cuff the unconscious man. Paramedics lifted him onto a stretcher and rolled him out of the bakery.

Ivy let out a shaky breath.

Beside her, Ruth trembled.

"It's over," Ivy said softly, wrapping an arm around her. "You're safe now."

Ruth's shoulders sagged, chin dipping.

And as Ivy glanced at Gram—standing silent, his jaw tight, fists still clenched—she knew this wasn't over.

Chapter Twenty

Then

Ivy pressed her fingers to the cold glass, watching the city lights smear across the window in fleeting streaks. Her cheek still burned where Harry's hand had struck, but the deeper ache came from somewhere else —something heavy and unmoving lodged in her chest. She wasn't a child, not anymore, not after everything. But the system still treated her as if she were, shuttling her between strangers.

She didn't bother asking where Emily was taking her. It wouldn't matter. The destination never did. Each new house might start out quiet or kind, but eventually the cracks would show. Ivy had stopped expecting anything else.

The car turned off the main road, and Ivy sat up, her attention caught by the buzz of traffic. The further they drove, the denser the city became—brick buildings towering over narrow streets, flashing billboards cutting through the early dusk, and sidewalks crowded with people moving in every direction. Honking horns, the whoosh of passing buses, and the occasional wail of a siren filled the air, replacing the quietness of country roads she had once known.

Emily eased the car past a row of storefronts, their neon signs casting shifting colors against the pavement. Ivy's gaze darted from the glint of streetlights bouncing off rain-damp sidewalks to the sight of a man pushing a cart filled with blankets, his face lost beneath the hood of a tattered sweatshirt. At a stoplight, a group of teenagers laughed on the corner, their voices loud and carefree as they huddled near a food truck, the scent of fried dough drifting through the cracked window.

When the car finally slowed and pulled to a stop, Ivy stared for a beat, trying to catch up. Ahead of her loomed a building unlike anything she'd ever seen. It rose high into the sky, its surface gleaming with steel and glass that seemed to shimmer even in the darkness. Ivy swallowed hard, her gaze traveling up the towering structure.

Emily turned off the engine and glanced at Ivy. "We're here," she said, as if one wrong word might shatter the fragile quiet between them. "You'll stay at my place tonight. I didn't want to take you anywhere else —not after everything you've been through today."

Ivy stared at her, trying to untangle the meaning behind the words. Emily's place? Since when did caseworkers bring kids home with them? The idea felt off, unfamiliar. Her instincts pricked with warning.

Ivy didn't ask questions. Gratitude warred with suspicion, but she kept her thoughts to herself.

She followed Emily into the towering building, past the doorman who greeted them fondly. The lobby stretched wide, its polished marble floors gleaming under soft, golden lights. Ivy kept her eyes down, her shoes scuffing against the perfection of it all. The air smelled floral, overly sweet, as if the walls themselves had been sprayed with something expensive.

The elevator ascended in silence, the numbers glowing and shifting as they climbed higher. Ivy kept her eyes on the panel, her thoughts racing. What was Emily like outside of work? Did she have a quiet, put-together life in this sleek building, far removed from kids like her? Was this invitation something Emily truly wanted, or was it another part of the job—another task no one else was willing to take on?

When the elevator finally dinged and the doors slid open, Ivy stepped out, her sneakers sinking into the thick carpet. The hallway stretched ahead, lined with muted artwork and elegant sconces casting a soft, warm glow. It didn't feel real—this place, this moment. Everything about it seemed too quiet, too polished, too far from the world Ivy had always known.

Emily unlocked the door to her apartment and pushed it open, gesturing for Ivy to step inside. Ivy lingered on the threshold, her hand clenched around the strap of her bag—her one familiar thing in a world that kept shifting beneath her feet. When she finally stepped through, her shoulders sagged, the weight of the day—of the past few months—pressing down harder than ever. She was too tired to care about the perfect polish of this place, but it still hit her like a slap.

The apartment was ridiculous. Floor-to-ceiling windows framed the glittering Indianapolis city skyline, sleek furniture sat in perfect angles, and soft, golden light made the whole room look like something out of a dream. Or a nightmare, depending on your mood. And right now? Ivy's mood wasn't great.

"Wow," she muttered flatly, not bothering to mask the disbelief in her tone. She wasn't impressed; she was stunned. Who even *lived* like this? How could Emily—a caseworker—live in such a luxurious space?

Emily caught the look on her face and smiled, soft and understanding. Too soft. Too understanding. "It's okay," she said gently, gesturing toward the couch. "You're welcome here."

Ivy snorted under her breath. "Yeah, sure," she said, the sarcasm slipping out before she could stop it. She couldn't bring herself to care if it upset Emily. Tonight, her cheek still burned from Harry's blow, and she was bone-tired of pretending to be grateful, of acting like any of this mattered.

Emily paused, her brow furrowing, but she didn't call Ivy out on it. Instead, she led her further into the living room.

"You *actually* live here?" Ivy gestured around the room. She knew she should hold her tongue, but the exhaustion dragged the words out of her. "This is where you go after you tell kids like me that we're safe when we're really not?"

Emily sighed, the kind of sigh that said she wasn't going to fight back, no matter how much Ivy pushed.

"Yes, I live here," she said simply. "It's not exactly my choice. My dad wanted me somewhere safe, with a doorman and everything. It's not really my style, but it works."

"Rich father?" Ivy said, dry as dust.

Emily let out a short sigh. "He's very protective."

She dropped onto the couch with more force than necessary, sinking into the cushions. She knew she sounded bratty, but she couldn't stop herself. She was done pretending to be polite, done trying to smooth things over.

"It's just a place, Ivy," Emily said. "What matters is that you're safe. *And you are.* Tonight, you don't have to think about anything else."

Ivy slumped back against the cushy sofa, the fight draining out of her. Safe. Sure. But for how long? The apartment looked sterile, as if it was trying too hard to be something it wasn't—kind of like her. She didn't say another word, letting the quiet stretch between them. She wasn't ready to forgive Emily for living this shiny, untouchable life, and she wasn't ready to let herself feel okay.

Ivy stared at her. Emily always seemed so grounded, so real. But this place? It didn't match up. How could someone who lived surrounded by all this comfort and ease possibly understand what it felt like to have nothing? To feel like nothing?

Emily must have seen the conflict written all over Ivy's face because she sat beside her, her expression soft but determined.

"Ivy, I know this place might seem... different from what you've experienced. And, yes, it is. But please don't think for a second it means I don't understand, or that I don't care. I care. *Deeply.*"

Ivy's gaze dropped to the floor, her fists clenching slightly at her sides. She wanted to believe her, but the walls around her heart had grown too high, too impenetrable. Emily didn't stop, though.

She leaned toward her, trying to meet Ivy's eyes. "Yes, I'm lucky to have what I have. I won't deny that. My family has given me more than I probably deserve. But that's why I chose this path—why I chose to work with kids like you. I could've taken the easy route, but I didn't. Because I believe in what I do. I believe in *you.*"

Ivy looked up, caught off guard by the raw honesty in Emily's voice. This wasn't some hollow promise meant to ease guilt. Emily meant every word. Ivy saw it in her eyes, in the way her hands hung steady at her sides—no twitch, no retreat.

"You're not just another case to me, Ivy," Emily said. "You're a person—a strong, capable person who's been through more than anyone should. And I know it might not seem like it now, but you matter. What you want, what you feel—it all matters to me."

A tightness gripped Ivy's chest, as if someone had reached in and nudged a part of her she'd locked away. She wasn't sure what to say, so she settled on the truth. "It's... hard to believe sometimes. That anyone really cares."

Emily offered a small, encouraging smile. "Come on, let me show you where you'll sleep tonight."

Ivy followed her down the hallway, the plush carpet muffling their steps. Emily stopped in front of a door and pushed it open to reveal a guest bedroom. The space was inviting, with a soft bed dressed in crisp white linens and a window overlooking the glowing city skyline. A small lamp on the nightstand bathed the room in a warm, golden light, making everything feel calm and strangely peaceful. Safe.

"This is all yours for tonight," Emily said gently, placing Ivy's bag on the bed. "Settle in, take your time. I'll order us something to eat. You must be starving."

Ivy kept still. Her voice didn't trust her yet.

She walked to the bed and sat down carefully, her hands gripping the edge of the mattress. It was soft—softer than any bed she'd slept on in years. The kind of soft that could make you feel like you might sink right in and never come back out.

Emily lingered in the doorway, her expression kind but searching. "I'll be right down the hall if you need anything," she added.

The door closed quietly, leaving Ivy alone in this magazine-shoot bedroom. She lay back on the bed, staring at the ceiling as tears pricked the corners of her eyes. The events of the day churned in her mind, but there was something else. A sliver of safety. Fragile, yes. But there.

For tonight, it would have to be enough.

The morning sunlight poured through the tall windows, lighting up the apartment. Ivy sat at the kitchen island, her fingers curling around the edge of the smooth counter. The barstool beneath her was plush and too comfortable, like everything else in Emily's place—a little too good to be true. The events of the night before felt hazy now, but the knot of uncertainty in her stomach hadn't gone away. If anything, it had settled in deeper.

Emily moved around the kitchen with quiet confidence, the clatter of pans and utensils filling the otherwise still morning. The air was warm and carried the rich, familiar scent of eggs sizzling in butter, toast crisping in the toaster, and something brighter—the tangy sweetness of fresh-cut fruit sitting in a bowl within Ivy's reach.

"How do you like your eggs?" Emily smiled.

Ivy stiffened, caught off guard. No one had ever asked her that kind of question before—one that suggested her opinion mattered. "Uh... scrambled?"

"Scrambled it is," Emily said cheerfully, cracking eggs into a bowl and whisking them with a practiced hand. She added a sprinkle of salt and a dash of pepper, the sound of the whisk rhythmic and soothing. Within moments, she slid the fluffy yellow eggs onto a plate, added a piece of golden toast, and placed it in front of Ivy. A small bowl of fruit —strawberries, blueberries, and chunks of melon—joined the plate.

"There you go," Emily said, her smile soft and genuine. "Let me know if you need more."

Ivy stared at the plate, her fork hovering above the scrambled eggs. The meal was simple, yet it felt heavy in a way she couldn't name. It wasn't just the food. Emily's quiet, unwavering gaze carried no hint of the empty politeness Ivy had grown used to. There was something real there, something that unsettled her even as it warmed a part of her she had believed frozen for good.

Emily sat across from her with her own plate, her movements unhurried as she sipped from her coffee mug. She didn't push Ivy to eat, didn't fill the space with empty chatter. She sat there, patient and calm, until Ivy finally took a bite of her eggs.

"Ivy," Emily began gently, "I know you've been through so much.

And I know it's hard to believe things can get better. But I wanted to let you know I've found a foster home for you. A good one."

The fork froze in Ivy's hand. Her heart stuttered, and she looked up sharply, her throat tightening. She had heard those words before, over and over again. A "good home." A "fresh start." Each time, it had only led to more disappointment, more hurt. But Emily's tone... it made her pause. She sounded so sure, so certain.

"Really?" Ivy's stomach twisted as she searched Emily's face for any sign of doubt.

Emily's smile didn't waver. "Yes. Her name is Sarah. She's forty-five, recently divorced, and her three sons are grown and out of the house. She's been living on her own for a while and decided she wants to become a foster parent. You'd be her first placement. She's really looking forward to meeting you."

Ivy's mind churned with questions. Another home. Another stranger. Another chance to feel unwanted all over again. She should've been used to this by now, the cycle of hope and disappointment. But there was something in what Emily said, something that made her stop and listen.

"She's ex-Amish." Emily set her mug down. "She left the community years ago. I thought you two might connect because of that shared background. It's just her—no men in the house—so you won't have to worry about that."

Ivy's chest squeezed at the mention of the Amish. The strict rules, the quiet, the fear of her father's anger. She'd buried that part of herself as deep as she could, trying to forget, trying to move on. But now, here it was, staring her in the face again.

"Sarah seems really kind," Emily went on. "And I truly believe this could be a good fit for you. In fact, I almost think it's fate that Sarah recently decided to foster, and that this opportunity landed in my lap right when you needed it."

Ivy wasn't sure what to think. Fate? That seemed too hopeful, too easy. She'd been through so many foster homes in under three years, and each one had left her more disillusioned than the last. But she couldn't deny that what Emily was saying made her want to believe.

She set down her fork, her appetite fading.

"Thank you, Emily," she said quietly, looking up at her caseworker. "For everything. I know you didn't have to take me in last night... or find me a place. I'm thankful, and I'm sorry if I acted a little bratty last night."

Emily laughed. "Not even close to bratty. And you don't need to thank me, Ivy. I care about you. And I want to make sure you're in a place where you can start to heal, where you'll be safe."

Ivy shifted her weight, fingers curling around the hem of her sleeve. She wanted to believe this time that things could be different—but the words stayed trapped behind her teeth.

After breakfast, Ivy showered and dressed in one of the new outfits Gina had bought her for her birthday—jeans and a loose sweater. Again, the jeans pressed stiff and unfamiliar against her skin, but as she glanced in the mirror, a small thrill caught her off guard—unexpected, electric. She looked different. Older.

She ran a brush through her long hair, the brown strands falling straight down her back. It was the same way she'd worn it for years. But now, seeing herself in those jeans and that sweater, she had the sudden urge to change something else—something that would make her even more different from the girl she once was.

She stepped out of the bathroom and found Emily tidying up the kitchen.

"Emily?" she asked, hesitating in the doorway.

"Hmm?" Emily looked up with a smile.

Ivy bit her lip, feeling a little nervous about what she was about to ask.

"Do you think... do you think you could take me to get a haircut? Before we go to Sarah's?"

"A haircut?" Emily's eyebrows lifted in surprise. "Are you sure?"

"Yeah, I'm sure," Ivy said, more certain now. "I want a new look. I don't want to look the same anymore."

Emily's surprise melted into understanding. "Of course. If that's what you want, we'll do it. Let's go."

The salon buzzed with chatter and laughter, the rhythmic snip of scissors blending with the whir of blow dryers. Ivy sank into the chair, stiff and uncertain, her fingers gripping the armrests. She'd never set foot in a place like this before. The smells—shampoo, hairspray, something floral—wrapped around her, unfamiliar and a little overwhelming. The stylist ran a comb through her hair, and Ivy stared at her reflection as if she were a stranger to her own self.

"How short are we going today?" the stylist asked, her tone friendly and casual.

"Um. Right above my shoulders," Ivy said. She was ready for this. She needed this.

The stylist gave her a questioning look. "You're sure?"

"Positive."

"Okay then." She got to work, and Ivy watched as the long strands began to fall away, piece by piece.

With each snip of the scissors, a weight lifted, bringing a sense of control. When the stylist finished, Ivy looked in the mirror, and a small, hesitant smile crept across her face.

Her hair barely reached her shoulders now, the ends brushing her neck. The heaviness was gone, leaving her freed from her past. And that, more than anything, told her she might finally have a chance to start fresh.

"Do you like it?" the stylist asked, smiling at Ivy through the mirror.

"Yeah." Ivy couldn't contain her excitement. Her smile spread across her whole face. "I really do."

Emily was waiting at the front of the salon, and when she saw Ivy, her eyes lit up. "Ivy, you look amazing. You look so happy."

"I feel... good," Ivy admitted, feeling a bit shy about the compliment but also proud. It wasn't just the haircut—it was everything. The new look, the new home on the horizon.

She was shedding the weight of her past, little by little.

Chapter Twenty-One

Now

Ruth's old boss—Gary Lawrence, as Ivy had learned his full name—hadn't shown up since the night at the bakery. Two months after his arrest, he was out on bail, but the restraining order had done its job. Ivy still felt the occasional prickle of unease, but for now, Ruth was free, healing. That was what mattered.

Now, standing in the doorway of Gram's new apartment, Ivy crossed her arms, watching as he dropped the last box beside his bed. The space was small—barely enough room for the secondhand coffee table, a slanted bookshelf, and a kitchenette that looked like it had survived multiple decades. But it was his. A real home.

And while she was happy for him, something about it left her unsettled.

No more waking up to him sprawled out on her couch, grumbling about how her throw pillows were "aggressively decorative." No more late-night conversations over leftover pie. No more Gram a few feet away, separated by a single wall.

She had been good—so good—at pushing down whatever

feelings had been creeping in. There had been too much happening, too many other things to worry about. But now, Ruth was getting better. Gram had his own place. The chaos was settling. Maybe it was time to stop pretending she didn't care about him as more than a friend.

"Whew, this place is... cozy," Ruth's voice cut in as she strolled through the door, a box in her arms, her lips already curling into a teasing smile. "Didn't think you'd actually go through with getting your own place, Gram. Guess I owe Ivy five bucks."

Ivy stiffened as she turned to her sister. She hadn't bet on anything, but Ruth knew how to make things sound a certain way.

Gram brushed his hands off on his jeans. "I like proving people wrong. Besides, I was getting tired of Ivy's house rules. Did you know she doesn't let people eat straight from the fridge? Like, what kind of dictatorship—"

"I prefer to call it basic human decency," Ivy shot back, but the joke didn't land quite right.

"Are these for the bed?" Ruth held up the bundle of bedding.

"Yeah, toss them on there. I'll make it later," Gram said, giving Ruth a playful wink.

Ivy stiffened again, her stomach twisting when Ruth smiled— actually smiled—as she threw the pillows onto the bed. Gram had that effect on people. He was easygoing, the kind of person who could make even the worst day seem bearable. And Ruth... Ruth had been soaking up that warmth like sunlight.

Ivy had noticed. The teasing, the lingering looks, the way Ruth seemed to gravitate toward him. She wasn't blind to it.

A small flicker of jealousy sparked, but she shoved it down. Gram wasn't hers. He was her friend, her confidant. If he liked Ruth, and if Ruth liked him, Ivy had no right to interfere. They had both been through so much, and if they found happiness together... who was she to stand in the way?

She forced a smile and stepped further into the apartment, grabbing one of the now-empty boxes to break it down. "You've really done a great job saving up," she said. "Between the bakery and the furniture store, you've been working your butt off."

Gram shrugged, ever modest. "Wanted to make sure I could get a place of my own. It's not much, but I'm proud of it."

"And you should be," Ruth added, smoothing out the bedding with slow, deliberate hands. "You've been kicking ass."

Ivy glanced at her sister, catching the warmth in her tone and the admiration in her voice. Ruth had changed so much in the past couple of months. Healthier. Happier. And clearly drawn to Gram.

The unease tightened in Ivy's chest.

"Speaking of the furniture store," Ivy said, shifting the subject as she stacked the flattened boxes, "how's that been going? You seem to be doing well over there."

Gram grinned, strolling to the window and gazing out at the street below. "Better than I expected. Turns out, I've got a knack for convincing people they need a new couch."

Ruth laughed, the sound warm and full. "I bet you're great at it. You're a natural charmer."

Ivy's grip on the box tightened.

She had no right to let jealousy fester when she should be happy for them both. Gram had always been honest about wanting his independence, and Ruth deserved someone good in her life.

Still, the way Ruth's eyes lingered on Gram, the way he grinned back—it gnawed at Ivy, a slow, quiet ache.

But she wouldn't let it show.

"Gram's always had a way with people," Ivy said, keeping her tone light. She caught his gaze before turning away, busying herself with breaking down another box.

Ruth stepped beside her, grabbing a couple of the flattened boxes. "You okay?" she asked softly, searching Ivy's face.

Ivy forced another smile. "Of course. Happy to see you both doing so well."

Ruth studied her for a second longer, like she didn't quite believe her, but she let it go.

As the afternoon faded into evening, they finished setting up Gram's place. The small apartment, once empty, now had the beginnings of a home. Gram stood in the center of the room, surveying their work with a satisfied grin.

"Thanks for the help, guys," he said, leaning against the counter. "Couldn't have done this without you."

"You did most of the work yourself," Ruth teased, nudging him. "Ivy and I were there for moral support—and to look pretty."

Gram glanced between them, his green eyes playful. "Can't say I'm complaining."

Ivy stayed silent, watching the easy way they interacted. The laughter. The shared looks.

She shoved the bad thoughts down.

"All right," Ivy said, clapping her hands together. "I think we've done enough for one day. Gram, congratulations again on your place. You deserve it."

He walked over, pulling her into a hug. "Thanks, Ivy. Really."

Their eyes met, something unspoken passing between them.

Ivy swallowed hard, willing herself not to feel. Not to hope.

Because hope would only make it hurt more.

Chapter Twenty-Two

Then

The drive to Sarah's house was quiet, the air tight with everything left unsaid. Ivy sat in the passenger seat, fingers toying with the ends of her freshly cut hair, still adjusting to the unfamiliar lightness at her neck. The buzz she'd felt the night before—staying in Emily's sleek, pristine apartment, feeling like someone who *fit*—had dulled into something dense and unsettled.

As they turned off the main road, the world outside the window changed. The streets narrowed, lined with cracked sidewalks and leaning fences scarred with graffiti. Trash clung to the edges of the curbs, and houses sat in tired clusters, their paint peeling, and roofs sagging. Emily's grip on the steering wheel tightened, her lips pressing into a thin line as they entered a run-down mobile home park.

Ivy swallowed. She wasn't sure if it was the neighborhood making Emily tense or the fact that she had to leave Ivy here after letting her taste something better, something safer.

When the car rolled to a stop beside a single-wide manufactured home, Ivy exhaled slowly. This one was different. The yard was neat, the lawn trimmed, and the house itself was painted a soft cream, the bright yellow door standing out like a stubborn piece of hope.

Beside her, Emily hesitated, staring at the house with a crease in her brow. Guilt flickered across her face, barely masked before she turned to Ivy.

"This is a good home," Emily said, though the reassurance in her voice didn't quite land.

Ivy shrugged, her mouth twisting into a small, wry smile. "I've lived in worse."

Emily flinched, and Ivy immediately regretted saying it. She hadn't meant it as a jab, but the weight of it hung in the space between them.

"It'll be fine," Ivy added, trying to sound steadier than she felt.

Emily studied her, then gave a tight nod. "Let's go meet Sarah."

As Ivy stepped out of the car, she took one last glance at Emily, at the way her shoulders tensed as she locked the car. It hit Ivy then— Emily didn't simply feel guilty. She felt like she was failing her.

And Ivy wasn't sure which of them hated that more.

As they neared the door, it opened with a creak. A woman in worn jeans and a bleach-stained T-shirt stepped out, gray streaks in her ponytail. No makeup, no jewelry—only soft, kind eyes that eased some of Ivy's tension.

"Hi there," she said, offering a small wave. "You must be Ivy."

"Yes, ma'am," Ivy said.

Emily introduced herself, and Sarah's eyes lingered on the bruise shadowing Ivy's cheek before she stepped aside, allowing them in. The mobile home was simple but tidy, carrying the faint scent of lavender. Small touches of warmth filled the space—fresh flowers arranged neatly on the table, framed photos lining the walls, each one hinting at a life carefully tended despite its modest surroundings.

"Would you like some coffee or water?" Sarah moved toward the living room, her hands fiddling with the hem of her shirt.

"No, thank you," Emily said as she settled into one of the chairs with a warm smile. "I'm fine."

Ivy hesitated, her throat dry. "Water, please," she said after a beat.

Sarah offered a faint smile before disappearing into the kitchen. The tap sputtered on, breaking the silence, and Ivy shifted her weight, fingers brushing the strap of her bag.

A moment later, Sarah returned with a glass, and Emily got to the point. "Do you have Wi-Fi? Ivy needs to homeschool."

Sarah brightened. "Yes, the park provides free Wi-Fi. It's not fast, but it works."

A wave of relief washed over Ivy, and she could see that Emily seemed pleased as well. At least that was one less thing to worry about.

Emily asked a few more questions, her tone more serious now. "How's the neighborhood? Is it safe here? And the home itself—are there any issues we should know about?"

"Lots of questions," Sarah said. "I promise you I've met all the criteria DCS requires."

"Yes, of course." Emily leaned forward. "But I need to know if Ivy will be safe here."

Sarah gave a quick, affirmative tilt of her head. "The neighborhood isn't perfect, but it's quiet. I've been here for years without any trouble. As for the house, it's solid—no leaks, no faulty wiring, nothing like that."

Ivy sat quietly, watching the exchange. Emily seemed satisfied, her expression softening with a small breath of approval. Ivy couldn't help but notice that this was the longest Emily had stayed to assess a new placement. That meant something, didn't it?

"Could we see the bedroom?" Emily asked, glancing over at Ivy as if to gauge her reaction.

"Of course." Sarah motioned for them to follow her. She led them down a short hallway to a small room at the end. The bedroom was tiny, with enough space for a twin-sized bed, a small dresser, and a single window that let in a soft light. Small touches—a vase with wildflowers on the dresser and a small rug beside the bed made the room feel welcoming.

"It's not much, but it's cozy," Sarah said as she stepped aside.

Emily looked around, her expression measured. "It's a good setup," she said after a moment. "Thank you for showing us."

Sarah's hand rested lightly on the doorframe. "I hope you'll feel comfortable here, Ivy."

Ivy stepped further into the room, running her fingers over the quilt. Expectation hung in the air, dense and unspoken. Her gaze landed on the vase of flowers—small, deliberate, a gesture meant for her.

"It's nice," she said, not quite sure what else to offer.

Emily studied Ivy's face. "This feels like a good place for you," she said. "How do you feel about it?"

Ivy let her fingers drop from the quilt and looked at them both. "I think it'll work," she said simply.

Emily lingered, her gaze scanning the room once more before settling on Ivy. "If anything comes up, you call me," she said. "Don't wait. Promise me."

"I will."

As Emily left, Ivy stood in the doorway, watching her disappear. A strange emptiness settled in her chest, but resolve pushed past it.

Sarah shifted awkwardly before speaking, her words startling Ivy. "*Schwetz du Deitsch?*" (Do you speak Pennsylvania Dutch?)

The sound of the old language took Ivy aback, bringing a sudden rush of memories—Ruth, the garden, the farm, the chickens, Twinkles, sitting in the meadow and feeling the sunshine on her face. The good things. All the things she missed.

She hadn't heard anyone speak the Amish language since she left the community. Though the dialect Sarah spoke was somewhat different from the one Ivy had known, she could still understand. Like she'd been able to understand her relatives who'd lived in Ohio, but with guidance from her mom.

Ivy swallowed, feeling the past catch up to her in an unexpected wave. She had almost forgotten Sarah used to be Amish, too. The realization hit her with a strange mix of comfort and anxiety.

"*Ich denk' so,*" Ivy replied hesitantly. "It's been a long time."

Sarah smiled. "*Gute.* I wanted you to know we have something in common."

The shared language was a fragile bridge between them, a tether to a past Ivy hadn't expected to resurface.

Ivy hesitated, unsure if she should delve into something so personal so soon, but her curiosity got the better of her. "Why did you leave the Amish?"

Sarah's face tightened slightly, but she didn't seem surprised. "My ex-husband and I left together years ago. We didn't like how the church had so much control over our lives, dictating every little thing we did. We couldn't breathe without someone telling us if it was right or wrong."

Ivy remembered her parents arguing over the same stuff.

"We started to question things," Sarah continued. "Some of the decisions the elders made... they didn't sit right with us. It wasn't about the rules—it was the way they enforced them, the way they could turn the whole community against you if you didn't fall in line. It didn't feel... Christian, not the way we understood it."

Ivy could see Sarah's eyes held a deeply rooted pain; old wounds that had never fully healed. She knew leaving the Amish was never an easy choice, that it came with a heavy price—being shunned by family, losing the only life you'd ever known, stepping into a world that was often confusing and harsh.

"So, we left," Sarah said, her tone more resolute now. "We packed up and walked away. It wasn't easy—gosh, it was the hardest thing I've ever done—but we knew we couldn't stay. I wanted a different life, one where we could make our own choices, live our faith in a way that felt true to us."

"And your husband?" Ivy asked. "Did he feel the same way?"

"At first," Sarah continued. "But out in the *Englisch* world, he became angry. Bitter at how our families shunned us. The church we joined here fed his temper, and he became abusive toward me. I stayed for the kids, but I couldn't let them grow up thinking that was normal. So, we left him, too."

The strength in Sarah's story caught Ivy off guard. "That was brave of you."

Sarah smiled. "Didn't feel like it at the time. But sometimes, you have to do what's right."

A silence stretched between them before Sarah exhaled, shifting gears. "You must be hungry. I was thinking of making fried chicken and mashed potatoes for supper."

Ivy's stomach tightened, not with nerves this time but with a faint, warm memory. "That sounds really good," she said, surprising herself with how genuine she sounded. Fried chicken and mashed potatoes had been a staple at home. She'd spent hours helping her mother prep and cook meals—this one a favorite.

Sarah must have caught something in her expression because she said, "I know it's not the same as home, but I hope it feels a little familiar. The smells, the tastes—they help sometimes."

"Yeah," Ivy murmured. "I guess so."

"Then I'll make sure it's perfect." Sarah patted Ivy's shoulder.

Hope glimmered in Ivy's chest, tangled with the anger and hurt simmering in her mind. She wanted to believe this could be a refuge, a place where she could finally breathe, but that belief remained fragile and distant.

Each day—each foster home—pulled her further from her old life, leaving more space for painful thoughts. Her parents hadn't let her down—they had abandoned her in every way that counted. Her father's abuse left scars she could conceal under sleeves and collars, but the wounds inside her cut deeper, refusing to fade.

And her mother? The silence, the way she'd stood by and watched it all happen, had cut even deeper. She hadn't done anything.

As Sarah moved to the kitchen, Ivy followed, not wanting to be left alone in the new house. The smell of chicken sizzling in the pan filled the air, buttery and rich, blending with the starchy tang of potatoes bubbling on the stove. Ivy's chest tightened as the smells hit her.

Each scent carried a memory, vivid and unshakable. Memories from her Amish home and memories of cooking for Gram, Hannah, Maya, and Ashley in Sophie's chaotic house. How the kids would crowd the kitchen table, all talking over each other, and for a while, Ivy had felt needed. The noise of it, the responsibility—it had made her feel useful, even when the world outside that house felt like it might swallow her whole.

She pushed the thoughts aside as best she could. This wasn't home, but it was where she was now. And for now, it would have to be enough.

———

Ivy lay flat on her back, quilt twisted at her waist, eyes locked on the ceiling. Sarah's soft snores drifted through the thin walls. But Ivy stayed wired, thoughts spinning, that old ache curling tight in her chest. Sleep didn't stand a chance.

Laughter outside caught her attention. She sat up, ears straining. Voices, sharp and uneven, punctuated by occasional shouts and laughter.

Curious, she tiptoed to the window, pushing aside the curtain. A small group of teens huddled around a bonfire near the edge of the mobile home park. They looked about her age—thirteen, maybe fourteen—but rough around the edges.

She recognized the type—kids who had learned to be tough because the world had forced them to be. But there was something about their energy, their defiance, that drew her in. It had been so long since she'd had anyone to talk to, let alone a friend. The thought of walking over there terrified her, but the idea of staying alone in her room, trapped with her thoughts, was even worse.

After a moment's hesitation, Ivy grabbed her hoodie and slipped out the front door. The night air hit her with a rush of exhilaration as she made her way toward the bonfire, her steps light and careful. The laughter grew louder, mingling with the crackling of the fire and the occasional hiss of something tossed into the flames. As she approached, she could hear snippets of conversation—some teasing, a few crude jokes, the kind of banter that made it clear these kids were used to fending for themselves.

She hesitated at the edge of the firelight, unsure of how to make her presence known. But before she could decide, one of the girls, a tall brunette with ripped jeans and a face covered in makeup, spotted her.

"What's up, creeper?" the girl said. "Gonna hang out in the shadows all night?"

Ivy's cheeks burned, but before she could respond, a wiry boy with shaggy dark hair stepped in.

"Chill out, Jess," he said easily. "She's here to kick back—not start a war."

"Well, why's she hiding then?" Jess glared.

The boy turned to Ivy, his grin both mischievous and kind. "I'm Connor. What's your name?"

"Ivy," she said, her nerves on edge as she stepped closer.

"You new here?"

"Yeah. Moved in with a foster mom." Ivy gestured toward Sarah's house.

Connor lifted his chin slightly in acknowledgment. "Cool. Welcome to the circus."

One of the boys handed her a stick with a marshmallow. "S'mores initiation," he said.

The group chuckled, the tension easing slightly as Ivy carefully angled her marshmallow over the flames. The fire crackled, punctuated by bursts of casual banter that felt both welcoming and excluding all at once. She could tell they were used to each other, their rhythm natural, their jabs effortless.

But as Ivy began to settle into the moment, one of the boys— another wiry kid but with messy blonde hair and jittery energy—shot to his feet, brushing crumbs off his ripped jeans.

"Hey, check this out," he said, stepping back a few paces from the fire. The others paused, turning their attention to him as he flashed a cocky grin. Without warning, he launched himself into a backflip, landing with a slight stumble but catching himself.

Ivy couldn't help but laugh as the group erupted into a mix of cheers and groans. The boys teased him about his landing, while the girls giggled, shaking their heads. Even though the flip wasn't perfect, Ivy was impressed. She smiled, feeling more comfortable. Their unguarded, unfiltered behavior was refreshing.

And Ivy felt... light.

Carefree, even as she stared up at the stars and grinned.

Jess—the same girl who had given Ivy a hard time earlier—plopped down beside her on the log. This time, her expression wasn't laced with sarcasm but something more curious, almost thoughtful.

"So, where do you go to school?" Jess asked, popping a piece of gum into her mouth.

"I homeschool," Ivy said, pulling her hoodie a little tighter around herself as the night air grew cooler.

Jess raised an eyebrow, looking surprised. "Homeschool, huh? Lucky you. I wish I could do that. I've gotta go to school with these fools every day."

Ivy laughed, the bluntness of Jess's comment catching her off guard. "Is it really that bad?"

"You have no idea. The teachers are lame, half the kids are rich pricks from the other side of town, and the rest are... well, like them." She flicked her chin toward the group. "I mean, they're not all bad, but still... I'd kill to be able to skip it all and do my own thing."

Ivy didn't know what to say to that. Homeschooling had its own challenges—mostly the isolation—but she could understand Jess's frustration. The idea of being stuck in a place where you didn't really fit in, surrounded by people you didn't fully connect with, was all too familiar.

"I guess it has its benefits," Ivy said. "I don't get to meet many kids my age, though."

Jess chewed her gum thoughtfully, then shrugged. "Well, at least you're here now. That's something, right?"

Ivy gave a faint smile, a flicker of understanding passing between them. It wasn't much, but it was a connection, however small—something that felt surprisingly solid for once.

A voice cut through the night air—clear and commanding.

"Hey! You idiots, put that fire out before you burn down the whole damn neighborhood!"

Ivy's head snapped toward the sound, her pulse skipping a beat. The voice was familiar, though she couldn't quite place it. A figure emerged from the shadows near a nearby mobile home, moving into the glow of the firelight. He was older, probably around eighteen or nineteen, with shoulder-length brown hair that fell messily around his face. A cigarette dangled from his lips, the tip glowing faintly as he took a drag.

The group around the fire grumbled but started to kick dirt onto the flames, knowing better than to argue with him. Ivy watched him closely, something tugging at the back of her mind, a memory she couldn't quite grasp.

"Who's that?" she asked Jess.

Jess glanced over at the boy and then back at Ivy. "That's Gram," she said. "He lives in that trailer with four other guys. They get stoned a lot. He's kind of a jerk sometimes, but people around here don't mess with him."

The name landed hard, knocking the breath from Ivy's lungs. Gram. She hadn't thought she'd ever see him again, not after everything that had happened. But there he was, as real as the ground beneath her feet. Without thinking, she bolted up from the log she'd been sitting on and ran toward him.

"Gram!" she called out, shocked.

He turned at the sound of his name, his expression initially one of annoyance, but as Ivy skidded to a stop in front of him, a strange look crossed his face. His leaf-green eyes—so familiar, yet so different now—narrowed as he stared at her, trying to place her.

Recognition dawned slowly. "Little Amish girl? That you?"

Ivy nodded, a wild rhythm pulsing through her chest. "Yeah, it's me. It's Ivy."

Gram pulled the cigarette from his mouth, exhaling a stream of smoke as he continued to stare at her. "Damn," he muttered, shaking his head slightly as if to clear it. "I didn't think I'd ever see you again. What are you doing here?"

"I could ask you the same thing." The last time she'd seen Gram, things had been different. She'd been three years younger, more naive. Seeing him here, in this run-down mobile home park, was surreal.

Gram took another drag of his cigarette, looking her over with a mix of curiosity and something else she couldn't quite identify. "I guess you're not a little Amish girl anymore." His gaze drifted down her jeans and hoodie. "A lot's changed, huh?" he finally said. "You look different."

"So do you," Ivy said. Seeing him again reopened an old wound, yet also revealed a missing piece of herself she hadn't known was gone.

"Yeah… Guess we've both been through some stuff."

"Yes." She jammed her hands in her pockets. "I worried about you after what happened."

"You mean after I almost killed that pedophile in your room?" His smile didn't reach his eyes.

"You know, I always wanted to thank you for protecting me and the girls. I'm not sure what would have happened if you hadn't run in and stopped him." No matter how violently—but she wouldn't mention that part.

He shrugged. "No big deal. Had to spend some time in juvie. I got out a few months ago when I turned eighteen."

The fire behind them had been reduced to a smoldering pile of ash and embers, the other teens now half-heartedly joking and kicking at the dirt, their attention no longer on Ivy and Gram. But for Ivy, the world had narrowed down to the two of them, standing there in the dim light, caught between the past and whatever came next.

Ivy shifted on her feet, unsure of how to bridge the gap between the memories and the present. "I moved into a new foster home today," she said quietly, glancing back toward the mobile home she had snuck out of. "Her name's Sarah. That's her place over there."

Gram followed her gaze. "Yeah, I've seen her around. She seems... normal, which is more than I can say for most people around here."

As he spoke, his eyes narrowed, focusing on something that made his expression harden. Ivy felt a jolt of nerves as she realized what he'd seen—the bruise on her cheek, barely visible in the dim light but unmistakable to someone who knew what to look for.

"Did that happen at your last foster home?" Gram asked, his voice low and on edge.

Ivy hesitated, then gave a small tilt of her head and stared at the ground. She didn't want to talk about it, didn't want to relive those moments.

Gram's jaw tightened, and he took a long drag from his cigarette, exhaling slowly as if trying to calm the rage simmering beneath the surface. "I'm sorry you had to go through that, Ivy. But I'm glad you're out of there now."

"Yeah," Ivy whispered, forcing herself to meet his eyes again. "Me, too. Sarah... she seems different. It'll be better here."

His eyes seemed thoughtful as they rested on her. "That's good, Ivy. You deserve better." He paused, glancing at the darkened windows of Sarah's trailer. "But maybe you should head back before she finds out you're not inside. The last thing you need is to get in trouble your first night here."

"Yeah, you're probably right." She'd taken a risk coming out here, and she didn't want to mess up whatever chance she had at making things work with Sarah.

Gram gave her a small, almost protective smile. "Don't worry, we'll catch up. I'm not going anywhere."

"Neither am I," Ivy said, feeling a strange mix of sadness and relief as she turned to head back to Sarah's trailer. She took a few steps, then glanced back at him. "I'll see you around?"

Gram gave her a two-fingered salute. "Yeah, newbie. I'll be around."

With that, Ivy walked back to the mobile home, her heart still wreaking havoc under her ribcage from the unexpected reunion.

Chapter Twenty-Three

Now

Ivy locked up the bakery after another long shift, waving off Fiona with a tired smile. Fall had arrived, and with it came a whirlwind of pumpkin-shaped cookies, spiced pastries, and endless trays of Halloween treats.

Exhaustion tugged at her limbs. Time to close up shop and head upstairs. She couldn't wait to read the last chapters of the cozy mystery she'd started a week ago.

As she climbed the metal stairs, something felt... off. A strange, unpleasant scent lingered in the night air, but she brushed it off, assuming it was something from the neighborhood. Inside her apartment, she kicked off her shoes and stretched, taking a deep breath.

The balcony door was open, which seemed odd. But sometimes Ruth left it open when she'd left bread in the toaster for too long. Her sister's main meal preference was peanut butter and toast.

Ivy went to close the door, and the scent hit her again, stronger this time. She wrinkled her nose, recognizing it now. Weed.

Frowning, she stepped out onto the balcony, looking up at the ladder to the rooftop and then down at the street. Pedestrians walked by the storefronts. The smell grew more intense. Somewhere, someone was smoking a joint.

Shaking her head, Ivy shut the door and went into the kitchen for a glass of water and a snack. As she took a sip, a dull thud sounded from above. Her head snapped up. The rooftop patio. What the heck?

Someone was up there. Was it Ruth? Her stomach churned as worry began to gnaw at her.

After grabbing a flashlight and a kitchen knife as a precaution, she climbed the ladder that led to the rooftop. As she reached the top and stepped out onto the concrete landing, the scene that greeted her made her gasp.

Gram and Ruth sat in lawn chairs under the string of twinkling lights. They sat close together with their backs toward Ivy, their legs covered by a blanket. A small table sat near the center with empty glasses and a tray of half-eaten snacks.

And a half-empty bottle of vodka.

Their bodies brushed together in a far more intimate way than friendship. Ruth had her arm lazily slung over Gram's shoulder, her fingers playing with the ends of his hair as she giggled. Gram leaned into her touch, their heads tilted toward one another in a shared, foggy bubble of intoxication. Neither of them had noticed Ivy yet.

Then, Ruth brought a pipe pen to her lips and sucked in a breath. A stream of smoke curled up between them, dissipating into the night air. The distinct, pungent smell of weed clung to the breeze, and Ivy's stomach dropped.

Ivy didn't need to get any closer to know what was happening. The combination of their sluggish movements, the smell of marijuana, and the alcohol confirmed her worst suspicions. Ruth was high. And Gram —Gram, who'd promised to help her keep Ruth from slipping back into old patterns—stood beside her, every bit as lost.

Her stomach flipped as she watched Ruth lean in and kiss Gram, her lips lingering on his, and he didn't pull away. They were completely oblivious to her presence, caught up in their haze of intoxication.

A stabbing pain hit Ivy's chest, and a whirl of anger and betrayal rose up in her throat. She'd confided in Gram, trusted him to help Ruth stay on the right path.

And now? Now they were kissing—high, and with a half-empty bottle of vodka sitting next to them.

Suddenly, it made sense as to why they'd both slunk out of the bakery earlier than usual today despite how busy they'd been.

How long had they been going behind her back like this?

"Gram." Her voice trembled with fury.

Gram's head whipped around, his eyes wide with shock. He stood up quickly, almost tripping over the small joint he'd dropped at his feet. Stomping on it with his foot, he tried to extinguish the flame, fumbling as he blurted, "It's just weed, Ivy. It's not a big deal."

"Go home, Gram. Now." Ivy was louder this time, her anger making her shake.

Ruth, still swaying, let out a slurred giggle. "Ivy, don't be jealous. You're totally overreacting."

"I'm not overreacting, Ruth. I trusted you. Both of you." She shot a cold glance at Gram, her fury barely contained. "I shared with you how worried I was about her falling back into this, and this is what you do? You're fired, Gram. Get out. Don't come back."

Gram ran a hand through his hair, his guilt evident in every twitch of his face. He hesitated, as if he were about to argue, but instead, he whispered a weak apology. "I'm sorry, Ivy. I didn't mean to hurt you. I get it... I do."

Without another word, he brushed past her, leaving the rooftop. Ivy's legs felt wobbly, her stomach aching as she watched him disappear down the ladder.

Ruth stumbled slightly as she bent down to grab the bottle of vodka, her voice slurred and dismissive. "Fine, whatever. You're seriously overreacting. And if you wanted him, you should've made a move."

"This isn't about a kiss, Ruth. This is about me not wanting to see you drop back down that same path I found you in. Glazed over, high with needle bruises on your arms, stripping for an abusive asshole."

"God, don't be so dramatic, Ivy. You're no better than me, you self-righteous cow. Lose a couple of pounds, and maybe Gram will take an interest in you."

Ivy clenched her jaw, fighting back the urge to say something she'd regret. "Go to bed, Ruth. We'll talk about this in the morning."

Ruth didn't even glance at Ivy as she brushed past, dismissing her with a careless wave before disappearing back into the apartment, the bottle still clutched in her hand. She muttered something under her breath, but Ivy couldn't make out the words. It didn't matter.

Disappointment pinched through her, low and unrelenting with a bitter twist she should've seen coming.

She exhaled, forcing down the frustration trembling through her. When she finally climbed back down the ladder and stepped into the apartment, she locked the door behind her, double-checking it before leaning against the frame. The space felt colder now, hollow.

She didn't trust that Ruth wouldn't try to sneak out again—or worse, do something reckless. So, instead of retreating to her room, Ivy grabbed a blanket from the closet and curled up on the couch.

As she lay there, staring at the dark ceiling, doubt crept in. Had she overreacted? Had she been too hard on Gram? But then her mind flashed back to the first night she'd found Ruth at that club—the vacant, broken look in her eyes. That memory made Ivy's stomach churn. She couldn't let things spiral again. She wouldn't.

Something had to change.

Tomorrow, Ruth would have to make a choice. She either stayed clean, or she'd have to go.

Early the next morning, Ivy found Ruth crouched over the toilet, heaving violently. Sweat clung to her pale skin, her body trembling as she gripped the rim of the bowl. Ivy knelt beside her, gently gathering her sister's hair and holding it back.

Ruth groaned, slumping against the wall next to Ivy. Her breath was ragged, and she wiped at her mouth with a trembling hand. Dark circles shadowed her red-rimmed eyes.

"I feel like death," she rasped. Tears welled, making her look even more fragile. "I'm sorry, Ivy. I really am... for everything I said last night. I didn't mean it. And I didn't mean to kiss Gram. I don't even like him that way. I don't know what's wrong with me. I'm such a fuck-up."

Ivy exhaled slowly, steadying herself. She wanted to comfort Ruth, to tell her it was okay—but it wasn't.

Instead, she simply said, "You're not a fuck-up," and placed a damp washcloth in Ruth's shaking hands. "Come on. Let's get you back to bed."

Ruth nodded weakly. Ivy helped her up, guiding her back toward her room. She collapsed onto the bed, burying her face in the pillow as more tears spilled. "I'm sorry," Ruth mumbled, her voice muffled by the fabric. "I screwed up."

Ivy stood at the edge of the bed, arms crossed, her stomach twisting as she forced herself to stay firm. The years of abuse she'd endured—from their father, from the system, from the people who were supposed to care—had shaped her into someone who knew when enough was enough. She had spent too much of her life being powerless, being hurt. She couldn't let Ruth do it to her now, not in this way. Not when she'd worked so hard to build something safe for herself.

"Ruth," Ivy said, "I love you. But I refuse to be treated poorly under my own roof. I can't—I won't—let you drag me down. You have one month to stay clean, get a job, and then find your own place. After that, you're on your own. And if I find out you're using anything mind-altering before that month is up, I'll have to ask you to leave."

Uttering the words cut deep, but she knew she had to say them. If she didn't set boundaries now, she never would.

Ruth lifted her head, her tear-streaked face twisting with anger. "Fine," she spat, wiping at her face. "I'll move out as soon as possible. I never wanted your damn help anyway." She threw a pillow toward Ivy. "You're such a bitch."

Ivy flinched. She recognized this—lashing out, trying to turn it around, making her feel like the bad guy. But Ivy wasn't that scared, powerless girl anymore. She had a choice now.

And she was choosing herself.

"You don't get to hurt me because you're hurting," Ivy said. "Whatever happens next is up to you."

Ruth's glare burned into her, but Ivy didn't waver. She turned and walked out, her heart aching but her spine straight.

She'd survived too much to let herself be broken again.

Chapter Twenty-Four

Then

The next morning, Ivy sat at the kitchen table, staring at her laptop screen as she worked through her homeschooling assignments. She typed out her answers, the soft clicking of the keyboard filling the quiet space. Across the room, Sarah sat on the couch with her coffee and a book. It was nice—not the tense, suffocating silence Ivy had been used to in other homes, but an easy, comfortable one.

By midday, Ivy finished her last assignment and stretched, rolling her shoulders.

Sarah glanced up from her book and set down her mug. "Hungry?"

Ivy hesitated. "Yeah, I guess."

"Turkey sandwich sound good?"

"Yes, please," Ivy said, then watched as Sarah moved around the kitchen, pulling out the ingredients with practiced ease. It struck Ivy how comfortable this all felt—like she'd slipped into a rhythm that wasn't hers, yet somehow fit.

As Sarah assembled the sandwich, slicing the turkey and layering it with lettuce and tomato, she glanced over at Ivy. "You're pretty quick with your schoolwork. Do you usually finish this early?"

"Most days," Ivy said, taking the plate Sarah handed her. "It's not too hard. I get it done early so I have the rest of the day free."

Sarah leaned against the counter, a thoughtful expression on her face. "And can you do your schoolwork at any time of the day?"

"I suppose so. Why?"

"I was thinking... since you have a lot of free time, would you be interested in making some extra money?"

Ivy looked up from her sandwich, curiosity piqued. "How?"

"Well, I clean houses. Usually two or three a day, depending on the schedule. It pays pretty well. I could use some help to get the jobs done faster. If you're up for it, and if you can put off your schoolwork until about three or four, I'd love your help. And I'd pay you for your time, of course."

Ivy considered the offer, thinking about the possibilities. She was used to cleaning, after all—it was something she'd done her entire life. And the idea of earning her own money was appealing. She could buy more clothes, maybe ones that helped her fit in better. And more books, too, of course.

"I think that could be a good idea," Ivy said. "I'd like to help."

Sarah smiled. "Great. You can start tomorrow morning, if you want."

"Sounds good." She'd have to do her assignments when she got home. It could work out.

At dawn, Ivy followed Sarah to the car. The air was crisp, and Ivy pulled her hoodie tighter around her, her breath visible in the chilly air. As they passed a row of trailers, Ivy spotted a familiar figure sprawled across a picnic table.

Gram.

Even in the dim light, she recognized his tousled hair, his slouched posture. Empty beer cans littered the ground.

Ivy's steps slowed, concern gnawing at her as she looked at him.

Before she could say anything, Sarah tugged at her hoodie. "Ivy, you need to stay away from that boy and the others who live there."

"Why?"

Sarah unlocked the car door, scowling. "Those boys... they're into drugs and drinking. They act way older than they are, and they're heading down a dangerous path. I don't want you getting mixed up in that, understand?"

Ivy nodded, keeping her expression neutral. But she wasn't sure she could ignore Gram—not after everything.

As they drove past, Gram stirred, rubbing his face. He glanced toward the car, locking eyes with her for a second. The look on his face stopped her breath—a mix of disorientation and shame that cut through her. He didn't wave, didn't call out. He watched, a faint crease forming between his brows as the distance between them grew.

She hoped he'd be okay. But deep down, she knew—there wasn't much she could do for him now.

The drive to the first house took them out of the rough part of town and into winding roads lined with oversized houses and flawless lawns. Ivy stared out the window, wide-eyed. It looked like a movie set—perfect hedges, glistening windows, and tiled driveways that had never seen a crack.

Sarah pulled up to a massive house, the kind that made Ivy sit a little straighter. "This is the first one," she said, parking. "It belongs to an older woman named Bianca. She's picky, so don't rough anything up. And seriously—don't break anything unless you want to see a meltdown."

"Got it," Ivy said, nerves fluttering in her stomach. She couldn't help but wonder what kind of woman made people this cautious.

Sarah keyed in the door code, and they stepped into a showroom of a house. Polished hardwood gleamed under chandelier light. Ivy hesitated in the doorway, afraid to breathe wrong.

"Bianca usually stays in her room," Sarah whispered. "Let's keep it quiet and move fast."

They got to work—Sarah mopping and sweeping while Ivy dusted and vacuumed. Ivy was careful not to touch anything she didn't have to. The fear of knocking something over lingered in every movement.

They were nearly done, gathering supplies from the living room, when footsteps approached. Ivy looked up as an older woman entered—

silver hair styled to perfection, silk robe gliding behind her. She stopped short, eyes locking onto Ivy like she'd spotted a stain on her rug.

"And who is this?" Bianca asked, tone clipped. "You've brought someone new?"

Ivy froze, her stomach twisting under the woman's scrutiny. She opened her mouth to answer, but the words stuck, jammed somewhere between her chest and throat.

Sarah stepped in smoothly. "This is Ivy. She's helping me finish faster. Thought it'd be more efficient."

Bianca's eyes raked over Ivy. "Fine. But if she breaks something, it's coming out of your pay. And make sure she doesn't steal."

Heat flared in Ivy's face. "I don't steal."

Sarah offered a calming smile. "You don't need to worry. Ivy's solid. Raised the same way I was—work hard, tell the truth."

Bianca gave a skeptical sniff. "Last time, the mirror had smudges. Be more careful."

"I will," Sarah said, nodding. "It'll be spotless."

Bianca turned and disappeared down the hall.

Ivy's shoulders were still tight when Sarah leaned close. "Don't take it personally. She's like that with everyone. Let's recheck everything so she doesn't have a reason to nitpick."

"I'm fine," Ivy muttered, though her jaw ached from clenching it. "Let's just finish."

They went back through the house, redoing the smallest spots. Ivy worked harder, fueled by the sting of Bianca's words. By the time they finished, the place gleamed, and despite everything, Ivy felt a quiet flicker of pride.

Back in the car, Sarah gave her a nod. "You did great. The rest of the day won't be this bad."

"Thanks," Ivy said. "I can handle it."

The second house wasn't much easier. A middle-aged woman opened the door, her expression tight. She barely looked at Ivy, directing instructions to Sarah as if Ivy weren't there. While they cleaned, Ivy overheard her on the phone complaining about "the help" and how Sarah had shown up with "some poor girl this time." Ivy kept her head down, but the woman's gaze followed her, eyes lingering like she expected Ivy to mess up.

At the third house, an older woman with a thick accent launched straight into complaints about the last cleaning. Ivy felt her irritation spike, but Sarah stayed calm, smiling politely and promising to do better.

The day dragged. Every house brought fresh scrutiny, new demands, and more reasons to feel invisible. Ivy was exhausted—physically and emotionally—by the time the car turned back toward the mobile home park. She leaned her head against the window, watching the pristine houses blur behind them.

Sarah glanced over. "Long day, huh?"

"Yeah," Ivy murmured. "Didn't know people could be that rude."

When they pulled into the driveway of the mobile home, relief settled over her. Home. Finally.

Inside, Sarah dropped the cleaning supplies onto the kitchen counter with a sigh. "How about we take it easy tonight? I'll make something simple for dinner, and then we can chill and watch TV. We've earned it."

"I wish," Ivy said, slumping into a chair. "But I've got coursework to finish."

Sarah hesitated, then pulled a twenty from her pocket and handed it over. "You earned it. Today was a tough one, but you handled it like a pro. And if you keep helping out, there's more of this coming your way."

Ivy took the cash, tucking it into her pocket. Twenty bucks. It wasn't much, but it was something *she'd earned*. Felt kinda nice.

"Thanks," she said.

It still stung, the way people had looked at her, talked about her as if she didn't matter. But today, Ivy had kept up. She hadn't broken. And in her world, that counted for something.

Days blurred together, and Ivy's life settled into an endless grind—a routine that barely felt like living. Mornings were spent scrubbing strangers' houses with Sarah. Afternoons bled into evenings filled with homeschool assignments she could barely focus on. Her body ached, her brain fogged, but the growing stash of twenty-dollar bills kept her going. The pride of that helped.

She missed the kids in the neighborhood. Missed feeling like someone her own age. And Gram—he was slipping away. She spotted him a few times, always looking thinner, more distant. His green eyes had lost their light, his movements slow and disconnected. Something had dulled him—drugs maybe, or the kind of loneliness that settles deep. One morning, she caught him climbing into a rusted pickup with a few men and a truck bed full of lawn gear. Probably heading to a job. Probably not okay.

She didn't have time to check.

Schoolwork piled up. Some nights, she stared at her laptop screen, eyes glazing over as the words blurred into meaningless lines. She told herself she could catch up later. That sleep wasn't as important as survival.

But Gram's blank stare stuck with her.

And the work kept coming. House after house. Cruel remarks. Suspicious eyes. Every fake smile and clipped command chipped at her patience.

Then came Bianca's. Again.

The old woman stood in the driveway before they even parked, arms folded. Her eyes locked on Ivy, and the knot in Ivy's stomach pulled tight.

Something was wrong.

The moment they stepped inside, Bianca's agitation was impossible to miss. Her movements were quick and jerky, and her lips pressed so tight they practically disappeared.

Without a word, she led them to her bedroom and pointed at the carpet near the bed. A cluster of dark brown stains marred the otherwise pristine floor.

Sarah's eyes widened. "What happened?"

Bianca's face turned crimson. "I didn't make it to the bathroom," she snapped. "Diarrhea." She spat the word out like it offended her. "You need to clean it up."

Sarah hesitated. "Oh, um, of course, we can—"

"We'll clean it, but it'll cost extra." Ivy had had enough, and the words flew out before she could stop them. Weeks of scrubbing floors for rude clients, the exhaustion, the way people ignored them—it all boiled over.

Bianca's head snapped toward her. "Extra?" she repeated, incredulously. "You're already paid to clean."

"Not this," Ivy said, keeping her voice steady despite the shake in her hands. "Feces is a biohazard. It's not the same as vacuuming. Cleaning it takes extra supplies, so yeah, it costs more."

Bianca glared like she couldn't believe a thirteen-year-old had the nerve to talk back. "That's ridiculous. I've never been charged extra before."

Ivy crossed her arms. "Any other cleaning service would charge way more. We're only asking for an extra $100."

Silence stretched between them. Ivy's heart pounded, but she didn't back down. Maybe no one had ever challenged Bianca before. The thought sparked a surge of satisfaction within her.

Finally, Bianca let out a sharp huff. "Fine. But it better be spotless."

Ivy grabbed the cleaning supplies, not giving Bianca a reaction. Sarah gave her a wide-eyed glance but didn't say anything.

The rest of the job was quiet, but Ivy sensed something was off. As they packed up, Sarah finally turned to her with a serious look.

"Ivy, how did you know what a biohazard is?"

Ivy shrugged. "I read about it online."

Sarah sighed. "You weren't wrong, but don't ever speak over me again."

Ivy's stomach tightened. "I'm sorry. I didn't mean to—"

Sarah raised a hand, stopping her—not harshly, but firm. "I know. But this job is my only income. I didn't get to finish school. I can't afford to mess this up."

Ivy swallowed hard, the depth of Sarah's words settling in. "I wanted to help. I hate how they treat us."

"I know, kid. But next time, let me handle it."

Ivy nodded, but as they drove to the next job, Sarah's words lingered. This was all she had. No high school diploma. No safety net. No way out.

For the first time, Ivy noticed the cracks in Sarah's life—subtle but unmistakable. In the Amish community, everything had been laid out from the start: leave school young, marry, raise children. No decisions to make. Only a road already paved.

But... it didn't have to be that way.

Her thoughts drifted to Emily, her social worker, who always seemed so put together, so confident in her job. Ivy wondered if she could have something like that—something that gave her freedom.

The sun dipped lower, streaking the sky in golds and purples. Ivy leaned her head against the window, exhaustion giving way to determination. She had to finish school. She had to do better.

She refused to end up stuck, whether scrubbing floors for people who barely saw her or trapped in a life she didn't choose.

For now, she'd keep her head down and get through this. One day, things would change. She'd make sure of it.

Sarah went to bed early that night, tired and still griping about how Ivy had handled the situation with Bianca. Ivy sat at the kitchen table, staring at the twenty-dollar bill Sarah had handed her—the same amount she always gave her, even though Sarah had pocketed an extra hundred from Bianca today.

She wanted to feel guilty for speaking out of turn, for causing trouble, but it was hard to when the math didn't add up. Sarah hadn't hesitated to keep the extra money, so why did Ivy feel she was the one who had done something wrong?

She turned the bill over in her hand, her frustration simmering quietly. The lines between foster mom and boss were blurry, and it left Ivy confused. Sarah wasn't like the other foster moms she'd lived with. She was kind enough, sure, but she didn't feel like a mom. More like a coworker or maybe a distant roommate. Ivy paid for her own stuff, cleaned up after herself, and even helped with the cooking most nights.

This wasn't being cared for—it was a job.

A glimmer of light outside caught Ivy's eye. The teens were gathered around the bonfire again, their laughter carrying through the night. They looked relaxed, like they belonged there, like this moment was theirs. Watching them made something twist in Ivy's chest—a reminder of the loneliness that had been sitting with her lately.

She grabbed her hoodie before doubt could catch up and slipped on her sneakers. Cool night air brushed her face as she eased the door open. Her pulse pounded harder the closer she got to the group, nerves tightening, but she kept walking.

The laughter quieted, and heads turned to look at her. A few faces lit up with recognition. Jess, the girl Ivy had met last time, flashed a smile and gave her a wave. "Hey, look who it is! Ivy, right? Decided to crawl out of your cave again?"

Ivy managed a small smile, shoving her hands into her hoodie pockets. "Yeah. Needed some air."

Jess looked her over, her head tilting slightly. "You know," she said, her voice teasing but not unkind, "I've been meaning to ask—why don't you wear any makeup? You're old enough, right?"

Ivy hesitated, feeling a familiar pang of insecurity, but then decided to tell the truth. "I'm thirteen. But... I used to be Amish," she said quietly, focusing on the flames. "That's how I was raised until I was ten. We weren't allowed to wear makeup, have electricity, or have cars."

An awkward pause. Then, to Ivy's surprise, Jess grinned. "That's kinda cool. Means you've got a blank canvas. Let me do your makeup."

Ivy flushed. "I don't know..."

Jess waved her off, already pulling out her makeup kit. "Trust me."

The other girls leaned in, murmuring encouragement as Jess worked. Ivy sat still, unfamiliar with the gentle strokes of brushes. It was strange, but not unpleasant. She felt included, like she was building friendships here.

Movement stirred in the shadows, and Ivy's stomach dropped. Gram had stumbled out of his trailer, scowling. His hair stood in uneven tufts, his wrinkled shirt hanging crooked, like he'd rolled out of bed moments before.

Jess ignored him and tilted Ivy's chin. "Almost done."

She handed over a mirror, and Ivy barely recognized the girl staring back. Her eyes seemed larger, her lips tinted a soft pink. She looked older. Different.

Jess leaned over her shoulder, admiring her handiwork. "Told you," she said, pleased. "You've got great features—needed a little pop."

Her reflection startled her—subtle and polished, someone older, bolder. It wasn't a bad face, she supposed.

Jess's gaze shifted toward Gram, who was still watching them from the edge of his trailer. "Hey, do you know him?" she asked, her tone casual but curious. "I saw you go talk to him before."

Ivy lowered the mirror. "Yeah, we used to be in the same foster home a while back. He's harmless, really."

Jess nudged Ivy playfully with her shoulder, a mischievous smile on her lips. "I don't know, I think he's kind of cute in a trailer-park-boy kind of way."

Ivy chuckled, her cheeks warming at the memory of once thinking the same way. When they lived together, she'd seen Gram as a little rough around the edges but still handsome. And as the bonfire burned down, she decided to talk to him. Standing, she brushed off her jeans and walked over.

Gram eyed her face. "What's with the makeup?" he asked bluntly.

Ivy froze, suddenly self-conscious. "I wanted to try it." She glanced down and nudged a rock with the toe of her shoe.

He rubbed at his jaw. "I mean, you can do whatever you want," he said. "You don't need it, though. You've got that—natural beauty thing going on, you know?"

Warmth crept into Ivy's cheeks. "Thanks, I guess."

Gram scratched the back of his head, shifting awkwardly. "Anyway," he said, his gaze drifting back toward the teens, "I'm sick of those kids lighting up a bonfire every other night. It's too close to my place, and it's annoying."

Ivy raised an eyebrow, the corner of her mouth quirking up. "You sound like a grumpy old man, Gram."

His jaw clenched, but then he let out a low chuckle. "Yeah, maybe I do," he admitted, stuffing his hands in his pockets. "Been feeling older lately, that's for sure."

"What do you do for work?" Ivy asked, genuinely curious.

169

"Whatever needs to be done to pay my share of the rent," Gram replied with a shrug. "Tomorrow, my friends and I are getting paid to scrub graffiti off a building downtown. It's not exciting, but it pays."

"Good luck with that. I've been cleaning houses with Sarah." Ivy glanced at her chipped fingernails and dry hands, wondering if they still smelled like bleach.

"I noticed you've been leaving pretty early in the morning. Is she paying you?"

Ivy nodded, not wanting to get into details.

He looked at her like he was seeing her in a different light—less guarded, more real. "Take care of yourself, Ivy. Don't let anyone take advantage of you. And don't let those fucking kids get you into trouble."

"I won't," Ivy said, giving him a salute.

He smiled and shook his head. "Better get to bed. Another day, another dollar, as they say."

"'Kay, see you around, Gram." Ivy watched him walk back toward his trailer, then turned and made her way back to Sarah's mobile home.

When she slipped inside, she stiffened at the sight of Sarah sitting at the kitchen table, a steaming mug in her hands. Sarah looked up, her expression calm but serious.

"I saw you talking to one of those boys," Sarah said. "I thought I told you to stay away from them."

Ivy sighed, shoulders sagging. She was too tired to argue, too drained from the long day to explain that Gram wasn't as bad as everyone thought. "I wanted to say hi. That's all. He, uh, used to be my foster brother."

Sarah rubbed her temples as if trying to ward off a headache. "Ivy, I get it, but those boys are bad news. You don't need to get mixed up with them."

Ivy swallowed back her frustration. She wanted to defend him, to tell Sarah Gram wasn't a bad person. But she didn't have the fight in her tonight.

"And one more thing," Sarah added, her gaze shifting to Ivy's face. "You should wipe off that makeup before bed. It'll stain the sheets."

Ivy bit back a sigh, her cheeks burning with embarrassment. "Okay," she muttered, retreating to the bathroom.

Once inside, she stared at her reflection in the mirror, the older-looking girl staring back at her with tired eyes. She grabbed a washcloth and scrubbed the makeup off, watching as the dark smudges faded away, revealing her bare, familiar face underneath.

With a weary yawn, Ivy turned off the light and made her way to bed. She slipped under the covers, her body aching and her mind buzzing with a thousand thoughts. But as her head hit the pillow, the day's exhaustion pulled her under, and she fell into a deep, dreamless sleep, grateful for the escape.

Chapter Twenty-Five

Now

Ivy snapped the cash register shut, exhaling sharply as she rubbed her tired eyes. The last of the Halloween cookies had sold, marking the end of a chaotic month. The bakery had been a battlefield of pumpkin-spiced everything, ghost-shaped cookies, and fall-themed pastries, leaving her too exhausted to do much else.

Her part-time employees had barely been around, juggling school and home life. But the real weight pressing down on her? Ruth.

Ruth, who had spent more time holed up in her room than helping at the bakery. Ruth, who barely spoke to her anymore. The silence between them had stretched into something heavy and unspoken, and Ivy didn't have the energy to confront it. Not when she was already scraping the bottom of her emotional reserves to get through each day.

She pushed open the apartment door, expecting to see Ruth curled up on the couch, half-asleep with an old movie playing in the background. Instead, the place was eerily quiet.

"Ruth?" she called, stepping inside.

Nothing.

The back of her neck prickled as she moved toward Ruth's room. The door was slightly open, enough for Ivy to see the neatly made bed and the gaping emptiness where her sister's things should have been. Her duffle bag—gone. Her clothes—gone.

On the nightstand, a hastily scrawled note:

I'm sorry.

The words slammed into her gut. Her fingers tightened around the scrap of paper as her brain scrambled to process.

Ruth had left.

The air in the room felt thin, suffocating. With a shaking hand, Ivy grabbed her phone and dialed her sister's phone number.

Straight to voicemail.

She tried again. Voicemail again.

"Damn it, Ruth," she whispered, pacing the small space.

Where would she go? She had no money, no safe place to land. Panic clawed its way into Ivy's chest as her mind raced through possibilities.

Then, like a cold slap to the face, it hit her.

The strip club. She went back.

Ivy didn't want to believe it, but deep down, she knew. Grabbing her keys, she rushed out the door.

The strip club's neon sign buzzed in the dark, its sickly glow reflecting off the cracked pavement. Ivy stood at the entrance, her pulse hammering, nausea curling in her stomach. She clenched her jaw, forced a steady breath, then pushed the door open.

The place smelled the same as last time—sweat, cheap perfume, spilled beer. The bass thrummed through her bones, a sickening pulse that made her want to turn and run.

She forced her way through the haze of smoke and flashing lights, her heart hammering as she scanned the room.

And then she saw her.

Ruth.

No!

She was back on stage, wearing a bikini bottom and nothing more, her movements sluggish and off-balance. Ivy's heart broke at the sight. Ruth's eyes were glazed over, her smile vacant. She was high and lost all over again.

Ivy pushed through the crowd, her anger and fear propelling her forward. She reached the edge of the stage as Ruth stumbled slightly, catching herself on the pole before she fell. Her gaze landed on Ivy, but it took a moment for recognition to dawn.

"Ivy?" Ruth slurred, blinking as if trying to focus. She stepped down from the platform, swaying unsteadily as she approached her sister. The bright lights of the club cast harsh shadows on her face, and Ivy could see how far gone she was. Her pupils were dilated, and her skin had taken on a sickly pallor.

"What are you doing here?" Ruth mumbled, trying to smile, but it was weak, hollow.

"What am I doing here?" Ivy hissed, grabbing Ruth's arm. "What are *you* doing here? This isn't you. You're better than this."

Ruth laughed, a sharp, bitter sound. "I needed money, okay? I'm not staying with you forever, remember? Gotta fend for myself, right?"

"Not like this." Ivy's grip tightened on Ruth's arm. "You're high, Ruth. I told you I'd help you, but you can't keep doing this to yourself."

Ruth pulled away, staggering.

Ivy could feel her anger rising, but kept her voice even as she asked, "Did he come for you again? Gary? Did he force you to come back here?"

Ruth's eyes flashed with something—maybe guilt, maybe recognition—but then she shrugged, dismissing the question as if it were trivial.

"Nah," she said, her tone flippant. "I'm here on my own. I wanted to come back. At least here, people... want me. They might even need me."

Ivy's heart dropped. "You're not safe here, Ruth. He doesn't want you. He's using you. Can't you see that?"

Ruth's eyes darkened, a trace of vulnerability vanishing behind her anger. "You don't get it, Ivy. You don't get it at all."

"I do get it, Ruth," Ivy said, stepping closer, trying to reach through the haze clouding her sister's mind. "I've been there for you, and I still am. I want to help you. But you have to want to help yourself. Please, come home with me."

Ruth's lip quivered, and Ivy thought, for a second, that she might break through. But then Ruth shook her head, stepping back. "I can't. I don't want to try anymore. I like dancing." She laughed. "And I like being *high*," she sang out.

A crack of pain tore through Ivy's chest, sharp and deep. She reached out, her fingers stretching desperately, but Ruth turned and slipped into the shadows beyond the stage. Tears blurred her vision, stinging hot against her skin.

She'd lost her sister again.

And this time, she didn't know if she'd be able to bring her back.

Chapter Twenty-Six

Then

The knock came again, firmer this time.

Sarah frowned, drying her hands on a dish towel as she turned toward Ivy. "Are you expecting anyone?"

Ivy shook her head. "No, are you?"

Sarah's lips pressed together, uncertainty crossing her face before she stepped toward the door. When she pulled it open, Ivy's posture straightened at the sight of Emily standing on the porch.

Emily.

Relief and surprise washed over Ivy in equal measure. She hadn't seen her caseworker in a few weeks, and while she had gotten used to fewer check-ins, she was always glad to see a familiar face. "Emily! Hi."

Emily offered Ivy a small, reassuring smile, the kind that steadied more than it soothed. But beneath it, there was a trace of something else —purpose, maybe, or concern. "Hi, Ivy. Morning, Sarah. I'm not catching you at a bad time, am I?"

Sarah's posture stiffened as she stepped aside to let Emily in. "Not at all, Emily. What brings you here so early on a Saturday?"

Emily motioned toward the kitchen table. "May I?"

"Of course," Sarah said, her voice polite but suddenly careful.

Emily slid into the chair next to Ivy, folding her hands neatly on the table. "I wanted to check in and see how things are going." Her gaze darted toward Ivy, then Sarah. "I noticed Ivy's grades have been slipping, and I wanted to make sure everything is okay."

Ivy's spine went rigid, caught off guard. She hadn't expected that. Had Emily really been paying such close attention to her schoolwork?

She hesitated before glancing at Sarah, who looked back at her expectantly. Ivy's stomach tightened. She wasn't failing, but she knew she wasn't doing as well as she should. Feeling flustered, she scrambled for an answer. "I'm... I'm tired, I guess. I've been working with Sarah, and it's a lot."

Emily's expression sharpened as she turned to Sarah, her tone calm but firm. "Working? Why is Ivy working, Sarah? She's not old enough to hold a job, and she should be focusing on her schoolwork, especially since it's her freshman year."

Sarah's lips parted, as if she hadn't expected this to be a problem. "I thought it wouldn't be an issue for Ivy to make some extra money for herself. She seemed happy to help, and it's good for her to learn responsibility."

Emily's frown deepened. "Sarah, the money you receive for fostering Ivy is supposed to cover her needs. She shouldn't have to work to make ends meet for you."

Ivy sensed the tension rising, the energy in the room shifting. She jumped in before it could escalate. "It's okay, Emily. I wanted to earn my own money. It's not a big deal."

But Emily didn't look convinced. Her jaw tightened, and she turned back to Sarah. "How many hours is she working?"

Ivy shifted in her seat, her fingers curling around the hem of her shirt. She didn't want to get Sarah in trouble. She had a roof over her head, didn't she? Food to eat? It wasn't like she hated helping. But under Emily's sharp gaze, the truth felt heavier.

"Um," Ivy's voice wavered. "It's usually about five to eight hours a day." She hesitated, her stomach twisting as she added, "Sometimes more. Nine or ten, depending on the day."

177

Emily's face went still, the warmth draining from it. "I had no idea you were being put in this situation, Ivy. This is unacceptable."

Sarah bristled beside her. "We were both raised with a strong work ethic, Emily," she shot back, her tone clipped. "It's normal for children to help out. I'm teaching Ivy responsibility."

"This isn't an Amish community, Sarah," Emily countered. "This is foster care. Ivy is here because she needs a safe home, not to be treated like free labor."

Sarah's jaw tightened, the muscles in her face twitching. "Maybe I'm not meant to be a foster mom, then," she said, her voice quieter but laced with pride, anger, maybe even guilt.

Emily stood, pushing her chair back with controlled force. "Maybe you're not," she said, unwavering. Then she turned to Ivy, her frustration melting into something softer. "Ivy, go pack your things."

Ivy's throat closed up, breath shallow. "No," she whispered. "Please." Tears burned as they slipped down. "I don't want to go to another foster home. I can't do this again."

Emily knelt beside her, placing her hands gently on Ivy's shoulders. "I know, sweetheart," she said. "But I can't leave you here if it's not safe. I promise, I'll find you somewhere better. Somewhere you don't have to worry about working or anything like that."

Ivy shook her head, hands clenched at her sides. Her body trembled. She didn't want to do this again—start over, relearn a new place, tiptoe around new rules. She'd only begun to find her footing here, imperfect as it was. The idea of being uprooted again, of another stranger deciding her fate, made her stomach knot.

Still, deep down, she knew Emily wasn't the villain in this story. She was the one stuck with the hard decisions.

Ivy drew in a shaky breath and swiped at her cheeks. "Okay. I trust you."

Emily smiled sadly, brushing a tear from Ivy's cheek. "Thank you, Ivy." Then, more gently, she added, "Go get your things."

Ivy pushed herself up on wobbly legs and trudged to her room, her chest tight with uncertainty. She yanked her suitcase from under the bed, her movements stiff, robotic. Clothes, toiletries, schoolwork. She shoved everything inside without bothering to fold it. The whole process took less than five minutes. It shouldn't be so easy to leave a place behind.

In the kitchen, Emily held Ivy's backpack, her books and laptop already packed inside.

Sarah was gone.

Ivy's throat tensed as she scanned the living room, as if she'd find Sarah lurking in the shadows, offering some kind of explanation. But the house was silent.

A knot formed in Ivy's gut, a nauseating mix of panic and realization. Sarah hadn't even said goodbye.

Her fingers clenched around the handle of her suitcase, but she forced herself to lift her chin. No more pretending this was home. No more pretending she was wanted here.

She looked up at Emily, trembling. "Can I at least say goodbye to Jess and Gram? They're my friends."

Emily hesitated. "Okay, but please hurry. We need to leave soon."

Grabbing her suitcase, Ivy rushed out the door and ran toward Gram's trailer, her breath hitching with every step. She knocked on the door, calling out his name, but there was no answer. Frustrated, she knocked again, louder this time, hoping he might be inside.

But the trailer remained silent, and Ivy's dismay grew. She turned, glancing around the park, hoping to spot Jess or Gram nearby. A few neighbors were milling about, but none were familiar. Ivy didn't know which home Jess lived in.

Crap.

Her shoulders slumped, a wave of disappointment washing over her. She had hoped to see them to at least say goodbye, but it seemed she wouldn't get that chance. With a heavy heart, she turned back toward Emily's car, dragging her suitcase behind her. She tried to hold back tears, knowing she had to be strong, but the pain of leaving another home—another life—was almost too much to bear.

In the car, Emily gripped the steering wheel tightly, her knuckles white with tension as they drove away from Sarah's mobile home park. Ivy sat silently in the passenger seat, staring out the window, trying to process everything that had happened.

As they pulled into a gas station, Emily parked the car and turned off the engine. She turned to Ivy, her expression softening. "I'll be right back, okay? I need to make a quick call."

Ivy nodded absently, watching as Emily stepped out of the car and pulled out her cell phone. She paced a few steps away, her back turned to Ivy as she dialed a number. Ivy could see her lips moving, though she couldn't hear what she was saying. Emily seemed tense at first, her free hand gesturing as she spoke, her brows furrowed in concentration.

Ivy wondered if Emily was talking about her. Was she arranging for another foster home? Was she calling someone at the agency to report what had happened with Sarah?

But then, as if on cue, Emily's expression changed. Her shoulders relaxed, and a slow grin spread across her face. Ivy's curiosity piqued. Maybe it wasn't about her after all. Emily could have been talking to a friend or a family member—someone close to her. Ivy realized she didn't know much about Emily's life outside of her role as a caseworker.

After a few more moments, Emily hung up the phone and walked back to the car, a bright smile spreading across her face. She opened the driver's side door, slid into her seat, and turned toward Ivy, her whole expression lit with excitement.

"I've got some good news," Emily said. "I spoke with my supervisor, and we've worked something out. Ivy, how would you feel about coming to live with me?"

Ivy gaped in surprise. "W-What? Live with you?"

In that fancy apartment?

Emily's smile widened. "Yes, live with me. I know it's a bit unconventional, but I want to make sure you're in a safe and stable environment. I don't want you bouncing around anymore. I know it's hard, but I think we'd make a good team. I'm not sure you know this, but you're a special girl, Ivy."

Ivy couldn't find her voice. She'd never considered the possibility of living with Emily, her caseworker. It seemed almost too good to be true. "You'd... you'd really do that? For me?"

"Absolutely," Emily said firmly. "I care about you, Ivy. I want to make sure you have the chance to focus on your schoolwork and be a kid for once. No more working long hours, no more worrying about whether you're going to be safe or not. Just... a home. For as long as you want."

A rush of emotions hit Ivy all at once—relief, hope, and enough disbelief to make her question if she'd heard Emily right. Living with Emily? Someone who actually seemed to care, who didn't see her as a burden or a paycheck? It felt too good to be real, but also like something she didn't dare turn down.

"Okay," Ivy said quietly, the words coming out softer than she meant. A small smile crept across her face, cautious but real. "Yeah. I'd like that. I'd really like that."

Emily reached over, giving Ivy's hand a gentle squeeze. "I'm glad, Ivy. I think this could be a good start for both of us."

As they pulled back onto the road, Ivy leaned into the seat, letting out a breath she hadn't realized she'd been holding. The tightness in her chest eased a little. God, she hoped this one would work.

Chapter Twenty-Seven

Now

Ivy sped down the narrow country road, anger simmering, pulse beating relentlessly. The endless hours at the bakery and the emotional weight of Ruth's departure had left her on edge. But now, as she drove toward the remnants of her past, the anger was directed somewhere new—at the life she and Ruth had been forced to live. A life without a normal family.

It wasn't fair. It wasn't right.

The road in front of her wavered, distorted by the surge of memories crashing into her. Her father's biting words, his fists, the endless nights lying awake with a hollow stomach. Ruth's silhouette by the door, vigilant, protecting her while she stifled her sobs. Years of scraping by, never truly living—just surviving.

As the tires crunched onto the narrow dirt path that wound toward her childhood home, Ivy's pulse thundered in her ears. Each beat a question: Was her mother still there? Would she find the answers she'd come for? And did Ivy even want them? Her grip tightened on the steering wheel as the pull of her past dragged her forward.

The long, winding dirt road stretched out ahead of her, flanked by overgrown corn fields and dense trees. The white two-story house, once grand and full of life, was now a ghost of the past. The paint was peeling, the windows were dusty, and the yard had been overtaken by weeds. The barn to the left of the house looked weathered, barely holding itself together.

Ivy parked beside the barn, the gravel crunching under her tires, and stepped out of the car. The cool autumn air smelled of damp earth, and the scent took her back to when she'd helped her mother plant vegetables in the garden. She could still see her mother's hands in the soil, hear her soft humming as they worked side-by-side. Ivy's gaze shifted toward the garden, now overgrown and wild, and her chest tightened with bittersweet nostalgia.

The farm was run-down, a far cry from the home she remembered. She began walking toward the porch, her footsteps hesitant, memories swirling. The sound of a creaking screen door pulled her from her thoughts, and Ivy looked up to see a woman stepping onto the porch. The woman had her arms crossed tightly over her chest, her face shadowed.

"Get on out of here. We don't want anything," the woman called out.

Ivy stopped in her tracks, unsure of what to do or say. Before she could respond, a dog—a scruffy brown mutt—ran out from the porch and sniffed at her shoes. Ivy blinked. The dog looked like the runt of the litter she'd had as a child. Could it be the same one? Over ten years had passed. That was impossible. But the familiar sight tugged at something deep inside her.

She swallowed hard and took a step forward, ignoring the woman's hostile words. "I used to live here," Ivy said. "I'm looking for my mother. Her name is Lara Schrock."

The woman on the porch hesitated, her stance faltering as she squinted toward Ivy. Silence stretched between them. Ivy's pulse quickened. Then, finally, the woman lowered her arms and stepped closer to the edge of the porch.

"Ivy?" she said, her voice softer now, almost disbelieving. *"Is es du?"* (Is that you?)

Ivy's lungs seized, her pulse slamming against her ribs. She stepped forward, trying to make out the woman's features, to see her face clearly. Was this really happening?

The woman walked into the sunlight, revealing her face—weathered and worn, her hair streaked with gray. But beneath the lines of time, Ivy recognized her.

It was her mother.

"*Mamm?*" Ivy whispered in disbelief.

The woman—her mother—nodded slowly, her eyes filling with tears.

"Ivy," Lara said again, this time softer, as if testing the name, as if she couldn't believe it had finally returned to her.

Ivy stood frozen, the lost years between them hanging in the air. So many questions, so many raw emotions, all flooding her at once as she stood before the woman who had once been her world.

The woman who'd turned a cheek whenever her father had become abusive.

The woman who'd abandoned her and Ruth into the foster care system, never coming to retrieve them.

Lara opened the creaky door wider, motioning for Ivy to come inside. The once-bright house was now dim, illuminated by the soft twinkle of kerosene lamps. The scent of oil hung in the air, mingling with something warm and comforting—bread, perhaps—baking in the stove. It smelled like childhood, like home, yet foreign all at once. Ivy hesitated, standing on the threshold of her past, before stepping inside.

The house was quiet, almost too quiet. Ivy's gaze darted around, taking in the emptiness. No brothers and sisters running through the halls, no scolding from their father. Just her mother. And the dog, which had followed them inside, was now lying lazily by the hearth. The stillness was unsettling, like the house itself had forgotten what it meant to be full of life.

Lara shuffled over to the stove, adjusting the heat, before turning to Ivy. "*Setz dich,*" she said, pointing to one of the worn wooden chairs by the kitchen table. The language slipped from her lips so naturally, yet to Ivy, they echoed from a life she could barely remember."

"I don't speak that anymore," Ivy said, her voice firmer than she'd intended. "Only English."

Disappointment was shown in her mother's eyes. "Of course," Lara murmured, switching effortlessly to English. "Please, sit down. Do you want some coffee?"

"No, thank you," she bit out and pulled out one of the chairs to sit, her hands resting awkwardly in her lap. She couldn't help but notice the little details—the crocheted doilies on the table, the ticking of an old clock on the wall, the faint creak of the floorboards. Everything was familiar, yet nothing felt the same.

Lara sat down across from her, folding her hands on the table. Her eyes—those same blue eyes that matched Ruth's—studied her, as though trying to figure out how to start a conversation after so many years of silence.

"So," Lara said, "why are you here?"

The question hit Ivy harder than she expected. Why *was* she here? She'd spent the whole drive furious, determined to find answers, but now, sitting in front of her mother, the words tangled in her throat.

"I don't really know," Ivy admitted. "I guess I had to see for myself."

Lara's gaze didn't waver, but her expression shifted, as if she'd expected a different answer. She tilted her head slightly, saying nothing, leaving space for more.

Ivy's fingers curled around the edge of the table, her knuckles turning white. She hadn't come here for small talk. There was so much unresolved between them, so much pain she'd carried for years. And suddenly, the words she'd kept buried deep inside came rushing to the surface.

"Why didn't you fight for us?" Ivy asked, her voice trembling with the force of years of pent-up emotion. "You let us go. No letters, no visits, no explanations, nothing."

Her mother stiffened as she sat up straighter in her chair.

"I didn't have a choice." Lara scoffed, shaking her head as if Ivy's question had been absurd. "It wasn't up to me. It was up to your father. It was up to the police."

Ivy's jaw clenched. "You could have done something. You were our mother."

Lara's gaze flashed with something—anger, regret, frustration. "I was your mother, yes. But in this house, that didn't mean much. Your *dat...* you know how he was, Ivy. He controlled everything. I couldn't go against him. Not without risking—" She broke off, her hands trembling slightly before she folded them again in her lap, trying to maintain composure.

"Risking what?" Ivy demanded. "What could have been worse than losing your children?"

Lara looked away, her face tight with emotion. "You don't know how it was," she said quietly. "How hard it was with all of you children...and him. I had no power. I feared him as much as you all did. And now he's gone..."

Ivy swallowed the lump in her throat, her anger still simmering but mixing now with confusion and hurt. "We were your daughters," she said quietly. "You were supposed to protect us."

Lara's shoulders slumped, the fight seeming to drain out of her. "I tried as best as I could, Ivy," she said. "I urged Reuben to listen to the caseworkers, to get help so we could bring you back. He was always so stubborn. He didn't think anything was wrong with him. He was angry with the *Englisch* for stepping in, and he refused to listen to any of them. And I... I was afraid of losing any more of my children. Whenever I brought it up, he drank more, and cursed, and hit.... So, I stayed humble and did my best to be a good wife."

Ivy looked down at the worn wood of the table, her emotions churning into a storm she couldn't control. She'd spent years blaming her mother, resenting her for not doing more, for not standing up to her father. But now, sitting here, looking at the woman in front of her—broken, weathered, defeated—she realized maybe her mother had been a victim, too.

But that didn't make it hurt any less.

"I'm sorry," Lara whispered after a long silence. "For everything. I know it wasn't enough. But I didn't have the strength back then."

Ivy closed her eyes, summoning strength from the memories of Emily—the woman who had saved her, cared for her, and shown her real, unconditional love. Emily had been the family Ivy needed, the one who had healed parts of her heart she thought would remain broken forever. Ivy thought about how much love and guidance Emily had given her when she'd been so lost, how she'd made Ivy feel worthy again.

The warmth of those thoughts gave her the courage she needed to face the moment.

She opened her eyes and looked at her mother, seeing a tired, defeated woman before her—someone who had failed her, yes, but also someone who had been crushed under the weight of her own circumstances. Ivy realized she didn't have to carry the same burden forever. She could let some of it go.

Standing up, Ivy took a deep breath. "Thank you for letting me in," she said. "And for talking to me."

Lara's eyes widened slightly, as if she hadn't been expecting gratitude. Her fingers twisted together on the table, her expression unreadable. "Ivy... will you write to me?" she asked, voice tentative, vulnerable. "I want to know how you're doing."

Ivy paused, her chest tightening. She didn't know how to respond. She was still angry—there were so many unresolved feelings, so much pain that hadn't been addressed. But now, as she stood in this old house, seeing her mother in this different light, Ivy couldn't shake the feeling of pity. Of sadness for what could have been.

But that didn't mean she was ready to open herself up again. Not yet.

"I have to go," Ivy said finally, her tone distant but polite. She walked to the door, pausing by the dog, who wagged its tail as she patted it on the head. She thought of her old dog, the one she had cherished as a child, and the faintest smile tugged at her lips.

Without another word, Ivy opened the door and stepped outside, the cool air hitting her face. She didn't look back as she walked to her car.

She had come looking for answers. What she found instead was a woman—a mother—who had lost her own battles long ago.

Chapter Twenty-Eight

Then

Emily's apartment became a permanent solution—a home. It wasn't just a stop between foster houses, a place where she had to prove she was worth keeping. It was stable... safe. The couch was actually comfortable, the books were plentiful, and Emily always made sure Ivy had everything she needed.

With each passing year, Ivy changed. She turned fourteen, then fifteen, her confidence growing in ways she hadn't thought possible. She pushed herself harder in school, driven by Emily's belief in her and the quiet certainty that survival wasn't the endgame—she could create a life worth living. College was no longer an impossible dream.

Emily was always busy—long days spent helping kids like Ivy—but she never let Ivy feel like an afterthought. Even after exhausting shifts, she made time. They'd sit at the kitchen table, talking about everything from school to books, and in those moments, Ivy felt something she rarely allowed herself to believe in: belonging.

Then, one afternoon, everything shifted.

Ivy had been mindlessly scrolling through social media when a suggested friend popped up. Her breath caught. Ruth.

She froze, staring at the screen. The girl in the profile picture barely resembled the sister Ivy remembered. Ruth had makeup on, her hair styled, and she wasn't wearing Amish clothes. She looked... happy. Like she belonged to a world Ivy had never been part of.

Without giving herself time to overthink, Ivy tapped *Add Friend* and quickly typed out a message.

Hey, Ruth. It's Ivy. How are you? It's been a long time.

For the next several days, Ivy checked her phone constantly. Nothing. No response, no notification. The empty message thread gnawed at her. By the end of the week, she couldn't take it anymore.

"Emily," she said hesitantly one evening, watching as Emily worked through another pile of paperwork. "I found my sister Ruth on social media."

Emily's pen stilled. "You did?"

Ivy fidgeted with a napkin. "I sent her a message, but she hasn't answered. Do you think you could help me figure out what's going on?"

"Of course," she said. "Let me see what I can find."

Days later, Emily sat Ivy down, her expression grave.

"I found Ruth's file," Emily said. "She went into foster care around the same time you did. Moved through a few homes before ending up in a group home. She was released when she turned eighteen."

Ruth's file. Ivy gripped the edge of the table, willing herself to stay grounded. "Why didn't they send us to the same foster home?"

Emily sighed. "I don't know, Ivy. Unfortunately, siblings get separated all the time—lack of space, paperwork mix-ups, and sometimes simply bad luck. It's not fair, I know."

Ivy clenched her fists, her nails digging into her palms. "But she's my sister," she said, frustration lacing her words. "We should've been together."

If Ruth had been there—if they had faced the system side-by-side—maybe things would have been different. Maybe Ivy wouldn't have spent so many nights lying awake in unfamiliar rooms, feeling like a stranger in someone else's house. Maybe she wouldn't have had to force herself to trust new people over and over again, only to be let down. With Ruth beside her, maybe she wouldn't have felt so completely alone, so scared of what came next. The thought of all the things they could have endured together, of the comfort she never got to have, made her throat tighten.

Emily reached across the table and softly patted Ivy's hand. "I wish I could change that."

Ivy swallowed hard. Her thoughts raced. "What about my other siblings? Can you find them?"

Emily hesitated, then nodded. "I'll try."

For the next few days, Ivy hovered while Emily made calls, searched records, and scrolled through databases. But when she finally returned with an answer, Ivy knew before Emily even spoke that it wasn't the one she wanted.

"I couldn't find anything on your other siblings," Emily admitted. "There's no record of them in the system. It's possible they stayed with your family, or..." she trailed off, letting Ivy fill in the blanks.

Ivy sat back, her chest tightening. She'd expected some kind of answer. Something. But this—this was worse than not knowing.

"Thanks for trying," she muttered, staring at the table.

Emily leaned in. "Ivy, I know it's hard not to have your siblings with you. But you're doing so well now. You have a bright future ahead of you."

Ivy offered a faint tilt of her head, though the words barely touched the ache inside. She had a home now, yes. A future, maybe. But a part of her still felt lost, like a thread that had been cut too soon. No matter how hard she worked to rebuild, some pieces of her past stayed out of reach.

Time didn't stop, even when Ivy wished it would. She stayed on top of her grades, burying herself in schoolwork, but the past had a way of creeping up, clawing at the edges of her mind. No matter how much Emily tried to ground her, there was a restlessness Ivy couldn't outrun.

By the summer after her sophomore year, Emily's work hours had stretched even longer, leaving Ivy alone more often. Her friends—the few she'd managed to make here—were all off on vacations, posting photos of beaches and mountains Ivy couldn't even dream of.

The city felt empty, and she was sick of staring at the same walls, the same streets, the same reflection in the mirror.

After tearing through every book she owned, Ivy decided to hit the library. She needed something, anything, to fill the gnawing loneliness. But as she rounded the corner, the library's doors in sight, something else caught her eye—a group of teens leaning against a wall covered in bright, angry graffiti.

There were three of them—two girls and a guy—sprawled out like they owned the street. They weren't lounging or killing time; they were staking a claim, radiating the kind of confidence Ivy had never touched.

The first girl stood with her arms crossed, chin tilted up, eyes sharp and daring. She had the kind of presence that made people think twice before saying something stupid. Ivy instantly thought of Hannah—tough, unreadable, the type who could cut you down with a look.

The other girl moved like chaos wrapped in sunlight, all wild gestures and laughter loud enough to echo down the block. Her messy hair bounced with every word, like the world existed for her amusement. She floated more than walked, untethered, untouched by the weight most people carried.

The guy lounged like the bench belonged to him, arms slung wide, the picture of indifference. But his eyes—dark and sharp—moved constantly, sweeping the street like he was solving a puzzle no one else could see. Ready for whatever. Calculating.

Ivy halted mid-step, her heart stumbling. The air around them crackled—charged, waiting. A strange twist unfurled in her chest—half intrigue, half something more possessive. Whatever it was, it cut through the haze she'd been living in.

She shoved her hands into her hoodie, nerves tumbling like loose change in her stomach. Should she turn around? Probably. But something stronger tugged at her—some unseen thread she couldn't ignore.

After a beat's hesitation, she crossed the space between them, her steps casual in appearance but tight with tension.

"Hey," she said, trying to sound cooler than she felt.

The girl with the curls smirked. "Who are you?"

The guy gave a lazy chuckle. "Ten bucks says she's lost."

"Or stalking us," the other girl muttered, still arms crossed, still not impressed.

"I'm Ivy," she said, forcing a smile. "Not lost. Just... passing through."

"Yeah? And you thought we looked friendly?" The curly-haired girl snorted. "That's hilarious."

"No, I thought you looked like a circus sideshow I saw last year," Ivy said, surprised by her own boldness. "Turns out, they had better costumes."

That got a laugh—even from Scowl Queen, who cracked the tiniest grin.

"Okay, Ivy," the guy said, dragging her name out like he was testing it. "You got jokes. I respect that."

"I'm Lucy," the curly one said. "That's Brianna, our fearless mood-killer, and this is Niall. You crash the party, you stay for the weird."

Ivy smiled. "Sounds tempting."

They made room without really saying so—a subtle shift, a tilt of shoulders and space on the bench. It wasn't an invitation exactly, but it wasn't a rejection either.

Before long, she was laughing with them—really laughing. They tossed around stories that sounded half true, half invented on the spot, full of midnight bike rides, stolen slushies, and near run-ins with cops. Ivy didn't care what was real. It felt good. Fast and chaotic and alive.

Over the next few weeks, they became her hiding place. Lucy, Niall, and Brianna weren't perfect. They were loud, impulsive, and constantly daring the world to knock them down—but they had each other's backs. And when Ivy was with them, she felt like maybe she could stop being the quiet girl with the haunted past.

She could be someone louder. Wilder. Braver.

Someone who didn't flinch when the world looked at her.

One evening, when Emily was stuck working late again, Ivy found herself wandering the streets with her new crew. They didn't have a destination. They walked, talked, and let the city guide them. Eventually, they ducked into a narrow alley. Ivy leaned against the graffiti-covered brick as Lucy swung her backpack off her shoulder and rummaged through it. A sly grin spread across Lucy's face as she pulled out a bottle of tequila and held it up like it was a trophy.

"Here we go," Lucy said, unscrewing the cap with a flourish. She took a long swig and passed it to Niall, who drank like a pro before handing it off to Brianna. Brianna laughed as she tipped the bottle back, wiping her mouth with the back of her hand when she finished.

When the bottle landed in Ivy's hands, she froze, the sharp smell of alcohol wafting up to her nose. She looked around, her gaze lingering on Lucy's confident smirk and Niall's easy grin. They made it seem so natural, so normal, like it was no big deal. Ivy hesitated, but then the thought of being the odd one out gnawed at her. She lifted the bottle to her lips and took a sip.

The tequila burned like fire, scorching its way down her throat, but she swallowed hard, refusing to cough or show how much it stung.

"Not bad." She took another swig, this one going down a little easier, and handed the bottle back to Lucy.

As the bottle kept making its rounds, the warmth of the tequila spread through Ivy's limbs, loosening the tension she always carried. Her cheeks felt flushed, her lips tingled, and everything suddenly seemed funnier. She couldn't stop laughing, her voice blending with the others as their jokes became sillier and their stories more outrageous. The weight she'd been dragging around for years felt like it had disappeared, if only for the night. She felt lighter, freer, and unburdened.

"Hey, I've got an idea," Lucy said, her grin sharp and mischievous. "I know a place that'll tattoo us, no questions asked. Doesn't matter if we're underage. Let's all get one."

Ivy's head was still spinning from the tequila, her body warm and loose from the buzz. The idea sounded reckless, stupid, and exactly what she wanted.

"Hell yeah, let's do it!" she said.

Her thoughts flashed to Hannah and that bloody rose tattoo. Fierce, bold, untouchable—everything Ivy wasn't but wanted to be. Maybe she'd get a flower, too. Not a rose, though. Something smaller, wild, unpolished. A sunflower, maybe.

Yeah, that felt right.

The group stumbled into a grimy little tattoo shop tucked between a liquor store and a laundromat. The smell of antiseptic hit Ivy's nose. The buzz of the tattoo gun vibrated through the air, and Ivy's pulse quickened as she scanned the walls, covered in bold designs. Skulls, flames, birds in flight—it all seemed alive, daring her to choose.

They dumped their crumpled bills and loose change onto the counter, laughing as they counted out enough to cover the tattoos. When Lucy dared Ivy to get hers on her neck, Ivy laughed, her cheeks flushed and warm.

"Yeah, right," she said, rolling her eyes. "I'm not that hardcore. I'll get it on my wrist. That way, I can actually see it."

The tattoo artist, a broad guy with a beard that looked like it hadn't been trimmed in weeks, motioned for Ivy to sit. She slid into the chair, trying to act chill even as her nerves hissed under her skin. He prepped his equipment, the needle gleaming under the fluorescent light, and Ivy felt her bravado falter for a split second. But then she saw her friends grinning, cheering her on, and she leaned back, gripping the armrests.

The first touch of the needle sent a sharp sting through her wrist, and she flinched.

"Damn," she muttered under her breath, biting her lip to keep from showing how much it hurt. The alcohol wasn't dulling as much as she'd hoped. She stared at the ceiling, focusing on her friends' conversations and laughter.

When it was over, Ivy glanced down at her wrist. The small sunflower stood out against her skin, its petals delicate but determined, like it belonged there. Her friends crowded around, hyping her up, but the excitement didn't last long. As the tequila's buzz faded, reality crept in like a cold wind. Her wrist throbbed, each pulse a reminder of what she'd done.

She pulled out her phone and froze. The screen lit up with a string of missed calls and texts from Emily. Her stomach dropped, and panic set in. What was Emily going to say? Ivy knew she'd screwed up—big time. What if Emily kicked her out? What if this tattoo, this stupid, impulsive choice, ruined the one good thing she had left? The sunflower on her wrist stared back at her, mocking her.

Ivy mumbled a quick, "I've gotta go," before bolting out of the tattoo shop, clutching her throbbing, plastic-covered wrist. She ran, the sharp burn of tequila still lingering in her throat. She didn't stop until she reached Emily's apartment, her breath ragged as she fumbled with the keys. The door jolted open, and there Emily stood, worry etched deep into her face.

Emily's expression softened the moment she saw Ivy, and she rushed forward, wrapping her in a tight hug. "Where were you?" she demanded. "I was so worried—"

"I'm sorry," Ivy cut in, stepping back with guilt and fear roiling in her stomach. "I did something stupid. Really stupid." Her fingers trembled as she showed Emily her wrist and the sunflower tattoo. She couldn't meet Emily's eyes.

The tension in the room felt suffocating as Ivy braced herself for the worst—for anger, disappointment, or the ultimatum that she couldn't stay here anymore.

"You got a tattoo," Emily said at last, her voice calm but disbelieving.

Ivy finally found the strength to look at her. "So stupid, I know."

Emily's nose wrinkled. "And you've been drinking."

"Yeah. It was my first time. I wanted to try it and fit in. It got out of control. I realize that now. I'm so sorry."

"Ivy... I thought—" Emily stopped, running a hand over her face as if trying to steady herself. "I thought you'd been kidnapped or hurt, or worse."

Ivy fidgeted with her hands, guilt clawing at her chest. "I'm really sorry. I understand if you're mad."

Emily let out a long sigh. "I'm not mad, Ivy," she said in a gentle tone. "I'm relieved you're okay. I thought something terrible had happened to you. I was about to start calling nearby hospital ERs to see if they had a patient who matched your description."

"You were?" Ivy's eyes burned. No one, aside from Gram and Ruth, had ever cared this much about her.

"Yes, Ivy. You're my daughter. Well, foster daughter, but still. I'd be torn in two if I lost you."

"Really?" Ivy swiped her palm along her damp cheek.

"Of course, sweetheart. I love you. You're my everything."

Ivy broke down and fell into Emily's arms.

The quiet concern and love from her foster mom hit Ivy harder than any yelling ever could.

"I love you, too, and I'm so, so sorry," she whispered between sobs. "I wasn't thinking. I... I wanted to feel like I had control over something."

Emily stepped back, cupping Ivy's face. "I get it," she said. "We all hit moments like this. But drinking and tattoos won't hand you control, Ivy. They'll only tangle things more. We'll talk about it later, okay? Right now, I'm grateful you're safe."

"Thank you. I promise I won't make you worry about me again."

She pulled Ivy into another hug, holding her tight. "You know, I was thinking," she said. "One day, after you graduate from college, maybe we can finally do that road trip we always talk about. Drive cross-country, see the Pacific Ocean. What do you think? It's something we both can look forward to."

Ivy laughed at the change of subject, even as tears blurred her vision. The thought of that adventure—something they'd talked about extensively—created a warm ache in her heart. But more than that, Emily's faith in her future—the belief that Ivy could graduate from college and accomplish so much more—settled like a warm blanket. Ivy felt her throat tighten, gratitude swelling.

"I'd like that," she managed.

Emily squeezed her tighter, and Ivy let herself be held, feeling a rush of emotions swirl inside her—relief, gratitude, and the sting of guilt. But more than anything, she felt the deep comfort of knowing Emily was there for her, believing in her.

Ivy wasn't alone. She had a home and someone who cared enough to stay, even when she made mistakes.

Chapter Twenty-Nine

Then

Two years later, Ivy stepped onto the sprawling campus of Indiana State University, a pulse of adrenaline surging through her veins. Her hands tingled with anticipation, fingers tightening around the strap of her bag as she took in the sight of buildings and students milling around.

She clutched a campus map in one hand and her schedule in the other, trying to make sense of the maze of buildings and paths that all looked the same. With Emily's help and guidance, Ivy secured a scholarship—her good grades and her status as a foster child opening doors she hadn't dared to dream about before.

Today was her first day, and her nerves were a jumble of anticipation and apprehension. Boy, what would Ruth think of her now? Graduated from high school and now starting college.

The morning sky was overcast, causing a muted light to fall over the red-brick buildings and bustling walkways filled with students moving purposefully in every direction.

Ivy breathed deeply, trying to calm her nerves as she navigated the unfamiliar grounds.

She looked at her schedule again, attempting to match the building names with the map. But the more she looked, the more confused she became. The map twisted and turned in her hands like an unsolvable puzzle. She frowned, turning in a slow circle, hoping for some sign or landmark to guide her. But everything looked so similar, and everyone around her seemed to know exactly where they were going.

As she was about to give up and ask someone for directions, she heard a voice behind her. "Need a compass?"

Startled, Ivy turned to see a boy standing a few feet away, his face lit up with a playful grin. His dark brown hair framed his face in a way that looked effortlessly cool, and his caramel-colored eyes sparkled with amusement. He was tall and athletic, his faded band T-shirt and well-worn jeans giving him a casual, laid-back vibe. He looked at ease, like he belonged here, as if he had been navigating these paths for years.

Ivy blushed, embarrassed at being caught so obviously lost and flustered by how handsome he was. He wasn't like the teenage boys she'd known—there was something older in the way he carried himself, a quiet confidence that made her pulse skip as their eyes met.

"Uh, maybe," she admitted with a sheepish smile. "I'm trying to find my next class, but this map isn't making any sense."

He stepped closer, peering at the map in her hands. "Yeah, these things can be a bit tricky. Let me see." He took the map from her gently, his fingers brushing against hers. "Where are you headed?"

"Uhm, I'm looking for Gillum Hall," Ivy said, glancing down at her schedule.

"Oh, Gillum Hall is on the other side of campus. But don't worry, it's not too far. I can show you the way if you'd like."

Ivy's shoulders eased, and she offered a grateful smile. "That would be great. Thanks...?"

"Beckett," he said, extending his hand. "But everyone calls me Beck."

"Ivy," she replied, reaching out to shake his hand. His grip was warm and firm, and she noticed his eyes flicker to her wrist, lingering on the sunflower tattoo below her sleeve.

"Nice ink," Beck said with a curious tilt of his head. "Does it mean something?"

Ivy hesitated, then waved it off with a laugh that was half-dismissive, half-nostalgic. "A teenage mistake," she said lightly, though the truth felt more complicated, since it was from the night Emily had claimed Ivy as her daughter and expressed how much she'd loved and cared for Ivy. It had become more than a tattoo.

"Looks good on you," Beck said, his grin widening. Ivy fumbled for a response, but her tongue stalled. Heat crept up her neck, and she ducked her head, hoping he didn't notice.

"So," he continued, "first day?"

"Yeah, can you tell?" Ivy tucked a loose strand of hair behind her ear, her fingers brushing against her freshly cut bob. The shortest style she'd ever dared to get, the ends barely grazed her jawline, and she still wasn't used to how light it felt. The look was new, almost bold, and it left her feeling exposed but also... a little more herself.

Beck tilted his head toward the building behind them. "It's not so bad once you get used to it. Want me to show you around?"

Ivy noted the easy confidence in his posture and the kindness in his expression. "Sure," she said, slinging her bag higher on her shoulder.

Walking beside him, she couldn't help but think about how far she'd come—from plain dark dresses and prayer caps to jeans and cropped sweaters. She wasn't hiding or trying to be what someone else wanted her to be. She was here, taking up space, and it felt... good.

As they weaved through the crowds of students, Beck chattered away, pointing out various buildings and landmarks, giving her a mini-tour as they went.

"You know," Beck said, "on my first day last year, I got stuck in a rainstorm." He chuckled, glancing up at the overcast sky. "It was pouring, and I had no idea where my class was. By the time I found the right building, I was completely drenched. Definitely not the best first impression."

Ivy smiled, feeling her anxiety melt away with every step they took together. Beck's easygoing nature and friendly demeanor put her at ease.

He looked up at the clouds again and then back at her. "Looks like you're lucky today... so far."

She laughed. "I guess so. Hopefully, the rain holds off a bit longer."

"Fingers crossed." He glanced over at her and asked, "So, are you from around here?"

"Yeah, I'm an Indiana native. But I'm dying to travel after I graduate." Ivy gave him a small smile. She thought about telling him more—about her Amish past and her years in foster care—but decided against it. It felt too personal to share right now. And she wanted to seem normal for once. "What about you?"

"I'm here from Colorado," Beck said. "I'm on a baseball scholarship. I'll be riding it out until they figure out how bad I suck," he added with a cute half-grin.

Ivy laughed again, finding his humor infectious. "I'm sure you're not that bad."

He shrugged with a wink. "Guess we'll see."

By the time they reached Gillum Hall, Ivy felt like she'd known Beck for much longer than a few minutes. She stopped at the entrance, turning to face him. "Thank you so much for helping me, Beck. I really appreciate it."

"No problem, Ivy. It was my pleasure. If you ever need a compass again, I'll be around here somewhere."

"I'll keep that in mind. Thanks again."

As she headed into the building, she glanced back over her shoulder to see Beck walking away, his hands in his pockets, whistling a tune she couldn't quite place. She smiled to herself, feeling a little lighter, a little more confident, knowing that she'd already made a friend on her first day.

Emily would be so proud. Ivy would have to call her from her dorm room later today to tell her all about her first day.

After her classes were over, Ivy returned to her dorm room and found her roommate, Virginia, sitting cross-legged on her bed, a book in her lap. They had met a couple of weeks ago when rooms were assigned, and Ivy had immediately felt a connection with her. Virginia was a bit shy and seemed to prefer reading over socializing, much like Ivy herself. It was comforting to have a roommate who shared her love of books and quiet moments.

Virginia glanced up as Ivy walked in, nervous energy shining in her bright blue eyes. Her red hair tumbled in soft waves around her shoulders, and she brushed a stray lock behind her ear. "Hey, Ivy. How was your first day?"

Ivy set her bag down, kicking off her shoes. "It wasn't bad. A little chaotic, but manageable. I even made a friend," she said, trying to sound casual, though the admission made her smile.

Virginia's expression softened, though her fingers fidgeted with the edge of her book. "That's great. Um, there's this thing tonight—a back-to-school party at one of the sorority houses." She hesitated, trailing off. "I was thinking about going... but I don't really know anyone. I thought maybe you'd come with me? I mean, if you want to."

Ivy paused, glancing at her roommate. She could see the uncertainty in Virginia's eyes, the nervous way she tucked her hair behind her ear again. Ivy wasn't sure about going to a sorority party—it wasn't exactly her scene. But she knew what it felt like to be in a new place, to face the intimidating unknown. She couldn't leave Virginia hanging.

"Sure, I'll go," Ivy said, sitting down on the edge of her bed. "I've never been to one of those parties either, but it could be fun to check it out together."

Virginia's lips parted in a quiet sigh. "Really? You'd do that? I was worried you'd think it was a dumb idea."

Ivy nodded, trying to ignore the flutter of nerves in her stomach. "Hey, we're in this together, right?" she said, and the memory of Tara saying this same thing to her popped into her mind.

She'd learned so much from her foster siblings throughout the years.

"Besides," Ivy added, leaning back slightly, "it might be good for us to step outside our comfort zones. Worst case, we leave early. Best case, we make a new friend or two."

Virginia's smile widened, the tension easing from her shoulders. "Thanks, Ivy. I really appreciate it. We can head over around eight, if that works for you?"

"Eight's perfect," Ivy said. As Virginia returned her attention to her book, Ivy glanced toward her own small desk, wondering what the night would bring. She still wasn't sure how she felt about the party, but at least she wouldn't be going alone.

Ivy and Virginia stepped into the sorority house, and the sound hit Ivy with force—voices shouting over thudding bass, the floor practically vibrating beneath her feet. She glanced around to get her bearings.

The place was impressive—polished hardwood floors, a grand staircase strung with fairy lights, and walls lined with photos of beaming sorority sisters. She was walking into a different world, but one she wasn't entirely sure she wanted to be part of.

Clusters of people filled the living room, laughing loudly, holding plastic cups in shades of red and blue. The sharp tang of alcohol mingled with the overly sweet scent of perfume, creating an air that suffocated. A long table near the wall groaned under bowls of popcorn, chips, and half-empty bottles of liquor.

Ivy hesitated, scanning the room, her fingers brushing the collar of her sweater, suddenly feeling too warm. She felt like she'd wandered into someone else's life.

Next to her, Virginia lit up. "No way—that's Jenna! We had chem together junior year." Before Ivy could ask who Jenna was, Virginia was already gone, swallowed up by the crowd.

Ivy stayed where she was, throat tight, as the crowd pulsed around her. Virginia was gone, and now it was just her—adrift in a room full of strangers. Coming to the party was a mistake.

She drifted through the house, eyes scanning the crowd on the off chance she might recognize someone. But she already knew better. She'd been homeschooled, bounced between foster homes for most of her life. Her past didn't overlap with parties like this.

She slowed near the edge of the living room, debating whether to track down Virginia and bail—when a tap landed lightly on her shoulder.

She turned and found Beck standing there, his grin lazy and a little crooked—the kind that made it hard to think straight.

"You look even more lost than you did earlier," Beck said, those warm caramel-colored eyes raking over her in a way that made her belly flutter.

Ivy gave a breathy laugh. "Yeah, I feel a little out of place," she said, glancing around before her gaze darted back to him. "Not really my scene."

Beck stepped a little closer, his arm brushing hers. He set his cup on the table without looking away. "Then let's ditch it. Fresh air's better anyway."

Beck steered her through the crowd with an easy touch at the small of her back, his hand light but grounding. Outside, the cool night air swept over her skin—a welcome contrast to the heat and noise inside. A few people clustered around the fire pit, but it was quieter out here, more breathable.

He led her toward a gazebo tucked into the corner of the yard, its white frame glowing under strands of soft lights. Calm, quiet, private.

They sat, the bench creaking slightly beneath them. Ivy caught movement out of the corner of her eye—a few girls near the fire watching them, their gazes lingering on Beck a second too long. She didn't blame them. With his easy posture, broad shoulders, and that unshakable confidence, Beck stood out.

And now he was sitting here with her.

Ivy shifted slightly, Emily's advice playing in her mind: Make friends, but be careful. Boys don't always want what they say they do. Ivy had agreed at the time, quietly promising herself she'd tread carefully. She was new to all of this—boys, dating, figuring out who to trust—and honestly, she wasn't ready for anything more than friendship. Not yet.

Beck turned to her, his brow furrowed, concern flickering across his expression. "You okay? You seemed pretty anxious in there."

Ivy hesitated, caught off guard by the gentleness in his tone. "Yeah," she said after a moment. "I guess crowds aren't really my thing."

He gave a knowing shrug. "Same here. Sometimes it feels like everyone's trying too hard to impress each other." He leaned back, his hands resting casually on the bench. "Out here's better, don't you think? Under the lights of the gazebo."

Ivy glanced around at the quiet night, the faint murmur of music drifting from the party in the distance. She drew in a breath and let it out slowly, the calm washing through her. "Yeah, it is."

Beck skimmed her wrist, and a playful smile curved his lips. "That really is a cute tattoo," he said.

Ivy followed his gaze, her fingers brushing the sunflower's delicate outline. It was still one of her favorite things about herself, even if the memory of how she'd gotten it was a little embarrassing.

"It was the first and only time I got drunk," she admitted with a soft laugh. "Let's say it taught me a lesson. I've been nervous to drink since. I hated feeling like I wasn't in control of my senses. And that I'd done something I wouldn't normally have."

Beck's gaze lingered on the tattoo before meeting hers, his expression thoughtful. "I get it, but sometimes feeling out of control can help you realize what your center truly is. Do you know what I mean?"

Ivy shook her head.

"Like, after you got drunk and got the tattoo, where did you head afterward? To find your balance again?"

"My foster mom. Emily." And then she understood and grinned. "She's my center. I see what you mean. She grounds me. Balances me."

"Your foster mom. Is she 'your person'?" He finger-quoted *your person*. "Your emergency contact?" He chuckled.

Ivy loved his laugh, so free and light.

"Definitely," she said. "Who's yours?"

"My dad. He's my biggest fan—treats me like I can do anything. He's why I'm here on a baseball scholarship. Because I never wanted to let him down or think I'm not the superhero he thinks I am."

"Is that a lot of pressure?"

"Nah, because whenever I've messed up in life, and I have, he was there for me. Still cheering me on."

"Emily's like that, too," Ivy said, lifting her hand to show her tattoo. "Especially after I did this."

Beck gave her an adorable lopsided smile and brushed his finger over the sunflower, sending a strange rush down her arm. "It's pretty," he said. "It suits you. No regrets, right?"

"Right. Luckily, it's not a hack job. I would've hated myself if it hadn't turned out well."

"Hey, don't hate yourself, Ivy." Beck leaned back against the bench. "Trust what your gut's telling you. My dad's always going on about that. 'Beck, this is your life. Don't screw it up by second-guessing what you already know.'" He paused, eyeing her. "Sounds like you've got a good sense for things."

"Me?"

"Yeah, you."

"Um, thank you." Ivy smiled, accepting the compliment, though it was hard. "I guess I need to learn to trust myself."

"For sure."

For a second, Ivy found herself noticing the way the light from the gazebo caught the amber flecks in his eyes, making them glimmer like gold. She looked away quickly, feeling a flutter she wasn't sure what to do with.

"It's a good thing to learn," he added. "More people should trust their instincts."

"Definitely."

He kept watching Ivy, that easy smile still playing on his lips. "All right, let's play *20 Questions*," he said. "Think of something from your past—a person, place, or thing—and I'll try to guess what it is within twenty questions."

Ivy considered his proposal, her mind drifting back through her memories. Without even meaning to, she thought of her favorite horse, Twinkles. She hadn't thought of her in such a long time, but the memory was vivid, pulling her back to the simple, quiet days of her Amish upbringing. Twinkles had been her solace, a gentle creature she loved dearly. She used to spend hours brushing the horse's coat, feeding her apples, and whispering secrets into her soft mane. The thought of her old friend made her feel both nostalgic and a little sad.

"Okay, I've got something," Ivy said, a small smile playing on her lips as she focused back on Beck.

"Great," Beck replied, a playful gleam in his eyes. "First question: Is it a person?"

Ivy shook her head. "Nope."

"Okay, not a person," Beck mused. "Is it a place?"

"Not a place, either."

Beck tapped his chin thoughtfully. "Hmm... is it a thing you can touch?"

"Yes," Ivy said.

"Is it something that you used to own?"

She hesitated. "Kind of, in a way."

Beck raised an eyebrow, intrigued. "Interesting. Is it something that's alive?"

Ivy nodded. "Yes."

"Aha, we're getting somewhere. Is it an animal?"

"Yes," she said, feeling a bit amused by his determination.

Beck's eyes lit up. "Is it a pet?"

"Sort of," Ivy said. "I guess you could say that."

"Sort of? Interesting... Did you grow up on a farm?" he asked, his eyebrow raised.

"Yep. I lived on one when I was younger."

Beck looked thoughtful for a moment, then his face brightened as he made a guess. "Is it a chicken?"

Ivy laughed. "No, not a chicken."

"A cow? A goat? A dog?"

"Wait," Ivy said, "that's three questions. How many are we at anyway?"

"I lost track." He chuckled and then lifted a finger. "It was a horse, wasn't it?"

Ivy's eyes widened slightly in surprise. "Yes, it was a horse."

He grinned triumphantly. "Tell me about the horse."

Ivy hesitated, her heart tugging at the memory of Twinkles. She didn't talk about her Amish past much, especially with new people. But something about Beck's seemingly genuine interest made her feel like she could open up, at least a little.

"Her name was Twinkles. My parents used her for our horse and buggy. I used to take care of her, brush her, feed her. She was kind of like my friend back then."

"Horse and buggy? Wait, did you used to be Amish?" Beck's eyes widened, but there was no apparent judgment in his expression—only intrigue.

Ivy nodded slowly, unsure of how much to reveal. "Yeah, I grew up Amish. But I left when I was ten."

"Wow," Beck said. "That's fascinating. Why did you leave?"

Ivy felt her cheeks flush with embarrassment. The truth of her past was complicated and painful, not something she wanted to dive into at a party with someone she'd just met.

"It's a long story," she murmured, looking down. She didn't want to get into the details of her abuse. And she definitely didn't want to think about anything that would conjure another nightmare about Ruth. She'd had one the first night here on campus. As if the new surroundings with strangers had caused it.

"You know," she said, swallowing down at the knot forming in her throat, "I'm actually not feeling great. I think I need to head back to my dorm."

Beck's eyebrows squished together. "Of course, let me walk you back."

Ivy agreed, and after she said goodbye to Virginia, she and Beck made their way back to the dorms in a comfortable silence, the night air cool and refreshing against Ivy's skin. When they reached her building entrance, Beck turned to her, a soft smile on his face. He leaned in and gently kissed her on the cheek.

"I'm glad I got a chance to talk to you, Ivy. I like you. And I'd really like to get to know you better." Beck's voice dipped slightly, more serious now. "And, honestly..." He paused, gaze holding hers. "You're kind of stunning."

Heat rushed to Ivy's face, her chest fluttering. She opened her mouth, then closed it again, scrambling for something remotely coherent. "Th-thanks, Beck. I, uh... thank you."

He smiled at her stammering, clearly amused—but not unkindly. "I hope you feel better. Maybe we can hang out again soon?"

Her stomach flipped. "Yeah," she managed, brushing a hand through her hair in an effort to seem casual. "I'd like that."

He pressed a second warm kiss to her cheek, lingering long enough to make her knees feel a little unsteady.

"Goodnight, Ivy," he murmured, pulling back with a cute grin.

"Goodnight, Beck," she said as she turned toward the dorm.

Once inside, she closed the door behind her and leaned against it, heart pounding. Her skin still tingled where he'd kissed her. Whatever this new chapter held, one thing was already clear—Beck had made it a whole lot more complicated.

She took a breath, a smile tugging at her lips, and headed upstairs.

The weeks blurred into something golden and precious. Ivy lost track of time, but she could track her memories by Beck—by his lopsided grin, the way he always managed to steal the punchline from a story she hadn't finished, and how his hand always found hers under the table like it belonged there. They'd started with coffee dates and walks between classes, but somewhere along the way, things deepened. He kissed her like he meant it, like he wasn't in a rush for the next step but also didn't want to stop.

With Beck, she felt wanted in a way she didn't have to question. And she wanted him too—with the kind of fierce, fluttering ache that curled warm in her belly and lit sparks beneath her skin.

It was heady. Addicting. Ivy knew she was falling, maybe too fast, but Beck caught her every time she tripped.

Emily's calls sometimes went unanswered. Not because Ivy didn't care—but because she kept losing time, swept up in kisses that tasted like cinnamon gum and the way Beck's arms felt like a place she could exhale.

But Beck wasn't the only thing grounding her. In the quiet of her dorm room, Ivy found herself drawn to something she hadn't touched in a long time.

Baking.

It started with a box mix and a toaster oven—hidden behind textbooks and laundry she never folded. Chocolate chip cookies at first. Then cinnamon crisps. She got flour on everything: her laptop, her textbooks, her clothes. Virginia didn't complain once; she just started dropping off ingredients like silent encouragement.

Soon, Ivy had a reputation. People knocked at her door under the guise of study breaks or class notes, but really, they came hungry—and Ivy fed them. It made her feel... useful. Rooted. Like she had something to give that didn't cost her too much.

Beck, of course, was her official taste-tester. He always insisted on getting the first bite, grinning like he'd won a prize, even if his mouth was full.

One night, she walked over to his dorm with a paper towel-wrapped stack of still-warm peanut butter cookies. They ate them cross-legged on his bed, trying not to drop crumbles on the sheets. As she told him about her failed attempt at macarons—"they looked like melted buttons"—Beck shook his head, grinning.

"You know, even your baking disasters are better than anything I've ever eaten in the dining hall," he said. "Honestly, I'd pay good money for your sugar lumps."

"Nice." She laughed.

He reached for another cookie and added, "I'm pretty sure you could win hearts or start a black-market bakery with this stuff."

Ivy wiped a crumb off his lip and leaned in for a kiss.

They talked for hours—dumb childhood dares, secret fears, dreams too fragile to say aloud to anyone else. Ivy didn't notice when her guard slipped. With Beck, nothing needed bracing. No cleverness. No caution. She could breathe. She could be herself.

And maybe that was why the nightmares had stopped. When she was with him, the darkness didn't reach as far. He listened when she needed silence and held her when words didn't work. He never flinched at her past, never made her feel broken.

"You know," Ivy said, "Emily and I always dreamed of taking a road trip across the country. We've talked about it a lot. Neither of us has been to the West Coast, seen the Pacific Ocean, and I haven't been out of Indiana, so we want to drive to California, stopping and doing touristy stuff on the way, and then experience the beach for the first time. We're planning for it after I graduate."

Beck turned his head to look at her, a cute smile on his lips. "That sounds amazing. Maybe I could go with you guys? Unless I'm overstepping?"

Ivy met his gaze, a slow warmth spreading through her chest. The thought of sharing that dream with Beck stirred something deep inside her, a sense of belonging she hadn't realized she craved. It was as if he'd slipped into her world without her even noticing, filling a quiet space she hadn't known was empty.

"I think that would be wonderful," she said, her smile softening as their eyes held, a silent promise lingering between them.

Beck reached over and squeezed her hand. "Then it's settled. One day, we'll all drive out there together. Let me know when you're ready, and I'm in. I'll bring the snacks."

Ivy's smile stretched wider, a flutter of excitement blooming in her chest.

As the night wore on, the space between them shifted, slow and electric. Beck leaned in, his breath brushing her skin before his lips found hers—gentle at first, like he was asking a question. His hands slid up to cup her face, sweet and careful, and something in her sparked. Her pulse kicked up, her fingers curling into his shirt as she kissed him back, deeper this time, like something inside her had clicked free.

The easy sweetness between them deepened into hunger, urgent and unspoken. Silence stretched, but nothing needed saying. The room dissolved around them, every touch drawing them closer, more certain.

One moment blurred into the next until they were lying tangled on his bed, their clothes a forgotten pile on the floor. Beck moved with quiet attentiveness, checking in with every glance, every touch. Ivy had never let anyone in like this before. And still, with him, it didn't feel terrifying—it felt like exhaling after holding her breath for too long.

There were nerves, yes—new territory always came with fear—but it was laced with something exhilarating. Ivy had never let anyone this close, never let herself be seen like this. But Beck didn't look away. He met her, held her, like nothing about her needed fixing.

After, Beck pulled her close, his voice low against her ear. "I think I'm falling in love with you, Ivy."

The words hit soft and hard at once. Her throat tightened, warmth blooming all the way to her fingertips.

"I think I'm already there," she murmured, pressing a kiss to his shoulder, the scent of him—clean laundry and something only his—filling her lungs. They stayed like that, quiet, her cheek pressed against his chest, listening to the rhythm of his heartbeat.

Eventually, she pulled herself up, her limbs reluctant to leave the warmth of his body. She kissed him once more, slow and sweet, before slipping out the door.

The air outside was cooler, sobering. Her mind buzzed with everything they'd shared.

Back in her own dorm's hallway, she pulled out her phone.

Three missed calls from Emily.

The rush of guilt was immediate and sharp.

She hadn't been good about keeping in touch lately, too caught up in her new relationship to return Emily's calls.

Worried now, she quickly dialed Emily's number. Emily picked up on the second ring, her voice sounding tired but relieved to hear from Ivy. "Hey, Ivy."

"Emily, I'm so sorry I missed your calls. I've been... distracted," Ivy said, biting her lip. "Is everything okay?"

There was a long pause on the other end of the line, and Ivy's stomach twisted.

"Sweetie, we need to talk," Emily finally said.

"I'm doing well in all my classes, I swear," Ivy blurted out, thinking Emily might be worried about her grades. Thinking Ivy might be too invested in Beck.

And the truth was, she did feel in over her head after their evening together.

"It's not about that," Emily said, breaking Ivy's thoughts. There was a hint of sadness in her voice. "I know you're doing great, and I'm so proud of you."

"Then what is it? What's wrong?" Ivy held her fist to her chest.

Emily hesitated, and Ivy could hear her take a shaky breath. "I don't know. I think we should speak in person, but I don't know if I can make it out there."

"Just tell me," Ivy said. "Please. You can trust me."

"I know, I..." Emily blew a ragged breath into the phone. "I've been seeing some doctors, Ivy. I've... I've been diagnosed with stage four pancreatic cancer."

The ground opened up and dropped Ivy with a hard thud. Her breath stalled, and her vision blurred with tears as she processed what Emily had said. "What? No, Emily, that can't be right. Are you sure?"

"I'm sure," Emily said, her voice breaking. "I've seen an oncologist, and I've gotten a second opinion, and... it's advanced.

211

They're not sure how much time I have left. Maybe a few months, maybe a year."

A sob caught in Ivy's throat. She'd never felt so helpless, so terrified. "I'm coming home," she said firmly. "I'm coming home to take care of you."

"No, Ivy, you need to stay and finish your semester," Emily said, obviously trying to sound strong. "I don't want you to miss out on your education because of me."

"I don't care about that right now," Ivy said, the tears streaming down her face. "You've been my everything. I'm not staying here while you're going through this. I'm coming home, and that's final."

Emily was silent for a moment, and then Ivy heard a soft sigh on the other end of the line. "Okay, Ivy. If that's what you want."

"It is," Ivy said, resolute. "I'll be there as soon as I can. I promise."

"I know, sweetheart. I know."

They stayed on the line a little longer, both crying softly, neither of them wanting to hang up. Ivy knew that her life was about to change in ways she couldn't have imagined, but all she could think about was getting home to Emily and being there for her, no matter what.

Chapter Thirty

Then - *Two years later*

Ivy sat quietly by Emily's bedside, the soft light of the lamp casting a gentle glow over the room. Emily looked frail, her once-vibrant energy all but faded, but there was still a spark in her eyes as she glanced over at Ivy. It had been over two years since the diagnosis, far longer than the doctors had initially predicted.

Emily had fought bravely, enduring rounds of chemotherapy at Ivy's urging, along with trying every holistic approach they could find. They had both believed, at one point, that these methods were working, that maybe they had bought more time.

And they had—Emily had lived longer than anyone expected.

But now, it was different. Ivy could see the way her body no longer responded to treatment, and how Emily seemed ready to let go. She was tired. The fight had taken everything out of her.

"So," Emily said with a weak smile, "when are we going to get out of here and finally drive across the country to California? We still haven't seen that ocean."

Ivy smiled, though her heart ached. Emily had always managed to joke, even in the worst of times. "Soon," Ivy said, trying to keep her tone light. "We'll rent a convertible and drive with the top down. You'll wear a big floppy hat, and we'll blast some oldies while cruising down the highway."

Emily chuckled, though it was faint. "Sounds like heaven." But her smile faded, and her expression grew more serious. "But Ivy, I think it's time for you to do that trip without me."

Ivy shook her head, gripping Emily's frail hand. "Don't say that."

Emily's eyes softened, full of a quiet acceptance Ivy wasn't ready to hear. "Ivy, I'm tired. I've fought longer than anyone thought I would. The chemo, the holistic stuff... we tried everything, but it's time. I don't want to keep fighting. I'm in pain, and I'm ready to let go. It's time for hospice."

Tears welled in Ivy's eyes, but she blinked them back, refusing to cry in front of Emily.

She knew what hospice care was. They'd talked about it over and over again.

Accepting hospice care meant the fight was over and death was imminent. But hospice also meant Emily wouldn't be in pain anymore —she'd get the medication to ease her pain and to help her rest until she passed.

Ivy swallowed hard, swiping at the tears she couldn't hold back.

"You're going to be fine," Emily said firmly, despite her weakened state. "You're going to go on and do amazing things. But you have to promise me something."

"Anything," Ivy whispered, voice cracking.

"When I'm gone, you have to do it. Drive to California, see the Pacific Ocean. You need to live your life, Ivy, not simply survive it, like you've had to do for so long. Promise me you'll take that trip."

Ivy's throat tightened, and she could only nod at first, the words too hard to say aloud. But she swallowed back the lump in her throat and whispered, "I promise. I'll go."

Someday. Not anytime soon. Taking that journey would be too painful without Emily.

Emily's smile returned, though it was bittersweet. "Good. I know you will. And one other thing..."

There was a long pause before Emily spoke again. "I've left you some money," she said, her hand squeezing Ivy's. "It's not a ton, but it'll help you start your life. My parents helped me when I became a caseworker, so I wouldn't have to worry about finances while doing what I loved. I've been living off it comfortably all these years. And now I want you to have the rest."

Ivy stared at her, a fresh wave of emotion threatening to overwhelm her. "Emily, I can't—"

"Yes, you can," Emily interrupted. "This money is for you. I'm so thankful my career led me to you. I want you to find what you're passionate about and live it fully. Don't settle for anything less, Ivy. You deserve a life where you chase your dreams and passions."

Ivy choked back sobs. She couldn't even think of what her passion was right now. All she cared about was being there for Emily, seeing her through this.

She breathed in deeply, trying to calm herself before she said, "I'll do whatever you ask, Emily. I'll live my life, follow my dreams. But right now, I want to be here with you."

Emily smiled faintly, her eyes fluttering closed. "That's all I need. I'm so proud of you, Ivy. Don't ever forget that."

Ivy sat in silence, watching as Emily drifted off to sleep. She looked so peaceful, yet so frail, as if the fight had finally left her. She glanced at her phone and saw a text from Beck, sweet as always, checking in on her. He was going on with his life, graduating from college and moving back to Colorado to work for his family business.

"My baseball career's shot, but I'm okay with that," he'd said. "So's my dad. We've got other plans."

Ivy was happy for him, but her world had narrowed down to this room, this moment with Emily.

For over two years, this beautiful soul had been fighting to survive. And Ivy was so grateful for every second she could have with her mom.

Yes, Emily was her mother in so many ways aside from blood.

Emily's parents had insisted on a formal service. Luis and Tina.

215

Ivy had met them twice in the years she'd lived with Emily. Their parenting mode seemed mostly monetary and from afar. When Ivy had first met Emily, she'd said her father was protective, but Ivy soon realized she meant he wanted Emily living in a safe building so he wouldn't have guilt for not being in her life.

They didn't know what they were missing, Ivy always thought. But she never minded having Emily to herself.

With Ivy, however, the distance was even greater. They'd never really seen Ivy as their own—as their granddaughter. It was a cold, formal relationship. One that had always felt obligatory rather than familial.

And of course, though distant from their daughter for years, they'd spared no expense to ensure the ceremony was nothing short of beautiful. White lilies adorned every corner of the chapel, and the soft melody of a piano echoed throughout, creating a sort of somber elegance. It was the kind of service Ivy knew Emily wouldn't have cared for, but her parents wanted to honor her in the way they believed was right.

After the ceremony inside, where strangers looked into Emily's casket with varying emotions, the pallbearers carried her foster mom out to the gravesite.

Ivy hadn't been asked to speak, and she was grateful for that. She didn't know these people, and her memories with Emily were her own. The funeral concluded as people began to drift away from the gravesite.

Ivy stood there, her arms wrapped around herself as the autumn wind swept through the cemetery, stirring the leaves around her feet. She felt hollow, as if part of her had been buried with Emily. The memory of her voice, her laughter, her gentle encouragement—it all lingered in the air, out of reach.

Luis and Tina approached Ivy, their faces composed, but an air of discomfort lingered between them. They stopped a few feet away, expressions cool—detached rather than cruel. Luis acknowledged Ivy with the briefest lift of his chin, the kind of greeting meant for a stranger rather than the girl their daughter had once claimed as family. Tina looked at Ivy for a beat before turning her attention back to the gravestone.

"Well," Luis said, "thank you for everything you did for Emily. She appreciated you."

Ivy didn't know how to respond. Did they even know how much Emily had meant to her? How she had been the only real family Ivy had ever truly known?

Tina cleared her throat. "We'll be in touch about the estate," she said, businesslike, as though they were settling matters with a stranger.

With that, they both turned and walked away, their coats billowing slightly in the wind as they headed toward their car. Ivy watched them leave, feeling even more alone than she had before.

The cemetery cleared out, and Ivy remained by Emily's grave, her eyes fixed on the headstone. The words carved into the marble were simple: *Beloved Daughter, Friend, Caregiver.* They were beautiful words, but they didn't come close to capturing who Emily had been. She was so much more—Emily was her entire world.

Ivy's legs felt weak, but she didn't want to leave. Not yet. This was the last physical connection she had to Emily, and the thought of walking away from the gravesite felt like walking away from everything.

The wind picked up again, swirling leaves around her feet. Ivy tipped her head back and let the cool air sweep over her face, grounding her in the moment.

"I promised, Emily," she whispered. "I'll keep my promise."

She would take that road trip. She would find her way. But for now, she allowed herself to mourn, standing alone at the graveside, feeling the ache of loss settle deep into her bones.

The next several months were a blur for Ivy. The days passed slowly, painfully, with a heavy silence that settled into the corners of her life. She had stopped talking to Beck, had slowly cut ties with the small group of friends she'd made over the years, and she found herself retreating into the isolation of her grief. She didn't have the energy to explain herself, and she wasn't sure how to find comfort in others when the one person who had always been there for her was gone.

Clearing out Emily's apartment had been one of the hardest things

Ivy had ever done. She spent weeks sorting through every drawer, every box, every shelf. She cried constantly, the grief hitting her in waves as she came across little reminders of their life together—an old mug Emily always used, a blanket they had shared on movie nights, the framed photos of Ivy that Emily had proudly displayed. It was like saying goodbye all over again with each item she packed away. The apartment that had once felt so warm and safe now felt like a hollow shell, echoing with the absence of the woman who'd filled it with life.

The estate attorney's announcement that Emily had left her half a million dollars in inheritance should have been a moment of astonishment, a time for relief or even joy. But Ivy felt none of that. Instead, all she felt was a deep ache, a heartache that pulsed with the reality that no amount of money could ever fill the void Emily had left behind.

Emily's generous gesture, the safety net she'd given Ivy, felt like a reminder of how much Emily had planned for Ivy's future, even when Ivy herself couldn't see beyond the fog of her grief.

One afternoon, while sorting through the last of Emily's belongings, Ivy came across a stack of journals tucked away in a drawer. To her surprise, Ivy's name was written in Emily's neat handwriting on the top of the journal.

She hesitated, unsure if she was ready to delve into the private thoughts Emily had written down, but she was compelled to open the first journal—the one on top with her name next to a scribbled heart.

As Ivy began to read, she was startled to find the early entries were about her—about the day Emily had first met her, the "little Amish girl" in the hospital. Emily's words were full of compassion, of how much she wanted to protect Ivy, even though at the time, she knew she had to keep her job separate from her personal life.

Ivy's eyes blurred with tears as she read about the struggle Emily had faced. She'd written about how Ivy's bright blue eyes and dark brown hair haunted her thoughts after their first encounter.

"She's so intelligent," Emily had written. "So much potential, but so much pain. It's unbearable to watch her be shuffled around the system. But I can't let myself get too involved. I need to keep a professional distance."

But as Ivy continued to read, the entries began to change. Emily's resolve to keep things professional had slowly broken down, and Ivy read about the moment Emily decided to take her in. She described how she couldn't stand watching the innocent little girl suffer anymore, and how she had no choice but to become the one person who would look out for her.

Ivy wept as she relived their journey through Emily's eyes—how proud Emily had been of her achievements, how worried she'd been during Ivy's rebellious teenage years, and most of all, how much Emily had loved her. It was overwhelming to read these private thoughts, to see how much Ivy had meant to her, not as a foster child but as a daughter in every sense of the word.

When Ivy reached the last page of the journal, her breath caught in her throat. There, in Emily's familiar handwriting, was a note addressed to her:

My dearest Ivy,

If you're reading this, I'm already gone, but I need you to know something. You've always been stronger than you think. You've always been a fighter, and I know you'll keep being brave, no matter what life throws at you. I'm so proud of the woman you've become. Now, I need you to do something for me. Write down all the things you've ever loved—no matter how small—and pick one. Let that be your passion. Then, invest in it. Use some of the money I left you and build a life around that passion. You can do it, Ivy. I know you can.

I love you. Be brave.

Emily

Ivy sobbed as she finished the note, her tears soaking into the pages. She clutched the journal to her chest, overwhelmed by Emily's love and unwavering belief in her.

A quiet shift stirred in Ivy, a glimmer of hope breaking through the haze of the past few months. Emily had left her this journal with purpose—trusting she'd open it when she was ready to face forward.

Ivy wiped her damp cheeks and took a deep breath. She wasn't ready to leave her grief behind—not yet—but she could feel the stirrings of strength, the courage to at least start thinking about the future. Emily had believed in her, and now Ivy would try to believe in herself, too.

With a sigh, she closed the journal and placed it gently on the table beside her. Maybe it was time to start writing down those things she loved, those passions Emily had told her to chase. Maybe it was time to take the first step forward, like Emily had wanted her to do.

Chapter Thirty-One

Now - *Two years later*

Ivy stood behind the bakery counter, the scent of sugar cookies and peppermint fudge filling the air. Christmas music played in the background as Fiona and Mila packed the last of the holiday cookie boxes.

"Okay," Fiona said, nudging Mila with her elbow. "Worst customer of the season. Go."

"Oh, that's easy," Mila said, straightening up. "The guy who wouldn't leave until all three of us smiled at him."

Ivy groaned. "Ugh. *That* guy."

"Yep," Mila continued. "Stood right there by the register, glaring at us until we gave in. What a creep. I was polite, I was professional, but apparently, my face wasn't cheerful enough for him."

Fiona shook her head. "I *did* smile at him, but I guess it wasn't 'authentic' because he kept staring at me like it wasn't good enough."

"I think he wanted the kind of smile that makes doves fly in the background," Ivy muttered.

Mila snorted. "Oh, and then he *left a review.* Said, and I quote, 'The pastries were fine, but the staff made me feel unwelcome. A smile costs nothing, ladies.'"

Fiona scoffed. "A smile costs nothing, but leaving a review like that? Priceless."

Ivy crossed her arms, shaking her head. "Next time, I'm charging for smiles. You want me to show teeth? That's an extra fifty cents."

Mila gasped. "A *smile menu!* Small smirk? Fifty cents. Full grin? A dollar. A genuine, *sincere* smile with eye crinkles? That's gonna cost you at least five bucks."

Fiona wiped a fake tear from her eye. "And if you want a *laugh*—we're talking a *real* chuckle—that's premium pricing."

They dissolved into laughter, their shoulders shaking as the last of the holiday rush faded into the quiet of Christmas Eve.

Ivy laughed with them, but as she listened to them chat about their holiday plans, a familiar loneliness crept in. Soon, they'd be heading home to the warmth of their families waiting for them beyond the bakery doors.

And Ivy would stay.

She pushed the thought aside, focusing on the lingering laughter, letting herself enjoy the moment a little longer.

These were the only two friends she had. She hadn't dated anyone since Camron—too afraid to try, too wrapped up in her bakery to have time, too depressed.

She'd lost Gram. The moment she'd fired him and told him to leave her life, he'd listened. She'd expected him to fight for her friendship, to come back and try to explain things, but he hadn't. The ache in her chest from losing him had never fully faded.

She'd lost her sister, Ruth. After disappearing back into her old life, Ivy had heard nothing. No phone call, no text, no visit.

She'd lost Emily.

She'd lost her biological family.

And she'd lost each of her foster families.

Ivy squeezed her eyes shut, trying to think of happier thoughts, of all she'd gained in life. She'd been lucky in a lot of ways. And here she was feeling sorry for herself.

Get over yourself, Ivy.

Fiona cut into her thoughts, giving Ivy a hug and a wave before rushing out the door to go home to her boyfriend.

"Merry Christmas, Ivy!" Mila called out as she gathered her coat and bag. As she slung the strap over her shoulder, she hesitated by the door, turning back to Ivy. "Are you sure you don't want to come over and spend Christmas with my family? We'd love to have you."

Ivy's heart squeezed at the offer. She could see the genuine kindness in Mila's eyes, and for a moment, she considered it. But the thought of sitting around a table filled with people she barely knew, feeling like an outsider in someone else's family, brought back memories of her time in foster care.

She forced a smile, shaking her head. "That's sweet of you, Mila, but I'm all right. You go enjoy the time with your family."

Mila hesitated, a frown pulling at the corners of her mouth, but she nodded. "Okay, but if you change your mind, call me, all right?"

"I will. Thank you." Ivy waved as Mila stepped out into the cold, leaving her alone in the bakery.

As the door closed behind her, Ivy let out a soft sigh. She stared out the window at the snow-covered street, watching as couples walked hand in hand, families huddled together, and groups of friends laughed and joked as they carried their holiday goodies home. The warmth of the season seemed to be everywhere—except inside her.

She wiped her hands on her apron and slowly began to shut down the bakery. She turned off the twinkling holiday lights that had made the bakery feel magical all month, unplugged the Christmas tree near the window, and turned off the music. Silence fell over the bakery as she locked the front door.

The bakery had been her entire world for so long, her sole focus, her reason for waking up every morning. But now, she stood in the middle of it, staring at the empty tables, and felt an overwhelming sense of emptiness. Her life in this town, which had always been centered on keeping the bakery thriving, now felt incomplete.

What was missing? Ivy asked herself.

And then, like a spark in the darkness, she remembered something she hadn't thought about in a long time—Emily. And their dream.

She could see it now, so clearly: the two of them sitting on Emily's apartment balcony, sipping iced tea on a hot summer day, talking about life and adventures. Emily had always wanted to see the Pacific Ocean, and Ivy had promised that one day they would take a road trip across the country to see it together. It had been their dream, their escape plan. But Emily had passed away before they could make that trip, and Ivy had buried that dream deep within her, convinced she didn't have time for it.

But now, standing alone in her bakery, Ivy saw something she hadn't before. Time had always been there—she'd just refused to claim it. Caught up in working hard, staying responsible, and maintaining appearances, she'd forgotten how to live for herself.

Why hadn't she taken that road trip? Why hadn't she allowed herself the space to breathe, to dream, to explore?

Because she'd been stuck in the mindset that she had to work hard to prove her worth, to be perfect. The mindset she'd kept since her childhood—to be that good little Amish girl who had always strived to please her family, to please everyone around her.

But Ivy wasn't that girl anymore. She'd grown up. She was her own person. And she was tired of living her life according to everyone else's rules.

There was nothing to fear anymore, was there?

The bakery had served its purpose, but now... now maybe it was time to move on.

Ivy's heart was racing with the realization of what she had to do. She would wrap things up here and put her building up for sale.

She had built the bakery from the ground up, pouring every ounce of passion into it, and she loved it. But love wasn't enough to carry the strain of being both the baker and the boss. Ivy needed to step out of the rut, to shed the weight this town, this state, had pressed on her shoulders for too long. She craved open roads and unknown horizons. A new chapter. A chance to feel free, untethered, and young for the first time, chasing all the experiences she'd been denied as a child.

So, she'd take the profits, pack her bags, and head out on the road trip of a lifetime. She would finally drive across the country, like she and Emily had always dreamed, and see the Pacific Ocean.

It was a scary thought—she'd never left Indiana. She'd never been anywhere.

But it was time.

She didn't need to keep proving herself. She didn't need to be perfect. She needed to be free.

She was ready for a new adventure.

———

After locking the bakery for the night, Ivy climbed the stairs to her apartment, her mind buzzing with thoughts of what lay ahead. The stillness of the holiday season made her restless, but now she had something to look forward to.

A thrill sparked, buzzing like electricity beneath her skin.

She kicked off her shoes and sat at the small kitchen table, pulling her laptop closer. As the screen lit up, she took a deep breath and began typing. *Road trip: From Indianapolis to California.* She grinned, exhilarated.

This wasn't a dream anymore. This was a plan.

First, she jotted down the main stops she wanted to make. San Francisco was a must—Emily had always talked about seeing the Golden Gate Bridge, and Ivy had clung to that dream even after Emily passed. And then, she'd drive down the coast to San Diego. Ivy paused, imagining the Pacific Ocean stretching out before her, the salt air filling her lungs, the waves crashing against the shore. It would be a moment of freedom, a new chapter, something that belonged entirely to her.

To begin the trip, she traced the route on a map, her finger hovering over the different highways. She decided to take Interstate 70 west, cutting through Denver and the Rocky Mountains, where she could stop and breathe in the mountain air, and see the towering peaks she'd only ever seen in pictures. She could almost feel the crispness of the high altitude as she imagined herself standing there.

From there, she'd continue through Utah, maybe stopping at Arches National Park to see the red rock formations, the vast desert landscape stretching toward the horizon. She'd never been one for the outdoors, but this trip was about discovery, and she was willing to try anything.

The highway would lead her up to San Francisco, the crown jewel of her trip. Ivy smiled as she typed it into her notes—*Golden Gate, Fisherman's Wharf, Lombard Street.* She'd explore the city before driving down the scenic Pacific Coast Highway toward San Diego. The road, winding along cliffs that dropped into the ocean, seemed like something out of a postcard, and Ivy couldn't wait to see it for herself.

She added a note: *Wait until summer to sell the bakery.* She didn't want to rush Mila and Fiona out of a job, and the weather would be better, making the roads safer for the long drive. Summer felt like the perfect time to close one chapter of her life and begin another. She'd list the bakery in late spring, giving herself time to find a buyer and say goodbye properly.

Ivy closed her laptop and leaned back in her chair, staring at the map she'd drawn in her mind. She was finally doing something for herself, something that didn't have to do with keeping the bakery afloat or worrying about everyone else.

Another giddy smile spread across her face as she imagined the sun on her skin, the open road stretching out before her. It was still a few months away, but the anticipation filled her with energy.

This was her journey, her adventure, and she couldn't wait to begin.

In early June, Ivy stood outside the now-empty building that had once been her dream. In over a month, she'd be twenty-four, but sometimes it felt like she'd already lived a dozen lives. A scared Amish girl ripped from her family, a foster kid passed from house to house, a lost teenager who had found something close to love with Emily—only to lose her. Then, a young woman who had built something from nothing, carving out a place for herself, proving she could stand on her own. And now, she was walking away from it.

Emily would have been proud. Ivy could almost hear her voice, warm with approval. *You did it, Ivy. You built something real.*

But Emily would have reminded her that her life wasn't meant to stay rooted in one place. Ivy deserved more than survival—she deserved to see the world. She'd spent years clinging to what she had, but maybe strength didn't mean holding on. Maybe it meant knowing when to let go.

She exhaled slowly, pressing her fingertips against the cool metal of the door one last time. The bakery had been her anchor, the thing that kept her from floating away when everything else had felt uncertain. But she wasn't meant to stay tethered to one place forever. This—this moment of standing at the edge of the unknown—was exactly where she was meant to be.

The thought made her giggle. It felt like she was in a book, the kind she devoured late at night when she should've been sleeping. She could almost hear the narrator: *And so, she left everything behind, stepping into the great adventure ahead.* Speaking of books, she'd packed an entire suitcase full of them. Clothes were replaceable, but her treasured books? Never.

She turned, letting her gaze linger on the bakery. Selling the building had been easier than expected—someone had jumped at the chance to buy a thriving business—but it wasn't the money that gave her the most satisfaction. It was the freedom. The open road, the sheer *possibility* of what came next. No more long hours kneading dough, no more stress about orders and suppliers, no more late nights wondering if she was doing enough.

The apartment above the bakery was empty now, scrubbed of any sign that it had once been hers. No lingering scent of flour in the kitchen, no books stacked by the bed, no warmth left in the space she had called home. It was just walls and floors now, waiting for someone else to fill it.

She'd said her goodbyes to Mila and Fiona the day before—the two women who had become her family in ways she hadn't expected. She hadn't realized how much they meant to her until she was wrapping her arms around them, holding on a little longer than necessary. They promised to keep in touch, and she knew they would—but she also knew this was a turning point. She couldn't hold on to the past when the future was wide open in front of her.

The Jeep waited in front of the bakery under a pale morning sky.

Warmth lingered in the air, soft and welcoming, while the street lay still, as if holding its breath. Ivy ran her fingers over the driver's door, the memories of years spent in this town pressing close. She slid into the seat, the cool leather anchoring her. With a quiet goodbye to the life she'd built, she turned the key. Part of her ached to stay, but the rest of her longed for what lay ahead. With a steady breath and a grip on the wheel, she flicked on the ignition.

This was it. The beginning of something she couldn't quite picture yet—but she knew it was hers for the taking.

Her first stop was St. Louis—four hours away. A city she'd never been to, a place she could explore without any expectations. Maybe she'd see the Gateway Arch, wander through the streets with no destination in mind. After that, Denver. The Rockies. The open sky.

San Francisco was the end goal, but she wasn't in a hurry. She had no strict timeline, no real plan beyond stopping wherever she wanted, eating food from places she'd never heard of, and finally seeing the world beyond the narrow existence she'd once known.

Rolling down the windows, she let the wind whip through her hair as she pulled onto the road. The sun climbed higher, casting light on the path ahead.

For the first time in her life, she was completely untethered. No expectations. No rules. No one to answer to.

She was free. And she couldn't wait to see what came next.

Chapter Thirty-Two

Ivy had been driving all day, and she was over it. Her legs ached, her eyes burned from staring at the endless stream of brake lights, and she was pretty sure her spine had permanently fused with the driver's seat. The Rocky Mountains had promised breathtaking views, and sure, they were stunning—but they hadn't warned her about the soul-crushing traffic on I-70.

When the highway screeched to a near standstill and her GPS politely suggested an alternate route, she sighed, muttering, "All right, universe. I get it. Detour it is."

The exit sign for Frisco, Colorado, flashed past, and she took it without hesitation, eager to put some distance between herself and the highway apocalypse.

The moment she pulled into town, it was like stepping into another world. Frisco looked like something out of a high-end travel magazine—pristine streets lined with cozy cafés, rustic storefronts, and towering pines framing the skyline. Snow still clung to the jagged peaks despite the warm June air, and Dillon Reservoir shimmered in the distance, as if daring anyone to not be impressed. The crisp mountain air alone made the detour worth it, clearing out the lingering exhaust fumes from the highway and making her wonder if she'd ever really taken a full breath before.

She rolled down her windows, letting the cool air rush in. "I officially don't regret this."

Still, the day had drained her, and if she didn't get out of this Jeep soon, she might start having a full-blown existential crisis. A rustic lodge on Main Street caught her eye, all wooden beams and flower boxes, the kind of place that promised a decent night's sleep and, hopefully, a breakfast that involved real butter and fresh coffee.

She pulled into the lot and turned off the ignition, savoring the rare silence. Stretching her arms, she glanced at the mountains one last time before stepping out.

"Let's see if you're as charming as you look, Frisco," she muttered, grabbing her bag.

A comfortable bed, a good meal, and a night of peace before hitting the road again? Not a bad trade for nearly losing her sanity on I-70.

Ivy kicked the door to her room shut behind her, dropping her bag onto the nearest chair with a satisfied sigh. Finally, after a full day of driving, dodging traffic, and questioning her life choices while stuck behind a minivan going ten miles per hour under the speed limit, she could breathe.

First order of business: food. She ordered a sandwich and fries from room service, then flopped into the armchair by the window. The view overlooked Main Street, where string lights twinkled against the backdrop of the mountains. Stillness settled in her shoulders, the tension of the day easing at last.

A glossy magazine sat on the coffee table, boasting "The Best of the Rockies!" on its cover, as if personally inviting her to become a whole new version of herself—one who hiked before breakfast and didn't have a deep, committed relationship with caffeine. Amused, she flipped through it, skimming past articles about skiing, whitewater rafting, and some must-visit brewery that promised "mountain views with every sip."

Then she turned the page—and froze.

Right there, smiling up at her from a full-page advertisement, was Beck.

Her stomach did an Olympic-level flip. *No way.*

The boy she'd dated in college. Only now he looked like a man—broader through the chest and shoulders, his body honed with strength that hadn't been there before. His dark hair was longer now, messily swept across his forehead like he hadn't bothered to fight the wind. He stood tall on a paddle board, steady and sure, his grin less carefree and more like someone who knew exactly what he wanted. And how to get it.

The ad said he owned a rental business for boats, kayaks, and paddleboards. *Dillon Reservoir, Frisco, CO.*

Ivy leaned back, a jolt skipping through her—surprise, but not the bad kind. Beck. Here. Of all places. She remembered he was from Colorado, but still—what were the odds?

Memories nudged their way in—late-night study sessions that had somehow always turned into something much less productive. Long walks around campus, talking about nothing and everything. The way he used to tuck her hair behind her ear when he thought she wasn't paying attention.

The way they'd fallen in love.

She hadn't seen him since she dropped out of college to take care of Emily. There hadn't been time to think about Beck back then, and later, it had felt easier to leave that part of her life behind.

A knock at the door startled her out of her thoughts. Room service. She tipped the bellhop and set the tray on the table, but her eyes kept drifting back to the magazine.

Ivy ripped out the page, folding it carefully before tucking it into her bag.

Go see him? Pretend she never saw this?

She popped a fry into her mouth, chewing slowly. *Well,* she thought, *this trip was supposed to be about adventure.*

And running into a beloved ex in a picture-perfect mountain town? That definitely qualified.

The next day, Ivy wandered down Main Street in Frisco, the crisp mountain air biting at her cheeks despite the sunshine. The town's charm was undeniable—small, picturesque, and surrounded by towering peaks. Every shop she passed seemed to beckon with its cozy atmosphere and colorful window displays.

She ducked into one of the boutiques, smiling at the rows of knitted sweaters, scarves, and leather boots. A wave of warmth wrapped around her as she entered, the scent of lavender and pine mixing pleasantly in the air. As she browsed the racks, her fingers found a thick woolen sweater in a deep burgundy color and a long, rugged coat perfect for the unpredictable mountain weather. It would keep her warm during the chilly evenings, a necessity she hadn't anticipated when she'd packed for this trip.

After settling on a few pieces, Ivy drifted toward the jewelry display, where delicate, handcrafted earrings and necklaces sparkled under the lights. She picked out a modest pair of gold hoops—nothing flashy, but enough to mark this unexpected stop along her path.

As she approached the register, the silver-haired shop owner greeted her with a warm smile. "That's a lovely sweater," the woman said, her eyes twinkling. "You'll be glad you picked it up—these summer nights get colder than you'd expect, don't they?"

Ivy smiled back, adjusting the items in her arms. "Yeah, I didn't think it'd be this chilly in June, but the Rockies are full of surprises."

The woman chuckled as she rang up Ivy's purchases. "Oh, tell me about it. I've lived here for over two decades, and these mountains still keep me on my toes. We had a bear walk through town a couple of weeks ago. He was searching for food after his hibernation, I suppose. That's why we keep the garbage bins bear-proof. Not to worry, though. He's long gone."

Ivy couldn't help but be charmed by the woman's friendly demeanor. "Where are you from?"

The shop owner's eyes lit up. "I'm originally from Denver, but I moved up here with my husband after we retired. Best decision we ever made. Now, I spend my days chatting with strangers and pretending I'm not the local busybody."

Ivy laughed, feeling more at ease. "Well, you seem like a good busybody."

The woman winked. "I do try. Can't help but talk to folks passing through. You learn a lot about people that way."

Feeling a rush of bravery, Ivy decided to ask what had been tugging at her mind since the night before. "Actually, speaking of being a local busybody, I was wondering if you knew a man named Beck—or Beckett—Holliway? I think he lives here."

The woman paused as she tapped a finger against her chin. "Holliway, Holliway... Oh! I remember now. I knew a Michael Holliway. He passed away a couple of years ago. Lovely man, owned a rental place by the lake."

Ivy's heart skipped a beat. That had to be him. "Was Beck his son?"

The woman's eyes brightened. "That's right! His son took over the business. That's what I heard, at least. I don't know if I ever caught the young man's first name—my memory's not what it used to be—but I see him at the brewery down the street sometimes. He works there during colder weather when the rental place is closed. Very handsome young man."

Ivy smiled, her pulse quickening. That was definitely him. The coincidence—no, the fate—of finding Beck here, in this tiny mountain town, was too much to ignore. She remembered he lived in Colorado, but to end up in the same town where he lived and worked?

"Thank you so much," Ivy said as she paid for her purchases.

The woman smiled as she handed Ivy her bag. "Of course, dear. Enjoy your time in Frisco!"

With her purchases in hand, Ivy stepped out of the boutique, the chill in the air sharper than before. As she walked down the street, she pulled out her phone and quickly searched for the brewery the woman had mentioned. It was only a few blocks away.

Ivy wasn't expecting anything from this encounter—no hidden agendas, no expectations. She was simply curious about how Beck was doing after all these years. They'd once shared something special, but time had passed, and life had pulled them in different directions. Still, seeing his face in the magazine ad had brought a wave of memories back, and she felt a need to know how he was doing.

And, well, if he were single.

As she made her way toward the brewery, she took in the beauty of her surroundings. The mountains, the pine trees, the crisp air—all of it was new and refreshing. And though she wasn't sure what she'd say if she saw Beck, she knew one thing: It was nice to reconnect, even if only through a glimpse of his life now.

With a deep breath, Ivy pushed open the brewery door and stepped inside. The scent of malt, hops, and freshly brewed beer filled the air, mingling with the earthy aroma of wooden beams and the faint smokiness of the stone fireplace crackling in the corner.

The place was nearly full of people of all ages sitting around, talking and laughing.

She glanced around, looking for a familiar face. A long, sturdy bar ran along one side of the room, made of dark oak and polished to a soft sheen. Behind it, rows of gleaming copper taps lined the wall, each labeled with the names of the brewery's own craft beers.

Strings of soft, amber lights hung from the ceiling, casting an ambient glow over the space. Large windows on the far side of the room offered a breathtaking view of the snow-dusted mountains in the distance, their peaks standing tall against the clear blue sky. The brewery's seating was a mix of high-top wooden tables, cushioned booths, and mismatched chairs that gave the place a casual, welcoming feel.

In the center of the room, a large community table stretched across the floor, surrounded by a group of friends, sharing laughter, stories, and pints of beer.

A couple of bartenders worked behind the counter, pouring beers and chatting with customers—none of them were Beck.

Maybe he wasn't working today. Or maybe this was a bad idea.

Ivy considered asking someone about him, but before she could, a familiar voice rumbled behind her.

"Lost? Need a compass?"

She turned sharply, her pulse jumping as she came face-to-face with Beck.

His dark hair was longer, curling slightly at the ends like he'd just run his fingers through it. His caramel-colored eyes still had that same teasing glint, but there was something different about him—something settled, grounded. He wore a simple gray Henley, the sleeves pushed up to his forearms, and his smile was effortless, like seeing her was the most natural thing in the world.

Ivy opened her mouth, but before she could say anything, Beck stepped forward, wrapping her in a firm, familiar hug. The scent of pine, warm skin, and the faintest trace of soap washed over her, stirring something deep in her.

For a second, she hesitated. Then, instinctively, she melted into him.

"Damn," he murmured, voice low near her ear. "You really are here."

When he pulled back, his hands lingered on her shoulders, his gaze searching hers like he was making sure she was real.

"You look good," he said, his smile softening. "Really good."

Ivy swallowed, her throat suddenly dry. "You, too."

Beck smirked, like he knew exactly what he was doing to her. "Are you here alone?"

"Yeah," she said, still catching her breath. "Road trip."

His eyebrows lifted. "No kidding?" His hand slid off her shoulder, but he didn't step away. "Well, if you're sticking around for a bit, let me buy you lunch. Or at least a beer."

Ivy exhaled a breath she hadn't realized she was holding. "Yeah. That sounds nice."

Beck grinned and led her to a quieter corner of the brewery, away from the noisy groups. He disappeared behind the bar, returning with two pints of amber beer. As he set them down, she noticed his hands—rougher than she remembered, like they belonged to a man who worked outside, who built things.

"So," Beck said, settling into his seat, "tell me about this road trip. What's got you wandering the country?"

Ivy took a sip of her beer, stalling for a second. "You remember Emily?"

His expression shifted instantly, the teasing edge softening. "Of course. She was your person."

"She passed away," Ivy said, her fingers tracing the condensation on her glass. "A while back."

Beck's jaw tightened. "Damn, Ivy. I'm sorry."

She swallowed the lump in her throat. "She left me some money. I used it to open a bakery."

A slow smile crept onto his face. "That tracks. You were always baking in your dorm, making magic out of that tiny toaster oven."

Ivy laughed, the memory flooding back. "Hey, that thing was solid. I made cookies, mini cakes… even cinnamon rolls once."

Beck leaned forward, eyes twinkling. "And I ate every single one."

"Not every single one," she teased. "You had competition."

He tilted his head. "True. But I was your favorite test subject."

Ivy rolled her eyes, but she was smiling.

"So, how's the bakery going?" he asked.

"I actually sold it." She tucked a piece of hair behind her ear, suddenly nervous. "I wanted something new. A fresh start."

Beck studied her for a beat, then nodded like he understood. "What's next?"

"I'm using the money to take the trip Emily and I always talked about. San Francisco, then down the coast to San Diego."

His grin widened. "I remember you going on about that back in college. I think I even tried to invite myself along at one point."

"That's right! I forgot about that." Ivy tilted her head, half teasing, half testing the waters. "You know, you could still come with me."

Beck let out a low chuckle, taking a slow sip of his beer. "Tempting, but I've got a business to run. Peak season's coming up."

Ivy raised a brow. "Yeah, I actually saw that advertisement with your face plastered on it—that's how I found you."

"No kidding? I was wondering why you showed up here."

"Yep. Fate intervened. I got off the interstate thanks to a traffic jam, grabbed a hotel down the street, flipped through a magazine, and boom —there you were. Looking all rugged and responsible." She leaned in slightly, her tone teasing. "Then a nice lady at the boutique filled in the blanks and pointed me here."

Beck shook his head, grinning. "Not surprised. Small town, everyone talks. And yeah, I guess I'm the face of the business now." He tapped the edge of his glass. "Took over after my dad passed."

Ivy's playful expression softened. "I heard… I'm really sorry, Beck."

His shoulders rose in an easy shrug, but a shadow passed through his eyes. "Thanks. It was tough for a while, but it's been a couple of years now. Staying busy helps—running the rental place, picking up shifts here—it keeps me steady." A small, lopsided smile tugged at his lips. "Clearly, the baseball dream didn't pan out, but I'm good. Maybe even happy."

Ivy smiled. "That's the goal, right? Happiness?"

Beck studied her, then tilted his beer toward her. "To happiness, then."

She clinked her glass against his, their fingers brushing for a split second before she pulled away.

"So, how's the beer treating you?" he asked, his gaze sweeping over her face.

Ivy lifted her glass. "Strong. I don't drink often—maybe on special occasions."

"Well, this definitely counts."

Something about the way he said it, along with the way he looked at her, sent a shiver through her body. Like he was seeing her in a way he hadn't before.

Or maybe, in a way he always had.

The conversation flowed, effortless, easy. Ivy leaned back, the tension in her shoulders melting as she sipped her beer, warmth spreading through her limbs. The buzz crept in slowly, enough to loosen her up, enough to make her laugh a little too easily at Beck's jokes.

Before long, Beck excused himself to grab them some food, flashing her a quick wink before disappearing toward the bar.

When he returned, he set down two plates—warm pretzels, beer cheese, and sandwiches. Comfort food, simple and perfect.

"Figured we should get some food in you before that beer takes you down," he teased, his grin widening as he slid into his seat.

Ivy reached for her sandwich, her fingers brushing his. A small, sharp jolt shot through her, but she played it cool, biting back the smile threatening to form.

"Thanks," she murmured. "It's definitely hitting." She took a bite, then paused, her brows knitting together as a thought hit her.

"Wait... are you supposed to be working? Did I hijack your day?" She swallowed, suddenly feeling guilty. "God, I'm so rude."

"Nah, Ivy," Beck said, leaning forward, his forearms resting on the table, his voice softer, more intimate. "They're doing fine without me. I told them to call me over if it gets too busy. And you're anything but rude."

The way he said it, with that low tone, made her stomach flip. She took a breath, feeling the heat in her cheeks that had nothing to do with the beer. She remembered the feeling he gave her, and it'd only taken a conversation for it to revive itself.

"Okay, that's good. I..." She paused, the alcohol loosening her tongue. "Are you seeing anyone?"

His chuckle was low and warm. "Not recently, no. You?"

She laughed awkwardly, feeling vulnerable but also emboldened by the slight haze of alcohol. "No, I've been on a dry spell. I'm not great with men, apparently. Or people in general," she added with a soft sigh, thinking of how isolated her life had become.

"Are you kidding? That's not the Ivy I remember." Beck's gaze grew a little more intense as he watched her, his head tilting slightly. "I remember you were shy, but you've always been an amazing person, Ivy. Sweet, funny, clever, smart. Not to mention stunning. Maybe it's not you that's the problem."

Her cheeks flushed, the warmth spreading through her. She ducked her head, unable to help the smile that tugged at her lips.

"You always did know how to make me feel better," she admitted.

"I'm telling the truth." Beck's fingers brushed hers again as he reached for his drink, the touch lingering a little longer than necessary. "Maybe it is fate you ended up here."

Fate or not, it felt good to be here, with him, even if for a little while.

As Ivy finished her sandwich, she realized how comfortable she felt sitting there with Beck, talking about life and everything they'd been through. It was nice to reconnect with him again, to catch up, and to know that he was doing well. She hadn't come here looking for anything more than that—a chance to see an old friend who had meant a lot to her once.

But now, three hours later, they were still sitting at the brewery, chatting and laughing like no time had passed at all. Outside, through the large open windows, the sun had already begun to set, casting an amber glow over the mountains.

"I've got something to show you," Beck said, his eyes twinkling with a playful energy.

Curious, Ivy agreed, and they left the brewery, walking toward the Dillon Reservoir. The air was crisp and cool, and she was grateful she'd picked up that sweater and coat earlier in the day. As they strolled along the water's edge, Beck pointed toward a large wooden building by the shore.

"That's my place," he said, gesturing toward the marina. "I run the boat and paddleboard rentals. We've got fishing boats, a pontoon, kayaks, paddleboards, you name it."

They walked closer, and Ivy took in the view. The Rocky Mountains loomed in the background, their snow-capped peaks reflecting in the calm waters of the reservoir. It was breathtaking, the kind of scene that made her heart swell with a sense of peace and awe.

Beck unlocked the door to the rental building and led her inside. The space was full of kayaks stacked against the walls, life vests hung in neat rows, and a couple of fishing poles leaned against a counter. There was a faint smell of wood and lake water, which added to the rustic charm of the place. Beck seemed proud as he showed her around, explaining how business had grown over the last couple of years.

"This is amazing, Beck," Ivy said, genuinely impressed.

He smiled warmly, leading her back outside to the marina. They walked along the wooden dock, the soft lapping of water against the boats the only sound around them. The air had grown cooler, and Ivy wrapped her coat tighter around her.

"See up there?" Beck pointed toward a house perched on the side of a mountain. "That's where I live now. It's quiet, but I love it. Just me and the view." He glanced at her with a playful glint in his eye. "I might be looking for a roommate soon, though." He winked, the suggestion hanging in the air between them.

Ivy laughed, brushing it off as a joke. "Very funny," she said, though her heart did a flip.

But before she could say more, Beck leaned in and kissed her. His lips were soft, familiar, and for a moment, Ivy melted into the kiss, memories of their past relationship flooding back. The years between them seemed to disappear. It felt so easy, so right.

But then she pulled back, breathless, her heart racing for a different reason. "Beck, I... I wish I could stay longer," she said softly, regretfully. "I do. But I have to finish this road trip. I promised myself. I promised Emily."

Beck's expression shifted, understanding softening the edges. "I get it," he said gently. "You have to do this for you, and for her."

She gave him a grateful smile, touched by how well he knew her, even after all this time. "I'll be thinking of you, though," she admitted.

"And I'll be here, Ivy," Beck said, his voice sincere. "Like before, if you ever need a compass, you know where to find me."

They walked back to her hotel in comfortable silence, the night growing darker around them. When they reached her room, Beck kissed her one more time, slower, softer. "Have a safe trip tomorrow," he whispered against her lips.

"Thanks, Beck." Ivy watched him walk away, disappearing into the night, before she closed the door behind her.

As she lay in bed that night, Ivy couldn't help but feel both excited and bittersweet. Her road trip had barely begun, and there was still so much ahead of her. But for now, she was content, knowing she'd found a little piece of closure—and maybe even a new chapter—maybe someday.

Chapter Thirty-Three

A week later, Ivy found herself driving through the rolling hills of California wine country. The vineyards stretched out endlessly, row after row of lush, green vines laden with grapes. The sun was high, casting a golden glow over the landscape, and everything seemed vibrant —alive with possibility. The air was fragrant with the scent of ripening fruit and the earthy smell of the land. Ivy rolled down the windows of her Jeep, letting the warm breeze flow through her hair as she passed through the tranquil countryside. She marveled at the beauty, at how far she'd come—not in miles, but in spirit.

Soon, the vineyards gave way to the hustle and bustle of the city as Ivy drove into the heart of San Francisco. The city rose up before her, its iconic hills and colorful houses dotting the landscape. She navigated the busy streets until she found her hotel near the bay, her eyes widening as she saw the view from the front entrance—the Golden Gate Bridge, shrouded in mist, standing proud and majestic in the distance. It was midday, and the fog clung to the bridge in thick, swirling tendrils, giving it an ethereal, almost mystical feel.

Ivy parked her Jeep, checked into her room, and immediately walked over to the large windows that framed the view. Her breath caught as she stared at the bridge and the vast stretch of water beneath it. Tears welled up in her eyes. Emily would have loved this moment. She could almost hear her foster mother's excited laughter, feel the warmth of her presence beside her. Ivy wiped at her cheeks, a bittersweet smile forming as she stood there.

"You would've been so proud of me, Emily," she whispered. "We would have had so much fun."

But even as her heart ached with the absence of Emily, she felt an immense pride in herself. She'd done this. She'd gathered the courage, packed her bags, and ventured out on the journey that had once been their shared dream. Alone, yes—but not lonely. Empowered. Free.

Later that afternoon, Ivy walked down to Fisherman's Wharf. The salty air, mixed with the scent of fresh seafood and baking sourdough, made her stomach rumble. Tourists crowded the streets, taking photos and browsing the souvenir shops, but Ivy didn't mind the crowds. She felt like one of them—exploring, discovering.

She stopped at a stall and ordered a steaming bread bowl filled with clam chowder. The warm, savory aroma rose from the bowl as she took it to an outdoor seating area, finding a spot with a perfect view of the bay. The wind tugged gently at her hair as she savored her first spoonful, the rich chowder warming her from the inside out.

As she ate, Ivy couldn't help but laugh at the sight of a pelican nearby. The enormous bird was making bold attempts to claim a man's lunch, snapping at the air as the man shooed it away with a napkin. Undeterred, the pelican strutted around before swooping down to snag a piece of food a child had dropped. With a triumphant squawk, it flew off, food clutched tightly in its beak. Ivy giggled, shaking her head at the scene. San Francisco had its own way of keeping things interesting.

After finishing her meal, Ivy bought a ticket for a ferry boat tour that promised views of the Golden Gate Bridge and Alcatraz Island. As the boat pushed off from the dock, she leaned against the railing, the salty wind in her face as they moved across the bay. The water was a deep blue, and the boat cut smoothly through the waves.

The dense fog hung low over the bridge as the ferry approached it. Ivy felt a sense of awe as they sailed beneath the massive structure, the towers disappearing into the mist. The fog was dense, giving the scene an almost ghostly quality. She shivered in wonder at the sheer majesty of it all. This was the kind of moment Emily would have loved—something so beautiful and raw.

They continued past Alcatraz, the island looming in the distance, its infamous prison standing stark and silent against the rocky shore. Ivy gazed at the island, fascinated by its history, but her eyes kept drifting back to the water and the fog-shrouded horizon.

This place—this journey—was everything she had hoped for and more. Ivy felt small against the vastness of it all, but in the best way. She was a part of something larger now, a world full of beauty and mystery that stretched out far beyond the confines of her bakery and her past.

As the ferry made its way back to the dock, Ivy took one last look at the Golden Gate Bridge, its red-orange hue glowing faintly through the mist. The fog would lift, she knew, revealing the bridge in all its glory. Like her own journey—slowly but surely, the fog was lifting, revealing her own strength, her own path forward.

As Ivy drove down the Pacific Coast Highway, the jagged cliffs of the California coastline rose beside her, and the vast, shimmering ocean stretched out on her right, glittering under the midday sun. The beauty was almost overwhelming—the way the waves crashed against the rocks, sending white foam high into the air, the sound of the sea meeting the shore in an endless rhythm. It was her first time seeing the ocean in person, and it took her breath away.

The world suddenly felt so big, so expansive, in a way that filled her with both wonder and a sense of awe.

The life she'd known as a child, back in that tight-knit Amish community, felt impossibly small compared to this. What if her life had been different and she'd continued to grow up in that family and that Amish community?

She could picture it clearly: By now, she would have most likely been married, like so many young women in her community. Maybe she would've married a man she loved if she were lucky. But there was always the possibility that she'd end up with someone chosen more out of necessity than affection. Someone she simply had to tolerate, to bear.

Her life would've been dedicated to raising children, one after another, working tirelessly on a farm or in a small, predictable routine. She'd wake up every day knowing exactly what to expect, her world restricted to household chores, tending to her family, and adhering to the rules laid down by the church. Rules created by men—men who had no idea what it meant to be a woman, a mother, to feel the burden of expectations pressing down on you.

And if that life was acceptable, even fulfilling, for others—like her mother—then that was fine. But Ivy knew now, deep in her bones, that it wasn't for her. She wanted so much more. More than the boundaries of that small community. More than a life spent in quiet obedience, her every action scrutinized by elders who had no understanding of what it meant to live as she had to.

Ivy was glad, so deeply glad, that she had been freed from that future. She could have had a life like her mother's, but it wouldn't have been her life—it would've been one dictated by tradition, duty, and expectations.

Here, now, as she gazed out at the endless ocean, Ivy felt the expanse of possibilities stretching out before her. She was free to do as she pleased, free to live her life on her own terms, without the burden of having to answer to anyone but herself. She could choose what she wanted, when she wanted, and with whom. And that was empowering.

She sighed, letting the salty sea air fill her lungs as she drove on. The horizon stretched out in front of her, wide open, like her life. She could love whomever she wanted, travel wherever her heart took her, and live each day to its fullest potential if that's what she desired. No restrictions. No rules set by others.

And for that, Ivy was more grateful than ever. The coastline continued to unfold before her, each curve of the road a reminder of the freedom she had claimed for herself. She was living her life—really living it.

Chapter Thirty-Four

Two weeks had passed since Ivy arrived in San Diego. She'd fallen into a comfortable rhythm, spending her days exploring the beaches, local cafés, and letting the warm California sun rejuvenate her spirit. Everything felt lighter here, leaving her freer than she had been in years.

One bright afternoon, while sitting outside a quaint coffee shop overlooking the ocean, her phone buzzed. She glanced down at the unfamiliar number, her brow furrowing slightly. Her gut told her to pick up, even though she hesitated. Swiping her finger across the screen, she pressed the phone to her ear and answered.

"Ivy?" a voice crackled, shaky and uncertain on the other end.

Ivy froze. "Ruth?"

A deep breath sounded on the other end of the line. "Yeah... It's me."

For a long moment, Ivy didn't say anything, her mind racing. Why now? After everything. Why was Ruth calling?

"I'm—" Ruth paused as she blew a breath into the phone. "I'm pregnant, Ivy."

Ivy straightened in her chair, the bustling world around her suddenly dimming as her focus narrowed in on what she'd heard. "Pregnant?" she managed a whisper.

"I... I don't want to keep living like this. I can't raise a kid the way I've been living, you know?" Ruth's voice cracked, the vulnerability hitting Ivy like a punch to the gut. "I messed up. But I don't know what to do, Ivy. I don't know where to turn."

Ivy closed her eyes, pushing down the flood of emotions welling up inside her. She and Ruth had gone through so much—years of distance, anger, hurt—but hearing her sister so broken and pleading tugged at something deep inside her.

"I'll help you," Ivy said, trying to be calm even though her pulse raced. "We'll figure this out."

Ruth let out a breath that sounded like it was part sob, part relief. "I went to your bakery, but you weren't there. They said you sold it."

"I did, yes. I'm in California at the moment. In San Diego."

"Oh, I see. Ivy, I don't want to go back to that life. I don't want to drag a baby into that. I can't."

"You won't," Ivy assured her. "You don't have to. I'll buy you a ticket. Come here to California. We'll get you out of this."

Ruth sniffled on the other end of the line. "I don't deserve your help, Ivy. After everything..."

"That doesn't matter," Ivy said. "We're family. And you deserve a chance to start over, especially now. I'll send you the ticket tonight."

There was a long pause, and Ivy wondered if Ruth was going to change her mind. But then she heard a soft, "Thank you."

After they hung up, Ivy sat there in the sun, staring out at the waves, processing everything. Ruth. Pregnant. Desperate for help. Ivy had barely settled into her new life, but she knew she couldn't turn her back on her sister. Not now.

Within the hour, she'd booked Ruth's plane ticket to San Diego and started looking at rental homes. Ivy didn't know what the future would hold, but she was determined to give Ruth and her baby a better chance at life. She wouldn't let her sister go back to that dark place.

In the following days, Ivy found a small house outside the city. It was cozy, with a little garden and enough space for them to start fresh. She even got a job at a local bakery, falling back into the work she knew best —kneading dough, frosting cakes, and finding comfort in the rhythm and routine of the craft.

The house became their sanctuary. Ruth arrived soon after, but she was almost unrecognizable. There were dark circles under her eyes, her once-vibrant energy drained. She looked thinner, worn down by life. Ivy's heart ached to see her like this.

Ruth's pregnancy, far from filling her with joy, seemed to weigh her down further. Her movements were sluggish, and she often stared out the window for hours, lost in thought, barely responding when Ivy tried to make conversation.

But there was also a flicker of hope in her—the smallest glimmer of someone desperate for a second chance, someone who wanted more for the life growing inside her. That little spark gave Ivy hope, even when Ruth had her dark days, staying in bed for hours, sometimes crying, sometimes silent. The pregnancy was taking its toll, physically and emotionally, and Ruth's depression lingered like a heavy cloud, making it hard for her to see the future Ivy was trying so hard to build for them both.

One evening, as the chirp of crickets filled the warm California air, Ivy sat at the small kitchen table, flipping through a recipe book she'd picked up from the bakery. The windows were open, letting in the cool sea breeze, and the house was bathed in the gentle glow of the moonlight. Ruth had been quiet all day, withdrawn, spending most of her time curled up on the couch, and Ivy didn't want to push her. But tonight, there was a different energy in the air—an unsettling heaviness that Ivy couldn't shake.

Suddenly, Ruth's voice broke through the quiet. "Ivy, can we talk?"

Ivy looked up, surprised by the tone in her sister's voice—so serious, so fragile. She nodded and closed the book, pushing it aside. "Of course. What's going on?"

Ruth sat down across from her, her face pale, her hands trembling slightly. She took a deep breath, her eyes downcast, as if she were gathering the strength to say what had been haunting her.

Ivy listened, her breath locked in her throat, as Ruth trembled through the confession.

"It's about Dad," Ruth whispered, her blue eyes glistening with unshed tears. "When we were kids... when we were living on the farm... he... he used to come to me."

A sick feeling crept up Ivy's spine, a cold, hollow dread she couldn't place. Her fingers gripped Ruth's trembling hand, her own shaking now.

"In the barn," Ruth choked out.

The barn.

The nightmares.

The snake.

Ivy's breath hitched. A memory, long buried, clawed its way to the surface, splitting open like a wound she didn't know she had.

She was little. Maybe five or six. She wasn't supposed to go into the barn—Ruth had told her so, warned her over and over. But she had, creeping through the wooden doors, her bare feet soundless on the straw-covered floor.

And then she saw him.

Her father.

Like a snake wrapped around Ruth, holding her down. Ruth was struggling, her face twisted in pain.

Ivy's stomach lurched.

She'd tried to move, to scream, to run to Ruth. But the snake, no— their father—had turned his head then, cold, dead eyes locking onto hers. It, *he*, lashed out, screaming, teeth bared, sending her stumbling back.

Ivy had spent years brushing the nightmare off, a twisted mess of childhood fears. But she knew now—now, as Ruth sat in front of her, crying, confessing—it wasn't just a dream.

She had seen it. She had seen him.

Her father wasn't the snake.

He'd been worse.

"He told me that if I ever said anything... if I told anyone... he'd do it to the rest of you," Ruth whispered, her face crumpling in anguish. "I couldn't let that happen, Ivy. I couldn't let him hurt you, too. So, I stayed quiet. I let him... I let him do what he did to me, because I thought it was the only way to keep you all safe."

Ivy tried to swallow back a sob, but her emotions were too powerful. Her heart ached for her sister. All the pieces of their childhood, all the times Ruth had been so fiercely protective, suddenly fell into place. Ruth had been carrying this burden alone for so long, shielding Ivy from a darkness she hadn't even known existed.

Ivy's throat tightened, her words barely squeezing past the lump forming there. "Ruth, I'm so sorry," she whispered. She shoved her chair back, rounding the table in an instant, and dropped to her knees beside her sister. Without hesitation, she wrapped her arms around Ruth, holding her tightly, as if she could shield her from the past itself. "I'm so, so sorry. I'm sorry you went through that. I'm sorry he took—"

"I couldn't fight him off," Ruth said and collapsed into Ivy's shoulder, sobs racking her body, years of silence shattering in the space between them. Ivy held on, rocking her gently, her fingers tightening as if she could hold her together through sheer will alone.

"It wasn't your fault," Ivy said fiercely. "None of it. You didn't deserve any of it, Ruth. You were protecting us, but you should never have had to carry that alone."

Ruth pulled back slightly, her face streaked with tears, her breath coming in uneven gasps. "I didn't know how to tell you," she admitted, her voice hoarse, ragged. "I wanted to keep you safe. I thought... if I kept it buried, if I never said it out loud, it would stay dead."

Ivy cupped Ruth's face, brushing away the tears with her thumbs. "I believe you," she said, her own tears falling freely now. "And I am so, so grateful you trusted me enough to tell me. You don't have to carry this alone anymore. You have me."

They stayed like that for a long time, holding each other, the weight of Ruth's secret hanging between them, but no longer buried in darkness. Ivy stroked her sister's hair, whispering soothing words, letting Ruth cry until the tears slowed and her breathing steadied.

"I'm here for you," Ivy said firmly, pulling back to look her sister in the eyes. "Whatever you need, I'm here. You're not alone in this."

Ruth swiped at her tear-streaked face, her shoulders easing a little. There was something lighter in her expression now, something almost relieved. "Thank you, Ivy," she whispered. "For believing me. For being here."

Ivy leaned in and kissed her sister's forehead gently. "Always. You're my sister. You've always protected me... now it's my turn to protect you."

As they sat there, the past still lingered, heavy but no longer suffocating. Their bond—born from pain, yet strengthened by love—held firm. Healing would take time, but Ivy knew they would face whatever came next together.

Chapter Thirty-Five

The delivery room pulsed with exhaustion and relief, the air dense with something fragile and profound. The steady beep of monitors and hushed voices of nurses blurred into the background as Ruth sank into the pillows, damp hair clinging to her forehead, her breath uneven. She looked utterly drained, but when the nurse placed the wriggling, pink-faced baby in her arms, everything else faded away.

Ruth blinked down at her daughter, her lips parting in silent awe. Then, in a voice hoarse from labor and emotion, she whispered, "Daisy. I'm going to name her Daisy."

Ivy, perched at Ruth's bedside, felt something tighten in her chest. She hadn't realized how hard she'd been gripping Ruth's hand until that moment. She swallowed past the lump in her throat, nodding.

"Daisy," she repeated softly, letting the name settle between them. "It's perfect."

A faint, almost disbelieving smile tugged at Ruth's lips. With trembling fingers, she traced the curve of Daisy's tiny cheek. "We used to have daisies in the field behind the barn," she said, her voice distant, as if reaching through time. "They grew wild, no matter how much they got trampled. They always came back."

Something inside Ivy clenched. She remembered those daisies, too.

They'd been a bright spot in a childhood filled with too many shadows. A stubborn, sun-kissed rebellion against the bleakness of their home.

She reached out, brushing her fingertips over Daisy's impossibly small hand. The baby's fingers curled instinctively around her thumb, gripping tightly. The warmth of that tiny grasp sent a fierce protectiveness surging through Ivy, an immediate certainty that she would do anything—anything—to keep this little girl safe.

A few hours later, they returned home to their small, cozy house. Ivy had spent weeks preparing a space for Daisy, setting up a bassinet beside Ruth's bed, hanging a delicate mobile overhead. Everything was soft and warm, a stark contrast to the world they'd both grown up in.

Ruth moved slowly, almost hesitantly, as she placed Daisy into the bassinet. For a long moment, she stood there, staring down at her baby as if waiting for something to click into place. Ivy watched from the doorway, noting the way Ruth's shoulders sagged, the deep shadows beneath her eyes.

"She's beautiful," Ivy said. "You did so well, Ruth."

Ruth managed a small smile, but it didn't quite reach her eyes. "Thanks," she murmured. Then, without another word, she climbed into bed and turned away, curling onto her side.

Ivy lingered, her fingers tightening around the edge of the doorframe. Something gnawed at her, a quiet unease she couldn't stifle.

In the following days, Ivy did everything she could to support Ruth. She handled most of the late-night feedings, rocking Daisy in the early hours while Ruth slept. She sang to her, whispered stories of the life she hoped Daisy would have—one filled with love and laughter, free of fear.

Daisy was an easy baby, her tiny coos and sleepy sighs making Ivy fall harder for her every day. But Ruth... Ruth was slipping.

At first, Ivy told herself it was exhaustion. Childbirth was brutal, and Ruth had always been slow to show weakness. But then the distance became impossible to ignore.

Ruth rarely held Daisy for long. She'd take her for a few minutes, then pass her back, as if the weight of her own child was too much to bear. She spoke less, smiled even less. Some days, she barely got out of bed.

One afternoon, Ivy found her sitting on the edge of her mattress, staring blankly at the wall while Daisy slept beside her. Ivy's stomach twisted.

She sat down next to her sister, hesitating only a moment before reaching out. Her fingers brushed Ruth's arm, and she felt the slightest flinch beneath her touch.

"Ruth," she said carefully. "I know you're tired. But it's more than that, isn't it?"

Ruth's gaze darted to hers, then dropped. Her jaw tightened. "I'm fine."

Ivy exhaled slowly. "I don't think you are," she said, choosing her words with care. "I think you're struggling. And that's okay. It happens. I've read about postpartum depression, and—"

Ruth let out a sharp, humorless laugh. "Depression." She scoffed, rubbing her hands over her face. "I don't have time to be depressed."

"You don't get to choose," Ivy pressed gently. "It's not about time, Ruth. It's about needing help."

Her sister's face crumpled, her breath shuddering. "I'm supposed to be happy," she choked out. "I have Daisy. I love her, I do. But I feel... empty. Like I'm watching my own life from the outside and I can't make myself feel anything the way I should."

Ivy's throat burned. She scooted closer, wrapping an arm around Ruth's hunched shoulders. "You're not broken," she whispered. "You're not failing. You're carrying too much on your own."

Ruth shuddered under her touch. "I don't know how to fix it."

"Maybe we start with your doctor," Ivy suggested. "Talk to them. See what they say."

For a long moment, Ruth didn't respond. Then, with a slow, weary nod, she whispered, "Okay."

The crushing force that had been sitting on Ivy's ribs evaporated. She squeezed her sister a little tighter. "We'll figure this out together," she promised. "You've always been the strong one. Let me be strong for you this time."

Ruth's eyes filled with tears, and she leaned into Ivy's embrace, letting out a soft, broken sob. "Thank you," she whispered. "I don't know what I'd do without you."

253

Ivy kissed the top of her head, her own eyes wet with tears. "You don't have to know. You're not going to be without me."

———

Two weeks later, Ivy decided to take Daisy out for a walk while Ruth went to her doctor's appointment. The past few weeks had been challenging, but today the weather was perfect—the kind of day that begged for a stroll by the bay. The soft breeze carried the salty scent of the bay, and with it, some of the tension from the last few weeks began to loosen its grip on Ivy.

Carefully, she placed Daisy into her stroller. The tiny baby looked around with wide, curious eyes as Ivy tucked a light blanket around her. Ivy smiled at the sight—so small and so innocent, completely unaware of the struggle the adults around her were working through.

They walked slowly along the waterfront, the boats swaying gently in the harbor, their sails catching the soft breeze. The bright sunlight danced off the water, and the gentle rhythmic sound of waves lapping against the pier filled the air. Ivy pointed out the boats, speaking softly to Daisy, even though the infant was too young to understand.

"Look at that one, Daisy," she murmured. "One day, maybe we can go on a boat ride together. Would you like that?"

Daisy's eyes stared up at her aunt, her expression serene. Ivy couldn't help but smile. These moments made all the challenges feel worthwhile.

After a while, they found a shaded bench by the water, and Ivy settled in, adjusting the stroller so Daisy could see the view. Ivy leaned back, letting the cool breeze wash over her face, closing her eyes as she took a breath. It had been so long since she felt this kind of peace—a fleeting moment of calm in an otherwise unpredictable time.

"This is good for us, Daisy," she whispered, looking down at the baby, her entire soul infused with love. "We're going to be okay. All of us."

When they returned to the house later that afternoon, Ivy was surprised to see Ruth already there. Her sister was sitting in the living room, gazing out the window with a faraway expression. Ivy noticed that something seemed different about Ruth today—her shoulders were a little less tense, and there was a hint of calmness that Ivy hadn't seen in weeks.

"Hey," Ivy greeted warmly, pushing the stroller inside. "How was your appointment?"

Ruth turned to look at her, her eyes meeting Ivy's for a second before she looked away. There was something there, something Ivy couldn't quite place—an emotion hidden beneath the surface.

Ruth shrugged, her expression turning guarded. "It was fine," she said, her voice distant. "But I don't really want to talk about it."

Ivy studied her sister, wanting to press further, but something about the look in Ruth's eyes held her back. Instead, she offered a gentle smile.

"That's okay," she said, a little too cheerfully. "Whenever you're ready, I'm here."

Ruth's gaze drifted down to Daisy, who stared up at her from the stroller. A hint of a smile curved Ruth's mouth as she reached out, fingertips brushing the baby's cheek. Something eased in her face— brief, but real.

"Thanks, Ivy," Ruth said. "You know, it's okay for you to go back to work now. I'm okay to take care of Daisy on my own."

Ivy's chest swelled, warmth blooming—a powerful mix of love and hope. She wanted to believe things would get better—that whatever plan the doctor had given Ruth would help her heal. More than anything, Ivy hoped her sister knew she didn't have to do any of this alone.

As the evening rolled in, they both settled back into their routine. Ivy took care of dinner, preparing something simple while Ruth took Daisy to the nursery to rock her to sleep. There was still a long road ahead of them, filled with its share of challenges, but tonight, Ivy allowed herself to feel a tiny glimmer of optimism. Small steps mattered.

Everything was going to be okay.

Over the next few months, Ivy poured herself into her work at the bakery. She was now working full-time and had recently been promoted to manager—a position she hadn't expected but was determined to excel in. The little things she was learning would maybe one day give her the confidence to open another bigger bakery with more employees—a business that would provide for her new family.

She realized now the errors she'd made previously: taking on too much on her own and not delegating enough, not using the right software to bookkeep, ordering too much and having too many items on the menu.

They were all things that would've made her less stressed and have more time for herself and her personal life.

Now, she found comfort in organizing staff schedules and being more in tune with utilizing her team.

But still, her days would start before dawn and often stretch until evening, which kept her away from Daisy and Ruth. Even with the long hours, she never stopped thinking about what awaited her at home.

Every evening when she returned, she'd find Ruth with Daisy, her niece's giggles and baby babble filling the small house. Ruth seemed happier, and Daisy was clearly well-cared for, smiling brightly whenever Ivy walked in. But as much as Ivy tried to tell herself things were fine, she couldn't stop feeling something wasn't right. There was an air of tension around Ruth Ivy couldn't ignore.

One evening, Ivy came home to find Ruth pacing around the kitchen, Daisy settled in her bouncer nearby, watching her mother's every move.

"You okay?" Ivy held back a sigh as she placed down her purse and keys.

"Not really." Ruth stopped pacing and faced Ivy. "I'm kind of stir crazy. I think I need to get out and get some alone time."

"I totally understand," Ivy said, feeling a bit of relief. "I can watch Daisy for you, no problem."

"Great." Ruth blew out a breath, her fingers fidgeting. "I'll head to the grocery store and get a few things."

"That would be great. Can you pick up some coffee? We're almost out."

"Sure." Ruth grabbed the car keys and her purse and then rushed out the door, not saying goodbye to Ivy or Daisy.

Ruth was gone for over two hours and returned with only a handful of items and no coffee. She walked in quickly, setting the small bag of groceries on the counter, her eyes darting around the room.

"Hey," Ivy said, trying to keep her tone casual as she glanced from the sparse groceries to her sister. "You were gone a while. Everything okay?"

Ruth stiffened, her face darkening. "Yeah, it's fine," she said, avoiding Ivy's gaze as she put the items away one by one.

Ivy's concern deepened. "It's just... you didn't come back with much. And you were gone a long time."

Ruth turned to face her, her expression defensive. "Why are you always asking me questions?" she snapped. "I don't have to account for every second of my day to you. And I told you I needed some alone time."

Ivy took a deep breath, trying not to react to the sharpness in her sister's tone. "I'm not asking for an account of every second, Ruth. I'm worried. You seem... off. Like something's bothering you."

Ruth scoffed and rolled her eyes, still not meeting Ivy's gaze. She picked up Daisy, her movements tense, and held the baby close. "I'm fine, Ivy. It's a lot taking care of a baby twenty-four-seven. There's nothing wrong with me. I just had to run a couple of errands. You don't need to make it a big deal."

"Okay," Ivy said, holding her hands in front of her. "But I'm here if you need to talk about anything. You know that, right?"

Ruth huffed, shifting Daisy in her arms as if Ivy's words were nothing more than background noise. "Yeah, sure," she mumbled, then turned and headed down the hall to her bedroom, shutting the door firmly behind her.

Ivy stood in the kitchen, staring at the closed door. Uneasiness gripped her, squeezing her chest. Ruth had been distant for weeks now, and though Ivy had seen no obvious signs of drug or alcohol use, the strange behavior, the defensive attitude, the long absences—all of it sent her mind spiraling into worry.

As she cleaned up the kitchen, her thoughts ran in circles. Maybe it was postpartum depression lingering, she reasoned. She'd read it could last for months. But she couldn't deny the gnawing feeling that something else was going on, something Ruth wasn't telling her.

She sighed, running a hand through her hair as she leaned against the counter. Ruth had been through so much, and Ivy wanted more than anything to be there for her, to help her through whatever she was dealing with. But how could she if Ruth kept shutting her out, if she refused to let Ivy into her life beyond Daisy's milestones and moments?

As Ivy turned off the kitchen lights and prepared to head to bed, she made a silent promise to herself: She'd keep trying. She'd keep being there, keep watching out for her sister and her niece, no matter how hard Ruth tried to push her away. Because, in the end, they were all each other had. And Ivy wasn't about to give up—not on her family, and certainly not on Ruth.

Chapter Thirty-Six

Ivy sank onto her bed, pulling the blankets over herself. Her body was exhausted, but her mind wouldn't settle. The house was quiet—too quiet. Ruth was home, but she may as well have been miles away.

She reached for her phone, checking the time, but before she could set it back down, a message popped up from Beck. She smiled, feeling that familiar warmth that always seemed to accompany his texts.

They'd been texting and chatting almost daily since she'd moved to San Diego. What had started as casual reconnecting had quickly become a lifeline for her. Beck was her sounding board, her late-night laugh, and the person she turned to when her worries felt too heavy to carry alone. Even from states away, he'd become her rock.

Beck: *You wouldn't believe the tourist I had to cut off tonight. Thought he was some kind of VIP. Honestly, if I had a dollar for every "Do you know who I am?" I get...*

Ivy exhaled slowly, the tension in her shoulders loosening a little. Beck. He was always there, even when she wasn't sure she had the words to say what was on her mind.

Ivy: *The entitlement is strong tonight, I see.*

Beck: *Strong enough to make me question my life choices.*

A pause. Then, another message.

Beck: Everything okay on your end?

Ivy hesitated, her fingers hovering over the keyboard. She wasn't sure how to put it into words, how to explain the feeling that had been bothering her for weeks—the slow unraveling of something she couldn't quite name. But Beck had a way of making it easy to be honest, even with things she didn't want to admit to herself.

Ivy: I don't know. Ruth was off tonight. More than usual. I asked her if she was okay, and she barely looked at me. She got defensive. Shut down. She's been distant for a while, but tonight it felt worse.

A few seconds passed before his reply came.

Beck: Think she's using again?

Ivy's stomach twisted. She had been trying to push that thought away, to tell herself it was stress, exhaustion—anything but that. But seeing it in black and white, staring back at her, made it real.

Ivy: I don't know. I want to believe she's past that. I want to believe she's okay. But something doesn't feel right. I keep telling myself I'm overreacting, but I can't shake the feeling that I'm not.

Beck: You're not overreacting. You know her better than anyone. If something feels off, it probably is.

Her throat tightened.

Ivy: I don't know what to do. I keep thinking that if I say the wrong thing, push too hard, she'll pull away completely. And I can't lose her, Beck.

A longer pause this time.

Beck: Ivy, you've been holding her up for so long. But this? This isn't yours to carry alone. I know that's hard to hear, but you can't fix this by yourself. You've done everything you can, and I know you'll keep doing it because that's who you are. But she has to want it, too.

She let out a shaky breath, and then a sharp inhale through the nose, like trying to pull in composure.

Ivy: I don't know where the line is. When to push. When to back off. When to let go.

Beck: Then don't try to figure it all out tonight. Just breathe. Try to get some sleep. Worry about tomorrow when it comes.

Ivy swallowed, staring at his words. As if it were that simple. As if her mind wasn't already tangled in what-ifs and worst-case scenarios. But he was right—she couldn't solve this in a night.

Ivy: *I'll try.*

Beck: *Good. And if you need me, you know where to find me.*

Ivy: *Thank you. It really helps knowing I can lean on you. You really are my compass.*

Beck: *Always. Now try to get some rest. You've earned it.*

She smiled, her fingers brushing over the screen as she typed her goodnight.

Ivy: *Goodnight, Beck. Sweet dreams. And good luck with the VIPs.*

She set down her phone, feeling a little lighter. She closed her eyes, letting his words linger in her mind, reassuring her. With Beck's steadying presence, her worries seemed a bit more manageable, and sleep finally pulled her in, leaving her with a small, hopeful smile.

The room was dark and quiet, Ivy drifting between dreams and the lingering worries of the day, when a sharp, high-pitched wail shattered the silence. Her body jolted as she heard Daisy's cries reverberating down the hall.

Ivy waited, hoping Ruth would stir, that she'd hear the creak of a bed or soft footsteps padding to soothe Daisy. But the crying only grew louder, more desperate. Ivy sat up, frowning. Ruth was usually attentive, quick to respond to Daisy's cries, even if she was tired. Something was wrong.

Ivy slipped out of bed, stepping carefully to the door and opening it enough to peek down the dim hallway. The light from the living room cast soft shadows, but Ruth's room was dark, and there was no sign of movement. Ivy could hear Daisy's cries growing hoarse, frantic, and she felt a knot tighten in her stomach.

She walked down the hall, stopping outside Ruth's door, and pressed her ear against it, straining to hear any sign of life inside. Only Daisy's cries cut through the silence. Taking a breath, she knocked lightly, hesitantly.

"Ruth?" she whispered, hoping not to startle her sister but needing reassurance.

No answer.

Ivy knocked again, harder, the panic clawing at her throat now. "Ruth?" Her voice pitched higher, trembling. "Are you in there? Open the door!"

Silence.

Her pulse pounded in her ears as she twisted the knob and shoved the door open. The moment she stepped inside, the breath rushed from her lungs, her stomach caving in on itself.

Ruth lay sprawled on the floor beside the bed, motionless, her skin a sickly shade of gray. Her lips—God, her lips—had taken on a bluish tint. And on the bed, Daisy lay on her back, her tiny fists curled, her red, tear-streaked face scrunched in distress. Her cries were hoarse now, weak, as if she'd been screaming for hours.

Ivy's gaze snapped to the nightstand, where a needle glinted under the dim light, beside an empty bottle cap.

No.

Her stomach lurched. The world tilted.

No, no, no, no.

"Ruth!" Her own voice barely sounded like hers, raw with terror as she dropped to her knees beside her sister. She grabbed Ruth's shoulders, shaking her. "Ruth, wake up! Please—wake up!"

Nothing. No stir, no flutter of her eyelids.

Ivy's hands hovered, and she was unsure if she wanted to grab Ruth, to shake harder, or to scream. A sob wrenched from her throat as she fumbled for her phone with trembling fingers, barely able to see through the blur of tears. She stabbed at the screen, her breath ragged, her body shaking violently as the line connected.

"Nine-one-one, what's your emergency?"

"My sister—" Ivy's voice cracked. "She's not breathing! I—I think she overdosed, I don't know, she's—please, please send help!"

"Ma'am, I need you to stay calm. Is she responsive at all?"

"No, she's just lying here! She's—she's not moving, she's not—" Ivy's voice broke as she pressed a trembling hand to Ruth's chest. Cold. Too cold.

Daisy let out another feeble whimper from the bed, her little body shuddering with exhaustion.

"Where is your sister, ma'am?" The operator's voice was calm, grounding. "She needs to be on a firm surface."

"She—she's on the floor," Ivy choked out.

"Okay, I need you to start compressions. Put your phone on speaker, and I'll guide you through it."

Ivy obeyed, dropping the phone beside her and pressing her hands against Ruth's chest. She'd never done this before. God, why had she never learned this before? But she pushed down, counting between sobs.

"One, two, three, four—" Her vision blurred, her fingers numb, her chest squeezing tighter with each count.

"Come on, Ruth. Come back. Please—" A sob tore through her throat. "Don't do this, don't leave me, please!"

Her arms ached, her head spun, but she kept pushing, her cries blending with Daisy's weak whimpers.

Somewhere in the distance, sirens wailed.

But Ivy couldn't stop. Wouldn't stop.

Not until Ruth opened her eyes.

The paramedics arrived in what felt like both an eternity and an instant. Ivy stumbled back, clutching Daisy to her chest as they took over, watching with wide, tear-filled eyes as they continued CPR, their movements efficient, professional, but urgent.

The minutes ticked by painfully slow, each second a slice of agony as Ivy held Daisy close, pressing soft kisses to her tiny head, whispering words of comfort she wasn't sure were more for her niece or herself.

Finally, one of the paramedics approached her, his expression a mixture of sorrow and sympathy.

"I'm sorry," he said, breaking through the haze. "We did everything we could. She's gone."

The words crashed into Ivy like a tidal wave, stealing the breath from her lungs and leaving her hollow. Her knees buckled, the floor tilting beneath her, but she held on—held onto Daisy like an anchor, pressing the baby against her chest as if that could keep her world from completely falling apart. A choked sob wrenched from her throat, pained and broken, as her tears spilled over, hot and unrelenting.

No.

This wasn't happening.

Not Ruth. Not her fierce, stubborn, complicated sister—the girl who had once shielded Ivy from the worst of their father's wrath, who had whispered bedtime stories to her in the dark when the nightmares wouldn't let her sleep. The girl who had fought so damn hard to survive.

But she had lost.

Ivy swayed, gripping Daisy tighter, her fingers digging into the soft fabric of the baby's onesie. Daisy squirmed but didn't cry, as if she understood, as if she felt the weight of the grief swallowing the room.

"I'm so sorry, Ruth," Ivy whispered, rocking back and forth. "I'm so sorry, I—"

The rest of the words dissolved into sobs, incoherent and gasping.

Behind her, the paramedics moved with quiet efficiency as they prepared to take Ruth away. Ivy couldn't watch. She couldn't see them cover her sister, couldn't hear the final zip of the body bag. It was too much. Too final.

She turned away, shielding Daisy, shielding herself.

She pressed her cheek against the baby's head, inhaling that soft, powdery scent—so innocent, so untouched by the cruelty of the world. Daisy let out a tiny sigh, her warm breath brushing against Ivy's collarbone, and something inside Ivy cracked wide open.

A promise formed in the wreckage of her heart.

She would protect Daisy. She would be the one to fight for her, to love her fiercely, to give her the life Ruth had wanted so desperately to provide. Ivy had failed Ruth—hadn't saved her in time, hadn't done enough—but she wouldn't fail Daisy.

She couldn't.

Her fingers curled around Daisy's tiny body, holding on as if the baby were the only thing tethering her to the earth.

Somehow, some way, she would get through this night.

For Daisy.

For Ruth.

Chapter Thirty-Seven

Ivy cradled Daisy close, gently rocking her as she gazed over the small gathering. It wasn't what she'd envisioned when she'd written those letters to her siblings and mother. She'd spent hours drafting them, explaining what had happened to Ruth and hoping, maybe foolishly, that they'd feel compelled to come, to mourn her together. She'd even offered to pay for a few plane tickets or to pay for a driver to bring them here. But no one had replied. The silence had cut deep, even if she'd half-expected it.

But then there was Beck, standing by her side like he had been since he'd arrived in San Diego, a calm presence through her whirlwind of grief and responsibility. And Gram had come too, surprising her with his sincerity and the quiet strength he now seemed to carry. They were all she had here, but somehow, their presence steadied her.

After the service, Ivy took Ruth's urn and joined Beck and Gram. Beck was holding Daisy, who looked around with wide, curious eyes, unaware of the gravity of the moment. Ivy felt a pang of sorrow at the thought that her niece would grow up never knowing her mother.

Both men offered their sympathies, their words gentle but sincere. Gram's expression held a heaviness as he looked at her, his eyes reflecting years of shared history and regret. He cleared his throat and motioned to Beck, then turned to Ivy.

"Can we talk for a minute?" he asked, gesturing to the side.

Ivy carefully set the urn down. "I'll be right back," she said to Beck. He gave her a warm smile, his gaze drifting to Daisy, then returning to Ivy with a quiet steadiness that urged her on.

She took a breath, following Gram a few steps away. She hadn't seen him in so long, not since she'd asked him to leave. He looked healthy, more settled than she remembered, his shoulders straight and his eyes clear.

"Ivy," he said, a breath rushing out, "I... I needed to tell you that none of this is your fault. What happened to Ruth—it wasn't because of anything you did or didn't do." He paused, glancing down as if gathering his thoughts, then met her gaze again. "You did so much for her. You gave her multiple chances, and you gave me a chance, and I'm grateful to you for that."

A small, bittersweet smile tugged at Ivy's lips. "Thank you, Gram," she said softly, feeling an unexpected warmth in his words.

He took a deep breath. "I've been working on myself, Ivy. Got a good job now, something stable. And I'm seeing someone. She's got her life together, and it's been good. Feels like things are finally falling into place." He smiled, a hint of pride tugging at his features.

"That's good, Gram," she said, meaning it. "I'm proud of you."

His jaw tightened, then relaxed as his gaze shifted toward Beck, still holding Daisy. "He seems like a good man."

Ivy followed his line of sight, watching as Beck gently ran a fingertip over Daisy's tiny hand, his expression unreadable but filled with something that made Ivy's throat tighten.

"Yeah," she said. "He is."

Silence stretched between them, not uncomfortable, but weighted with years of history neither of them knew how to fix. Then, in a movement that surprised them both, Gram reached out and pulled Ivy into a hug.

It was brief, a little stiff, but real.

When he stepped back, he gave her one last look—something between an apology and a promise. "Take care of yourself, Ivy."

Then he turned and walked away.

Ivy stood there, watching him go, feeling the quiet shift of something that wasn't quite closure but wasn't quite pain either. Just change.

Turning back, Ivy found Beck watching her, his expression softer than she'd ever seen it. Daisy's tiny fists tugged at the fabric of his shirt, her round cheeks flushed from the cool air. He glanced down at her, murmuring something gentle that Ivy couldn't quite hear, but it didn't matter—the tenderness in his voice said enough.

Ivy stepped closer, her gaze drawn to Daisy. She reached out, smoothing a hand over the baby's fine hair.

Beck passed the blanket-swaddled infant to her, his hands lingering long enough to steady her hold. His warmth seeped into her skin, grounding her in the moment.

"You okay?" he asked quietly, searching her face, his thumb grazing the back of her hand before he let go.

Ivy inhaled deeply, adjusting Daisy in her arms. "Yeah," she murmured. "I think I am."

The words felt strange, but there was truth in them. She glanced down at Daisy, at the delicate rise and fall of her tiny chest, the way her little fingers flexed and curled against Ivy's sweater. A swell of fierce determination rose inside her, an unshakable certainty that she would do right by this child.

"I'm going to give her a good life, Beck," she said, her voice stronger now. "She deserves that."

Beck's gaze didn't waver. "I believe that. And she's lucky to have you." He reached out, squeezing her hand, his touch reassuring, solid.

Ivy swallowed past the lump in her throat. "I think I'm the lucky one."

She stood there, holding Daisy close, as uncertainty settled deep in her chest. The future stretched out before her, vast and unknowable. How was she supposed to do this—raise a child, start over, find solid ground when everything beneath her felt unstable? It loomed over her, daunting, and for a fleeting moment, she longed for Ruth's guidance. But Ruth was gone, and all Ivy could do now was take the next step forward.

Beck must have sensed the hesitation, the questions turning over in her mind, because he nudged her lightly with his elbow, a small grin playing on his lips. "You know," he said, "I'm still looking for a roommate."

Ivy let out a quiet laugh—soft, but real. It was the first time in days that something felt light, like maybe everything wasn't entirely broken.

"Are you now?" she mused, tilting her head as she looked at him.

His grin faded into something gentler, something more serious. "And... I happened to notice there's this spot in downtown Frisco. Right on Main Street. Cute little storefront, perfect foot traffic, and— get this—the town's in desperate need of a bakery."

She raised an eyebrow, watching him carefully. "So, you think I should just settle down in Frisco and open up a bakery?"

Beck shrugged, but there was a certainty in his expression, a quiet confidence that wrapped around her like a safety net. "I think you should do whatever feels right for you. But if you're looking for a place to land... this might not be such a bad one."

Ivy looked down at Daisy, her heart tightening as she traced a fingertip over the baby's tiny hand. Maybe she and Daisy did need a place to land. A fresh start. A home.

"I don't know yet, Beck." Ivy's voice was quiet, thoughtful, as she cradled Daisy closer. The baby nestled against her, warm and safe in her arms, unaware of the weight of Ivy's uncertainty. "I need to think about what's best for her." She hesitated, watching the way the last light of the day painted the horizon in soft golds and purples. "I want to give her a life better than what Ruth or I had. One filled with love and stability. A place where we can build something good."

Beck didn't rush her. He never did. Instead, he reached out and gave her shoulder a reassuring squeeze, his touch solid, grounding. "Take all the time you need, Ivy," he said. "Just know that if you decide Frisco's the place for you two, I'll be there. Waiting."

She turned to him then, emotion tightening her throat. "Thank you, Beck. Really. For everything."

His grin softened, a quiet understanding passing between them. He glanced down at Daisy, his thumb brushing lightly over the baby's rosy cheek. "I think you're already giving her an amazing life, Ivy," he said.

"Whatever you choose next will only make it better. And if that choice includes me..." He exhaled, shaking his head with a small, self-deprecating laugh. "I love you. I don't think I ever stopped loving you."

Ivy's breath caught. The words settled deep, pressing against the ache she hadn't fully acknowledged, the longing she hadn't let herself feel. She turned toward the setting sun, the vastness of the sky stretching out before her, endless and uncertain.

"You don't have to say it back," Beck added, lifting a hand before she could speak. "Or even think it back. I know you've had a rough time lately. I want you to know where I stand."

She swallowed, her grip tightening around Daisy. Beck had been her anchor in the storm, the one steady thing when everything else had crumbled. She wasn't sure what came next. But at last, her steps felt purposeful—she was moving toward something, not away.

"I appreciate you so much." Ivy looked up at Beck, her heart both hesitant and hopeful. She didn't have all the answers. But she had Daisy. She had Beck. And maybe she had the start of something that could feel like home.

Ivy pulled the rental car onto the gravel driveway, her pulse thrumming in her ears as she stepped out, cradling Daisy close against her chest. The urn was tucked tightly under her arm, its weight both grounding and suffocating. This place—her childhood home—stood before her like a relic of another life, familiar yet foreign, suspended in a haze of memories that threatened to pull her under.

The yard was alive with children's laughter, their voices ringing through the humid summer air. It felt surreal to see them here, running through the grass she'd once sprinted across barefoot, playing in the same dirt that had caked her own hands and feet as a child. It was like stepping into a distorted dream—one where the past and present overlapped, where time had moved forward, but the ghosts of what had been still clung to the air.

And then she saw them.

Under the sprawling oak tree sat her siblings, gathered around a long picnic table. Jonas, Esther, Leah, Joseph, and Eli—older now, but their faces still unmistakable. Each one froze mid-conversation as their gazes snapped toward her, expressions shifting from shock to something colder, something unreadable.

Jonas sat at the head of the table, as their father once had. His posture was easy, his smug expression twisting Ivy's stomach. Around them, their spouses sat in quiet observation, their gazes shifting between Ivy and Jonas as if waiting for his lead.

No one moved. No one spoke.

The unspoken message landed hard, dragging her thoughts down with it.

She wasn't welcome here.

Ivy's steps faltered as a trio of young boys darted past her, their laughter fading the moment they caught sight of her. They gawked, their wide eyes brimming with curiosity. An *Englisch* woman in jeans and a sweater was an unfamiliar sight on this land—land that had once been hers, too.

Her gaze landed on one of the boys, and recognition struck like a slap. Jonas's son. The last time she had seen him, faint bruises had darkened his face. Now, a cast wrapped around his arm, and the remnants of more bruises shadowed his cheek. A fresh wave of nausea curled in her stomach. She didn't have to ask how he'd gotten those injuries. Some things here hadn't changed at all.

She swallowed the sick feeling rising in her throat and forced herself to move forward, gripping Daisy a little tighter. Summoning the courage she wasn't sure she had, she spoke.

"Where's Mom?"

The words hung in the air, fragile yet sharp.

Across the yard, Esther rose slowly from the picnic table. Her face had softened with time, but hesitation clouded her features. Ivy could see it—the war in her eyes, the pull between memories and the many years spent apart. For a fleeting second, she thought Esther might step forward, might reach for her, offer something that resembled comfort.

But she didn't.

Instead, she held herself back, her expression guarded. And then, in a voice barely above a whisper, she said, "Mom passed away two months ago."

Ivy staggered, the breath torn from her lungs. She gripped Daisy tighter. Her mother was gone. Just like Ruth. Another thread of her past, cut. She had known this place would no longer feel like home, but she hadn't realized how much of it had already slipped away.

She forced herself to meet Esther's gaze. "So did Ruth."

A flicker of something—grief, regret, something nameless—passed through Esther's eyes, but it was gone before Ivy could grasp it.

"I sent you letters," Ivy said, the words trembling with a mix of accusation and disbelief. "I sent them here."

Esther's lips pressed together, her gaze shifting downward. "I know," she admitted. "We couldn't make it."

Ivy blinked, waiting for more—for an explanation, an apology, something.

Esther exhaled, glancing toward Jonas, whose watchful eyes had never left them. "We had to help Jonas move his family into the house," she said, the words careful, rehearsed. "He'll be taking over the farm now."

Of course he would.

Ivy felt something inside her fracture, sharp and irreversible.

Ivy's gaze landed on Jonas, who lounged in his chair with the same smugness he had always worn, like a second skin. His eyes met hers, dark with amusement, arrogance simmering beneath the surface. He knew why she was here, but he didn't care. He never had.

She held his stare, something hot and bitter twisting inside her. A part of her had foolishly hoped that time might have softened this place, that the years would have washed away the worst of it. But standing here now, looking at Jonas, she realized nothing had changed.

The farm had passed from one tyrant to the next.

Looking around, she took in the children running through the yard. A pang of sadness filled her as she spotted the little boy again, his cast a stark reminder of the cycle she had fought so hard to escape. Ivy swallowed, her throat tight. She wouldn't dwell on it, not now. She couldn't.

She took a steadying breath, forcing herself to keep her voice calm.

"I'd like to spread Ruth's ashes where the daisies grow behind the barn. Then I'll be gone."

Esther glanced back at Jonas, as if waiting for permission, before giving Ivy a subtle nod. "That's fine," she murmured. Then, leaning in close, she whispered, "I'll distract him. Tell him something... anything. I remember how Ruth loved those daisies."

Ivy's chest tightened with gratitude. "Thank you," she whispered.

She walked quietly past them, heading toward the back of the barn, the weight of the urn in her arms growing heavier with each step. Behind her, she heard Esther, louder and strained, as she tried to keep Jonas's attention away from her. Ivy cast one last look over her shoulder, watching as Esther whispered something in Jonas's ear, her body blocking his line of sight.

With Daisy cradled in one arm and the urn in the other, Ivy moved to the field where the daisies grew wild and free, like they had when she was a child. The sun was setting, casting a warm golden light over the field, illuminating the delicate petals. She knelt down, her heart aching, and opened the urn, letting Ruth's ashes scatter into the breeze, drifting down to rest among the flowers that had always seemed so resilient, so unbroken.

She closed her eyes, feeling the presence of her sister, of the girl who had once been her fierce protector, who had sacrificed so much. She whispered a quiet goodbye, her voice choked with tears.

"You're free now, Ruth," she murmured. "And so am I."

Standing, she looked down at Daisy, who gazed up at her with wide, innocent eyes. Ivy knew she couldn't erase the pain of the past or undo what had happened to her and Ruth. But she could create something new, something better for Daisy. And as she walked back to her car, leaving the farmhouse, the barn, and her family behind, a sense of lightness settled over her, as if she were finally stepping out from under a shadow.

When she reached the car, she looked back one last time, then climbed in, fastening Daisy safely in her car seat. Turning the key, she took a deep breath, feeling a calm settle over her.

Now she could move on.

Chapter Thirty-Eight

Two years later

Ivy stood at the wide kitchen window, cradling a warm mug between her hands as she gazed out over Dillon Reservoir. The early-morning sun stretched its golden fingers across the water, turning the surface into a rippling sheet of light. Out on the lake, Beck sat in his fishing boat, his relaxed posture a quiet contrast to the excited movements of Daisy beside him. Even from here, Ivy could see her daughter's tiny hands flailing, pointing at something in the water, her bright orange life vest making her look like a little firefly against the blue expanse.

Beck laughed—a deep, easy sound that carried across the lake—and Ivy felt her heart swell.

God, she loved this man. She loved this life.

A life that felt solid, real. A life she had built with intention, with love, with the sheer will to carve something good out of the wreckage of her past.

The bakery she owned in town had become more than just a business—it was a place filled with warmth, with the comforting scent of cinnamon and fresh bread, with friendly faces who had come to know her by name. Her days were simple but full, laced with the kind of contentment she never thought she'd have. And every night, she had Beck, holding her close, grounding her in a way she never realized she needed.

She should have been at peace.

But her gaze drifted to the envelope sitting on the table. The letter inside had arrived the day before, the handwriting young and uncertain but unmistakably familiar. Ivy exhaled slowly, setting her mug down as she reached for it, her fingers brushing over the creased paper before she unfolded it again.

"We hear Mom and Dad talk about you and your life out west. We don't know you much, Aunt Ivy, but we think we'd like it there with you. Can we come live with you?"

The words were simple, written in a child's scrawl, but they carried an unimaginable weight. Ivy's heart broke as she read the plea for help between the lines. She could almost feel their longing and the quiet desperation that came from living in a place where safety and freedom were not guaranteed.

She knew too well what they were going through, the loneliness of being trapped in a place that didn't allow for dreams, where the future was defined and limited by rules that felt like walls.

And in some cases, walls that didn't allow safety from the very people who were supposed to protect you.

Ivy swallowed, closing her eyes as a mix of anger and sadness welled up within her. She wanted to save them, to take each of her nieces and nephews and bring them here, give them a chance at a different life, a life filled with choices and kindness.

But she didn't have the resources. She was just one person, with a modest income and a three-year-old to raise. She didn't know how to fight against something so large and so rooted. Yet she felt a stirring within her, a resolve she hadn't felt in years. She couldn't ignore their plea, and she wouldn't.

She opened her eyes, staring at her laptop screen. Her fingers hovered over the keyboard, her mind racing with everything she wanted to say. She didn't have all the answers, didn't know if she ever would, but she knew one thing for certain—she couldn't keep quiet anymore.

The silence had stretched on for too long.

She thought of the letter from her niece or nephew, the desperation hidden between the lines. She thought of the bruises she'd seen on Jonas's son, of Ruth's whispered warnings when they were young, of all the children still trapped in the cycle of obedience and fear. She thought of herself, of the abuse, of being taken away from her biological family, and thinking it was her punishment.

Too many people who didn't know the truth—people who romanticized the Amish, who believed the stories about simple living, about faith and family and wholesome traditions. And that may be the case for some communities. But it wasn't for Ivy, and now her nieces and nephews.

Normal people didn't see what lurked behind those closed doors. They didn't hear the screams swallowed by barns, the prayers that went unanswered, the cries for help that never came.

Ivy remembered the article about abuse in the Amish community that Fiona, her previous employee, had shown her. That article had reached a particular audience. Yet, abuse was still happening.

Maybe if Ivy told her story—and Ruth's story—a larger audience would see it. She could only try.

With a steadying breath, she placed her fingers on the keys and typed:

The Silent Scars of Amish Life: What the World Doesn't See

She stared at the title for a long moment, letting the depth of it settle over her, then she started writing. Words spilled from her faster than she could process them. Her childhood. The fear. The powerlessness. The way their father's voice had wrapped around them like a noose. How Ruth had tried to protect Ivy only to be failed by a world that looked the other way. How Ivy had barely escaped herself.

She poured everything onto the pages, her hands shaking as she typed. This wasn't about her or Ruth or the children they used to be—this was about all of them. Every child still locked inside a world that told them their suffering was God's will.

She didn't know if anyone would publish it.

She didn't know if it would make a difference.

But she had to try.

Ivy typed the final word and exhaled, her fingers trembling slightly as she pulled her hands back from the keyboard. She leaned back in her chair, rubbing her tired eyes before glancing at the clock. Three hours had passed. She hadn't even noticed.

The front door creaked open, and the familiar sound of Beck's footsteps filled the quiet house.

"All right, little fish," Beck murmured, warm and low, "nap time."

Ivy turned to see him standing in the doorway, barefoot and sun-kissed, Daisy cradled against his chest. Her damp curls clung to her forehead, her tiny fists gripping his shirt as she stared up at Ivy with sleepy, half-lidded eyes.

"You should've seen her out there," Beck said, shifting Daisy slightly in his arms. "Tried to convince me she wasn't tired. Five minutes later, she was tipping sideways."

Ivy smiled, standing as Beck stepped closer. Daisy let out a soft, contented sigh, her cheek smushed against his shoulder.

Beck leaned in, pressing a slow, lingering kiss to Ivy's forehead. "You okay?" he asked, quieter now, like he already knew she wasn't entirely ready to answer.

Ivy glanced back at her laptop, the words staring back at her, heavy with truth. Then she looked at them—Beck, Daisy, the life she'd built. Safe. Stable. Loved.

"Yeah," she whispered. "I think I am."

She'd fought to give Daisy a better life, had carved out something balanced, something safe. She'd broken the cycle.

And now, maybe, she could bring light to something that needed to be seen. Something that needed to be stopped.

This was just the beginning.

Acknowledgments

My heartfelt thanks to JoAnn Collins of Twin Tweaks Editing, Imogen Grace, and Shauna Brongo for your keen eyes and skill in catching my errors. I'm deeply grateful to my dear friends Sherri and Patrice for being the first to offer feedback and for your encouragement. And a special thank you to Kim and Menno for your belief in my work.

About the Author

Viola Estrella, a 2010 RITA® finalist and award-nominated author, is best known for her romance novels—but her latest work, *Little Amish Girl*, was inspired by her own family history. The youngest daughter of a family that left the Amish community in the early 1970s, Viola weaves a heartfelt story rooted in resilience and change.

When she's not crafting characters or managing her day job, she can be found at home in Colorado with her husband and their two spoiled dogs—who are convinced they run the household.

To read more about Viola, visit her website: www.violaestrella.com

Join her newsletter to get news on upcoming cover reveals, new book releases, and a chance to sign up for her ARC (Advanced Reader Copy) list: https://dashboard.mailerlite.com/forms/1604677/157563245601752193/share

Also by Viola Estrella

Urban Fantasy
ANGEL VINDICATED - Abby Angel: Book One
ANGEL UNLUCKY - Abby Angel: Book Two
Abby Angel Book Three - Title coming soon

Paranormal Romance
BEWITCHING YOU - Bewitching Women: Book One
HAUNTING YOU - Bewitching Women: Book Two
FINDING YOU - Bewitching Women: Book Three
BEWITCHING WOMEN TRILOGY
BETWEEN ASH & ETERNITY - Guardian Angel Series Book One
BETWEEN LOVE & VENGEANCE - COMING SOON!

Contemporary Romance
SLOANE'S LIST

Book Club Questions (Contains Spoilers!)

1. What were your initial thoughts about Ivy as a ten-year-old? Did your perception of her change as she grew into adulthood?

2. Which foster home experience impacted you the most, and why? How do you think each shaped Ivy's independence?

3. How did Ivy's foster mothers (Mrs. Anderson, Sophie, Gina, Sarah, and Emily) deepen or take away from the book's themes of belonging, independence, and trust? And in what ways did they take away that trust?

4. In what ways did Emily's death shape Ivy's path forward, both emotionally and in the choices she made for her future?

5. Did it alter her views on family, love, or stability?

How might Ivy's journey have been different if Emily had lived?

How did Ivy's encounters with people from her Amish life challenge or strengthen her?

In what ways did Ivy's early experiences affect her ability to form friendships and romantic relationships as an adult?

How does the novel explore the balance between belonging and self-reliance?

Why do you think the author chose the title *Little Amish Girl*, even though much of the story is set outside the Amish community?

What did you think of Gram's role in Ivy's life? How did he challenge or support her growth?

Camron has his own flaws and complexities. Did you feel he was good for Ivy, or was he another obstacle she had to navigate?

Beck ends up being a strong character in Ivy's life. How did your feelings toward him evolve as the story unfolded?

What did each man (Gram, Camron, and Beck) teach Ivy about herself, if anything?

How did Ivy's early experiences with her father's abuse and alcoholism shape the way she connected—or struggled to connect—with people later in life?

In what ways did those early wounds influence her ability to trust, set boundaries, or form healthy relationships?

Did you see moments where her past made her misinterpret someone's actions or intentions?

How did her journey show the long-term impact of childhood trauma, and where did you see her begin to heal from it?

If Ivy had ended up with Gram or Camron instead of Beck (or stayed single), how would that have changed the ending?

Ivy's confrontation with her biological mother is a pivotal moment in the story.

What emotions did you see driving Ivy in that scene—anger, longing, grief, hope?

Do you think this confrontation brought her closer to closure, or open new wounds?

How did Ivy's relationship with her sister Ruth evolve throughout the story, and what did it reveal about the long-term effects of trauma?

In what ways did Ruth's decline—from protective older sister to someone lost in addiction and self-destructive choices—affect Ivy's sense of family and loyalty.

Do you think Ivy saw Ruth as a cautionary tale, a mirror of what her own life could have been, or both?

How did Ruth's struggles complicate Ivy's feelings of love, disappointment, and responsibility toward her?

Do you think Ivy successfully broke free from the emotional patterns of her childhood, or does some of it linger?

Do you think forgiveness is necessary for Ivy's healing? Did she achieve it by the end of the story?

Printed in Dunstable, United Kingdom

76583710R00170